10/93

SANTA MARIA PUBLIC LIBRARY

D0975009

Santa Maria Library

FIC M
Wilcox. Collin.
Find her a grave   /
1993.___

38

OFFICIALLY NOTED

FIND
Her a Grave

FIND
Her a Grave

COLLIN WILCOX

A TOM DOHERTY ASSOCIATES BOOK
NEW YORK

This is a work of fiction. All the characters and events portrayed in this book are fictitious, and any resemblance to real people or events is purely coincidental.

FIND HER A GRAVE

Copyright © 1993 by Collin Wilcox

All rights reserved, including the right to reproduce this book, or portions thereof, in any form.

This book is printed on acid-free paper.

A Forge Book
Published by Tom Doherty Associates, Inc.
175 Fifth Avenue
New York, N.Y. 10010

Edited by Teresa Nielsen Hayden

Library of Congress Cataloging-in-Publication Data

Wilcox, Collin.
    Find her a grave / Collin Wilcox.
        p.   cm.
    "A Tom Doherty Association book."
    ISBN 0-312-85244-4
        1. Theatrical producers and directors—United States—Fiction.
    2. Private investigators—United States—Fiction. 3. Mafia-
    -Fiction.   I. Title.
    PS3573.I395F56   1993
    813'.54—dc20   93-26557
                                                              CIP

First edition: December 1993

Printed in the United States of America

0 9 8 7 6 5 4 3 2 1

This book is dedicated to
Tottie and Gardie
All those years . . .

1985

TUESDAY, JULY 9th
3:15 P.M., EDT

Bacardo leaned forward, tapped the driver on the shoulder. "Switch on the radio, Eddie. Remember, no rock and roll." Bacardo waited until the music came up, then turned to the man beside him. Both men wore dark suits, white shirts, ties, and black loafers. Bacardo's loafers were brass-buckled; Caproni's were tasseled.

"You've never done this before, right?" Even though music now filled the Lincoln's interior, Bacardo spoke quietly, discreetly.

Caproni shook his head. "Never."

"The way it goes," Bacardo said, "we leave the car in the parking lot. Eddie's done this before, he knows how it goes. When we're parked, Eddie gives you the car keys. You take the keys, open the trunk, take out the suitcase. Then—this is important—you keep the keys in your pocket. If Eddie has to move the car, which he won't, he's got a duplicate set of keys. Got it?"

Caproni nodded. His dark eyes were fixed on Bacardo's face. Waiting avidly for the rest of it:

"At the gate, you give up the suitcase. There'll be two guards—flunkies—and a lieutenant. Harrison, that's the lieutenant's name. A guy about fifty, about two-twenty-five, reddish hair, bald, with a pot that's just starting. If there's any question, give me a look. Harrison's the one that gets the suitcase. He also gets the keys. The way it works, we take everything out of our pockets, for the scanner. Harrison knows the keys he wants. He picks up the keys off the conveyor belt."

"So Harrison gets the suitcase and the keys, both."

Bacardo nodded. "Right. And then he disappears. That's the last we see of him. While we're inside, Harrison unlocks the suitcase and empties it out, checks off everything. It'll take him maybe fifteen, twenty minutes, no more. Meanwhile, we do our business, me and the don. While we're doing business, Harrison takes the suitcase out to the car, puts it in the trunk, gives Eddie the keys. And that's that." Bacardo smiled, spread his large, knob-knuckled hands. He was tall, gaunt, loosely made. Like his hands, his face was large and rough-cut. It was a peasant's face: heavy brow ridges, an outsize jaw, an amorphous mouth. The body, too, was peasant-bred, defying the efforts of even the most skillful tailor. Bacardo's complexion was mahogany brown, his ancient Sicilian heritage. His unruly hair was dark and coarse and thick. His eyebrows, too, were spiky-thick, and his jowls were dark with underlying stubble. His black eyes revealed nothing. Like all mafiosi, Bacardo was clean-shaven.

"After we're through the scanner," Bacardo said, "a guard'll take us to the administration building in a golf cart. The don'll be waiting for me in the warden's office. You'll be in a conference room right down the hallway. You'll probably talk to Gerald Farley. He's captain of the guard, maybe the number-four man in the prison. Maybe he'll have someone with him, maybe not. Maybe you'll be patted down for a wire, maybe not. This is your first time, so they probably *will* pat you down. Anyhow, you've got to figure that Farley'll be wearing a wire. Right?"

On cue, Caproni nodded. "Right."

"Mostly," Bacardo said, "what Farley'll give you is just a lot of shit to make him feel important. He's a windbag, but he's no dummy, so you've got to watch yourself. One thing you've got to remember, and that's not to talk about the suitcase."

Caproni nodded again. "Got it."

"What you'll get from Farley, the only thing you have to pay attention to, is how it's going with our guys. Usually there's no complaints. Our guys, the capos, they're all in one cellblock.

Which, naturally, everyone calls 'Mafia Row.' There's eleven guys there now, including the don. In the rest of the prison, there's maybe twenty-five soldiers and button men. They're also our responsibility. If one of them fucks up, we take care of it. Us, not the guards. That's the deal. The guards don't fuck with us, we don't give them any problems. Our guys do their time, behave, get out, go back to work. You know all this."

Caproni nodded. The Lincoln was slowing, stopping for a red light. Even though there was no traffic in either direction, the driver came to a full stop, turned, then smoothly accelerated to a conservative forty-five. Looking at the sign on the light pole, Caproni saw FREDRICKSVILLE, 5 MILES. And, yes, in the distance the beige buildings of the prison were dimly materializing, built along the top of a bluff that was the landscape's only distinguishing feature; the rest was marshlands. Caproni glanced at the digital clock on the dashboard; the time was 3:25 P.M. The radio was playing something from the forties: a love song with mournful lyrics. Was it Sinatra?

"The way it works," Bacardo said, "just so you'll know, the don only talks to the warden or the captain of the guards. Nobody else—no guards, no inmates. And nobody talks to the don directly. Anything that's important enough for the don to make a decision, it goes to Augie first. He's the don's cellmate."

Caproni nodded, then decided to say, "Can I ask you something?"

Bacardo shrugged. "Ask."

"The don's been in for—what—five years?"

"Right."

"Out of—what—a fifteen-year sentence?"

"Right."

"So how come? I mean—" Perplexed, Caproni shook his head, spread his hands. "I mean, Christ, that was a frame-up, the don's trial. It was like Luciano and Genovese all over again. I went to the don's trial a few times. And those two guys the DA dug up, they could hardly remember their lines. The don, it looked like ten to one he'd walk on appeal."

Grimly, Bacardo looked straight ahead as he said, "In the first place, it wasn't the DA. It was the state's attorney. And the feds, if they want you bad enough, they'll get you. Christ, you talk about Luciano and Genovese. Those two, between them, who knows how many guys they had whacked. So the feds got Luciano for pimping, for God's sake—fixing Frederico up with a seventeen-year-old girl so stupid she didn't know enough to keep her mouth shut. And Genovese, Christ, convicted on a nickel-and-dime drug deal—street-corner stuff."

"And now Don Carlo."

Still staring straight ahead, Bacardo made no reply. The subject was closed.

4:05 P.M., EDT

The wall behind the warden's desk was covered with pictures, most of them photographs in narrow black frames. Advancing a step, Bacardo looked closely at a snapshot of a cabin cruiser with—yes—Warden Donovan at the helm, one hand resting on the traditional oaken ship's wheel. Wearing, yes, a yachtsman's cap, Donovan was smiling, squinting into the sun. Two men and three women shared the cockpit with him. The men were bare-chested, rolls of middle-aged fat overhanging their belts. The three women matched the men: overweight, cheerful-looking, settled. Donovan and one of the men clutched cans of beer, raised in a salute. From the design of the cockpit and the lines of the woodwork, the boat appeared to be a Ranger.

How many suitcases full of money and dope had it taken to buy the Ranger? Donovan, they said, was only a few years from retirement. How much had he—?

From behind him Bacardo heard the click of a latch, the

metal-on-metal sound of a door swinging on its hinges. He smiled as he turned to face Carlo Venezzio. The smile was genuine; more than anyone's, Venezzio's life was part of his own.

As always, Venezzio wore neatly pressed, dark-colored slacks, burnished loafers, and a white silk shirt, open at the neck. The feel of silk on his skin, Venezzio had once said, was half as good as sex.

As he pushed the door closed, he greeted Bacardo, gestured to the long leather sofa where they always sat, one at either end. A man of medium weight and height, sixty-five years old, Venezzio lowered himself slowly to the couch, bracing himself with both hands, one hand on the back of the sofa, one hand on the cushion. Watching the other man, Bacardo was aware of differences: a pallor of the face, an uncertainty of gesture, a tightening of the mouth, an underlying grimace about the eyes.

It had been two weeks since Bacardo's last visit. In those two weeks something had changed. Something significant.

But the voice, thin and reedy, was the same: "So. Caproni. How's he working out?"

Bacardo shrugged. "So far, so good."

"He's ambitious. Too ambitious, maybe."

"Sure. But he's smart. And he listens. He pays attention. I give him something to do, I know it'll get done."

"Okay." Venezzio nodded. "Let's see how he works out. You need a number one, Tony. Someone to take the load off."

Bacardo nodded in return. Between them, words had always been few. For a long moment, in silence, Bacardo covertly studied Venezzio. If the man in the street had to choose, "accountant" would be Venezzio's label, not "mafioso." Or, more like it, "CPA." With his narrow, pinched face, his small, compressed mouth, his mild stare, and his no-style glasses, Venezzio looked and acted like a quiet man, no ambition, no trouble to anyone. Only the eyes hinted at the truth: watchful, hard-focused eyes that saw everything, blinked at nothing. His only vanity was his thick head of brown hair, only lightly flecked with gray. When he passed a mirror, Venezzio almost always took a silver comb from his pocket, ran it through his hair, then turned his head from side to side, checking the result. Once a week, without fail, Venezzio had his hair trimmed, always by his personal barber.

"So," Barcardo finally decided to say, "anything?"

At the question, Venezzio's mouth briefly up-curved, the mockery of a smile. But behind the glasses with their tinted lenses, an optical necessity, Venezzio's eyes were steady, constantly registering small, significant calculations and corrections, the moment-to-moment pulsations of the machine within the man. Over the years, how many men had died when Venezzio's calculations had gone against them?

"How do I look?" Venezzio asked.

It was a puzzle of a question, a test, one of the don's little games—the game that never ended, loser beware.

Having expected the question, Bacardo decided to say, "You look tired, Carlo. And a little pale."

With his eyes fixed on Bacardo, Venezzio smiled again: the same hard, bitter smile. "Pale, eh? I look pale?"

Bacardo made no reply, and once more they regarded each other in silence, both men probing, balancing risk against gain, the endless game. Finally Venezzio looked away, let his eyes lose focus as he spoke in a voice Bacardo had never before heard:

"All my life, I've been healthy. I never had problems, except for that ulcer, thirty, thirty-five years ago. I always took care of myself, you know that. I quit smoking when I was—what?—twenty-five. Maybe thirty, no more. Okay, I used to drink, that's no secret. But nothing like most guys drink, nothing heavy. You know."

Gravely, Bacardo nodded. "Yeah, I know."

"And when I turned fifty or so, I cut out the hard stuff. And I watch my weight. Two meals a day, that's it. You know."

"Sure."

"All that," Venezzio said, "that's on one side. And then there's the old man—my dad. He was never a drinker, either. And, Christ, he could bend iron bars, I bet, when he was fifty."

Remembering, Bacardo smiled. "Yeah—your dad. Nobody fucked with your dad."

"Yeah . . ." Still with eyes gone blank, Venezzio spoke absently, from far away. Then, with infinite regret: "So then, when he was fifty-two, he had a heart attack."

"Ah . . . yeah." But more than that, Bacardo knew, he must not venture.

"Probably now," Venezzio said, "these days, they could've saved him, all the equipment they've got, and the drugs, and everything. But then, back then—" Grimly, as if he were remembering an ancient grudge, Venezzio shook his head.

"Back then, yeah . . ." As Bacardo said it, images returned: the limousines in the funeral procession, the church in the old neighborhood, packed. And, yes, Don Carlo, tears streaming down his cheeks. Maria had been with him then—Maria, the daughter of a don, beautiful in black. And their two children, so young, so round-eyed.

There was more, Bacardo knew. . . something more. Never would Venezzio speak of his dead father like this, not without a purpose, without a plan.

A heart attack . . .

These days, they could have saved him.

The pallor of Venezzio's face, the effort it had taken, lowering himself onto the sofa. All of it meant something.

"I thought maybe you heard." As he said it, Venezzio's eyes were hard-focused, probing, boring in.

Careful to keep his own gaze steady, keep his hands at rest, under control, Bacardo spoke softly, cautiously: "I heard nothing, Carlo. Nothing."

There was a last uncompromising moment of scrutiny, the final test. Then, also speaking softly, as if admitting to something shameful, Venezzio said, "Five days ago, I had a heart attack."

"Ah . . ." As if he, too, experienced the pain, Bacardo touched his chest over his heart. Then: "A small one, though. A warning."

Venezzio shrugged. "I guess that depends on who you talk

to. The nurse said it was a warning. The doctor, he didn't say that. He said the next one—" He shrugged again. Venezzio was speaking as he always spoke: without inflection, revealing nothing. But, deep behind the eyes, something had gone dead—or, if it was fear, come alive.

As both men sat facing each other, the silence between them began to lengthen past the breaking point. Bacardo realized that he must be the first to speak.

"Lots of guys, you know, they have a heart attack and it's no problem. They just watch themselves, eat right, exercise, and they live forever."

No response. Nothing but the eyes, boring in.

Bacardo drew a deep breath, began again: "What we've got to do is get a good doctor to look at you. These prison quacks, what'd they know?"

As if to dismiss the subject, Venezzio gestured, an indifferent response. "Sure. But what'd *any* of them know? Something like the heart, it's a crapshoot." Then, a familiar mannerism, Venezzio took a ballpoint pen and a small notebook from his shirt pocket. They were about to do business.

"One thing," Venezzio began, "is that our guys inside here, they know what happened. You understand?"

Slowly, meaningfully, Bacardo nodded. "Yeah, I understand."

Venezzio clicked the pen, wrote in the notebook, turned the pad for Bacardo to see:

Tony G., written in Venezzio's cramped, precise hand.

"You want . . . ?" It was a question that would never be completed, not in words. Not here, in the warden's office, almost surely bugged. Venezzio nodded—once. For Tony Gallino, it was the death sentence.

"Soon?" It was the only question that was allowed. The meaning: would the council be consulted, one slim hope for Tony G?

"Soon."

Meaning that, no, the council would not be told—or asked.

Meaning that, for Don Carlo's heart attack, Tony G. must

16

pay. It was coincidence, nothing more. To prove that Don Carlo was still *capo di tutti*, it was necessary that an example be made of someone. For years, systematically, Tony G. had been skimming, mostly gambling receipts. So Tony G. had drawn the short straw, bad luck for Tony.

Acknowledging the order, Bacardo nodded—once. Signifying that he would pick one man and do the job himself.

Many years ago, still in their teens, they'd tried to hijack a Puerto Rican poker game, he and Tony G.—the "two Tonys." They'd carried switchblades and iron pipes wrapped in friction tape. One of the players had pulled a gun, an enormous long-barreled revolver, the first gun Bacardo had ever faced. He'd run—and stumbled. And fell. Tony G. could have gotten away clean, but instead he'd turned, come back, shouted something in Spanish to the Puerto Rican with the gun. The Puerto Rican had started, staring at Tony G. Then, amazingly, the Puerto Rican had begun laughing, a wild, loud laugh. Then, with the gun, the Puerto Rican had—

"—something else," Venezzio was saying. Still he spoke quietly, evenly—all business. Expectantly, Bacardo looked at the other man. Awaiting orders.

Once more, Venezzio wrote on the pad.

Janice Frazer.

Instantly, Bacardo sensed the significance of the two words, written on the same page beneath *Tony G.* It was the turning point, Venezzio's final accounting. Kill Tony G., and that point was made.

Leaving only Janice Frazer, the name that was never spoken, the woman who never was. Janice, and one name more—the name Venezzio was writing now: *Louise.*

"Yes," Bacardo said, "I understand." As he said it, the memories returned, taking shape and substance: Janice Frazer, the incredibly beautiful peaches-and-cream waitress, no more than nineteen years old. He and Venezzio had been together when Venezzio had first seen her. Venezzio had been twenty-nine, married to Maria for less than a year, with one child on the way. Maria had been nineteen, too, the same age as Janice.

But Maria was the daughter of a Mafia don; Janice was a runaway teenager from the Midwest.

And Louise was the love baby Janice bore—the baby Janice took with her when she left New York.

At twenty-nine, Venezzio had only been eight years away from the top job, *capo di tutti*. Luciano couldn't stop him, and neither could Genovese.

Only Janice Frazer could have ruined his chances—Janice and her love baby. Louise.

"We never talked about them," Venezzio said. "But everyone knew. You, and everyone else. You knew."

"I—" Uncertain how to say it, Bacardo broke off. Then: "I saw her a few times, dropped off a couple of envelopes, like that. After she had her baby."

"Ah . . ." Venezzio nodded. "Yeah. Right."

"We never talked about her, though, you and me. Not really."

Gesturing to Bacardo's pocket, Venezzio said, "Turn it on."

Nodding, Bacardo withdrew the small pocket radio he always brought with him. He found a music station, golden oldies, and put the radio between them on the couch.

"A little louder," Venezzio ordered.

"Say when."

"That's fine." For a moment they listened to the soft, syrupy strains of "Deep Purple." Then Venezzio began to speak.

"I never lost track of Janice. You know that."

Bacardo nodded, a slow, measured inclination of his large, rough-featured peasant's head. "I knew that, yeah."

"Until she had the baby, it was all right to have her in New York. But when she had the baby, she started making demands. So I had to send her away. I waited until the baby—Louise—was six months old, but then Janice had to go. Especially when, Jesus, Maria had Carlo Junior just about the same time. Carlo and Louise, they're both the same age—thirty-five now." Venezzio shook his head, an expression of memories remembered with regret. "Life's funny, you know. Very funny."

"Funny. Yeah."

"Janice took the kid and went out west. She had relatives out there. So every once in a while, I'd—you know—drop in on her, you know what I mean."

This, Bacardo knew, was the story no one else had ever heard—the story no one would ever hear again.

This was a story with a purpose.

"Maria, you know—" Venezzio drew a deep breath, began to shake his head. "Maria, as soon as she had Carlo, she started laying it to me. I was pretty much—you know—just starting out then, climbing the ladder, and whenever I did something she didn't like she'd go to her old man. Don Salvatore always spoiled her, I knew that when I married her. I always figured one reason he never got married after Lucia died was because he was hung up on Maria. Fathers and daughters, you know—it happens."

"Yeah, I know what you mean."

"But, anyhow, by the time we had Maria—that tells you something, you know, the mother naming her daughter after herself—by that time, that was pretty much it for the marriage. We lived together, went through the motions, but that's all."

"Like almost everyone."

"Yeah." Venezzio smiled, a thinning of his lips, no more. Never had Bacardo seen Venezzio really smile. Or laugh. It was, someone had once said, the secret of his success. If a man smiled, he could forgive. But Venezzio never forgave. Or forgot.

"But you always had—" Bacardo pointed to Janice's name in the notebook lying beside the transistor radio.

In response, Venezzio nodded. "Yeah. Right. I always kept track of her—her and the little girl. And I have to say, speaking of fathers and daughters, I always liked it, being with the girl. She was someone to—you know—give presents to, take to Disneyland, like that."

"Sure." Bacardo said it quietly, sympathetically. Then: "Did you ever go to that other one? Epcot Center?"

"No."

"Amazing. Really amazing."

A short silence fell as they listened to Tony Bennett winding up "That Old Black Magic," one of Bacardo's favorites. Then Bacardo decided to ask, "So how're they doing now?"

"Well . . ." Venezzio pointed to Janice's name. "She's dead. She died about a year ago." He spoke without inflection, without emotion. "She went out west, like I said. For a while—a few years—she did all right, she and Lou—she and the little girl. I took care of them, saw they had everything they needed. If I couldn't make it, I'd send someone, make sure she was all right. I sent you, I remember, once or twice."

"Twice."

"Yeah. Twice. And for a while—years—she *was* all right. They had a nice house, and the little girl did fine in school and everything. You know—the way most people live, with white picket fences, and a garden, and bicycles on the lawn.

"But then she started to drink—" Venezzio pointed to Janice's name. "When she was a girl, her mother drank, and her father was never around. That's why she left home, because her mother was a drinker. So then, Jesus, *she* starts drinking."

"That happens. It happens a lot. The parents are boozers, so are the kids."

"Yeah, well—" Venezzio gestured, an expression of helplessness, of futility. "Well, that's what happened. She drank herself to death, ruined her liver."

"She seemed real nice," Bacardo offered. "Always real—you know—cheerful, very friendly. Some women—beauties—they aren't friendly. They figure they got the looks, that's it."

Looking away, lost in memory, Venezzio made no reply.

"Did she always have the house with the white picket fence?"

"Always. She always kept it nice, too. And you're right, she was always cheerful. Some people, you know, they get mean when they drink. Or else they start slobbering. Not her, though. Maybe she'd get a little loud, but that was all."

"What about the little girl? She's thirty-five, you said. Is she married?"

"She was married, with a child of her own. She's been married twice. Once it was a divorce, and once her husband died. It was out in Los Angeles. She doesn't live there now, but that's where she lived when—" He left the rest of it unsaid. But a glance at Venezzio's face revealed the rest of it: with a divorce behind her, and now widowed, Venezzio's daughter was struggling, needed help.

"What I've been doing," Venezzio said, "I've been thinking about this. You understand what I'm saying?"

Gravely, Bacardo nodded.

Venezzio picked up the notebook, slipped it in his shirt pocket. He gestured to the radio, which Bacardo switched off.

"What I want you to do," Venezzio said, "is think about this too. I want you to figure out a plan, if something happens with my heart. You understand?"

"I understand. Sure. No problem."

"You think, and I'll think. Come back in ten days, and we'll talk."

"Right."

"Okay . . ." Venezzio nodded, allowed his eyes to momentarily close as he drew a deep, ragged breath. Then he raised his hand, wearily signifying dismissal. Meaning that Bacardo should go to the door of the office and summon a guard.

"Tell him to get a golf cart," Venezzio ordered. "I feel like riding."

"Sure." Bacardo rose, hesitated, then decided to touch Venezzio's shoulder, in sympathy.

FRIDAY, JULY 19th
2:20 P.M., EDT

"No golf cart," Bacardo said.

Venezzio nodded as they walked through the door to the small exercise yard, a featureless expanse of concrete surrounded by prison buildings with closely barred windows. Overhead, in the clear, bright July sky, a small formation of birds whirled against the sun. At Venezzio's request, the exercise yard had been cleared for Bacardo's visit.

"No golf cart," Venezzio answered. "When we talked it was—what—ten days ago?"

"Yeah. Ten days."

"Well, the day after you were here, a couple of heart specialists came."

Bacardo nodded. "I know. I just got the bill."

"How much?"

"Plenty. The trip, everything, Jesus, it was something like seven thousand dollars. And then there was another bill from the lab. Those guys, we could take lessons."

"Yeah, well, whatever it was, it's worth it. They really gave me confidence. And they told me the bill would be stiff, for all the business they lost coming here. So pay."

"I already paid. I took care of it personally."

"All right. Good." Venezzio gestured, and they began walking slowly together.

"So what'd they say?" Bacardo asked.

"They said to start exercising. There's a treadmill thing that I can hook myself up to, all computerized. I get on that thing, and start walking, and I do what the dials tell me to do. They say walk, I walk. They say stop, I stop. And there's a tape. When the tape runs out, I send it to the doctors."

"So you feel—what—okay?"

"Better than okay. I'm eating two meals a day, no meat but a little fish and skinned chicken. No booze, not even wine with dinner. And I feel fine. I've lost six pounds since I saw you." As he spoke, Venezzio changed their direction. Soon they were in the center of the yard. With their backs to the windows of the buildings that surrounded them on three sides, the only place of concealment for directional mikes, they could talk business.

"Tony G." Venezzio said. "So far, so good, eh?"

"Tony wasn't so well liked, it turns out."

"Who'd you take along? Caproni?"

Bacardo shook his head. "I decided to take Maranzano. He's—well—he's steady, on something like that. Besides, Caproni and Cella, they get together once in a while."

"Cella. Yeah. I was going to ask you about Cella. It's been—what—six days since Tony died?"

"Yeah. Six."

"Did you talk to Cella afterwards?"

"The next day. We had clams, pasta, a bottle of wine. Great lunch. Fuchini's, you know." In tribute Bacardo shook his head. "The way they do clams, with garlic and white wine, you wouldn't believe it."

"So Cella's all right about Tony G."

"As far as I could see, no problems. He insisted on picking up the check. Absolutely insisted. So that says something. Plus, he sends you his best regards."

"Ah . . . good." Venezzio nodded. Then: "Tony's funeral, I hear it was first-class."

Bacardo considered. "It was okay. I mean, everything we could do, we did. But I was expecting more people."

"His family—what, three children?"

"Four."

"Take care of them. The whole works. College, everything."

"Right."

"Let's walk a little. We can walk along the wall. If they're using a shotgun mike, it's still okay along the wall."

"Sure."

As they began to walk, Venezzio said, "About Louise, what we talked about last time."

"You're thinking you want to get enough money to her so if anything happens to you, she'll be okay. Is that it?"

"She and her kid, yeah. Her little girl. Christ—" Venezzio shook his head. "Christ, she's fifteen already. *Fifteen.*" In wonderment, he shook his head.

Bacardo smiled. "So. You're a grandfather."

Another incredulous shaking of the head.

"So she was—what—nine, ten, the last time you saw her?"

"Nine."

"What's her name?"

"Angela."

"Nice name."

"She'll be twenty-five before I get out of here. And I'll be seventy-five."

"Well," Bacardo said, "I'll be sixty-five."

"Jesus. Time. That's the real enemy, you know. Time."

They walked in silence for several paces. Finally Bacardo said, "Well, it shouldn't be so hard. Get some money together, start feeding it to her. She invests it right, she'll be all set. Both of them."

"Except that I don't want her to have anything until I die. It'll be—you know—like a will, for her."

Startled, Bacardo looked at the other man. In their organization, nothing was written down. Ever. No records were kept. Ever.

"I don't mean a real will. Relax."

"Ah . . ." Bacardo nodded.

"What I mean, Louise's no good with money. She gets with some guy, he starts sucking away, and pretty soon she's broke. So I want to fix it so she'll have it when I die, but not before. Or anyhow, not till I say it's all right."

"How're you going to do that?"

24

"I thought you were figuring out something," Venezzio said.

"I was. But I wasn't figuring on any delay. I thought you were talking about now, give it to her now."

"Okay. Forget about the delay. What'd you figure?"

"Well, I was figuring maybe get together some money, but mostly jewels. Unmounted jewels, that's better than gold."

Venezzio nodded. "Okay. So then what?"

"Well, where's she live? In California?"

"Right."

"Okay. So we collect, just to say something, let's say a couple of hundred thousand in old money. Then we get, say, eight hundred thousand in jewels. *Good* jewels."

"I was thinking a million and a half. But the jewels, that's good." Approvingly, Venezzio nodded. "They're better than cash, if there's inflation. And lighter than gold." He nodded again.

"And easier to sell, if you do it right. Gold, there's a paper trail a lot of times."

"Okay," Venezzio said. "We get the jewels. Then what?"

"Well, I was thinking she should get maybe five safe-deposit boxes, in different cities, whatever. And—"

"I don't know." Dubiously, Venezzio shook his head. "Safe-deposit boxes—all it takes is a judge and a court order, and the feds're all over you."

"Yeah, but she's clean, isn't she?"

Emphatically, Venezzio nodded. "She's clean. Absolutely."

"Okay—well—safe-deposit boxes, that's only one idea I had. The other idea, I had something fancy."

Venezzio frowned. "Fancy? What?"

"We give her a house, and hide the stuff in it. You know—in the walls, under the floor, whatever. When the time comes, I tell her where to look." Bacardo spread his hands. "No problem."

As Venezzio considered, he gestured for them to turn, begin another lap, walking parallel to the wall. Finally he shook his head. "It might leak out. You know—carpenters, whatever."

"We must have somebody can hammer a nail. That's all it'd take."

"I want only one guy in on this. You. Or maybe one other guy, if we need him. But I've got to know this other guy. And I don't know any carpenters."

"This whole thing, it isn't easy. I mean, if you want me to put a million five together, get somebody to ride shotgun, and we get on a plane and I fly out to California, or wherever, that's one thing. But if you want to stash the stuff until, God forbid, you die, that's something else. And you can't write it down, 'open on my death,' anything like that. So that means when the time comes—maybe a year from now, maybe five, ten, twenty years from now—I find her and I say—"

"No. That's wrong. We're just talking about when I'm in here. Ten years. No more."

"Okay. Ten years. So what'm I going to do, put the stuff in my hall closet for ten years? Do I want that responsibility? Let's face it, some of the guys—Cella, let's say, he finds out . . ." He let it go ominously unfinished.

"No," Venezzio said. "I'm not saying any hall closet. But the stuff's got to be safe."

"For ten years, safe? Without even Louise knowing?" Bacardo shook his head. "Things happen in ten years. Let's say, God forbid, you should die in here. So then Cella decides, hey, he'll whack me, make his move. So what then? Where's Louise then, if—?"

"Wait." Venezzio held up a hand. "Wait, I think I know a way."

"Hmmm." Deliberately, Bacardo let the skepticism show. Was Don Carlo losing it?

"I'm going to figure someplace for the stash. I'll decide on one guy to handle it. He'll know where he's stashing something, but he won't know what it is. All he'll know is that he's doing something for me. So—" Venezzio broke off, letting the words catch up to the thoughts. His eyes had sharpened, working out the plan, seeing how it would go. His voice, too, was sharpening: "So you'll collect the stuff, and get it ready. So then our guy, the one I pick, he gets the bundle from you. He doesn't know what's in it, and you don't tell him. It's just a bundle, period. He takes the bundle, does what I tell him to do. So after he's done the job, you come here. I give you four or five words, whatever. Then I tell Louise to come here, later. I'll give her four or five words, too, to put together with the words you've got. So you put them together, and you know where the bundle is."

Slowly, thoughtfully, Bacardo nodded. "Yeah, that could work. That could work fine."

"Okay, then." As he spoke, Venezzio gestured to the door that led to the administration building, where a guard waited to pass them through. Now Venezzio's voice was fading; in his eyes, the deal-making glint had dulled. "Okay, so you start getting it together—a little cash, maybe fifteen, twenty gold coins, but mostly jewels. Diamonds, mostly. Use Fineberg. You can't do better than Fineberg. But pay him twelve percent, no more. Otherwise, he gets his legs broken. Right?"

Bacardo nodded. "I agree. Fineberg."

"I'm not kidding, though, about the legs. The last time we did business together, he was right on the edge. Tell him that. Then remind him about Tony G., about what can happen."

"I don't think I have to remind him. I think he knows."

"Just make sure he knows."

"I'll make sure."

"The jewels—Fineberg knows: big ones, unmounted. He'll know. A million dollars, you can hold in one hand."

"I know."

"So—what—six months to get the stuff together, play it safe?"

"Maybe eight, nine months. Business is off, you know. There's a lot of our guys with not much to do. So they start asking questions, looking around, thinking about the angles."

"Well, whatever. Nine months, a year, whatever. But keep your ass covered. This one, it's got to be done right."

"Sure. Of course." Bacardo let it show, his irritation that the other man would think he had to spell it all out.

And, as if he was tuned in, his special gift, Venezzio said, "Sorry, Tony. I'm—suddenly I'm tired. You understand."

"Sure, I understand. No problem."

"Okay. So we're all set, then."

"All set."

"Don't forget what I said, about Fineberg."

Bacardo nodded, but decided not to reply. *Was* Don Carlo losing it? Or was he just tired, after the heart attack?

They were almost to the door, which the guard was opening with his key. "About Cella," Venezzio said. "Keep in touch with him. Make sure he understands about Tony G."

"Sure. I already told you, he understands."

"Just make certain. War, we don't need."

"War?" Bacardo broke stride, looked at the other man. *"War?"*

"Just keep in touch with him. Next time, you pick up the check for lunch. Got it?"

"Got it."

TUESDAY, OCTOBER 22nd
8:20 P.M., EDT

Respectfully, Bacardo would remain standing until Cella had been seated. One of Cella's bodyguards held his chair. The other bodyguard stood at the door of the small private dining room.

"Thank you," Cella said. The bodyguard nodded to Cella, nodded to Bacardo, then stepped back. The room's only windows opened on the dead-end alley that ran along the side of The Chop House. Since the alley windows were steel-shuttered, both guards could withdraw, take tables in the restaurant, one close to the door of the private dining room, one close to the restaurant's front door. Their waiter was Sal Raffetto, a member of the Magglio family. Completely reliable, Raffetto was known to both Cella and Bacardo. The Chop House's private dining room was not wired, had never been wired, would never be wired. It was an agreement guaranteed by all five New York families.

As the bodyguards withdrew, Raffetto entered, gave his greeting, presented the menus.

"So," Cella said, smiling cordially across the table at Bacardo. "So eat. Enjoy. A bottle of Chianti?"

Returning the smile, Bacardo nodded. "Fine."

Cella gave the wine order to Raffetto, who withdrew. In his late fifties, Cella was perfectly groomed, a slim, silver-haired man with the long, narrow, finely drawn face of an aesthetic. He was always seen wearing an impeccably tailored gray suit, a white shirt with silver cuff links, and a dark tie. Sicilians, Cella's family had come to America when their only son was five years old. Mother and father had worked hard to see their son graduate from college—or from a Catholic seminary. A quiet, serious, often brooding student, Benito had been admitted to Columbia when he was only sixteen, and in his sophomore year had elected to major in theater arts. He was a compelling actor with a gift for projecting menace, and he soon became a protégé of Columbia's principal professor of drama. But in his junior year Cella was accused of aggravated assault on a prostitute. The state's case failed when the prostitute refused to testify, but Cella was forced to leave college. Without hesitation, he turned to crime. By age thirty, a trusted member of the Gentile family, Cella began specializing in loan-sharking. Soon he was supervising a dozen companies the Mafia had forced into bankruptcy and then bought for pennies on the dollar. In 1975, after Joseph Gentile was murdered as he left a whorehouse, the Gentile family became the Cella family. It was an open secret that, wearing his customary gray suit, Cella had rolled down the rear window of his Mercedes and pulled the trigger on Gentile himself, a single shot to the head from a distance of more than fifty feet, at night. Discussing the remarkable feat of marksmanship, admiring the steadiness of hand, one of the dons had dubbed Cella "The Undertaker." The name stuck, but only out of Cella's hearing. To satisfy the Mafia coda, at age thirty Cella had married an immigrant Italian girl. Ten years later he sent her back to Italy, childless, a psychological ruin. After her banishment Cella returned to prostitutes, exchanging hundred-dollar bills for the violent pleasures of sadism.

Cella waited until the wine had been poured and the waiter had withdrawn. Then, gracefully, he raised his glass. "To Don Carlo." The words were softly spoken, precisely measured. Cella's pale gray eyes were hard-focused on Bacardo, an intensity that confirmed the significance of the words he had just spoken.

"His health," Bacardo said solemnly, acknowledging that, yes, he understood the deeper meaning of the toast. It was confirmation that Venezzio's status as *capo di tutti* was secure, unthreatened. One of the five New York dons, Cella was offering to keep a weakened Venezzio in power.

Cella placed his wineglass on the table, took a moment to consider, then decided to say, "How *is* Don Carlo's health, Tony? It's been three months now. What'd the doctors say?"

Also setting his glass aside, also taking a measured moment to consider, Bacardo looked directly into the other man's eyes as he said, "The doctors tell him to do what he always does, only do it slower, that's all."

"Ah . . ." Cella nodded. "Good. That's about what I thought. And his mind, of course—sharp as ever."

"No question." Bacardo spoke firmly; his eyes were steady.

"When he had Tony G. whacked, that was smart. That helped us all. You told him that." It was a statement, not a question.

Bacardo nodded. "Of course. I told him immediately."

Nodding in return, Cella raised his glass, fastidiously sipped the wine. "Tony was getting to be a problem, no question."

Bacardo made no response.

Cella returned his wineglass to the table with a gesture of finality. The preliminaries had been concluded.

"How old is the don, Tony?"

"He's sixty-five."

"Ah, right . . ." Cella inclined his narrow, finely boned head. His silver-gray hair was full cut, meticulously styled. "And you're—what?"

"Fifty-five."

As if the answer had been expected, Cella nodded. Then, after a moment's hesitation: "Your son—Tony Junior—I'm sorry. It—Christ—this business is hard enough, without something like that."

At the words, Bacardo's rawboned face froze. His splintered gaze looked through Cella's eyes, not into them. Even as a small boy, his son had often cheated at games, had once been caught taking money from his mother's purse.

Two years ago, Tony Jr. had been caught again—skimming

COLLIN WILCOX

the organization's off-track take. It was an offense for which no appeal was possible; even Venezzio could not have changed the council's death sentence. For a year afterward, except when it was absolutely necessary, Bacardo's wife had not spoken to him or looked at him directly.

"I don't mean to open old wounds, Tony. I just wanted you to know that how you handled yourself, it was just right. It took a lot. Everyone knew it, how much it took."

Sitting rigidly, his gaze still fixed far back in time, Bacardo made no reply. He could only endure.

"Here." Cella lifted the bottle of wine, replenished Bacardo's glass. It was a small gesture of peace, an offering.

Bacardo thanked him politely, but did not raise his glass. Cella let a last long moment of silence pass before he spoke again, this time in an even, controlled voice:

"The reason I invited you, Tony, is that it's time Carlo and I got a few things out on the table. You agree?"

Carlo, this time. Not *Don Carlo*. Was it a signal? The next moments would tell.

Bacardo decided on a sip of wine before he nodded. Saying simply, "I agree."

"This place—" Cella gestured at the room. "It's okay?"

"It's fine."

"There's a button on the floor. When I want the waiter, I step on it."

"Ah." Bacardo smiled. "Good. I'm glad you told me."

"Otherwise, there's no bugs. Guaranteed."

"I know."

"So." Cella tapped his fingertips lightly on the gleaming white linen tablecloth for a moment, then began: "So, like I said, Tony G., that was okay. The other dons, they understood. Carlo had to do something, and he did. But something like Tony G., whacking a capo without putting it to a vote, usually you only get one free ride from the council. Right?"

Revealing nothing, Bacardo nodded—once.

"So you'll tell him that," Cella pressed. "You'll tell him what I said. Just to keep us square, me and Carlo."

32

." "

." Once more, an invitation, Cella gestured to
.. half-empty glass.

"Thanks. No more."

Cella refilled his own glass, sipped. Then: "So that takes care
of the Tony G. thing. What I really wanted to tell you—what I
want you to tell Carlo—is that I've got a proposition for him. A
quid pro quo, the diplomats say."

Bacardo frowned. "Quid pro *what?*"

Cella smiled, raised a slim, elegantly condescending hand.
"A deal. Tell him a deal."

"A deal. Yeah."

"Tell him—" The final pause. "Tell him that I'll support
him, do everything I can to keep him in the top job. Remind
him that we've never—*never*—had problems, Carlo and me."

"Well, that's—"

"But then," Cella cut in, "when he goes—retires, whatever—then I expect his people to support me like I supported
him. He's got—what—ten years left, inside?"

"Right. It was a fifteen-year sentence."

"Okay. Well, he's doing a good job running things from inside. Genovese did it, and so did Charlie Lucky, from Italy. But
something like the heart, you never know. So what I'm saying
is, when Carlo's out of it, one way or the other—then it's my
turn. Tell him that's the deal."

Careful to show no emotion, no approval, no disapproval,
Bacardo said, "I'll tell him."

"Good." Cella's voice was brisk with finality. "So—" Smiling broadly now, he raised his glass. "So, to Don Carlo. Good
health."

"Good health."

1986

WEDNESDAY, MAY 14th
3:45 P.M., EDT

It began as it always did: the crushing weight in the upper chest, the shortness of breath. Then the pain: slivers at first. Daggers, thin and sharp. In moments, he knew, the pain would congeal into a solid mass, growing, spreading, reaching upward to the base of the neck, like strangler's hands.

From the pocket of his shirt Venezzio took the plain white envelope that was always there, quick to his hand, a reflex now: feel the pain, reach for the envelope, take out one tiny nitro pill, put it under the tongue. Secure the flap of the envelope with its life-or-death contents, carefully return the precious envelope to his pocket.

And then, his latest doctor had said, relax. Lie down, close the eyes, breathe deeply. "Think of something pleasant," the doctor had said. "Think of when you were a little boy."

A little boy . . .

How old was the doctor, a specialist, flown in from New York? Forty? Dr. McCoy, the best in the business, according to Bacardo. Dr. McCoy, a tall, smooth-talking Ivy Leaguer, a scrubbed little kid from the suburbs, say shit when he stepped in it and get his mouth washed out with soap.

"I'll have to analyze the test results," McCoy had said. "Then I'll tell Mr. Bacardo. Will that be satisfactory?"

Five days it had been before Bacardo had come. And then "inconclusive" was the best McCoy had made out of the tests.

The first attack, almost ten months ago, hadn't damaged the heart; the first doctors had said that much.

But the second attack, eight months later—that one, McCoy

said, was inconclusive. Meaning, Venezzio knew, that anything could happen—anytime.

Think of when you were a little boy . . .

Lying on his bunk, arms and legs limp, staring at the riveted metal of the cell's ceiling, Venezzio drew a long, deep breath, then let his eyes slowly close. Yes, the nitro was doing the job; the pain was slowly fading, diffusing. From his chest, the weight was lifting. Five minutes more and he could sit up, stand, walk as well as ever. Thank you, nitroglycerin.

A little boy . . .

McCoy had said it because, for him, boyhood had meant sunshine and laughter, tennis lessons at the club, swimming parties, bike rides down golden lanes.

Not trash littering the sidewalks. Not overflowing sewers. Not the shouts and screams and threats and clangor of the slums. Not the narrow cobblestone streets where the sun never shone, in perpetual shadows cast by the tall brick tenement walls.

Genoa, in the twenties . . .

His father had a withered leg, mangled beneath a horse-drawn cart. His mother lived most of every week at the house of a prosperous Genoese banker, where she washed clothes and scrubbed floors. In the corner of their tiny kitchen his father had kept a wrist-thick length of tree branch he'd cut many years before. There were twig stubs at the end of the branch. Many times, lying in bed between his two sisters, one older, one younger, he'd heard the crash of the branch, followed by the high-pitched chirp of the injured rat—followed by another crash. And another. Followed finally by silence. Except that, in the silence, he could hear his father panting from his exertions, dragging his withered leg as he returned the branch to the kitchen corner, then dragged himself back to bed. His father had—

Wood tapped twice against the bars of the cell. "Mr. Venezzio?" It was Farley's voice. Farley, captain of the guard, back from vacation. Captain Farley, the only guard permitted to talk directly to him. Venezzio opened his eyes, braced his elbows, rose to a sitting position, legs swung over the end of the bunk, feet on the floor. After an angina attack, keeping up appearances, it was necessary to speak briskly, move decisively:

"Jerry! How was the vacation?"

"Fine, thanks. We went to the Grand Canyon."

"Ah . . ." Venezzio nodded. Now the pain was almost gone, a mild discomfort, nothing more. It was only necessary to buy a few minutes more before he could get to his feet, go into his act: the indestructible mafioso, for thirty years *capo di tutti*. If the President was the most powerful man in the world, then he was the most feared.

A few minutes more . . .

"Did you drive, Jerry?"

"Yeah." The guard, big and blubbery, bulging inside his uniform, nodded. It was an expression of heartfelt exasperation. "Yeah. But never again. Two kids, forget it. Not only that, but we pulled a trailer." Once more, Farley shook his head.

Venezzio smiled, rose to his feet, stood motionless for a moment. Yes, the pain was passing—had passed.

"You've got a visitor," Farley said. "Where d'you want to see her?"

Her, Farley had said.

Meaning that, finally, Louise must have come. Louise, accompanied by Bacardo. For days, he'd expected them. Why hadn't Bacardo called the prison, left a message, given him notice?

The answer, he knew, lay with Louise, not Bacardo. Never had Louise kept appointments, kept to a schedule.

"Is the little yard clear?"

"Yessir. And there's a golf cart."

"What about the weather?"

"It's fine. Fifty-seven, according to the radio. But this time of day, you know, that little yard's in shadow."

"Okay." Moving slowly, carefully, Venezzio went to his

free-standing closet, selected a light poplin golf jacket. From the small desk he took his notebook and a ballpoint pen. "Okay," he repeated. "Let's go."

"Yessir."

4:10 P.M., EDT

Frowning, Louise turned up the collar of her coat. "It would've been warmer in the warden's office."

"This won't take long." Venezzio switched off the golf cart's electric motor, stopped the cart in the center of the small exercise yard. The yard hadn't yet been policed after the lunchtime tour; cigarette butts and food wrappers littered the area. A few feet from the cart, Venezzio saw a condom, used.

"Are you getting enough exercise?" Louise asked. "I saw a heart specialist on a talk show—Larry King, I think. He said it's very important after a heart attack to get on an exercise schedule. But he said it has to be supervised. Very carefully supervised."

"I do as much walking as I ever did. I just go slower."

"And weight." She looked him over. "Maybe you should lose some weight."

Exasperated, he sighed. "My weight's fine, Louise. A hundred sixty, stripped. That's it."

"I know. But maybe you should—"

"Louise. Wait." He held up his hand. "What about you? Your last letter, you said you were going to move. Then you left it, didn't write any more about it. So what's happening?"

"Did we come out here to talk about me?" Her voice rose a querulous half-note. "You said there was something important. I'll bet it's fifty degrees, no more."

Ignoring his daughter's complaints, Venezzio spoke with labored patience. "When you think about moving, you should think about Angela. She's—what—sixteen?"

"Angela's sixteen—and I'm thirty-six. And it's been two years since Jack died. I rented my place because I had to get out of the house, because of the creditors. I never intended to stay forever. I—"

"What I'm saying, a girl's sixteen, a teenager, she wants to hang around with her friends. You already moved once, a year ago. Now you're going to move again. But you should—"

"Dad. Please. I've heard all this. And Christ, I don't have to be reminded about teenagers. But you're talking like I'm throwing Angela out in the street."

"If you move," Venezzio said, speaking with flat finality, "that's all right. You want a bigger place, a better place, that's fine. But—" He waited for her to look at him directly. Then, firmly repeating: "But you stay in the same neighborhood, that's all I'm saying. For God's sake, you live in Beverly Hills. Find a place there, somewhere close, where Angela can—"

"Will you listen a minute? Will you please quit giving orders, and listen to me, for a change? Will you do that?" As she said it, a new note entered her voice, a note of entreaty. Looking at her closely, he saw uncertainty in her face. Uncertainty, and something else. Was it desperation?

A man? Was that it: a new man? Another new man? *I'm thirty-six*, she'd said. The words had been a plea, he realized that now. Once more, Louise had lost her way. At thirty-six, her body had begun to thicken. And, yes, sag. Around her eyes, the wrinkles were beginning, deepening. All her life, Louise had been a beauty who didn't—couldn't—believe she was beautiful. So, all her life, she'd gone with the wrong man—the wrong men. Like her mother, she had the cornflower-blue eyes and the flaxen blond hair and the full, buxom bloom of a farm girl.

Except that Janice's mother hadn't come from farm folk. She was born in the slums of Cleveland, where her father died in a barroom brawl when Janice was ten. Janice's mother had then lived with a succession of men, and they'd all beat her. So Janice's mother had begun to drink—and drink.

Just as Janice had begun to drink—and drink.

Forced to leave New York, Janice had gone to Sacramento, where she'd raised her baby. When Louise was in grammar school, Janice had begun to drink—and drink. Once Venezzio had tried to cut off the envelopes stuffed with money. Either Janice must join AA, he'd told her, or there'd be no more money, ever. Her baby would be taken from her. Defiant, a drunk's don't-give-a-damn bravado, Janice had threatened to go to the newspapers and tell her story: MY DAUGHTER'S FATHER IS CARLO VENEZZIO.

With the deepest regret, Venezzio had ordered one side of Janice's face slashed. It must be done, he'd told Bacardo, with a very sharp single-edge razor blade, right out of the package. Then, immediately, she must have the best of surgeons to stitch up the face.

Louise had been ten years old when her mother was slashed. Because a mistake was made, the little girl had heard her mother's screams. Never before had Bacardo displayed such heartfelt remorse.

When she returned home from the hospital, Janice began to drink again, more heavily than ever. But Venezzio no longer cared. He began sending the envelopes again, but he no longer cared what happened to Janice, so long as she never again threatened to go public. When she died of drink, two years previously, his only concern had been for Louise.

Louise, and now Angela.

"Okay . . ." Venezzio nodded. "Okay. I'm listening."

"What I'm thinking—" As she said it, Louise's eyes began to slide off, a sure signal that she was anxious, unsure of herself. "What I'm thinking is I—I might move to San Francisco."

As if she'd made a bad joke, he snorted. Then, flatly: "In a couple of years, when Angela's ready to go off on her own, then you can go to San Francisco. But I won't let you—"

"It's a *man*. I met a *man*." She spoke in an anguished voice, as if to confess some shameful flaw. Her eyes begged him for understanding.

"A man, eh?" Venezzio's voice registered both disdain and bored indifference. "This man—are you going to marry him?"

"W-we haven't talked about getting married. It's—it's not what everyone does, you know. It's not what *you* did with Mom."

"We don't talk about me, Louise." He spoke very softly. But his dark eyes, boring in, were remorseless.

"I—" She faltered, tried to avoid his eyes. "I know. And I didn't mean—"

"This man. What's his name?"

"His name is Walter Draper." She tried to speak defiantly— but succeeded only in masking a whine. "And he's very successful. He's got a restaurant in San Francisco. We can't very well—"

"Is he married, this Walter Draper?"

"No. He—he was married. But he's been divorced for years. Three years, I think."

"Children?"

She nodded. "Two. But they live with his ex-wife."

"So what're you thinking—that you'll move in with him? Is that it?"

"Walter's got a house. A big house, in San Francisco. He wants me to live there."

"That's you. What about Angela?"

"Well, of *course* Angela," she flared. It was her first display of temper. "Angela *likes* it in San Francisco. She likes it a lot."

"She likes it for a weekend. But she's spent her whole life in Los Angeles."

"Angela's got her life to live, but I've got my life, too. I've got *needs*. I've got—"

"What you've got, Louise, is hot pants. What you've also got is a screwed-up life. It's not all your fault. Your mother and me, it would've been better if we'd never got together, let's face it. But we *did* get together—and you were the result. I don't know what your mother told you about what happened after you were born. She probably told you that I forced her to take you and get out of town. And that's right, that's what I did. The reason I did it was because someone in my position, I can't afford scandals, can't afford publicity. I can't—"

"I *know* all this," she broke in. "You've got to marry right. So you married, and you've got two children, my age. I *know* that. But—"

"Hey." His voice dropped ominously, his gaze hardened dangerously. In that moment, instantly gone, she glimpsed the essential Carlo Venezzio. Her father. The man who ordered other men killed. Many men.

The man who might have ordered her mother's face slashed—that poor, sodden woman, now dead these last two years.

"Hey," he repeated. "Don't interrupt. Okay?"

Sullenly, she made no reply.

"What I started to say, I realize you've had a tough life, in lots of ways. Your mother was a drunk, there's no other word for it. She drank herself to death. Plus, I was never around. And now, this—" He gestured to the prison walls. "This doesn't help, me being locked up. I understand that. But you've always been taken care of. *Always.* And you always *will* be taken care of, just so long as you don't screw up."

"What's that mean?" she asked bitterly. "Does that mean you'll keep on having money dropped off just so long as I do what you want me to do? Is that it?"

"Louise . . ." Again, the low note of warning, the evocation of darkness, of death. "Don't take that tone with me. You want to talk about these things, we'll talk. That's why you're here. But don't push me. You understand?"

"Okay." She gestured, a conciliatory wave of one hand. "Sorry. But *isn't* that what you're saying?"

Elaborately patient, Venezzio said, "Think back, Louise. Will you think back? You married a playboy when you were only nineteen. A pretty boy, you married. A lightweight. A goddam druggie. I knew he'd be trouble. I *told* you."

"You had Jeff checked out." It was an accusation.

Venezzio shrugged. "Him, and your second husband, too. The first one, Jeff Something, at least his father was loaded. But—"

"Rabb," she said, her voice tight and bitter. "His name was Rabb. Angela's last name. Your granddaughter. Remember?"

"Rabb—okay." Condescendingly, Venezzio nodded. "Okay. Rabb. Right. Then that second guy—that actor— Christ, he was in the hole when you married him. Broke. Completely broke. He was—what?—twice your age, and already washed up. And you—"

"Jack was sweet. He was just—just vulnerable."

"Sweet." Venezzio snorted. Mocking her now: "*Sweet?*"

"He always liked you. He was fascinated by you."

For a moment Venezzio made no reply. Then, contemptuously: "Jeff Rabb. Was he sweet, too? Coked out of his skull, was he sweet?"

"That was only at the end," she muttered. "At first, we had fun. We had a lot of fun."

"Fun." The single word dripped with scorn. "Kids, having fun. What'd he have, a red Ferrari, something like that?"

For a moment she said nothing. Then, driven to say it, to take the risk: "It was either marry Jeff or else get an abortion." Avoiding his eyes, she spoke softly, a confession.

"Ah . . ." As Venezzio said it, the memory came back: Janice, nineteen years old, stubbornly refusing to have her baby taken—the baby she'd named Louise. "Ah . . ." he repeated, nodding. "Yeah. I see." Then defiantly: "Nobody said anything about that."

"Nobody knew," she answered.

"Your mother—she didn't know?"

"Only Jeff knew."

"Jeff Rabb . . ." Venezzio considered, finally nodded. Acknowledging that, yes, she'd confided in him. Finally confided in him, as a child should.

But he, in turn, could only nod, could only say, "Well, anyhow, he's out of your life. And the actor, he's been dead— what—a couple of years, now?"

"I wish," she said, "that you'd at least call him by his name. Jack Castle. Maybe you never saw him in the movies. But lots of others, they saw him. He was—"

"Listen. Louise." He turned on the golf cart's uncomfortable seat to face her squarely. "What's past, let's forget about that. It's now, that's what I want to talk about."

"Walter, you mean. Me going to San Francisco." She spoke resentfully, bitterly. "Is that what we're going to talk about?"

"Goddammit, forget about Walter. Forget about San Francisco. Will you do that? Will you forget about men just for a minute, and pay attention? Christ, we've been talking for a half hour, give or take. And all we've done is argue. So will you listen? This exercise yard, you know, doesn't exactly belong to me." He let a single quick beat pass before, with an effort, he said, "Please, Louise. Will you listen?"

At the words, startled, she raised her eyes to his. Had he ever said please to her before this moment? Exploring, perhaps venturing to hope, each searched the other's eyes. Then, defensively, she shrugged. "Go ahead."

He began speaking in a slow, measured voice, a father instructing his daughter: "The first thing you've got to know is that I've got nine more years in here. That's the first thing."

In response, she nodded. Yes, she understood that.

"And the second thing is, I've had two heart attacks in the last eight months. Those're the facts. The way I understand it, though, my heart's okay. Not great, but okay. But these goddam doctors, they do a lot of guessing. I could drop dead tomorrow, or I could live to be a hundred, who knows? All I know is, I'm sixty-six now, and I'll be seventy-five before I get out of here—*if* I get out of here. Now—" He paused, took two long, deep breaths. Yes, he was tiring. Meaning that he wanted to get it done, give her the words, then get back to his cell and lie down. "Now," he repeated, "I always expect the best and prepare for the worst, that's something my old man always said. And, surprise, he had a point." He allowed himself a brief smile, tentatively shared with his daughter. "So I'm preparing for the worst, which is that I don't get out of this place alive." He broke off again, watched his daughter's face, looking for a reaction, a hint of sympathy. There was nothing.

"So the question is," he went on, "what'd happen to you if I died? And the answer is, right now, it'd be anybody's guess. One thing's for sure, though. You aren't going to start getting any checks from insurance companies if I die, nothing like that."

She nodded. "I know."

"People talk about Communism," he said, "they don't realize that our organization's always had it. Like it or not, that's what we've got. Communism. Everything belongs to everyone—and no one. Everything belongs to the organization, in other words. The reason is, if we put anything in writing, we're screwed. Houses, even cars, they're all owned by dummies. Companies, usually—small corporations. The money comes in, the money goes out. But none of it sticks. Take me. As far as the feds're concerned, I import olives. As far as the IRS's concerned, my company pays me maybe twenty-five thousand a year—on which I pay taxes. That's what happened to Capone, you know. Income taxes."

"I know that."

"Luciano and Genovese, they were both *capo di tutti*—and both of them died with chicken feed in their pockets. Vito, he was always good with money. He saw that his family was taken care of when he died. But Charlie Lucky, he didn't give a shit. He lived like a king, over in Italy after they finally deported him. But that was it for Charlie. When he died, and the undertaker was paid off, then it was like you'd change the channel of a river. All that money, diverted."

Once more, she nodded. The next few minutes, she knew, could change her life.

"So then there's me and Maria. My wife." He was looking at her intently. An answer, then, was required: an acknowledgment that, yes, she understood about his official Mafia family.

She nodded. "I—I know about them."

"When I die," Venezzio said, "the organization'll take care of Maria. And if she wants to, she'll send some to the two kids—our children. That's up to her. But, either way, the organization'll take care of her. Personally, for all the shit she's given me, I'd as soon see Maria on Times Square, hustling. But there're the children—and grandchildren, too. Maria, she poisoned all of them against me. I've got grandchildren I haven't even seen, don't even know their names, all thanks to Maria, that bitch. But the organization doesn't like divorces. So—" He drew a long, deep breath. "So, like I said, Maria'll be taken care of, when I die."

"Envelopes, you mean."

He nodded.

"For Maria. Not for me."

Once more he spoke heavily, ponderously: "That's what I want to talk to you about. That's why you're here. To talk about afterwards, if I die in here."

She made no reply, but only watched him—and waited.

Now he spoke briskly, concisely, plainly having already decided exactly what he wanted to say. "What I've done is to tell Tony Bacardo to get together some jewels—diamonds, mostly—and some gold. Not much gold, because it's so heavy. It's taken Tony about six months to get it all together. And when he was doing it, collecting it all, he was taking a risk. The other dons, if they ever knew about this, well—" As if he were pronouncing a benediction—or a death sentence—he shook his head.

She nodded. "I understand. It's a risk."

"You're damn right it's a risk. And not just for Tony, either."

"For you? A risk for you, too?"

Grimly, he made no response.

"Wh-what about for me? If—" She licked her lips. "If it all comes to me, and they find out I've got it . . ."

Once more his silence said it all—and more. Then, speaking matter-of-factly, Venezzio said, "Do you know about that plastic pipe they use for plumbing? PVC, it's called. They use it for sewer lines a lot."

Puzzled, she frowned. "Sewer pipe? Did you say sewer?"

Impatiently, he nodded. "It's white or black. Plastic. You put it together with a special glue, and that's it. It'll never rot, never leak. And once everything's glued together it takes a saw to get it apart. Plus, it's light. You understand?''

Hesitantly, she nodded. ''I—I've seen the stuff, I guess. But I never paid any attention.''

''Well, you can go to any hardware store, look it over. But what I'm talking about, these jewels, Tony's sealed them in a piece of this sewer pipe. It's white, and it's about a foot long, maybe four, five inches diameter on the inside, something like that. It's got caps at the ends, all sealed up. Tony's got it now. But in a few days, a week, something like that, I'm going to have someone pick it up from Tony. This guy, call him Pete, he'll take the package and he'll hide it in some safe place.'' He paused, watching his daughter's face, letting her catch up, take it all in. Always, Louise's face had been expressive; she'd never been able to keep a secret, never been able to lie, not really. What Louise was thinking, it was always right there in her face. Janice had been like that: not really very smart, but always transparently truthful.

''You with me so far?'' he asked.

Hesitantly, she nodded. Yes, she understood. But she was going slowly, cautiously feeling her way. ''Louise is good-natured,'' Janice had once said. ''But she's no great brain.''

''The thing is,'' he explained, ''only Mar—only Pete and I'll know where the package is hidden. But only Tony and me—and you, now—know what's in the package. And—'' A beat, to focus her attention. ''And only I know the whole story, both sides of it.'' Another beat. ''Right?''

''But then how do I—I mean—'' Once more, hesitantly, she broke off. Then, more resolutely: ''But if you should die, then how—'' She bit her lip, began to shake her head.

He took his notebook and pen from a jacket pocket. He wrote three words, then held the notebook angled so she could see the words he'd written: *''Don't say anything out loud,''* he whispered. *''There's directional microphones. They can pick up a pin drop. So just look. Memorize these three words.''* Holding the notebook, he watched her lips move, mouthing the words.

"Okay?" He closed the notebook.

"Y-yes." She spoke cautiously, her voice pitched low. Fixed on his face, her eyes were large and anxious. "But how—?"

"Tony. He's got three words, too. If I die, the two of you get together. He'll come to you, where you live. So you should just sit tight, wait for him. The two of you, you'll go get the package. Tony'll help you, tell you what to do."

Tentatively, she nodded. Then, venturing cautiously: "But what if Tony finds out my three words, and then he—"

"He won't," Venezzio interrupted curtly. "Forget it. There's only one person I trust, and that's Tony."

"But you'd be—I mean, you couldn't—"

"I'd be dead, is that what you're trying to say?"

Chastened, she nodded.

"The answer is, Tony's already out on a limb on this one. A couple of guys in New York—dons—if they knew about this, Tony'd die. It's what I said before, about whose money it is that bought those jewels."

"But you're the boss. You run things."

"I run things as long as I play by the rules. It's the same for me as anybody else. I don't kid myself. There's one of the dons—Cella—if he doesn't like what I do, the decisions I make, well . . ." Venezzio shrugged, looked away.

"Will he take over, after you? Is that what you're saying?"

Venezzio nodded reluctantly. "Yeah, that's what I'm saying." It was the first time he'd said it out loud, admitted that, yes, Cella was waiting—and watching. At the thought, he felt a sudden weariness, a quick, piercing chill. Without looking at his daughter, he flipped the toggle that switched on the golf cart's electric motor. "It's getting cold."

"I know," she answered. "I know."

MONDAY, MAY 19th
1:10 P.M., EDT

"Here." Maranzano pointed ahead through the windshield. "Turn right."

Behind the wheel, Fabrese nodded, flicked the Oldsmobile's turn indicator.

"Fifteen, twenty minutes," Maranzano said, "and we're there."

"Do we both go in?"

Maranzano shook his head. "It's only when Bacardo does it that two people go inside."

"That's when they're carrying," Fabrese said. "You know—suitcases." As he said it, Fabrese looked aside at Maranzano, briefly searching the other man's face for a reaction. Keeping his eyes straight ahead, Maranzano made no response. Always, with Fabrese, there was an angle, a hustle. Fabrese was almost thirty-five years old, and still a soldier, nothing more, driving the car and asking questions he shouldn't be asking, looking for yet another angle, another way in. But their organization was like any other business. By age forty, you were either on the fast track or else you were passed over, given the shit jobs, an embarrassment. Couldn't Fabrese see it? Couldn't he see what was happening, who was on the fast track, who wasn't? Like today. Right now. Right here. Two days ago, Maranzano had gotten the word from Bacardo: Don Carlo had a job for him. Meaning that today at two o'clock he was to be at the prison gate, stating his business: an appointment with Mr. Venezzio. "Don't call him *the don*," Bacardo had cautioned. "Not when you talk to the guards."

He would be taken to the don. He would be greeted according to his rank: a new capo, not yet forty years old, a comer. Then, saying as little as possible, he would receive his orders, learn of his mission.

"Remember," Bacardo had warned, "keep looking in his eyes. The don doesn't trust anyone who doesn't look him square in the eye."

In a half hour, probably, he would be back in the car. Fabrese would be waiting to drive them away from the prison.

Fabrese, his driver . . .

At the thought, covertly, he smiled. *Perks*, they were called. Little things that meant nothing—and everything. *It's who opens the doors for who*, Luciano had said once. *That's what it's all about, who opens the doors.*

2:20 P.M., EDT

Seeing Maranzano walking between the rows of parked cars, Fabrese leaned across the front seat, tripped the door latch, pushed the passenger door open. Maranzano was moving as he always moved: compactly, purposefully, with his head slightly lowered, his short, muscular arms tight to his sides, like he was ready to throw a quick punch. Maranzano was one of those short, stocky men who looked bigger than he really was. His head was large, covered with thick black hair, always perfectly barbered. Everything about his dark, Sicilian face and head was thick: a short, thick neck, thick nose and brows, thick lips, a wide, thick jaw. His small eyes were black, sunk deep in the face.

As Maranzano slipped into the car and pulled the door closed, Fabrese started the engine, backed out of the parking place, began driving away from the prison. They drove for a time in silence. Finally Fabrese said, "So how'd it go?"

"It went fine."

"The don—how's he doing? I mean, everyone knows he's had heart trouble. They say—"

"He looks fine. As good as ever. Better, maybe."

"How much longer has he got inside? Nine, ten years?"

"Something like that, yeah."

"He's—what—sixty-five, something like that?"

"Yeah."

Fabrese looked at the other man, studied the dark, closed face, those black eyes that seemed never to blink. Appearance, he knew, was important. You looked like a mafioso, people paid attention. Never mind Venezzio, who looked like he could be a tailor. Never mind Cella, who looked like he should be teaching school—or hearing a confession. And Bacardo, who looked like a farmer—and thought like one, too. But the old-timers—Luciano and Costello and Anastasia—they looked the part. And, now, Maranzano: another Sicilian who looked the part. And, yes, acted the part. *Think big*, he'd once read. *Think success*. Meaning that the way you thought about yourself, your self-image, that's the way people saw you.

So here they were: him doing the driving, Maranzano trying out his new job. Maranzano, the family's newest capo.

They'd grown up in the same neighborhood, hung around the same places. Pitched pennies together, rooted for the Yankees, chased the girls. Always, from the first, they'd wanted to be what they were right now: connected, part of the organization, their thing. *La Cosa Nostra*, the papers had called it.

Except that he'd been ordered to wait in the car, a flunky, while Maranzano, in his new suit and gleaming white shirt and fifty-dollar tie, had just seen Don Carlo.

Had it been one on one, the don and Maranzano? Had it been—what—a ceremony, congratulations from the big man, something every new capo got?

Or had it been a job?

"Bacardo wants to step down," Don Carlo could have said. "He wants to retire, take it easy, maybe go to Florida, where it's warm." And then the question, asked in Venezzio's thin, reedy voice: "So I was thinking about you, to take Bacardo's place. I'm thinking new blood, the newest capo, the new number one. What d'you say?"

Fabrese took his foot from the accelerator, let the car slow for the four-way stop ahead. At the intersection he saw a gas station, a fruit stand, and a boarded-up restaurant. In the desolate, low-lying countryside that surrounded the prison, there were no other structures in sight, no other signs of life.

As the car came to a stop, Maranzano pointed to the gas station. "Pull in there, see if they've got a pay phone."

Resentful of the other man's clipped tone of command, Fabrese answered in kind, short and not so sweet: "Right."

"Where're the quarters?" Maranzano asked, still talking like a capo, not like a friend from the old days.

"In the glove compartment." Fabrese brought the car to a stop on the concrete apron of the gas station, close beside a weather-beaten phone booth.

"Sit tight." Maranzano put a handful of quarters in his jacket pocket, swung the passenger door open, walked to the phone booth, called Bacardo, who was waiting for the call.

"Hello, Tony." To be sure Bacardo recognized his voice, Maranzano spoke very distinctly.

"How're you doing?" Yes, Bacardo knew who was calling— and why.

"I'm fine. We're all set here."

"You know what to do, then."

"No problem."

"When d'you want to come by?"

"How about tomorrow morning? Eight o'clock?"

"So early?"

"I thought I'd pick it up, then go right to the airport. But if you want to make it later—" He let it go unfinished.

"No. Eight's fine. I'll give you some coffee. And a blintz, too. I've got a great bakery for blintzes."

Maranzano decided to chuckle, one capo to another, free and easy, trying it out: "Blintzes. That's Jewish, Tony."

"Okay. Snails. Whatever."

"I—ah—" Maranzano hesitated. "I was wondering how big it is? How heavy?"

"It's about five inches by twelve inches, a tube. The weight—I'm no good at guessing weight. But I'd say maybe ten pounds, give or take."

"That's fine. I was thinking, is all, if it's fifty pounds, something like that, then I'd have to make plans."

"No. Fifteen pounds. No more."

"Well, that's fine. So—eight o'clock. You're sure that's okay, so early?"

"It's fine. Eight o'clock."

TUESDAY, MAY 20th
8 A.M., EDT

"Very nice," Fabrese said, bringing the Oldsmobile to a stop in the wide combed-gravel driveway. "Has he got his own dock?"

"I think so. He's crazy about boats."

"It's hard to imagine, Tony belonging to a yacht club, all those Ivy Leaguers."

Ignoring the remark, Maranzano glanced at his watch: good, exactly eight o'clock. "I'll just be ten, fifteen minutes. Then we've got to haul ass for the airport. Ten minutes after ten, my flight leaves. So that's nine-thirty I've got to be there."

"The rush hour—" Fabrese shook his head doubtfully. "I don't know. It'll be an hour and fifteen minutes to Kennedy."

Without comment, Maranzano swung open the passenger door and walked down the driveway. Fabrese watched him move, that cocky, compact walk, eyes straight ahead, concentrating. Every day, Maranzano was coming on stronger, pulling the feeling closer around him, getting deeper into his part: the capo, don't fuck with the capo. Yesterday, a trip to the prison, everything hush-hush. The conference with Venezzio, the man himself. Followed by the phone call from the gas station, probably to Bacardo, passing the word along to Venezzio's top gun outside, no time to waste. And now, ahead, Bacardo coming out on the front porch of his big two-story brick-and-stone house on the water, shaking hands and gesturing for Maranzano to come in. Bacardo, still in his pajamas and bathrobe.

Them that had, got. And Maranzano was getting. Fast. Two

weeks ago he'd been a soldier, taking orders, driving his own car, holding doors for the dons, even for the capos, if that's the way it worked out. Sometimes, like Luciano had said, that's what it all came down to: who held the doors for who, and who had to smile, whether the joke was good or bad.

Ten, fifteen minutes, Maranzano had said.

Fabrese turned in the seat to look at the sun coming off Long Island Sound, the water sparkling beneath a clear, high sky. He'd heard about Tony Bacardo's boat, a big cabin cruiser. Someday—someday soon, maybe—Maranzano would be invited out on that boat, drinking beer, wearing a yachting cap, one of those blue caps with the embroidered ship's wheel and anchor, hot shit.

Now Fabrese twisted, looked into the back seat where Maranzano had put his suitcase and his topcoat. He'd been wearing the topcoat when he came out of his apartment building, carrying the suitcase. Before he'd gotten into the car, in front, he'd taken off the topcoat. He'd carefully checked the inside pocket, then he'd folded the topcoat neatly, laying it across the rear seat cushion, with the suitcase on the floor.

Meaning that, in the inside pocket of the topcoat, Maranzano had probably put his airline ticket.

Ten, fifteen minutes . . .

Coffee, maybe, with Bacardo, a few minutes to get their signals straight, make sure Maranzano understood whatever job Venezzio had given him—whatever job would take him out of town.

Out of town where?

The answer, Fabrese knew, could be imprinted on the airline ticket.

It was unusual for a New York capo to go out of town on business.

So unusual that Cella, for one, might want to know.

He turned, looked at the house. From any one of a half dozen windows, it would be possible for someone to see him as he rested his right arm casually on the back of the front seat—

—and then, still casually, dropped the arm down behind the seat—

—as he was doing now.

For a long moment, watching the house, his arm behind the seat, concealed, he sat motionless.

Then, as his fingers found the topcoat, camel hair, soft to the touch, he moved his head again, to look at the coat. Working awkwardly with only the one hand, he folded back one of the lapels to expose the inside breast pocket. Yes, there it was: the airline ticket envelope.

Aware of the risk—aware that, yes, he was going hollow at his center, beginning to tremble—he drew the envelope clear of the pocket. Still using only one hand, fumble-fingered as a child, he managed to open the envelope, take out the itinerary slip that accompanied the ticket.

Flight 235A to San Francisco, the printout read. And: *Flight 87 to Sacramento.*

In the margin of the itinerary slip, four words had been handwritten: *Janice Frazer, Fowler's Landing*. It was Maranzano's scrawl.

Carefully he refolded the envelope, returned it to the pocket, refolded the topcoat's lapel. Then, drawing a long, shaky breath, he turned back to face the house, both hands resting once more on the steering wheel. Safe.

WEDNESDAY, MAY 21st
11:57 P.M., PDT

With the tiny flashlight Maranzano shone a slim beam of light on the ground. With his free hand he carefully brushed the fresh dirt away from the newly laid square of sod. He switched off the flashlight, straightened, looked carefully around, slowly pivoting. The night was still, the sky overcast. Holding up his wrist, he checked the time: midnight. The whole job, from the time he'd arrived, had taken twenty-five minutes. It was longer than he'd estimated; the ground had been hard and dry, the digging had been slow. Lying at his feet, the plastic shopping bag rustled faintly in the gentle breeze. He stooped, picked up the small collapsible shovel, began to turn the large knurled nut that would collapse the shovel to backpacking size. He laid the collapsed shovel on the ground, picked up the plastic bag, upended it, shook out the dirt left from the sod. He put the shovel and penlight in the bag, used the paper toweling he'd brought to clean the dirt from his hands. Then, with time passing, each minute a risk, he picked up the plastic bag. He began walking to the gate. He'd left it closed but unlatched. His rental car was parked a few feet from the wrought-iron fence, perhaps a hundred feet from the gate. He'd parked the car on the grass in the shadows cast by a small grove of trees.

When he was still thirty feet from the gate, he saw headlights. The car was coming slowly, making steady progress down the narrow, uneven road that led past the gate. A large tree grew close beside the pathway he was on. He must move fast enough to reach the tree before the car's headlights picked him up—but not so fast that the movement would attract attention. "In the dark," Bacardo had told him once, "if you move too fast, they'll see you." He'd been only twenty when Bacardo had told him. He'd been the lookout when Bacardo and two others went in after Tommy the Cork. They'd found Tommy in bed—with a boy.

When he was five feet from the tree's shadow, the oncoming car's headlights dipped down, then bobbed up—and caught him. Instantly immobilized, he waited until the headlights dipped again. Then, two strides took him into the shadows, hidden behind the trunk of the tree. Safe.

Safe?

No, not until the car passed would he be safe.

Carefully, he lowered the plastic shopping bag to the ground. His .38 was thrust into his belt, on the left side. The gun had a two-inch barrel, easy to conceal but useless beyond fifty feet, even in daylight.

By now the driver had seen Maranzano's car, parked in the grass beside the fence. Had it been a mistake to park the car so far from the gate?

Soon he would know.

Because, yes, the car was slowing, stopping. The headlights shone for a moment after the engine died, then went out.

Revealing, across the car roof, a police patrol car's light bar, plain in the pale light from the sky.

Slowly, the driver's door swung open, and the driver laboriously climbed out. He was a big, slow-moving man who stooped, reached inside the dark car. When he straightened, he was adjusting a wide-brimmed Smokey the Bear hat on his head. With a long flashlight in his left hand, the policeman began walking toward Maranzano's car. As he walked he unsnapped the safety strap of his holster, then continued with his hand resting on the butt of his service revolver.

Still in the shadow cast by the single tree, Maranzano used his right hand to slip an ice pick from its homemade leather sheath slung beneath his left arm. After a moment's thought he slipped the ice pick point first into the left sleeve of the light wool jacket he wore, adjusting the pick so that the handle was cupped in his left hand. Then, leaving the plastic shopping bag where it lay, he stepped boldly away from the tree, began walking toward the gate, dragging his feet noisily on the gravel pathway. As he pushed open the gate he called out cheerfully, "Looking for me, Officer?"

"This your car?"

"Well," Maranzano said, walking along the fence toward the policeman, "yes and no, I suppose is the answer. I rented it in Sacramento. Why? Has one like it been stolen?"

Suddenly the flashlight came on, focused blinding-bright on his face. *"Hey."* He put indignation in the single word, the pissed-off taxpayer protesting. Repeating: "Hey, you *mind*?"

In response, the flashlight beam dropped, focused now on his torso. But the voice from behind the light came cold and hard: "What're you doing here, this time of night?"

He moved his head in the direction from which he'd come, smiling as he said, "I was coming along that goddam levee road, and the next thing I knew, I could hardly see the goddam hood ornament, all that ground fog."

"That's the levee road. This is here. What're you doing here?"

"I'm lost, is what I'm doing here. I'm looking for Fowler's Landing. Can you help me out?"

"But why're you parked here, is what I'm asking. And where were you when I drove up?"

Maranzano sighed loudly, another pissed-off-taxpayer protest. "Well, Officer, if you really have to know, I was taking a shit. My stomach, the last hour or two, it's tied up in knots. So—" He shrugged, man-to-man admitting, "So I was out beating the bushes, you might say, looking for some paper on the ground." Now, man-to-man smiling: "You ever have to shit, and you don't have any paper?"

The flashlight beam had fallen waist-high now, an accommodation. Yes, it would all work out. And, confirming it: "I've got some newspaper in the car."

"Well, thanks anyhow." The smile was wide open now, as

friendly as he could make it. "But I'm all set now. Some litter-bug, thank God. But if you don't mind, if you can spare some of that newspaper, maybe I'll take it along. Just in case."

"Sure. No problem."

"Thanks, Officer. I appreciate it."

"What's your name?"

"It's Matuska. Frank Matuska. That's Polish."

"Ah—Polish." The policeman nodded. Then, politely: "Just let me see some identification, Mr. Matuska. Then I'll get that newspaper and you can be on your way."

"Oh. Sure." Careful not to do it too suddenly, he began a movement with his left hand, to reach in his left hip pocket for the wallet that contained his fake ID. But the handle of the ice pick rested in the palm of his left hand. Could he reach the left hip pocket with his right hand? No, it was not possible. Could he support the ice pick with the little finger of his left hand, using the other three fingers and thumb to withdraw the wallet? No. Never.

"What's the problem?" As he spoke, the policeman moved back one cautious step, then another. He'd opened six feet between them, guarding against a knife attack. Now his right hand was in motion, dropping toward the butt of his holstered revolver. The flashlight beam was focusing on Maranzano's left arm, still half concealed behind his back.

"It's this button. They're new pants." As he spoke, Maranzano used his right hand to unbutton his jacket, exposing the revolver thrust in his belt.

"Hey!"

The flashlight was falling away, leaving sudden darkness between them. Maranzano's hand was on the butt of his revolver, jerking it from his waistband. The policeman was crouching, an indistinct blur after the flashlight's glare. Maranzano fired point-blank: one shot, and another, double action.

"Ah." It was a sharp, sudden sigh. "Ah, Jesus. Don't." Now the policeman was trying to keep his balance, keep standing. He raised his left hand, as if to ward off a third shot. His right hand was pawing awkwardly at his revolver, still in its holster.

Maranzano took a step forward, pulling the trigger with the muzzle of his pistol less than a foot from the policeman's torso, lined up on the heart. With the third shot, the policeman dropped instantly to his knees, then fell heavily on his face, lying motionless. Standing over the body, Maranzano decided on a fourth shot to the temple. "The insurance shot," Bacardo called it. "The executioner's pop."

TUESDAY, MAY 24th
10:15 P.M., EDT

"No dessert?" Bacardo asked. "You sure?"

Maranzano raised an affable hand, then patted his hard, flat stomach. "Thanks, no. The first time in my life, I'm starting to watch what I eat."

"What d'you weigh?"

"Stripped, a hundred seventy." He smiled. "That's on a good day."

"A hundred seventy, though . . ." Bacardo looked over the younger man sitting across the table. "Your height and build, that's okay."

"*That's* okay. No more, though. I've made up my mind."

"Well, what about a brandy?"

"How about an espresso?" Maranzano countered.

"Espresso. Fine." Bacardo waved to the waiter, ordered two espressos. Then: "You're probably wondering why I asked you tonight. And the answer is just—you know—get acquainted, let some of the guys see us together, get them used to the idea, now you're a capo. Diplomacy, I guess you'd say."

"And it's appreciated, Tony. It's appreciated very much." As he said it, Maranzano was conscious of the satisfaction, the privilege, calling Bacardo Tony.

"Also," Bacardo said, "I wanted to tell you that Don Carlo appreciated it, how you took care of that thing for him."

"That cop—" As if to thrust the thought angrily away, Maranzano gestured, a quick chop of his muscular hand. "A rube cop. Jesus."

Bacardo was ready with a reassuring smile. "The difference

between rube cops and New York cops, you know, there's not much juice out in the sticks. So they got no choice but to be honest. The other way, there's no advantage."

Maranzano nodded, smiled appreciatively, waited for the waiter to serve the espresso. Then, looking around the restaurant, he asked, "Where's Eddie? I don't think I've ever seen you without Eddie."

"He had a root canal today. He wanted to come, but I said no. He's on painkillers, feels like shit. And there's something I've got to do tomorrow, I need him. So I told him to stay home tonight, take it easy."

"Does Eddie live out on Long Island, too?"

"He lives fifteen, twenty minutes away from me. Most of the time he's got my Caddie, keeps it overnight."

"Ah . . ." Approvingly, Maranzano nodded. "Yeah, I see. That's good. Perfect."

Bacardo sipped the espresso, frowned, added sugar. "Jesus, this stuff stands right up, eh?"

"I know."

Bacardo stirred in the sugar, asking, "What about Fabrese, speaking of drivers? How's he working out?" The question was casually asked, but Bacardo's eyes flicked quickly, catching the other man's reaction.

"Well," Maranzano answered, "you want the truth, it seems to me that he asks too many questions."

"Yeah . . ." Heavily, Bacardo nodded. "Yeah, I can see that. What d'you want to do, keep him on for another couple of months, then put him back on the street, something like that?"

"A couple of months—yeah." Maranzano's answering nod was equally judicious. "Yeah, I guess so. He drives all right, there's nothing wrong with his driving. But I just wonder, if there was a problem, something came up, I don't know where Jimmy'd be."

"Maybe under a table."

"Yeah, well." Maranzano shrugged, sipped his coffee. "Well, I wouldn't be surprised."

"Okay." Bacardo signaled the waiter for the check, dropped

money on the table. Explaining: "I've got to be going. Long Island, you know, driving myself . . ." He shook his head, then pushed back his chair. "You got your car?"

"No. I went home first, and Fabrese took the car to the parking garage. That's Manhattan, you know. Having a car—I wouldn't ever have one, if it wasn't for business."

"So you took a cab."

"Right."

"Well, then, I'll take you home, drop you off."

"Aw—no. There's no need, Tony. It's no problem, taking a cab."

"No." On his feet, Bacardo gestured to the restaurant's rear exit that led to a small parking lot. "No, come on. We can talk. There's something else that I want to talk to you about."

"Well, fine."

Together they walked to the exit, then out to the parking lot. Always polite, Bacardo was unlocking the Cadillac's door for him. Quickly, Maranzano slid into the car, found the latch for the driver's door, pushed it open. Bacardo got in behind the wheel, settled himself, closed the door, looked at the man beside him. "Hey." Bacardo twisted the key in the ignition, brought the engine to life. "Hey, buckle up there."

"I never buckle up in the city."

"You ride with me, you buckle up. Most accidents happen within a couple of miles of home. That's the statistics."

"Okay, okay." In amiable mock surrender, Maranzano raised his hands, then went about the business of fastening his belt. Saying finally: "There. All set."

"Good." Bacardo nodded, put his foot on the brake, moved the shift selector to "R," carefully looked back through the rear window—

—glanced down at Eddie Caproni, crouched in the darkness behind the front seat. Waiting. Ready.

Bacardo turned to face front. He kept his foot firmly on the brake, immobilizing the car, to give Eddie the best chance.

There was a hiss as the slim plastic-coated steel cable looped over Maranzano's head. Instantly Maranzano threw himself forward, fighting the bite of the noose, his fingers clawing at his throat. But Caproni had both knees braced against the front seat, back bowed, hauling on the noose. Because he was strangling, Maranzano's eyes were bulging. Because he was fighting to keep the noose tight, biting deep into the skin of his victim's neck, Caproni's eyes were bulging, too.

1990

THURSDAY, APRIL 12th
10 A.M., PDT

She crossed the living room to the telephone, answered on the second ring.

"Is this Louise?" It was a man's voice, deep and thick.

"Yes."

"This is Tony, Louise."

"Tony . . ." The single word lingered, not quite a question. Tony Bacardo, that big, awkward, slow-talking, even-tempered man. She'd last seen him when he'd taken her to her father at the prison hospital. Ever since, she'd been expecting this call. All the time was gone now. Everything, gone.

"It's—it's about your father, Louise. Don Carlo."

"Ah . . ."

Her father, that man some called a monster. Dead. Surely, dead.

Without realizing that she'd done it, she was sitting on the sofa. Would she choke up? Cry? Was that what was expected now?

"He's dead," she finally managed to say.

"Yes."

"When did it happen?"

"It happened last night sometime. They didn't tell—" A pause. "They didn't tell the family until early this morning. Eight o'clock, I think. Our time."

"Was anyone with him when he died?"

"I don't know. He was in the prison hospital, where he died. And they have their rules."

"I thought he ran the prison." It was an accusation.

"Well, that's true—as long as everyone understands each other. He could have his own doctors, things like that. But he couldn't have visitors in the hospital. It's security."

"What about his—" How should she say it? How *could* she say it? "His family, what about them? His children?"

"Well, Maria—his wife—she wouldn't've visited him, even if they'd let her. And his children—the two children he had with Maria—I don't know. Maybe Maria said stay away, and that's what they did. I think that's probably what happened."

"What about the funeral?"

"I haven't heard anything. But the way I think it'll go, Maria'll sign all the papers, and our organization will take it from there, pay the bills and everything. There's an undertaker—Sigler and Sons—they know how to do things."

"Will you tell me when the funeral is?"

"Are you planning to come, make the trip?"

"Yes. Sure. Angela, too. We'll both come."

There was a long, heavy silence. She knew the meaning of that silence, knew what Bacardo was about to say.

"I'm not so sure that'd be a good idea, Louise. Our organization, the top guys—the capos, and the dons—it's like they're politicians, you know. They *are* politicians. That's what it's all about with us. Your dad, he had every politician in New York in his pocket. Senators, judges, you name it."

"But my father still went to trial, went to prison."

"That's different. That's federal. He was framed by the feds, the same way Luciano and Genovese were framed. The feds want you bad enough, you got to be careful."

"Once he told me Maria gave the feds what they needed."

"We can talk about that when we get together, Louise. This is Thursday. The funeral'll probably be Monday or Tuesday. Then there's some things I've got to do. Something like this, Don Carlo dying, there're things have to be settled. You understand?"

"Yes," she answered. "Yes, I understand." As, once more, she felt it: the ageless weight of the Mafia, bearing her down, imprisoning her. "What you're saying, they don't want me to come to the funeral. Is that it? My own father."

"Louise—listen. It's what I said. It's politics. That's all. Politics. Christ, you and Angela, you're all the don cared about. You know that."

She made no response.

"The business we've got with each other, Louise—the words we got from the don, you and me—that was a risk for the don. A big risk. You should understand that, how big the risk was. He wouldn't've done that for anyone else. Never."

Still she made no response.

"So—" Bacardo spoke hesitantly, tentatively. Then, with finality: "So I'll see you in a week, maybe ten days, something like that. I'll come out there, and we'll do what the don wanted us to do. You understand?"

"I understand." She said it grudgingly.

"And about the funeral, listen, you send flowers to Sigler and Company. Send a big floral piece—you know, two, three hundred dollars, like that. Charge it to Sigler. And you tell them it's from 'Louise and Angela, rest in peace,' something like that. You do that, and I guarantee your piece'll be right up front, the closest to the casket. You understand?"

Suddenly weary, suddenly unutterably drained, she nodded to nothing, to no one. Saying: "I understand."

"Don't say anything on the wreath about—you know—whose father he was, nothing like that."

As he said it, the last of her strength flared, focused on one final protest. "You had to say that, didn't you? You just had to say that."

TUESDAY, APRIL 17th
11:15 A.M., EDT

As the organist began playing the overture to *Othello*, Don Carlo's favorite opera, Cella turned, whispered to Bacardo, "When we go to the cemetery, you ride with me. My car'll be right behind Maria's car."

"I've got to tell my driver," Bacardo whispered in return.

"He's already been told."

With his eyes on the casket, Bacardo nodded.

12:40 P.M., EDT

Cella leaned forward, touched the button that raised the limousine's glass partition. As the glass went up, Cella pointed to the tiny bar. "Drink?"

"No, thanks."

"Likewise." Cella unbuttoned his morning coat, settled back. "So what'd you think? Good service?"

"I thought the priest did better than the monsignor."

"No question. The pope should put that old fart out to pasture somewhere."

Bacardo smiled, but said nothing. Until the funeral procession began to move, both men had made small talk broken by awkward silences. Finally, as they moved away from the curbside, Cella said, "I hope your wife doesn't hold it against me, taking you away like this."

"She couldn't care less. She's only here because I'm here. Truth to tell, Don Carlo made her nervous. She never liked him."

Cella's laugh was spontaneous, appreciative. "Carlo made a lot of people nervous. It's the secret of his success."

Bacardo's answering chuckle was also quick, also appreciative.

"I wanted our people to see us together," Cella explained.

"Sure . . ." He let the single word linger, then said, "Thanks. I appreciate it."

They rode for a time in silence. Then, with his eyes forward, Cella spoke softly, precisely, significantly:

"So. Do you want the Venezzio family, Tony? The job's open."

Also looking straight ahead, also speaking softly, precisely, Bacardo answered, "No, thanks, Benito. I—" Suddenly he broke off. *Benito*, he'd said. Not *Don Benito*, but simply *Benito*, the first time he'd ever done it, an unpardonable familiarity. Take the don's job, and he could call Cella *Benito*. Turn down the job, and it was *Don Benito*. Forever.

"I've thought about it," Bacardo admitted. "You realize that. And Don Carlo, he told me he'd do what he could for me with you and the council. But I'm sixty years old. Ten years ago, when they locked Don Carlo up, I admit I thought about it. But sixty—" Wearily, Bacardo shook his head. "Sixty, that's no age to try and go all the way, start taking chances."

Fingering a pearl stickpin, then stroking his impeccably styled silver-gray hair, Cella nodded in return. "I think it's the right decision, Tony. It shows class. That's why you're respected, you know that. I don't know anyone who doesn't respect you."

Bacardo nodded, but made no reply. The funeral procession was on the expressway now, picking up speed.

"So," Cella said, his voice rising on a note of crisp finality. "So you don't want Don Carlo's family. So how about coming to work for me?" Smiling cordially, he turned to face the other man squarely. Signifying, Bacardo knew, that they'd come down to it, the make-or-break moment, no turning back—no mistakes allowed.

"You might not want to move up, Tony. But I do. I'll say it right out: *capo di tutti.* And for that, I need a new number one. Sal, he's fine. He's honest, and he's got heart. But he doesn't have respect, not like you. Sal's a second stringer."

Also turned to face his companion squarely, Bacardo nodded: a calm, measured response. "Sure. That's great. I'd like that."

"Okay, then. It's a deal."

Solemnly they shook hands. Then they embraced, the Mafia seal of brotherhood. Finally they drew back, and, as if they were embarrassed by the necessary expression of affection, both men once more turned to face front.

"What about Sal?" Bacardo asked.

"There's a good spot for him down in Atlantic City. It's all set." As he took time to reflect, Cella's colorless eyes wandered. Then: "Your wife, she's going to the cemetery. Right?"

Puzzled, Bacardo nodded. Repeating: "Yeah. Right."

"The reason I asked, I'll give Sal a ride back into town, after the ceremony. I'll give him the word then. He likes Atlantic City. The ocean—he's crazy about the ocean. Plus, his girlfriend's giving him a hard time. So it'll be fine. No problem."

Bacardo smiled, decided no comment was required.

"Let's give it a week or two, give Sal a chance to get used to the idea."

"Maybe two weeks might be better."

"Two weeks is fine. Get on that boat of yours, take a cruise." As Cella said it, the limousine slowed for the expressway exit.

"I was thinking maybe I'd go out to California for a few days. A week, maybe. Then maybe I'll come back, take a cruise. There's something I've got to take care of out in California. Maybe it'll only take a day or two. Then I'll come back, maybe take a ten-day cruise." Pleased at the prospect, Bacardo nodded. Effortlessly, it seemed, everything was working out.

"Listen, whatever time you need, no problem. Just—you know—keep in touch."

"Fine."

"And listen." Cella touched the other man's arm, smiled into his eyes, the well-known Cella charm. "Listen, call me Benito, okay? Maybe not—you know—in public. But there's just the two of us, it's Tony and Benito."

2:40 P.M. EDT

Cella waited for the glass partition to rise. Then, gesturing to the limousine's tiny bar: "How about a drink, Sal? Don Carlo, rest in peace." A twisting of Cella's thin lips signified that the toast was ironic.

"Are you having one?"

"Today," Cella answered, "I'm having one."

"Then I'll have one. Scotch on the rocks, please."

Cella made the drinks, handed one to Salvatore Perrone, a small, formal ceremony. Both men saluted each other, then gravely drank. Staring reflectively into the depths of his glass, Cella allowed a moment of silence to pass as the limousine waited its turn to join the procession leaving the cemetery. Finally he said, "Tony isn't interested in moving up."

"I never thought he was," Perrone answered. Like Cella, Perrone was a slightly built man of medium height. His hair was sparse, his face was narrow and deeply lined. A knife scar ran from the corner of his right eye down to the point of his chin. He spoke in a low, expressionless voice. Whatever emotion Perrone felt, it was never reflected in his dark, watchful eyes. He never laughed, almost never smiled. Unlike Cella, Perrone was visibly uncomfortable in his rented morning clothes.

"And you don't want Carlo's family."

Sipping his drink, Perrone considered. "The other dons, I don't think they'd let it happen, you putting me in there when you move up to *capo di tutti*. You'd have too much power. Every vote, you'd have two of them locked up—two out of five."

Cella nodded, pretended to consider the point as he sipped the Scotch. The limousine was inching forward, still caught in traffic. Finally he said, "I'm going to think about it. Don Carlo dies, I show a profit. There should be some way for you to come out, too. Maybe a family of your own, out of town."

Perrone made no response, neither by word nor gesture. This, he knew, was only a probe: Cella moving the chess pieces.

Cella finished his drink, put the empty glass in the rack, smiled reflectively. His voice was thoughtfully measured as he said, "It's funny, about people. You and Tony, neither of you're interested in moving up."

Perrone shrugged. "It's like animals, the animal kingdom. There's always got to be a top dog. Some guys—you and Don Carlo—it's natural for you to fight for the top job. But me and Tony, we're not interested. Simple as that."

"I suppose you're right. My folks, they could never understand why I even went into the organization." He smiled, adding, "Maybe it's just as well that they didn't understand."

Making no reply, Perrone finished his own drink, put his glass in the rack. The limousine was moving faster now; ahead the expressway overpass was coming into view. For a time, the two men rode in silence, each at ease with the other, no conversation required. Finally Cella spoke:

"About Tony. There's something going on with Tony."

Perrone turned to look at the other man's face, but made no response, let nothing show. Over the years, Perrone had learned to watch—and wait.

"When I took Tony to the cemetery," Cella said, "I had two things on my mind. I wanted to—you know—show respect for

Carlo. I mean, I'm sure not going to ride with Maria, that bitch. So that left Tony. You see."

"I see. Sure."

"Also, I wanted to make sure he wasn't thinking about taking over the don's family."

No reply, only a watchful silence.

"But," Cella said, speaking softly, deliberately, "something's going on with Tony. I want you to check it out."

Still no reply.

"When Venezzio had his first heart attack—that was almost five years ago, now—the first thing he did, of course, he had Tony G. taken out, to show he was still boss."

"Tony G. was living on borrowed time, the son of a bitch."

"I'm not saying he wasn't. But the thing is, Tony G. was a capo, just like you. And when a don wants a capo whacked, the four other dons have to go along. That's written in stone."

"Which is why Don Carlo did it. To show it *wasn't* written in stone, not for him."

"Okay, but why'd he have Frankie Maranzano whacked?" It was a delicately timed question, suggesting an intriguing puzzle.

Somberly, Perrone nodded—and said nothing. Some questions were too dangerous to answer.

"A year after his heart attack," Cella said, "give or take, Maranzano saw Venezzio. Alone. No Tony, nobody but Venezzio and Frankie, out in the yard. Everyone figured it was because Frankie was just made capo, and Don Carlo wanted to show that Frankie was in, had some juice with the big man. Politics, in other words."

Perrone nodded—and waited.

"But then, ten days later, whatever, Frankie gets whacked. It was the same thing as Tony G. Venezzio gave the word, and Frankie goes down, never mind what the council said. Or, more like it, didn't say."

"You didn't know about it, know it was coming?" Puzzled, Perrone frowned. "The council didn't know?"

Silently, Cella shook his head. "No, they didn't know."

"Everyone figured Frankie made a big mistake, maybe before he made capo. Everyone figured that had to be it."

Cella allowed another delicately timed silence to pass. Then, softly: "The mistake Frankie made was going out to California, to take care of something for Venezzio. That's the only mistake Frankie made."

Perrone's frown deepened. "California?"

"You didn't know about that?"

Perrone shook his head. No, he hadn't heard.

"Don Carlo sent Frankie out to the West Coast. Frankie was there for a couple of days. When he got back, he went straight to Venezzio. They went out into the yard again, talked for a few minutes. Don Carlo gave Frankie the big hug. A couple of days later Tony and Frankie had dinner, and Tony gave Frankie a ride home. Good-bye Frankie."

"Frankie must've screwed up out in California."

"Either that, or else Don Carlo didn't want anyone to know why Frankie went to California. Ever."

Judiciously, Perrone nodded. "Yeah—Venezzio did that before."

Now it was Cella's turn to remain silent while Perrone considered the possibilities. Finally Perrone said, "So what're you thinking, about Frankie's trip?"

"I think he was setting up something for Don Carlo. Something secret, maybe a West Coast connection for running money through Las Vegas. But whatever it was, I figure Frankie tried to cut himself in, maybe cut Don Carlo out."

"Jesus." Perrone shook his head. "I don't know. Frankie wasn't any genius. But he wasn't that dumb."

"Well, something sure as hell went wrong for Frankie."

"Huh . . ." Perrone let his eyes wander thoughtfully away. The limousine had slowed to a crawl; ahead, outlined on the rising arch of an overpass, the late-afternoon expressway traffic was bumper-to-bumper. It could be another hour before they got back to Manhattan.

Another hour that Carlo Venezzio had been in the ground.

Meaning that, for another hour, Cella had been *capo di tutti*, with no one to challenge him.

Meaning that now, Cella was giving him his first order: find out why Frankie Maranzano died. Find out what he'd done in California years ago that had cost him his life: a first-class hit, no expense spared. Jimmy Hoffa, say hello to Frankie Maranzano, rest in peace.

"What you said about Tony, something going on with him," Perrone said. "What'd you mean?"

"I mean," Cella answered, "that maybe tomorrow, maybe the day after, Tony's going out to the Coast. Just like Frankie did, four years ago."

"And you want me . . ." He decided to let it go unfinished, leaving the last line to Cella:

"I want you to find out what Tony does out there. Don't stir things up. But contact our people out there, buy some drinks, keep your eyes open. Take as long as you need. And keep in touch. Anything you find out—anything—give it to me, right away."

Perrone nodded. "Right away."

"This is a sensitive time, Sal. You understand that."

"Yes, I understand that."

FRIDAY, APRIL 20th
6 P.M., PDT

"Is this Louise?"

Yes, it was his voice. Tony Bacardo. "A week, ten days," he'd said. Since his last call, this was the eighth day.

"Yes. Tony?"

"Yes."

"Where are you?"

"I'm in San Francisco. I got in about an hour ago."

"Well, where're you staying?"

"At a hotel. I just checked in, got settled."

What should she say? What was she meant to say? Eight days ago, he'd told her he would call again. But instead of calling from New York, he'd come to San Francisco.

Three words, her father had told her to memorize.

How many words had Tony Bacardo memorized?

"Louise?"

"Y-yes."

"Is everything okay?"

There was a risk for the don, he'd said. *A big risk.*

In the past eight days, the words had been burned into her consciousness, a constant refrain. If there was a risk for her father, then there must be a risk for her.

Mafia gold . . . another refrain, like an MTV title.

"Louise?" Insistently now. Demanding an answer.

A big risk . . .

"Yes. I—sorry—I'm just surprised. I mean, you said you'd call. But I didn't think . . ." She couldn't decide how to finish it.

"I'm at the Hilton, downtown. It's six o'clock. I'll rent a car, and be at your house in about an hour. You're on Thirty-ninth Avenue. Right?"

"Y-yes. Thirty-ninth near Noriega."

"What's that? A house? An apartment?"

"It's a house."

"All right. I'll see you about seven. Will you be alone?"

"I—there's Angela. My daughter. She's been staying with me."

"How old is Angela?"

"She's twenty."

"Does she know about this, why I'm here?"

"I told her a little."

"A little . . ." In the two words, disapproval was plain.

"I—she's the only one I can talk to about it. When he died, I told her about it. Some of it."

"But the words—does she know the words?"

"No, I didn't tell her the words."

But I want to tell her, she almost said. *I've got to tell someone. I'm scared, and I've got to tell someone.*

"Have you had dinner?"

"We're just ready to sit down."

"All right. I'll see you in about an hour." The line clicked, went dead.

7:05 P.M., PDT

Fabrese watched the Ford Taurus come up the ramp. The driver was a young Chicano girl, black eyes, black hair, her face a pert, dusky oval. She stopped the car in front of him, set the parking brake, smiled as she got out of the car, held the door for him. She wore a Hertz uniform. Beneath the short brown skirt her legs were smooth and muscular. How many propositions a week would a girl like that get, bringing rental cars up the ramp to visiting tourists?

Fabrese slid in behind the wheel, decided to give the girl a dollar—decided to smile when she thanked him. Before he got under way, Fabrese spread the map of San Francisco on the seat beside him. At the Hertz office, they'd marked his route with a yellow highlighter: left on Post, right on Stockton, right on Geary. Follow Geary all the way to Thirty-ninth Avenue.

At seven o'clock, the traffic in downtown San Francisco was light. The cars moved more slowly than they moved in Manhattan, and the drivers had better manners.

Four years ago, with only a few days to live, Maranzano could have driven this same route. Maranzano, less than a month a capo—Maranzano, with the whole world on a string, a big red balloon, his for the taking.

Maranzano, with only a few days to live.

Maranzano had still been in his thirties when they'd made him a capo.

Young when he made capo.

Young when he died.

A trip to the prison, paying his respects, getting the Mafia hug from Don Carlo. Then the trip here, to California.

Then the dinner with Tony Bacardo, Maranzano's last dinner. Rest in peace.

California . . .

See California, and die.

Fowler's Landing, Maranzano had written on the airline routing slip. *Janice Frazer*.

How many had put it together, figured it out?

For years, there'd been the whispers: Don Carlo's two families, one family for the flash, one family for fun. Maria, herself the daughter of a Mafia don, royalty marrying royalty. Maria, beautiful in black, standing at the head of Venezzio's grave, watching the casket being lowered into the ground.

Janice Frazer . . .

Until he'd seen it written on Maranzano's airline routing slip he'd never heard the name. Until Maranzano had died, three days after he'd come back from California, Fabrese had hardly been curious. But then it had been like a blinding-bright searchlight, suddenly switched on. Maranzano had gone to see Venezzio, gotten his orders. Then Maranzano had gone to Bacardo, picked up a small red nylon flight bag with something inside, not too heavy, not too light. Maranzano had carried the nylon bag and his suitcase to the airport, flown to California. Three days later, he was back. The next day, Fabrese had driven him to the prison again, to see Venezzio. It had been a cordial meeting, in the prison yard. Meaning that, yes, Maranzano had done the job, done what Venezzio had told him to do with the package.

Meaning that, because the job was so secret, Maranzano had to die. "Mafia insurance," it was called: the silence that only death could insure.

Maranzano, dead.

Venezzio, dead.

Meaning that, now, he could be the only one alive who knew where Maranzano had gone four years ago.

Where he'd gone, and why.

Except that, at first, there'd been no why. Only where, and when. Janice Frazer had been a name that meant nothing; Fowler's Landing had been just as meaningless.

It had been an accident, nothing more, that had given him the first clue. Abe Zwillman, eighty-five years old, the last of the Jewish tough guys, had been talking about the old days: the wars of the thirties, when Charlie Lucky and Vito Genovese had shot their way to the top, then changed everything, put the organization on track, made it what it was today, big business.

For Abe, everyone bought the drinks. Everyone bought, and then everyone listened to Abe's stories, the good old days, buy a gun, make your bones, buy a striped suit with wide lapels, watch them smile and tip their hats. It had been just after Maranzano had died. As always, Abe had been telling the old stories. Then there'd come a phone call, orders for three soldiers who were listening to the old man spin his tales. Leaving just Fabrese and Abe Zwillman, who was still talking, still remembering the old days. It had been Fabrese's chance, and he'd taken it, asked the question: What about Fowler's Landing? What about Janice Frazer?

"Fowler's Landing?" Abe had asked, his leathery face creasing, puzzled. He'd never heard of Fowler's Landing.

What about Janice Frazer?

"Ah . . ." Abe had nodded, swallowed his cheap red wine, the only kind he ever drank, nodded again. "Janice Frazer," he'd said, his eyes losing focus, remembering. It had been almost forty years since Janice had come to town, had her baby, left town. Tony Eboli had been driving for Venezzio then—and Abe and Tony had been friends, drinking buddies. So when the time had come for Janice to leave New York, Tony had been the one who'd driven her to the train station.

And because they were friends, Tony had asked Abe to come along, help out with the tickets, whatever. He'd even held the baby, a little girl, while Janice had gone to the bathroom at the train station.

"I even remember the baby's name," Abe had said. "She was named Louise, after Janice's mother."

Nineteen, twenty years later, Abe Zwillman went on, the organization had sent him to Las Vegas, to see about skimming at the tables. He'd been there for two years, hated every minute of it. Then, winding back on his own story, an old man, drinking and rambling, he'd told about meeting Louise, the woman he'd once held in his arms when she was a baby. She'd married a man named Rabb, she'd said, the son of a Hollywood producer. And, yes, Louise had a baby of her own.

Louise Rabb, Carlo Venezzio's daughter.

Louise Rabb, who now lived at Thirty-ninth Avenue, near Noriega. Just four blocks ahead, according to the route they'd drawn at the Hertz office—that yellow road that could lead anywhere.

7:20 P.M., PDT

Louise stepped to the window, drew back the curtain a cautious two inches. But, in the gathering dusk, the car she'd heard in the street outside wasn't slowing, wasn't stopping. She stepped back from the window, released the curtain.

"About an hour," he'd said—almost an hour and a half ago. Were mafiosi usually on time? Or, as she'd once heard, did they purposely keep to no schedule, should enemy gunmen be waiting?

Mafiosi . . . a band of ruthless Italian men who ruled the world from the shadows. Most mafiosi were Sicilian. Yet her father, the boss of bosses, had been born in Genoa. He'd first been arrested at age twelve, he'd once told her. So, when he'd come to America, two years later, he'd already been tested. Because being arrested, he said, was part of "the life." It was one of the few times he'd ever told her about life inside the Mafia. To be arrested—to do good time—was often the first real test, sometimes the only test that mattered. Because when they arrested you, they always offered a deal. Turn state's evidence—squeal—and you could go free. But the stand-up guy, her father had said, served his time, didn't squeal. When he was in jail the stand-up guy had respect. While on the outside, if he was connected, his family was provided for.

Just as, all her life, her mother had been provided for.

Her mother, and now her.

Now her, waiting for a man named Tony. Just as, all her life, her mother had waited for the men with the envelopes. They'd never come inside the house, those mysterious men. They'd always stayed on the porch, their faces in shadow. A few words, a polite nod, and the man was gone.

She was standing close to the front door. There was a small table in the entryway with a gold-framed mirror above it. She went to the mirror, stood close, looked at herself. When Tony Bacardo had called, they'd been eating dinner, she and Angela. She'd finished the meal, asked Angela to clear the table while she did something with her hair, then changed from jeans and an old plaid shirt to slacks and a loose-fitting sweater. She'd intended to do something about her face. But her skin was coarse, and there hadn't been time to do much with foundation. So she'd settled for eyebrow pencil and lipstick.

Her father's skin had been fair, his hair light brown, not Sicilian black. Genoese, he'd once said, were often fair. Therefore, her complexion was fair. Once he'd told her that, of the three children he'd fathered, two of them recognized by the church, she was the child who had always looked the most like him. They'd been at Disneyland, eating banana splits, when he'd told her. At the next table, plainly uncomfortable in their three-piece suits, her father's two bodyguards had been sipping ice cream sodas.

She'd been ten years old then. Her father had been forty.

Just as, now, she was forty. Louise Frazer Rabb Castle. And now, because it was easier for Angela, Rabb again, the name of Angela's father.

Her first marriage had been a pointless mistake: two teenagers, Beverly Hills brats with too much money and too many cars. Except for Angela, the baby she'd almost given away, it had been a pointless mistake. Her father had warned her. Just as he'd warned her not to—

Suddenly the door buzzer sounded, the front door, only a few feet from where she stood. Her first reaction was to back away, as if danger threatened.

Danger?

Or a fortune?

When he'd called, almost an hour and a half ago, she'd gone to the front door, made sure it was locked and bolted. Even as she'd done it, she'd wondered why. Her father, one of the most powerful men in America, had only trusted one man completely. That man was Tony Bacardo, who looked like he should be riding a tractor, a dirt farmer.

Tony Bacardo, on the other side of her front door.

Once more, the buzzer sounded.

"Tony?"

"Yes, Louise."

"Just a second." She turned the lock, worked with the stubborn dead bolt. Finally the door came open. Revealing the tall, awkward figure of Bacardo. He was dressed as she'd always seen him, in an expensive suit that didn't quite fit him. Like a servant presenting himself, he held his hat in his hands. It was a felt fedora, a hat that no one in San Francisco would wear, except to a funeral in the rain.

"I'm sorry to be late. My car—Avis—the damn thing wouldn't start."

"Ah." She smiled, nodded, stepped back. "Come in." Should she call him Tony, this man who'd come to help make her life whole? Mr. Bacardo?

With his hat in his hands, he followed her into the living room. It was an ordinary room in an ordinary house in an ordinary neighborhood. The living room was crowded with expensive furniture, the only relics she'd salvaged from the life she'd once lived in Los Angeles.

"Sit down—please." She gestured to an elaborate copy of a Louis XVI sofa. He thanked her, put his hat carefully on a mirror-topped coffee table. As she sat to face him, she was aware of movement behind her, instantly tracked by Bacardo. Angela stood in the archway.

"This is my daughter, Angela. She's—ah—been staying with me. This is Mr. Bacardo, Angela. He and your grandfather were—" She broke off. How could she finish it? What were the words? Business associates? Partners in crime? Successful gangsters?

Or should she say, *"Mr. Bacardo probably gave the order to have Walter's legs broken after Walter tried to rape you."*

On his feet, Bacardo was telling Angela how glad he was to meet her, after hearing about her for so long. As he said it, Bacardo's eyes paid unspoken tribute. At age twenty, a natural tawny blonde with a slim, lithe body and exquisitely shaped breasts, her hair loose and long and free, Angela was a classic California beauty.

For a long, awkward moment they held their positions, Bacardo and Louise seated, Angela standing uncertainly in the archway. Bacardo's face was implacable, impassive. He was waiting. Finally Louise rose, went to Angela, spoke over her shoulder to Bacardo: "Excuse us just a minute." With Angela following, she went down the narrow central hallway that led to the single bathroom and the two back bedrooms. At the door of Angela's room, she spoke to her daughter. "I told you what this is about. We'll talk later."

Angela shrugged. "Sure." Then, irrepressibly smiling, a lilt in her eyes, she dropped her voice, whispering, "He's a creepy-looking guy, isn't he? I mean, he's like that statue. *The Man With the Hoe.* Remember? Or maybe those old monster movies. You know—*klomp, klomp, klomp.*"

"Angela—" Gently, she pushed her daughter into the bedroom. "Close the door. And put some music on, or the TV."

"Or else, huh?" Angela was still smiling.

Louise turned, walked back into the living room as the rock music began from Angela's bedroom.

"Nice girl," Bacardo said. "Pretty. Very pretty. And polite, too."

"Thank you."

"She's your only child."

"Yes . . ." As she said it, she looked at him, searching for the predictable male response to Angela: the lust that none of them could ever conceal. But in Bacardo's eyes there was no lust. There was only concentration, fixed on her.

"That music," Bacardo said, leaning toward her and lowering his voice. "She's back there listening to the music. Right?"

Louise nodded. "She's in her room. Yes."

"You told her to stay there, stay in her room."

She nodded again.

"You and me—this has got to be private, just between us.

You understand." He spoke slowly, distinctly, giving each word weight. His dark, watchful eyes never left her face.

Yes, she understood.

"Before we get into it," Bacardo said, "there's something I've got to ask you. It's not like I'm trying to—you know—give you the third degree, nothing like that. But we've got a job to do, you and me. There could be risk. The don told you that, told you there could be risk."

"He told me, yes. But he said you'd handle it."

"Yeah, well, that's why I'm here, to handle it. First, though, we should talk. Doing business with someone, it's good to know all you can about the other person. You see what I'm saying?" Earnestly, he searched her face.

"Yes, I—I see."

"Okay. So—" He gestured. "So give me the high spots. You know." He smiled: a slow, lumpy smile. "Your life story in a couple of sentences. Like that."

"Well, my mother left New York when I was tiny. She came to Sacramento for a while. She had relatives near there. Then she went to Los Angeles. That's where I grew up, down in Los Angeles. By the time—" She broke off. Then, drawing a deep, determined breath: "By the time I was fourteen, fifteen, my mother had started to drink. A lot. So I—" She shrugged. "I ran wild, let's face it. And when I was nineteen, I married a guy named Rabb. Jeff Rabb. His father was a movie producer—among other things. A promoter. He—" She paused, looked directly at Bacardo, a question. "Is this what you mean? Is this what you want to know?"

Bacardo nodded, gestured with his plowman's hand. "Go ahead."

"Well, the reason we got married, I was pregnant. So when I was twenty, I had Angela. When I was twenty-five, I got divorced. A couple of years later I married Jack Castle. He was an actor." She looked at Bacardo, hoping for a reaction to the name, for recognition. But, as always, there was nothing. No one remembered Jack Castle. "He was a supporting actor—if you saw him, you'd recognize the face. He did a lot of TV—soap operas, mostly. He was a lot older than I was, and he died when I was thirty-four. Angela was fourteen." She sighed, shook her head. "That was a hard time. Jack made good money, but he always spent more than he made. He wanted to live like a big star, I think. And he gambled, too. He didn't leave anything behind but a lot of unpaid bills and a lot of happy bartenders."

"So you lived all your life in Los Angeles. Until now."

Reluctantly, regretfully, she nodded. "I was married to Jack for seven years. We had our problems, mostly because of the way he spent money. And he drank, too. He drank a lot. But we had a good life. Jack knew how to live, and he was always good to me. Always. But then, about a year after Jack died, I met a man named Walter Draper." As she said it, her eyes fell, her voice dropped, her shoulders went slack. "He had a restaurant here, in San Francisco. Two restaurants, in fact. And he wanted me to move up here, move in with him. He'd just been divorced—for the third time. That should've warned me. He said he'd had it with marriage. No more. But—well—Walter was exciting. He made a lot of money, and he spent a lot. He even had his own airplane. And we—well—" She hesitated, then ventured, "We got along. Sexually, I mean. That part—the sex—was great. Except that when Walter drank—got drunk—the sex got rough. And the longer we were together, the rougher it got."

"You moved in with him, then. Here. In San Francisco."

"Right. My father warned me—begged me not to do it. He was worried what it'd do to Angela. And, God, he was right. She was only sixteen when we moved up here. At first, I thought it'd be all right for Angela. She liked San Francisco, still does. Walter used to take her flying, and she loved that. She even learned to fly. She got a license and everything. And she liked her high school, too. She made lots of friends. She's—well, you saw her. She's beautiful. So, of course, the boys started coming around. And girls, too. Angela has always been good at that—not making the other girls jealous, because of her looks.

"But then—" Louise waved a dispirited hand. "It all started to come apart, after a couple of years. Until finally, one night, Walter went wild. He—he went after both of us. Me, and Angela, too. Angela, you see, had moved out, once she graduated from high school. She couldn't stand it, living in the same house with Walter. She moved in with her boyfriend. But then she had a fight with her boyfriend, and she moved back in. Just temporarily, just until I could help her find her own place. But then, the second night after she came back, Walter got drunk. He went after both of us. Me and Angela. He—" Suddenly her voice caught. Fighting tears, she began to shake her head. Would she cry? Bawl?

"That's all right," Bacardo said. "Never mind that."

With great effort, she raised her head, looked at him directly. Yes, Bacardo had known. Of course Bacardo had known. She'd told her father what Draper had done. A week later Draper was in the hospital, both legs broken at the knees, plus internal injuries.

"So you and Angela moved in together. Here."

She nodded. "Yes. For now, anyhow." As she said it, she guessed at the reason for his questions. He wanted to know whether there was a man in her life—or in Angela's life. She saw him look at his watch, then shift on the sofa to square his body with hers. The time had come to transact business.

"Your father—" Bacardo paused, searching for the words. "He told me to get in touch with you as soon as I could after he died. He told you about it—told you what we have to do."

"The—" She swallowed, dropped her voice. "The jewels, you mean."

"That's right." Heavily, with a note of finality, he nodded. "The jewels. He told you what we've got to do. We've got to tell each other the words..That'll tell us where the jewels are. Then we have to get them. And then you've got to figure out what to do with them."

Hesitantly, she nodded. From the back bedroom, the sound of music had ceased. She saw Bacardo's eyes shift as the silence lengthened. Until, yes, the music began again.

"Do you have a safe-deposit box?"

"Yes. But it's Friday night. And the banks're closed tomorrow."

"Well, it might not matter." Bacardo rose, went down the hallway until he could verify that Angela's door was closed and the music was still loud. Now he returned to the sofa. Leaning toward her, he spoke quietly, carefully measuring the words: "What Don Carlo told me to tell you—the words—they're—" A final pause. Then: "They're 'behind the stone.' "

Behind the stone . . .

"Ah—" Unaccountably stunned, momentarily numbed, she could only nod. For almost four years she'd known the words—her three words. And now those years had fallen away; a lifetime had been reduced to mere seconds—

—these seconds, when only she knew where a fortune in jewels was buried.

Not Bacardo and her. Just her.

Until she told Bacardo, gave him her three words, it was her fortune. In all the world, only she knew.

But once she told Bacardo, then he would know. How could she stop him if he wanted to dig up the jewels, keep them for himself? If she tried to stop him, he'd kill her. Killing was Bacardo's business, his stock-in-trade.

But he'd gone first. If he meant to take the fortune for himself, would he have gone first?

Sitting across the coffee table from her, he waited. Calmly. Impassively.

"It's—" She faltered. Her hands, she realized, were clamped so tightly on the arms of her chair that the muscles of her forearms ached. Her throat had gone dry. Suddenly she was perspiring heavily; her sweater was damp at the neck and armpits.

She cleared her throat. Once. Twice. Then, in a voice that

was no more than a harsh whisper: "It's—the words—they're 'my mother's grave.' "

For long moments they sat motionless, simply staring at each other, as if they were alone in time and space, suspended. Then Bacardo spoke:

"Behind the headstone of your mother's grave."

Hardly aware of it, she was slowly nodding, her eyes still fixed on Bacardo.

"And where's that?" Bacardo's voice was low. He was frowning: two deep creases between his dark, spiky eyebrows. "Her grave, I mean."

"It's in Fowler's Landing. That's near Sacramento."

"How far is it from here?"

"About seventy-five miles, I'd say."

"This Fowler's Landing. What's it like? What kind of a place?"

"It's a small town. It's on the San Joaquin delta south of Sacramento. There're maybe three thousand people in the town, something like that. It's rice-growing country, some of it. My mother was born there. That's where she wanted to be buried."

"When did your mother die?"

"About six years ago."

Bacardo nodded thoughtfully, let his eyes wander away. A six-year-old grave in a little town. Three thousand people. One graveyard, probably, and three or four cops.

It was here, then, to California, that Maranzano had come, four years ago, here that he'd buried the plastic pipe with the jewels—

—here that he'd killed someone. A policeman, Bacardo had always suspected.

First a policeman at Fowler's Landing. Dead.

Then Maranzano, three days later. Dead.

Would Maranzano have had to die if he'd done the job clean?

Across the mirrored coffee table, Louise sat motionless, rigidly, as if her body was frozen in her chair. Was she afraid? Did she know that, four years ago, a young capo had died to protect the secret of her treasure?

He looked at his watch: eight-thirty.

Seventy-five miles . . .

In two hours he could be in Fowler's Landing. But at ten-thirty, in a strange town, how could he hope to find the grave-yard? In the dark, how could he find Janice Frazer's grave? A stranger in a strange town, asking directions to the graveyard, then wandering among the headstones, flashlight and shovel in hand, looking for the grave with a fortune in jewels buried behind the headstone.

My mother's grave . . .

For four years, Louise had known those three words. How often had she visited the grave in those four years?

Six words . . .

She'd already had three words, the most important words. What had she thought was the whole message? *On top of the casket of my mother's grave? At the foot of my mother's grave? Ten feet north? Twenty feet south?*

He must know. First, before he did anything, made any decision, he must know what she'd done—what she'd done, what she'd tried to do, therefore what she might do.

"It's been four years," he began. "You've been to visit her grave, in four years."

Hesitantly, cautiously, she nodded—once, then twice. She knew he was probing, calculating, deciding.

"Did you see anything that made you think there was something buried behind her headstone? Fresh dirt, anything like that?"

She frowned, considered, finally shook her head. But she'd lowered her eyes. What was it that he saw in her face, turned away from him now? Was it fear? Was it greed—the treasure, the closeness of it? Sometimes the sight of great wealth—stacks of money, handfuls of jewels—could turn men to stone. Stone men, with bright, burning eyes. Greedy men.

Dead men.

"You knew the jewels were there, somewhere near your mother's grave."

"Yes," she answered. But I couldn't—" She faltered, began again: "There was no way I could try to get it. Even if I'd known where it was, I'd've been afraid."

Bacardo considered the answer, finally nodded. "Afraid, yeah—you're smart to be afraid. In our organization, you know, nobody feathers his own nest, even the dons. They take what they need—what they want—and pass the rest on. So your father, he took a chance collecting those things for you."

She raised her eyes, looked at him fully. "Are we taking a chance, too?"

"That much money—more than a million dollars—you're taking a chance." His voice was dead level; his eyes were dead calm.

"Ah . . ." She nodded. Yes, there it was: the tremor of fear in the single word. And, yes, he could see fear shadowing her eyes now, working at her face.

"There's a don named Benito Cella—that's the Cella family. Cella's about sixty now, the same age as me. And he'll be the *capo di tutti* now. The boss of bosses. Like your father was."

"Yes." She nodded. "Yes, I see."

"I was Don Carlo's *capo di capo*—his chief of staff, you might say." As he said it, he smiled to himself. Never before had he used those words: chief of staff.

"So now," he went on, "Don Benito has got to think about me. I can't stay in the Venezzio family. The new don, he'd want his own *capo di capo*. So Cella, he's going to move his own *capo di capo*—a man named Salvatore Perrone—out of town, set him up someplace else. Atlantic City, maybe, something like that. Then Cella'll move me into Perrone's spot. See?"

Tentatively, she nodded.

"So while Cella's supposed to be making the arrangements, I'm supposed to be taking a vacation, taking a break, giving Don Benito a little room to maneuver."

"Yes . . ."

"Except that people like me, in my line of work, there's no such thing as a vacation. I mean, you want to go out to Las Vegas for a weekend, do some gambling, even that's not a vacation. Because, see, you'd always be met by someone at the airport, and you'd stay at the right hotel—free—and you'd call a couple of people, buy some drinks. And when you do that, buy drinks, whatever, you talk business." He spread his hands, shrugging. "It's just the way it happens."

"Did—" She broke off, then ventured: "Did someone meet you when you came here? To San Francisco?"

Holding her gaze, he shook his head. He spoke slowly, deliberately: "No one met me. But they know I'm here."

"Are they—do you think they're following you?"

Still speaking slowly, gravely: "They could be."

"Now? Right now?" Involuntarily, her eyes fled to the front entryway and the door.

"If I go out of town, even for a day, I always tell someone where I'm going, where I'm staying."

"So . . ." Once more, her eyes moved, this time to the living room window that opened on the street. "So they *could* be following you."

"I've got a rental car, and I was careful, coming here. That's all I can tell you."

"But if they do follow us, and they see us digging up the treasure, what'll they do?"

Instead of answering he said, "This Fowler's Landing. What kind of a place is it? Is it on a main highway?"

She shook her head. "No. It's off by itself, one road into town, one road out. The delta, you know—it's a strange place. No hills, not many trees. Just water everywhere you go, in channels, mostly. And fog. Almost every night, there's fog. Thick, pea-soup fog."

"The graveyard where your mother's buried—is it in town?"

"On the outskirts, I'd say. North of town a mile or two."

"Let's say we went there tomorrow afternoon. You're carrying flowers to put on your mother's grave. While you're doing that, I'm digging."

As she heard him say it, an image of the graveyard materialized: overgrown and neglected, sad. Some of the gravestones were leaning, some had already toppled over. Her mother's gravestone was one of the most ornate, a granite obelisk, paid for in cash from one of her father's envelopes. There was an old-fashioned wrought-iron fence, and a gate to match. The road out from town bordered the graveyard on the west side. Beyond the graveyard the road continued on to a small settlement on Richardson's Slough where sportfishermen could dock their small boats and buy bait or beer or sandwiches. On a Saturday afternoon in April, most of the traffic in Fowler's Landing would be going on to Richardson's Slough.

"Well," Bacardo was saying. "What d'you think?"

She shook her head. "Someone would see us. The road out of town runs right along the fence."

"Then we'll have to do it at night. Tomorrow night, or Sunday night."

"I—" Suddenly her throat closed. *We*, he'd said. *We!* "Will I go with you? Is that what you mean?"

"You don't want to go?" His dark, deep-set eyes watched her steadily.

"I—" She couldn't finish it. *Did* she want to go?

"You'll trust me with it? You'll trust me to bring it back to you?" His face was unreadable. He was testing her. But why? Even if she went with him, she couldn't keep him from taking the treasure. She had no gun—no man—only a daughter that she must protect from harm.

Angela. Until that moment, she hadn't thought of Angela. What if Bacardo got the jewels, and brought them here? What if the Mafia were watching? They would kill all three of them. She, Bacardo, and Angela, all dead, their blood everywhere, pooled on the floor, splashed on the walls, soaking the carpets.

"I have to know, Louise. I've got to have someone with me. I can't do it by myself. I've got to have a lookout, backup. You drive, don't you?"

"Y-yes. Sure. But—"

"Well?" he demanded.

"Y-you say they know you're here. In San Francisco. So they could be following you."

"You're Don Carlo's daughter. You couldn't go to the funeral. So here I am, to pay my respects." He shrugged, spread his hands. "That's what they'll think. Period."

"But—" Helplessly, she began to shake her head. "But I—I wouldn't be able to help you if anything went wrong. I can drive, sure. But—" She broke off. Then, a whispered confession: "But I'd be scared, Tony. I *am* scared. Right now. Right this minute, I'm scared. Angela—what if—?"

He raised a hand to silence her. "It makes sense that you're scared. It's okay. I wanted to make the offer, ask you to come, so you wouldn't think I'd hijack the stuff. But the truth is, I need someone who can use a gun. If you or Angela was married, had a man . . ." He let it go unfinished, an unspoken question.

Deeply regretful, she shook her head. "There's no one. I haven't got anyone. And Angela moved out on her boyfriend. He hates her now. Really hates her." Now it was her turn to question him with a look. "Don't you have anyone?"

His face hardened; his eyes had turned to stone. "I had two sons. One of them—" He broke off, set his jaw, dropped his voice. "One of them is dead. And the other one is a doctor. A pediatric doctor."

They looked at each other silently, one final wordless exchange. Then, without ceremony, Bacardo rose. Just as, from the back room, the rock music wound down.

"Tomorrow morning," Bacardo said, "I'm going to drive up to Fowler's Landing, see what it looks like. You think about this. We'll both think about this. When I get back, I'll come here. Have you got a shovel? A good flashlight?"

"I've got a flashlight. No shovel. I haven't been here long enough to—"

"Well, in the morning, buy a shovel. And some flashlight batteries. Maybe another flashlight, too—a good one." As if he were anxious to leave, he turned toward the front door. From Angela's bedroom, the music began again. As Bacardo's hand touched the doorknob, Louise spoke: "Tony?"

He turned, looked down at her. Said nothing. In his face, there was nothing but calm calculation: the professional, solving the kind of problem he was in the business of solving.

She spoke hesitantly. "Angela. I've got to tell Angela."

For a moment he made no response. Plainly, he was calculating, considering the odds. Finally: "Whether you want to tell her everything—the words and everything—well, that's up to you. Think about it, though, before you tell her, that's all I'd say. You understand?"

"Yes. I understand."

9:45 P.M., PDT

"I can't believe it," Angela said. "It—it's like a movie, for God's sake." She stood over her mother, who was sitting round-shouldered on the sofa, as if the story she'd just told had exhausted her.

"Are you sure about this?" Angela demanded. "Your father, did you believe him when he told you about the jewels?"

Except for a lifting of her shoulders, her mother made no response. There was nothing left to say—and no strength left to say it.

A fortune in jewels and gold . . .

If her mother had it right—if Tony Bacardo, mobster, was telling the truth—then there were still dreams that came true, fantasies that still came to life. But her mother sat as if she had been convicted of a crime and was waiting for her sentence.

Aware that she was standing too close, an intimidating posture, Angela stepped back, then sat facing her mother.

"What'll we do, Angela?" Her mother's voice was low, without expression, unaccountably without hope. Had life beaten her mother so far down that a fantasy—a fortune—only made the burden seem worse? Was her mother asking her for help? Role reversal, it was called. The daughter became the mother, ready or not.

"If he goes by himself," Angela said, "and if the treasure's really there, what's to keep him from taking it to the airport and going back to New York? This man—God—he makes his living breaking laws. He's a professional criminal. Do you really think he'll hand over a fortune in jewels, then tip his hat and say good-bye?"

"I—" With great effort, Louise raised her head. "I think he will, Angela. Somehow I think he will."

"But, Christ, he—"

"He won't go alone, though. He's already said that, said he wouldn't go alone to get the jewels."

"So who's he going to take along? Another gangster?"

"No." Louise shook her head. Then, as if to rouse herself, come back, she drew a deep breath. "No, he wouldn't do that, I don't think. He's worried about the Mafia, you see. The jewels never really belonged to your grandfather. They belonged to the Mafia. Or, at least, the money that bought them belonged to the Mafia. So—"

"I'll go with Bacardo."

Instantly Louise's head came up, her eyes came alive. For an instant Angela glimpsed the woman she'd once known: determined, willful. "No, you're not going."

"Well, *you're* not going. So who else is there?"

"Angela—" Yes, there it was: that note of parental anger, their role reversal reversed.

"You're *not*, Mom. You *know* you're not going. So if I don't go—drive his goddam car for him, act as lookout, whatever he wants, then who *will* go, for God's sake? What'll we do, hire a—a hit man? Christ, I'd trust Tony Bacardo before I'd trust someone I could hire for a couple of hundred dollars."

"The Mafia knows he's here," Louise said. "And if they follow him . . ." Ominously, she let it go unfinished.

Unable to remain seated, Angela rose, went to the fireplace, stood looking down into the dead embers, both hands resting on the mantle. She was slim and tall; her unbelted jeans sculpted lean flanks and buttocks. Her dark blond hair fell loose to her shoulders. She wore a khaki safari shirt, her favorite. She was barefooted.

For more than a minute the tableau held: the mother sitting motionless, staring woodenly at her daughter, who said nothing.

Then, still staring down into the cold fireplace, Angela said, "I've got an idea."

"An idea?" It was a hesitant question.

"I think I know someone."

SATURDAY, APRIL 21st
10 A.M., PDT

"This," Bernhardt said, "is the first test." With a sweep of his arm he included the twenty-odd hopefuls sitting in the theater's first three rows, clustered close to the center aisle. "Here you are. It's a beautiful Saturday morning in April. You could be walking on the beach, or hiking up Mount Tamalpais, or maybe doing the laundry or else sleeping in, to recover from all the crap your boss has handed you during the week. But instead here you are, sitting in a windowless theater, when the sun's shining brightly outside."

Opting to project an air of amiable benevolence, he smiled down at the upturned faces, some of them old, some of them young, almost all of them attentive, a few of them transparently anxious. Sitting on the edge of the stage with legs dangling, hands spread wide at either side, Bernhardt had assumed the traditional get-acquainted posture of the director upon first addressing the random group of aspiring actors from which he must select that brave handful who would face the footlights on opening night.

Bernhardt was a tall, lean man with a long, lean face. The face was Semitic, darkened through the ages by ancestors whose forebears had lived beneath an uncompromising sun shining down on an uncompromising land. His hair was dark and thick, flecked with gray and worn long and careless. His forehead was high, his nose was generously curved. Beneath dark, thick eyebrows, behind gold-rimmed aviator glasses, his dark eyes were in constant, restless motion. His face was deeply creased, a reassuring pattern of lines that suggested intelligence, perception, and energy. He wore what he always wore when he directed: a pullover sweater, vintage corduroy slacks, and middle-aged running shoes.

"Little theater is—" Bernhardt broke off, searching for the word, the phrase. "It's transitional, that's the best word I can think of. Some of you—the ones with acting talent, whatever that is—you might have a good shot at going on to Broadway, or the San Francisco equivalent. And yes, some of you will decide to give Hollywood a shot, with all the attendant risks and rewards. But the rest of you—which is to say those of you who're either blessed or cursed with no acting talent—" He broke off again, taking time to sweep the upturned faces with eyes that touched each face in turn, a preface to what must come next: "Well, you'll either opt to stay on here, painting scenery and rustling up props, or else you'll find something better to do with your spare time. *All* your spare time, for the next two months, probably." Once more, watching them for reactions, he smiled. "I'm forty-odd years old, and I've been doing theater for a long, long time. I'm hooked, in other words. Just like a few of you, certainly, are also hooked." He waited for the predictable response: the small smiles, the sidelong looks, the shifting on seats that badly needed reupholstering.

"I've discovered," he continued, "that at this stage—call it get-acquainted time—you're interested in knowing something about me." Now his gaze questioned them. And, as always, they nodded. Yes, they wanted to know more about him.

"Briefly," he said, "I grew up in New York City. I'm Jewish, as you've doubtless surmised. My father was a bombardier during World War Two, and he was killed over Hamburg. My mother was a modern dancer. We had a loft in Greenwich Village; that's where she taught dance. She was also involved in lots of causes, mostly in favor of women and against war. Her father was a small clothing manufacturer. He played the harpsichord, and he was a wonderful man. He sent me to good schools—including Antioch College, in Ohio. That's where I got hooked—changed my major in my sophomore year from Political Science to Theater Arts. Antioch has a first-class little theater—they call it the Yellow Springs Area Theater—and in my senior year I had the very great pleasure of acting in two plays that I wrote myself."

A subdued ripple swept the ranks of the aspirants, a well-earned tribute that Bernhardt always secretly savored.

"After I graduated," he continued, "I went to New York, of course. And, of course, I started making the rounds reading for parts. Eventually I got a few walk-ons, with the promise of better things to come. While I was doing that, I was revising my plays—and writing another one. The two plays that were produced in Yellow Springs were two-acters. The one I wrote in New York was three acts. It was called *Victims*. And—lo—after a couple of years knocking on doors, I finally found someone to produce it." Once more he paused, waiting for the response, this one more forthcoming, therefore more satisfying.

"It only ran three weeks off Broadway, Thursday through Saturday," Bernhardt said. "But the reviews—well—critics are generous the first time around. Which is to say that I've still got those reviews." He smiled, dipped his head, an aw-shucks turn. "All three of them." Once more, one last time, he waited for the predictable response. But now came the conclusion, the inevitable, regrettable wind-up, no more calculating the laugh lines, nothing left but the bitter truth: "Then, though, I had some problems. Personal problems. And, well, it was time to leave New York. I went to Los Angeles for a year, but it didn't work out. I had a few power lunches, and got my playwright's ego stroked. I got a few bit parts in a couple of B movies, too. But that was it for me and Hollywood. I wasn't raised to spend part of every day driving on freeways. So I came to San Francisco. I love it here. Literally, from my first day in this city, I knew it was for me. It's been more than ten years now, and I still love San Francisco. However, unlike New York or Los Angeles, it's impossible to make a living in the acting profession here, let alone the directing profession, or the playwrighting profession. Even actors who work in equity houses here have to have an outside income, usually. Moonlighters, in other words." Once more he broke off, let the fateful words sink in, watched for the reactions. A few in his audience registered consternation, others registered exasperation. Others appeared to be indifferent.

"Some of us do commercials," Bernhardt went on. "I suppose they're the lucky ones. Then there's always cab driving, of course, and waiting on tables, the traditional solutions. And, meanwhile—" Bernhardt raised his hands, a graceful gesture that included them all. "Meanwhile, here we are at the Howell Theater. Which is, in my opinion, the best little theater in California. Some of us are hiding out, some of us are still pursuing our dream. And all of us—" Bernhardt moved his right hand to lift a bound copy of *East*. "All of us are going to cooperate in the absolutely best-ever nonequity production of *East*, which I think is an excellent play. If the play should close in its first month, the Howell will lose money—yet again. If, however, we're successful in conveying the magic of *East* to our audiences, and if, therefore, the play should run for five or six months, then the members of the cast and the volunteer staff might make, say, a thousand dollars each. The director—me— might make five thousand. With luck." As he said it, delivered the tag line, he looked once more at the upturned faces. Among them, was there the collective willingness and the tenacity and the infernal spark that he could somehow combine into a successful play?

In the front row a middle-aged woman with a mischievous face and bad posture raised her hand, a question.

With his business concluded, elapsed time about a half hour, Bernhardt smiled benign encouragement. Questions were always a promising start.

"Do you moonlight?" she asked, mischief sparkling in her eyes.

"Yes," Bernhardt answered. "I do."

"May I ask what you do?"

"Certainly," Bernhardt answered promptly. "I'm a private investigator."

"*What?*"

Pleased at the spirited reaction and the general exclamation of surprise, Bernhardt grinned, spread his hands. "Think about it. Flexible hours and pretty good money, if you have the right clients. Plus, for an actor, investigating is a natural. There's a lot of playacting involved, you know. Otherwise known as little white lies. Bullshitting, in short."

2:15 P.M., PDT

"And after Tony Bacardo left last night, your mother told you about the treasure. It was the first time she mentioned it to you. Is that right?"

Angela nodded.

"But she didn't tell you the precise location of the treasure—just that it's buried up in the San Joaquin delta."

"Right."

"So only she and Bacardo know the precise location of the treasure. They didn't find out until last night, when they put the six words together."

"Yes."

Nodding thoughtfully, Bernhardt let a silence fall. They were in his office, once the front bedroom of a turn-of-the-century flat that he had rented on Potrero Hill. Bernhardt sat behind the vintage carved-oak library table that served as a desk; Angela Rabb sat on an aging Victorian love seat that Bernhardt realized he must either junk or have reupholstered.

Whenever he was puzzled or apprehensive or experiencing unspecified pangs of emotion, Bernhardt was unable to sit still. He rose, walked to the generously proportioned bay window that looked out on Vermont Street. Since it was Saturday afternoon, technically not a workday, he still wore the same Icelandic sweater and wrinkled corduroy slacks he'd worn earlier at the theater. Bernhardt was a tall, lean man, slightly stooped.

Standing with his hands thrust deep in his pockets, he looked out at two small boys, Andy and Eugene Ralston, who lived across the street. They were skateboarding down the steep slope of Vermont Street, seemingly courting certain injury, if not a messy death.

A million dollars in jewels . . .

The Mafia . . .

He'd first met Angela Rabb two years ago, when she was only eighteen. She'd come to the theater with Ramon Rodriguez, who'd been in his midtwenties. Ramon had been serious about acting, and Angela had been serious about Ramon. She came to the theater with him and helped backstage. Sometimes she'd volunteered to usher and take tickets. Only once had they really talked, she and Bernhardt. As always, she'd come to the theater with Ramon for rehearsal. But that night it had been obvious that she and Ramon weren't getting along, and during a rehearsal break, drinking diet Coke from the machine, Bernhardt had invited her confidence. Unpredictably, she'd begun to cry. Before anyone could see her crying, he'd guided her through the wings and into a prop room, locking the door behind them. In minutes, she'd told her story. It began with her mother, who'd moved in with a sadistic restaurant owner named Walter Draper. One night, Angela said, her voice choked by the memory, her eyes moving furtively, Draper had gone for both of them, first her mother, then her. No, it hadn't been an actual rape. Angela had known what to do, how to fight him off.

The next day Angela had moved out, gone apartment hunting with Ramon Rodriguez. They'd been in love—they thought.

But after a year she and Ramon had broken up. Determined to make it in Hollywood, Ramon had gone to Los Angeles. Angela had moved in with her mother, who was living alone—again. Bernhardt had asked Angela why Draper had let her mother move out, just like that. Usually, he'd said, men like Draper wouldn't let their women go so easily. "He didn't have a choice," Angela had answered cryptically.

And now, a half hour ago, a year after the fact, Angela had told him why Draper hadn't had a choice. When he'd learned that Draper had attacked his daughter and granddaughter, Carlo Venezzio had sent men to break both of Draper's legs at the knees—after they'd beaten him almost to death.

Aware that he'd stood at the window too long, Bernhardt returned to his chair behind the desk. Saying: "I really should be talking to your mother. Why didn't she come with you?"

"Bacardo's gone up to the delta to look things over. It's about seventy miles one way, I think. He probably left this morning. He said he'd contact us when he got back. He told Mom to be home."

Bernhardt looked at his watch: two-thirty on a bright, clear Saturday afternoon in April.

Carlo Venezzio, boss of bosses . . .

Everything about Angela's story could be checked. Either Draper had been attacked, or he hadn't. Either Venezzio was in prison, or he wasn't. Either he'd had a heart attack, or he hadn't. Either he'd had an affair with a beautiful waitress in New York forty years ago, or he hadn't.

Leaving, however, the one essential point dangling, impossible to check: Did the Mafia know about the treasure buried somewhere in the delta near Sacramento? As the question surfaced, Bernhardt visualized the San Joaquin delta: a desolate, low-lying terrain crisscrossed by a random network of waterways, a land favored only by millions of birds, a few corporate rice growers, assorted fishermen and houseboaters: bayou country without the picturesque trees and swamps. Why, Bernhardt wondered, had Venezzio chosen the delta?

Did he want to know?

Yes, he wanted to know.

The timeless lure of buried treasure, the attraction of potential profit, the tug of simple curiosity: whatever it was, yes, he wanted in. Didn't he?

"So." Bernhardt settled himself behind his desk, decided to make a judicious steeple of his long, bony fingers, decided to take the role of the confessor, the advisor, the savior for hire. Maybe.

"So," he began again, slipping into the with-it cadence of the post-teenager. "So, why're we having this conversation, Angela? What do you think I can do for you?"

"Well, I—I told you what Bacardo said. He won't go after the treasure alone."

"Let's suppose," Bernhardt said, piecing together his thoughts as he spoke, "that I *did* do it. And let's suppose something went wrong. Bacardo and I, let's say, are apprehended by the police with the jewels in our possession. What I'm wondering is, could I be liable to prosecution? On the one hand, I'm not stealing anything. I'm merely helping Bacardo carry out Venezzio's wishes that your mother collect her inheritance. But the money that bought the jewels was Mafia money. So—" Bernhardt spread his hands, shook his head. "So I don't know how I'd stand with the law, if the worst happened. And that's always my first consideration, when I take on a case: how vulnerable I'd be legally."

Angela made no response; she simply looked at Bernhardt as if she were waiting for him to decide her fate. Her eyes, Bernhardt noticed, were a light, clear hazel. Beneath a light blouse, her breasts were superbly shaped.

"And then," Bernhardt said, "there's the question of money. My fee, in other words. I get fifty dollars an hour, plus expenses, once I decide to take on a client. I also take the first day's payment in advance. Four hundred dollars, in other words."

For a moment Angela made no reply. Then, a rueful, reluctant admission: "My mother doesn't have any money, and I don't either. I don't know about Tony Bacardo, whether he'd pay for your time."

"It's not my time. It's my neck. I don't know much about the Mafia. But, based on what I do know, I sure as hell don't want to tangle with them. Their intelligence is better than the FBI's and their enforcement is about a hundred percent. If they decide someone has to die, then he dies. It might take years. But he dies."

With the solemnly spoken words, silence fell between them as they stared at each other. Finally Angela ventured: "Could we do it on—?" She frowned, searching for the word. Now she appealed to Bernhardt: "You know—the way lawyers work sometimes. They take a percentage if they win a case."

"Contingency." As he said it, Bernhardt let his eyes thoughtfully wander. For two years, free-lancing, he'd worked for Herbert Dancer, San Francisco's most prestigious, most expensive agency. When he took contingency work, which was seldom, Dancer charged thirty percent. At least.

A million dollars in jewels, Angela had said. *Plus some gold coins.*

"Yes." Angela nodded. "That's it. Contingency."

"Hmmm."

5:30 P.M., PDT

Three cars ahead, Fabrese saw Bacardo signal for a right turn. Yes, he was entering the Hilton's parking garage. The meaning: Bacardo was keeping the rented Oldsmobile, wasn't turning it in. The conclusion: Bacardo still had more business in San Francisco.

Fabrese let his own rental car slow, cautiously falling back. Passing the Hilton, he turned right, then right again, driving slowly through the congested Saturday evening traffic: shoppers and tourists, wandering. He pulled the Taurus into the right lane of Sutter Street, outbound, stopped the car, switched off the engine.

The time had come to decide. Up to now, it had been enough to hang back, follow Bacardo, make sure that, yes, Louise Rabb was the woman Bacardo had come to see. Meaning that, yes, she was Carlo Venezzio's daughter.

Add it all up, then, this one last time. Put all the rumors together with everything he knew—and everything he could guess:

Forty years ago, Venezzio had just been married, he and Maria. Then he'd met the waitress named Janice Frazer. Proving, some said, that, yes, Venezzio could feel something.

But, even though Venezzio was already a don then, and moving up, he couldn't let the woman stay in New York, not with her baby. So he'd sent her back where she'd come from. Over the years, Venezzio's couriers kept the woman named Janice Frazer supplied with money. When Venezzio went out to the Coast and visited the woman, there were always bodyguards outside the house. So, slowly, the rumors had spread, became common knowledge: Yes, Janice Frazer lived in Los Angeles with her daughter. Yes, Janice Frazer had become a drunk. Yes, she'd died a few years ago, been buried somewhere in California. Where, nobody knew.

Until now, nobody knew.

Until now, a few hours ago, nobody in the organization had known. Nobody but Venezzio and Bacardo—and, yes, probably Maranzano.

The three of them, and now him. Jimmy Fabrese.

Him.

In prison, Venezzio had lived like a king on Mafia Row: specially cooked meals, errands run, silk shirts, a phone always available.

But even kings got heart attacks.

It was almost a year after the first heart attack that Maranzano had gone to the prison, talked to the don. And then, the next morning, they'd gone to Bacardo's house, picked up something in a red nylon flight bag, taken it to the airport, where Maranzano had boarded a flight to California.

California, and then Fowler's Landing.

Just as, yesterday, Bacardo had come to San Francisco.

Just as, today, Bacardo had gone to Fowler's Landing—

—Fowler's Landing, and the graveyard.

The graveyard, and the grave of Janice Frazer.

A grave for Janice Frazer, then a grave for Maranzano, less than a week after he'd returned to New York, mission accomplished. See California and die, Mafia insurance. The bigger the job, the bigger the risk, rest in peace.

Once more, Fabrese checked the time. Would Bacardo's next stop be Thirty-ninth Avenue, Louise Rabb's house? What would he tell her? What would they say, what would they decide? Had Bacardo realized he was being followed? Certainly Bacardo expected the organization to keep track of him; it was part of the life for someone like Bacardo. So, even if Bacardo knew he was being followed, he would probably have ignored the tail. Anything else would have been suspicious. To anyone who wanted to know, Bacardo was simply visiting Janice Frazer's grave, a deathbed promise he'd made to Venezzio, Hail Mary, full of grace.

In that delta country, there were almost no trees, nothing but flat, low-lying land with a few towns scattered along the edges of the main waterways. He'd been able to fall back a mile and still keep Bacardo's car in sight. When Bacardo had finally stopped at the graveyard, Fabrese had been able to conceal his car in a small grove of trees less than a hundred yards from the wrought-iron gate. He'd been able to see which grave Bacardo had visited.

Janice Frazer's grave.

Janice Frazer, 1930 to 1984. A short, hard-luck life.

Bacardo had only stayed for a short time. He'd put flowers on the grave, then stood with head bowed, as if he were reciting a prayer. Then he'd returned to his car and driven back to San Francisco. He'd driven slowly, conservatively. Imitating Bacardo, Fabrese had gone to the grave, stood with his head bowed, facing the headstone. Even though there was no one to see him, he'd moved his lips, as if, like Bacardo, he'd been saying a prayer—

—a prayer to find a fortune.

A fortune compact enough to fit in a small red flight bag.

A fortune hidden somewhere in Fowler's Landing.

He started the Taurus's engine, checked traffic, carefully pulled out into the traffic on Geary Street. The drive to Louise Rabb's house, even in traffic, would take less than a half hour.

6:10 P.M., PDT

She'd just picked up the remote control wand, about to switch on the TV, when she heard it: the front-door buzzer. Like a shriek from the firepits of hell, the sound echoed and re-echoed, piercing the center of herself.

Bacardo.

It had to be Bacardo, come back from Fowler's Landing. Angela would have used her key, come right in.

Louise rose from the couch, placed the wand on the TV set, turned to face the front entryway. She'd been waiting for hours, alone in the house. Every hour, every minute, waiting for Angela to return, had drawn her nerves so painfully tight and raw that, once, she'd grown short of breath. She'd been in the bedroom, changing from a sweatshirt and jeans into a skirt and sweater, one of her best cashmeres. Somehow she'd felt that, for whatever the next hours might bring, she must be dressed like a lady, someone to be respected.

Bacardo at the door. It had to be Bacardo.

Or was it someone tracking Bacardo?

The police?

A Mafia hit man?

Once more, the buzzer sounded, longer this time, more insistent. She smoothed down her skirt, pushed at her hair, drew a long, deep breath, walked into the entryway, faced the door. Moving closer, she put her eye to the magnifying peephole.

It was a man. A stranger. About forty, bareheaded, he wore

a three-piece suit, dark brown. The suit looked expensive. The man was staring straight at the door. As if he knew she was there, he lifted his chin, squared his shoulders—and waited, smiling slightly.

She put the night chain in place, twisted the dead bolt, let the door come open on the chain.

"Mrs. Rabb? Louise Rabb?"

"Yes . . ."

"I'm Frank Profaci," Fabrese said. "I worked for your father. I have to talk to you for a few minutes."

"Talk? What about?"

"I've just come out from New York. I've come from—" He stepped closer, carefully lowered his voice. "I come from Mr. Cella. Benito Cella."

Benito Cella . . . the man Bacardo had warned her about.

Should she tell the stranger to come back later, after she'd talked to Bacardo?

No. It might make him suspicious.

If only Angela were with her. Angela, who had been so steady, so calm last night after Bacardo left. Angela, only twenty—suddenly a woman. When she was Angela's age, she'd been married for a year—married and pregnant, just one little mistake, out on a weekend boating party to Catalina. And so, thank God, Angela had come into her life.

"Are you going to let me in or not?" Fabrese demanded. "I don't have much time. I've got to call New York after we talk, and there's three hours' difference."

She had no choice. She had to let him in, had to know why he'd come. Otherwise, on the phone, what would he say?

"Just a minute." She closed the door, freed the night chain, opened the door, stepped back. Irrationally, her first thought was that she was glad she'd changed into a skirt and cashmere sweater. If only she'd taken more time with her face, her hair.

He was a small, slightly built man. His head was narrow and bony, his features compressed. It was a face that seemed never to smile. His black hair was thick and stylishly barbered. His movements were tense and guarded, as if he were venturing into enemy territory. He was impeccably dressed: an expensively cut, meticulously pressed suit, gleaming brown shoes, a necktie precisely knotted. His shirt was light beige, with a stiff white collar.

"Please." She gestured him into the living room, where he sat on the same love seat Tony Bacardo had sat in last night. When he sat down, the newcomer plucked at his trouser creases, crossed his legs, touched the knot of his tie. Then he turned his full attention on her. With his small black eyes boring in, she shifted uncomfortably in her chair, crossed her legs, took a fresh grip on the arms of her chair.

When he finally spoke, his voice was thin and uneven. "The reason I came, I wanted to warn you." His body language, too, was uneven. Was he frightened—as frightened as she was? Was it possible?

"Warn me?"

"About Tony Bacardo—about what he's doing out here."

"I—I—" She realized that she was shrinking back in her chair, as if to escape what must surely come next: Mafia justice, kill or be killed. "I don't know what you're—"

"Come on, Louise. I know he's in San Francisco. He's at the downtown Hilton right this minute. And he was here last night. He stayed for about an hour." Now his voice was rough; his eyes were turning hostile: killer's eyes. Suddenly images of the past returned: the shadowy figures who came to the door, handed over the envelopes, then disappeared into the night. First the men had given the envelopes to her mother. Then, these last years, they'd given the envelopes to her.

But this man—Profaci—carried no envelope.

Instead, beneath the perfectly fitting suit, he carried a gun. Without doubt, he carried a gun.

She must speak. Only if she spoke could she save herself. But save herself from what? Why? After all, Carlo Venezzio had been her father.

The king is dead, long live the king. It was an English expression. She'd never understood its full meaning. Not until now had she understood.

"I—yes, he was here last night. But—"

"Is he coming back here? Now? Today?"

"I don't know." Because it was the truth, she earnestly repeated it: "I don't *know*."

"Well." Now, unexpectedly, he shook his head, an expression of regret. "Well, Louise, the reason I want to know, I want to warn you. That's why I'm here. To warn you."

She swallowed. "Warn me?"

"About Tony Bacardo."

"Ab—" Suddenly her throat closed, choking off the rest.

He nodded. Then, as if he were puzzled, he frowned, looked her straight in the eye. Saying: "Your father and Tony, they had a deal. Or, more like it, Don Carlo *thought* they had a deal." Watching her covertly, he fell silent. But she made no reply.

"After Don Carlo had his heart attack, he started to think about you. I mean, he knew Maria and his two kids would always be taken care of. But that left you, after your mother died. And Don Carlo always had a soft spot for you. So, naturally, he wanted to take care of you after he was gone. You know— you saw him, in prison. He—" Fabrese hesitated. Should he take a chance, try for a long shot?

Yes, he would try. "Don Carlo told you about it—told you what he and Bacardo planned for you, when you saw him in prison."

As he said it, he saw the words register in her face, her eyes, the twist of her mouth. He'd gambled—and won.

"You—" Plainly puzzled, she flinched. "You know that— know what my father told me?"

He nodded. Now playing a winning hand, he could pick up the beat, go to work on her. Get in and get out—before Bacardo rang the doorbell.

"I guess I was your father's number-two man." Pretending puzzlement, he looked at her. "I'm surprised he never mentioned me to you. Bacardo was always number one. But Tony—well—" Fabrese shook his head, sighed. Then, as if to confess: "Tony, it looks like, he's on the take."

"I—I don't understand."

"It's simple. With Don Carlo gone, Tony's without a job. He's unemployed, you might say. He needs money."

"He—he needs money?"

"Listen, Louise." Fabrese leaned impatiently forward, glanced at his watch, gleaming gold. "I don't have a lot of time. So let me lay it out for you. Okay?"

"Y—yes. Okay."

"Your father got a package together—call it your inheritance. Or, more like it, he told Bacardo to do it. Then they got a capo—his name was Maranzano—to bring the package out here. Maranzano brought it to Fowler's Landing."

As he pronounced the words, Louise realized that his eyes were locked with hers, searching her face for some reaction, some clue.

Fowler's Landing . . .

Except for her father and Tony Bacardo, who else inside the Mafia could have known about Fowler's Landing?

Proving that, yes, the man sitting across the coffee table had been close to her father.

Proving?

No, not proving. In this world of shadows, there was no proof. There were only more shadows—and, yes, ghosts.

"And now," he went on, speaking softly, almost gently, "Tony's here in San Francisco. Which is why I'm here."

"I—I don't understand."

"I already told you, I came from Don Benito—Mr. Cella. He'll be the new *capo di tutti*. And he wants me to tell you that it's all right with him if you get the package. He's willing to square it with the council. Otherwise—" As if even the thought of what could happen saddened him, he shook his head. "Otherwise, you could have problems. Big problems. You know that, don't you?"

She nodded, saying, "Yes, I know that." She spoke as if she were reciting words that were strange to her, lines that were only half memorized.

"But if Tony gets the package, keeps it for himself, that's

skimming." Once more he shook his head. "And whoever skims, takes money from the organization—well—he has to die. You understand that."

She made no response.

"The way your father told me," he said, "you and Tony both know where the package is—where Maranzano hid it. Right?"

"I—" She began to shake her head. Then, helplessly, she nodded. Whispering: "Yes. Right."

"And when're you planning to get it?"

"I—I'm not sure."

"But it'll be just him—just Tony—that'll get it," he said.

"I'm not sure."

"Well . . ." As if he were sorry for her, he once more shook his head. "Well, I'll tell you, Louise, I'd go with him when he gets it, if I were you. Otherwise, sure as hell, Tony's going to take the package and run. That'll leave him dead. And it'll leave you broke."

"Broke?"

He shrugged, rose to his feet. "Afraid so. Tony gets killed, we're not going to give you the stuff, once we get it off Tony. You can see that, can't you?"

"Yes," she whispered, "I can see that."

7 P.M., PDT

"I'm sorry." Bernhardt rose, strode across the small, over-furnished room to the fireplace. He turned back to face the two of them: Angela, twenty and beautiful, Louise, forty and frightened. "I'm sorry," he repeated, shaking his head, "but there's something missing. It just doesn't add up."

Louise turned to her daughter, who was looking hard at Bernhardt. Neither woman spoke. In Louise's face, Bernhardt saw nothing but uncertainty and isolation: forty years that had ended in defeat. In Angela's face, even though it was youthful, he saw more complexity, more resolution—more hope. In World War II, boys no older than Angela flew bombers into Germany and fought hand to hand in the jungles of the Pacific islands.

"This second guy—Profaci," Bernhardt said. "He claims he's representing the big shots in New York. But if that's so, then why does he make a big point of warning you that Bacardo might cheat you? Why should he try to help you? Why isn't he trying to get the treasure and take it back to Cella?"

Angela nodded agreement. "That's true, Mom."

Mutely shaking her head, Louise made no reply.

"I think," Bernhardt said, "that Profaci's using you to get to Bacardo."

Louise shook her head. "No. He doesn't have to use us. He knows where Tony's staying. It's the Hilton. He—"

"I don't mean he wants to find Bacardo," Bernhardt interrupted. "I mean Profaci wants to drive a wedge between you and Bacardo. He wants you to suspect Bacardo's motives."

"I think so too," Angela said.

Bernhardt returned to his chair, sat facing the two women sitting side by side on an ornate love seat that complemented the room's furnishings: expensive, garishly reproduced antiques, many of them painted off-white, trimmed with gold leaf. Whatever house this furniture was meant for, it wasn't this one: a cramped, one-story stucco row house, one of the cookie-cutter thousands built during the thirties in San Francisco's Sunset District.

Bernhardt drew a deep breath, then admitted, "I'll tell you the truth, ladies, I'm not sure I want to get involved in this. And I'm not sure you should get involved, either. Even if we take these guys at their word, then what we've got is Bacardo trying to help you without the Mafia knowing about it. But according to Profaci, the Mafia *does* know. Or, at least, suspects." He shook his head. "It's just too dangerous."

"I've got about three thousand dollars in the bank," Louise said. "And that's it. That's everything." She spoke softly, reluctantly. "For all of her life, my mother took money from my father. If she hadn't had him—those men, with the envelopes—she'd never have made it. And the truth is—" With great effort, she met Bernhardt's eyes squarely. "The truth is that, without those jewels, I won't make it, either."

"You're only forty." Bernhardt kept his voice neutral, kept his eyes level. "You've got half your life in front of you."

She smiled: a small, bitter smile that left her eyes without animation—without hope. "My father was a gangster and my first husband was a drug case. My second husband died owing every bookie in town. And my mother, she was a drunk. I came to San Francisco to live with a man who tried to—"

"Mom. Come on." On the love seat, Angela moved closer, touched her mother on the arm. "You can't blame yourself because Walter—"

Bernhardt broke in. "I think I should leave. After you've talked with Bacardo, if you want to, you can call me, and we can talk. But I have to tell you that I don't see where I fit in." He rose, waited for them to rise. "It sounds like Bacardo's looking for a backup man. A hired gun, in other words. And—" His deeply etched face registered a self-deprecating smile. "And that's not me, ladies. I'm sorry, but that simply isn't me."

10:15 P.M., EDT

Boiatano listened, nodded, spoke into the phone: "Just a second, Sal." And to Cella he said, "It's Sal."

"Ah." Cella nodded, waited for the phone to be given to him. "Sal. How's it going? What's happening?"

"It's all right to talk?"

"I'm at The Chop House. No problem."

"I got in yesterday afternoon. I took Augie with me, I guess I told you that."

"You told me."

"I called ahead, made three or four calls Thursday. So Ricca and Genna and Adamo met us at the airport. They had two cars, very thoughtful. Everyone out here, they're for you, for *capo di tutti*. They—you know—volunteered that, didn't wait to be asked. Today—Saturday—they had a big lunch for us at Fisherman's Wharf. Great place—a view you wouldn't believe, right on the water. And the lunch, there were twenty-four guys there. I counted. All the top guys out here. And some came from L.A. And Vegas, too. Like I said, they really laid it on. I thought you'd want to know."

"Yes, sure." Cella nodded, pleased. "Very good."

"Ricca and me, we rode together from the airport. So we could talk. I guess that was the hardest part. I mean, I don't know Ricca all that well. So I couldn't come right out with it, tell him I wanted to hear about it, if our friend started making funny moves out here."

"So our friend wasn't at the lunch."

"No. I don't know where he was. But he sure wasn't at Fisherman's Wharf."

"Our friend called, checked in. He's staying at the Hilton. The downtown Hilton."

"Yeah, I already knew that."

"Tell me again, the guys that were at lunch. Go slow."

As Perrone obeyed, Cella stopped him frequently, time for thought. Finally Perrone said, "That's all I can remember. There were—what—a half dozen capos. Maybe more."

"That's fine. Just fine, Sal. You've got a good memory."

Pleased, Perrone answered modestly, "I try."

"So what about our friend?"

"I told Augie to keep track of him. But nothing—you know—heavy. Augie's got two cousins out here, so that was lucky. They're both young, but they're eager. Smart, too. So they got right on our friend, beginning this morning, early. It was perfect, see, because Augie could lay back, stay out of sight."

"Augie uses his head."

"I think so, too. I always thought so."

"I'm going to keep him in mind, give him some jobs all on his own, see how he does."

Perrone decided not to respond.

"So what'd Augie find out?"

"What Augie found out," Perrone said, "is that, about nine-thirty this morning, our friend got in his car and started driving. Augie was covering the lobby of the Hilt—of the hotel, and his cousin was in a car outside, covering the garage. So then, just when our friend drove out of the garage, and Augie was getting ready to follow him, Augie saw Jimmy Fabrese. He was—"

"Wait." Cella frowned. Then, an embarrassment, he was forced to ask, "Jimmy Fabrese? I know the name, but—" He let it go unfinished.

"He drove for Frankie."

"Frankie Maranzano?"

"That's right."

"Ah . . ." As if he were pleased by some sensation, perhaps an excellent forkful of food, Cella nodded his measured appreciation. "Yeah, I see." A moment passed, for reflection. Then: "Was Fabrese driving for Frankie when . . ." Once more, he let it go unfinished.

"He drove Frankie to the prison both times, when Frankie met Don Carlo. So if anyone knew about Frankie—why he went to California—it had to be Fabrese."

"And when Frankie disappeared . . ." Another pause.

"Fabrese didn't drive Frankie that night. It was Bacardo. After they had dinner, Frankie left the restaurant with Bacardo, just the two of them."

"And now Jimmy Fabrese . . ." The final pause.

"Right. It looks like he's out here riding shotgun for our

friend. Or anyhow, that's what he did today. Wherever our friend went, Fabrese was following him."

A long, silent moment. Then, reflectively, "So where'd they go this morning?"

"All I know is that they went out of town. Across the Bay Bridge toward Oakland, that's all I know. When Augie saw Fabrese, he decided to be careful, lay back. But then there was an accident on the bridge, and Augie lost both of them."

"Fabrese—how do you rate him?"

"As much as I know about him," Perrone said, "I don't like him. I don't like him, and I don't trust him."

"Why would our friend trust him, do you think?"

"Maybe he doesn't have a choice."

"What's that mean?"

On the line from California, Perrone chuckled. "I'm not sure."

"Well, find out."

"Right."

7:20 P.M., PDT

"My God, Mom." Exasperated, Angela slammed her hand down flat on the kitchen counter, turned to confront her mother, who was standing at the sink. Louise was staring down at nothing, head bowed, shoulders slumped. "My God," Angela repeated, you've got to *decide*. Don't you *see* that? You can't have it both ways. Either you trust Tony Bacardo, or you don't. You trust him, or you trust Profaci. But whichever you decide, you've got to do it now. Right now."

Louise pushed herself away from the sink, went to the small round table in the breakfast nook, sank into a chair. She spoke in a low, listless voice: "I've already trusted Tony Bacardo. Don't you see that? I gave him the words."

"You didn't have a choice. You had to tell him."

"I *did* have a choice. Right up to the second I told him, I had a choice. But I was wrong to do it. I should've waited. I should've talked to you first. That's what I should've done."

Angela went to her mother, sat at the glass-topped table, gently took her mother's hands in hers, waited for her mother to lift her head, meet her gaze. She spoke softly, gently: "You're talking to me now, Mom."

Louise began to shake her head, an empty gesture of utter defeat. "God, I've made such a mess of things. I—everything I've done, it's turned out wrong."

"That's not true. When you and Jack were married, those were good years. He was fun."

Smiling almost timidly, Louise ruefully shook her head, resigned. "Good years—it's true. Jack drank too much and he was the most insecure man in the world, and he spent two dollars for every one he took in. But you're right. He was fun." Now, half smiling, she squeezed her daughter's hand. "Actors. You know about actors."

Angela's answering smile shared her mother's mood of reflection. "Yeah, I know." Then, embarrassed, Angela took back her hands, sat up straighter.

Now, they both knew, was the time for her mother to speak.

In a leaden monotone, reciting, Louise said, "It's buried behind the headstone of my mother's grave."

For a long moment Angela made no response, as if she hadn't heard. Then, gravely, she nodded. "Thanks, Mom." She nodded again, cleared her throat, blinked. Repeating softly, "Thanks."

Louise shrugged, bit her lip. "I should've told you last night. I should've told you before I told him."

"You told me now." Suddenly Angela went to the cupboard, took down two glasses. "Want a drink of water?"

Louise shook her head. Then, suddenly, she spoke in a high

plaintive voice, a child's anguished plea: "What're we going to *do*, Angela?"

Angela filled a glass, drank, set the empty glass on the counter. "It comes down to Tony Bacardo. Did he come here to help you? Or did he come here to take the treasure for himself?"

Louise nodded. "I know."

"You trusted Tony. You trusted him enough to give him the words. And he—"

"My father trusted him. I just—just did what my father told me to do."

"What about Profaci? Do you trust him?"

"No," Louise answered. Then, as if she were puzzled, she repeated, "No, I don't trust him. There's something about him that—that's creepy. Maybe it's—I don't know—maybe it's that he looks like a killer. It's something in his eyes. He looked at me, it was like he was thinking about how easy it'd be to kill me. That's the way it felt. It felt like—"

"You realize," Angela interrupted, "that if Tony Bacardo shows up, then that cancels out everything Profaci said."

Louise frowned. "I don't see what you mean."

"If Bacardo's after the jewels, then he bought a shovel and went up to Fowler's Landing and dug up the jewels. By now, he's on his way back to New York. He's—"

On the wall beside the refrigerator, the telephone warbled. At the first ring, Angela took it from its cradle. "Hello?" She listened briefly. Then: "Yes. Just a second, please." She covered the mouthpiece as she gestured with the phone to her mother. "It's him. Bacardo."

7:50 P.M., PDT

"This Profaci," Bacardo said. "Describe him."

"He's thirty-five, forty years old," Louise answered. "Not real big. Not small, exactly, but not big, either."

"About—what—a hundred sixty, something like that?"

Hesitantly, Louise nodded. "I guess so, yes. He had dark hair, and his face was sort of all pushed together. An ugly face, really. Small, and ugly. And he was nervous. Very jumpy."

"How was he dressed?"

"He was dressed very nice. A three-piece suit. Brown, I think. He looked flashy."

"What time did he come here today?"

"About six o'clock."

Bacardo looked at her speculatively as he calculated: six o'clock . . . about a half hour after he'd returned to the Hilton from Fowler's Landing. In silence, Bacardo considered the two women, one a blooming beauty, the other thickening, fading. One was strong and willful, the other hoped only to survive. Sitting on the same spindly antique love seat he'd occupied the night before, Bacardo let his eyes wander away. In New York, for a job like this, he could choose from fifty men, give one of them a call: "Get a car, bring a flashlight and shovel, pick me up. Bring a piece." They'd drive to the cemetery, do the job in an hour, give or take. If there was ever a leak, one shot would take care of it. If there was a problem with the law, a call to the precinct captain would square it.

But in California—San Francisco—Fowler's Landing—there was no one to call.

He'd come to San Francisco yesterday. He'd called The Chop House, left a message that he was staying at the Hilton, downtown.

Meaning that, playing the percentages, Cella would have him followed this weekend. Meaning that, when he returned to New York and saw Cella he'd say that, yes, he'd seen Louise

Rabb, Don Carlo's daughter. She wasn't allowed at the funeral; what else could he do but give her Don Carlo's last words? And, yes, he'd visited Janice Frazer's grave, paying the don's last respects, his dying wish.

Meaning that there'd be no need to lie.

Until he went for the jewels, there'd be no need to lie.

Until he went for the jewels, nobody died.

If he went for the jewels.

"Profaci," Angela was saying. "You know him?"

Bacardo's large mouth twisted briefly, a grim smile. "No," he answered, "I don't know any Profaci. At least not the Profaci that came here tonight."

"But—" Anxiously, Louise leaned forward, searched his face. "But he said he worked for my father. He said you and he were important to my father."

Suddenly aware of the weariness he felt, jet lag plus the long drive to Fowler's Landing and back, he slowly shook his head. "There's no Profaci, Louise. He gave you a fake name."

"But—"

"He probably works for someone out here, that's my guess. Or maybe someone in New York. Anyhow, somebody wants me to know that they're watching me. Which I already figured."

"When we—when you get the jewels," Louise said, "will they follow you then?"

"That depends on a lot of things. Very complicated things. It depends on how much they know—and how much they suspect. So far, all I've done is talk to you, and then visit your mother's grave. Even if they suspect your father left something for you, there's no reason for them to connect that with your mother's grave."

"Not until you go back to the graveyard," Angela said.

"If I go back, I'll go at night."

" 'If' . . ." Angela was looking at him steadily. Waiting for his reply.

Instead of answering the unspoken question he turned to Louise. "You told Angela about it—gave her the words?"

"I—" Nervously, Louise nodded. "I—I wanted to. I felt like I had to tell her. It's—I guess it's like a will, or something. I mean, what else've I got to leave her?"

"Yeah . . ." Reluctantly, he nodded. "Yeah, I can see that."

The three of them shared a bleak silence before Angela spoke to Bacardo: "You said 'if' a minute ago. What'd you mean?"

"I mean," he answered, "that I've got to think about this. We've got to know what it means, that this guy showed up here this evening just about the time I got back in town."

"Does it mean that he followed you to Fowler's Landing?"

"It's not *whether* he followed me. I expected someone would probably follow me. It's *why* he followed me."

" 'Why'?"

"Is he a free-lancer? Or is he connected? That's what I've got to know."

"Connected?"

"With the organization." Plainly distracted, Bacardo looked away as he spoke. Then, feeling his way: "This private detective—what's his name?"

"Alan Bernhardt."

"What's his story?"

"He's very talented," Angela said. "And very nice. He's an actor, really—and a director, in little theater. He's had a play produced, in New York. But there's no money in little theater. So he moonlights."

Once more Bacardo's mouth twisted into a wry smile. "I'm not interested in how talented he is, or how nice he is. I'm interested in how smart he is. And how tough."

"He's smart," Angela answered promptly. "Very smart."

"How about tough?"

Angela considered, then decided to retort, "I don't know about tough. But I trust him." She looked at her mother. "*We* trust him."

"And there's no one else," Bacardo said. "No one else you trust." As he spoke, he glanced at his watch: eight o'clock on a Saturday night. In Manhattan, at The Chop House, his people were drinking together, laughing, laying bets on the next day's games, looking over each other's girlfriends, making good-natured comments, the old story. Suddenly he realized that, like the two women, he was alone, no one to trust, a stranger in a strange city. And strange cities could be dangerous cities.

"Can you call this Bernhardt, set up an appointment for me?"

"Now?" Angela asked. "Tonight?"

"Now."

8:10 P.M., PDT

In the far corner of the room, Crusher lay with his head between his paws. The Airedale's soft brown eyes were fixed reproachfully on Bernhardt.

"I can't stand it. I've got to feed Crusher."

Across the table, Paula smiled. "When he realizes we're giving him leftovers, he'll understand why you waited."

"Except that there aren't any leftovers." Bernhardt looked at the dish that had contained the fettucini with crab and capers in white cream sauce.

"Put his dog food in the fettucini bowl. He'll appreciate the gesture."

"Good idea." Bernhardt rose, took up the dish, gestured for Paula to remain seated. "I'll get the ice cream."

"Just one scoop for me."

"Likewise."

"There're cookies in the cupboard."

"Right." With Crusher prancing anxiously at his side, attention riveted on the fettucini bowl, Bernhardt walked into the kitchen, scooped dry dog food into the dish, added water. Sternly, he commanded the dog to sit until he'd put the dish on the floor. Then, released, Crusher bounded for the dish, began to eat. As Bernhardt turned to the refrigerator, Paula came into the kitchen with their dirty dishes. Bernhardt watched her stack the dishes in the sink and run water into them. She wore a bulky-knit, loose-fitting sweater, blue jeans, and shearling slippers. Her dark shoulder-length hair was caught in a casual ponytail, Bernhardt's favorite hairstyle. Because her jeans were soft and tight and provocative, she called them her Saturday-night jeans.

They'd known each other for less than a year, and the relationship was just beginning to settle. Saturday nights, Paula stayed over. Unless they were invited out to dinner, they preferred not to battle for a parking place, or a place in a ticket line, or a table at a restaurant. Instead, after they'd cooked something special and eaten it appreciatively, always with a fifth of red wine, they went into the living room with brandy snifters and watched a movie on Bernhardt's VCR. They sat side by side on the couch, cuddling as they sipped the brandy and commented on the movie and occasionally petted Crusher, lying at their feet.

As Paula turned away from the sink, Bernhardt stepped close, put his hands on the Saturday-night jeans, and drew her close. Their first kiss was companionable. Then, interested, she came closer. Kissing him again, more interested now, she held her hands away from him, smiling as she said, "Wet hands."

"Hmmm . . ." Slowly, he moved his own hands down her flanks, then drew her closer, began to move with her, at first subtly, then more urgently—

—as, from down the flat's long hallway, from his office that fronted on the street, his business phone rang.

Muttering an exasperated obscenity, he involuntarily moved away from her. Explaining ruefully, "I might have to get that. There's one call I promised to take. I haven't had a chance to tell you about it."

As, yes, from down the hallway he heard a woman's voice on his answering machine.

"That's her, I think. Sorry." He kissed Paula's forehead,

walked toward his office. Yes, Angela Rabb was leaving her number and asking him to call. Standing in the rear hallway, Crusher looked indecisively from the receding figure of Bernhardt to the figure of Paula, who was occupied putting cookies on a plate. Predictably opting for the possibility of food, Crusher entered the kitchen and began begging for cookies. In the study, Bernhardt punched out the number on the tape.

"Angela?"

"Ah—Mr. Bernhardt."

"Alan."

"Alan. Yes."

"What's happening?"

"Tony Bacardo wants to see you."

"Why?"

"I—I'm not sure. But—"

"When?"

"As soon as you can make it, Alan." Her voice was low, hushed by the timidity of hope. "Tonight, if you could do it."

"Tonight . . ." He let the reluctance come through. "I could do it tomorrow, probably. Sunday. But tonight . . ." He let it go dubiously unfinished.

"I know. I hate to ask you. But he—he's been up to the delta, and now he's back. And he—well—I think he might just—just go back to New York. I think that unless he can talk to you— unless you and he can agree, work together—then I think he's going to go. That's what I think."

"Is that what your mother thinks, too?"

"Yes, it is. She thinks the same thing."

"Jesus . . ." Irritably Bernhardt gritted his teeth, shook his head. Why did it happen, not once but several times, that he'd fallen for the oldest cliché of all: the damsel in distress, pleading for help? He looked at his watch as, behind him, he sensed a rustle of movement—accompanied by the click of Crusher's toenails. Eyeing him quizzically, Paula was standing in the doorway, Crusher at her side. Never had the Saturday-night jeans seemed so provocative.

"All right." Bernhardt drew a deep breath—and gave Paula

an apologetic look. "All right. I'll talk to him. But I warn you, Angela, I'll tell him exactly what I told you."

"I—I know. But I can't walk away from this, Alan. It could be my mother's whole life. It could mean—"

"How does it work, with Bacardo and me?" Somehow, interrupting her so abruptly, he felt more decisive, more in control.

"He's at the Hilton, downtown. Room twelve thirty-six. He wants you to call him first. From the lobby. Not from outside. From the lobby."

"Twelve thirty-six," he repeated, writing it down.

"Will you call us after you talk? Please?"

"Of course." He hesitated, then decided to say, "Lock the doors and draw the drapes. You understand."

"Yes, I understand."

9:40 P.M., PDT

"If the jewels were so accessible," Bernhardt said, "I don't understand why you didn't shake whoever was following you and get them today."

"If I shook him," Bacardo answered, "it'd look like I had something to hide. That's the last thing I want. As far as our people're concerned, I'm in San Francisco to pay my respects to Louise after her father died. Because she couldn't go to the funeral, you see."

"But won't your people wonder what you were doing up in the delta?"

"Louise's mother is buried up there. So it makes sense that I'd visit her grave, pay the don's respects." Bacardo let a moment pass as he watched Bernhardt's reaction. Then: "Besides, the stuff's buried. So there's some digging. It's better done at night."

"Is there a lot of digging?"

Bacardo shook his head. I don't think so. Not a lot. But some."

"Couldn't you have waited until dark, then, and—?"

Bacardo sharply shook his head, moved restlessly in his chair. When Bernhardt had knocked, Bacardo answered the door with a cocked Colt .45 automatic in his hand. With Bernhardt inside, Bacardo had bolted the door, eased off the pistol's hammer, placed the .45 on a side table beside his chair. Now Bacardo was staring at the gun, frowning as he said, "It won't work to do it in daylight. And at night there's no way I'd do it without a lookout—a wheelman, who can shoot." Even though Bacardo's body language betrayed tension, his voice was matter-of-fact: the professional, discussing job-related problems.

"Is that why I'm here? To apply for a wheelman's job?"

Bacardo's gaze shifted from the .45 to Bernhardt's face. Plainly, the big, awkwardly moving man with the deeply lined face was looking for something in Bernhardt. Something essential. Finally he shook his head. "No," he said quietly. "No, that's not why you're here."

Bernhardt decided to make no response, decided instead to wait—and watch.

"Louise told you about the guy who knocked on the door. Profaci, he said his name was. He told her he was a capo in Don Carlo's family—the Venezzio family. Right?"

Bernhardt nodded. "Right."

"But I don't know any Profaci, at least nobody who looks like the guy Louise described."

"He told Louise to be careful of you," Bernhardt said. "He said you'd cheat her."

Ominously—watchfully—Bacardo made no reply.

"I told her, though," Bernhardt continued, "that if you came back to her from the delta, then that proved you weren't out to cheat her."

"I had those jewels in my house for two weeks before

Mara—before they were brought out here. If I'd wanted to take them, that was the time."

After a moment's thought, Bernhardt decided to probe. "Venezzio was alive then. Now he's dead. That's got to make a difference."

At first Bacardo made no response. Then, speaking in a soft, dangerous voice: "What're you saying, Bernhardt? Exactly?"

Concentrating on keeping his eyes steady, his voice firm, Bernhardt said, "I'm not saying anything except that this thing is suddenly getting very goddam complicated."

As if the answer satisfied him, Bacardo nodded, then shrugged. Saying: "Anytime there's a lot of money involved, things get complicated. It's just the way it happens."

"You said I'm not here because you want me to drive for you."

Once more, Bacardo nodded. "That's right."

"Then why *am* I here?"

"Until I know who this Profaci really is, and why he rang Louise's doorbell, there's no way I'm going after the jewels."

"Your people, you mean. You've got to know whether they sent him."

Bacardo nodded.

"Do you think Profaci followed you up to the delta?"

"I've got no idea. All I'm doing is taking out insurance. Life insurance."

"You mean—" Bernhardt swallowed. "You mean insurance against your people, what they might do?"

"Yeah . . ." Bacardo nodded heavily, ironically. "Yeah, my people." As he said it, the slightly twisted smile returned. Then, as if he were reminiscing, he said, "I guess maybe you remember years ago, there was a guy named Valachi. Joe Valachi. You remember him? It was on TV. He was—you know—just a soldier, a nobody. A bullshit artist, that's all he was. But he was also nuts, thought people were out to get him. So he went to the feds, for protection. Naturally, they said they'd protect him if he talked. Which he did, on nationwide TV, in front of a Senate committee—guys looking for votes, that's what it was all about. Except by that time, for Valachi, it was either talk or die. So there he was on TV, singing for his supper.''

''I remember that,'' Bernhardt said.

''He was the Cosa Nostra guy, that's what the papers picked up on. You know, like they were really on to some inside stuff. Except that Cosa Nostra means 'our thing.' The papers, of course, they had to add something, jazz it up. So they said 'La Cosa Nostra,' which means *the* our thing. Funny, eh?''

It was, Bernhardt realized, a confidence of sorts. A tiny sliver of light cast on the dark interior of the Mafia. Therefore he must smile appreciatively, must nod knowingly. ''Yeah,'' he answered. Finishing lamely: ''Funny.''

''Anyhow,'' Bacardo said, now speaking at a faster cadence, ''the reason I got started on that, sometimes when we're fooling around, bullshitting, we say that our thing is like the IRS.''

''The IRS?''

Bacardo nodded. ''The IRS, you know, if you beat them out of a dollar, they'll spend thousands to get you.''

''Ah—yes. I see what you mean.''

''With us,'' Bacardo said, ''somebody takes a dollar—skims—he gets his hand broken, let's say. If he doesn't get the message—if he keeps at it—he'll end up dead.''

Once more, Bernhardt swallowed, nodded, decided to remain silent. Thoughtfully silent.

''Which is why,'' Bacardo said, ''I'm bowing out.''

''Bowing out?''

''I've got to know where I stand—who sent this Profaci guy, or whatever his real name is. And the easiest way for me to find out what I need to know is to go to New York, talk to the head man. So that's what I'm going to do. Tomorrow.''

''But what about Louise? The jewels?''

''I figure,'' Bacardo said, ''that I've done all I can. I came out here, and Louise and I told each other the words. I went up there to Fow—to the delta, and looked things over. If you'd've been willing to do it—and if this asshole Profaci hadn't shown up, whoever he is—then you and me might be on our way to get the jewels. But now—" Bacardo shrugged. "It's a new ball game."

"So why'm I here? If we aren't going for the treasure, then why am I here?"

"You're here," Bacardo said, "because I wanted to talk to you, look you over."

Listening to Bacardo say it, Bernhardt felt it begin: that schizoid, split-image shift, the playwright looking over the private detective's shoulder, always in search of new material. But would this scenario ever play: two mismatched men in a luxury hotel room, one man a rawboned mafioso, the other a Jewish intellectual?

Bernhardt decided to smile, decided to wait. Did mafiosi ever smile, transacting business? From the look on Bacardo's face, the answer was never. Murder, after all, was serious.

And murder, Bernhardt realized, was the subject of this meeting, now almost an hour old—an hour's tour among the shades and the shadows of the underworld, a once-in-a-lifetime glimpse into a baroque, bizarre landscape that existed unto itself, a government within a government, a culture within a culture, all of it held together by a code of honor and blood oaths and, overhanging it all, *omertà*, the Mafia's code of silence.

Silence, or death.

"If you're trying to decide whether I'm the one to get those jewels," Bernhardt said, "the answer is probably no. I'm no hero. I'm no dummy, either."

"Are you very tough?"

"No," Bernhardt answered, "I'm not very tough. I'm stubborn, but I'm not very tough. The last time I hit anyone, I think I was twelve years old."

"I'm not talking about hitting. I'm talking about shooting. Killing."

"I know that's what you're talking about."

"And?"

"And the answer is that I've killed one man and crippled one woman. And I've had nightmares ever since. Especially about the man. I turned him into a human torch." As he said it, Bernhardt realized that he was angry. By what right had Bacardo become privy to his nightmares? Paula, yes. But not this stranger sitting within easy reach of his pistol.

Now Bernhardt saw Bacardo slowly, gravely nod. Signifying what? That Bernhardt had passed muster? In the Mafia, he knew, the expression was 'making his bones,' the most meaningful qualification for advancement within the organization.

"Have you told Louise you're going to leave town?"

"No," Bacardo answered. "Like I said, I wanted to talk to you first."

"Look me over."

"Right."

"Okay, you've looked me over, and I've looked you over. And my conclusion is that neither of us is willing to risk his neck to help Louise and Angela get their treasure."

As if he were carefully considering the point, Bacardo frowned thoughtfully. Then, still thoughtfully, he nodded. Admitting: "Yeah, I suppose that's right."

"My problem," Bernhardt said, "one of my problems, is that nobody's got the money to retain me."

"That's now. If you deliver—get the stuff—Louise'll take care of you. She's got to."

"I've only been running my own shop for less than a year. But I've learned that I've got to take retainers. I learned the hard way."

"How much retainer would you take to do this job?"

"I haven't thought about it. For ordinary jobs I take two days' compensation up front. That's eight hours a day, fifty dollars an hour. But this job, Christ, there's a risk factor. A *real* risk factor."

"With me gone, there could be less risk."

"Maybe."

For a moment Bacardo sat silently, his long, angular body an awkward fit for the elegantly styled armchair. Then he rose, went to the bureau. He rummaged in the top drawer, found an envelope. He closed the drawer, turned, handed the envelope to Bernhardt. Gingerly, Bernhardt accepted the envelope, which was unsealed.

"That's five thousand dollars," Bacardo said. "That's between us. Louise doesn't know anything about it. If you're smart, you'll take a lot more, once you get the jewels."

"That's if I live."

"If you live. Right."

Weighing the envelope in the palm of one hand, Bernhardt said, "I'm curious. Do you think I'm up to the job?"

"I don't know." Bacardo spoke as if he were earnestly searching for the answer to a problem that puzzled him. "You wouldn't last long in my business, I can tell you that. But I can see you're stubborn. Maybe that's enough. I just don't know."

Making no response, Bernhardt looked down at the envelope. The envelope had a seductive heft. "What d'you think the value of the jewels is?" he asked. "Just a rough guess."

"A million dollars." Still standing, Bacardo yawned, then reached for the .45, which he held pointed down, uncocked. The message: their business had been concluded. Bacardo was ready for bed.

"I want your address," Bernhardt said.

"Why's that?"

"Because I haven't decided whether to keep this." As he spoke, he slipped the envelope into an inside pocket.

"Don't send me a check," Bacardo warned. "No checks."

"I know." Bernhardt dug in another pocket, came up with a notepad and a ballpoint pen. "It'd be a cashier's check." He handed over the pen and notebook.

With pen poised over the notebook, Bacardo frowned. Then: "What I'm going to do is give you a phone number. You'll get a machine. It'll tell you what to do. Just do what it says." He wrote numbers on the notepad, and handed it back.

"But I'd need an address, before I could—"

Bacardo turned his back, strode to the door, and stood with his left hand on the draw bolt. The right hand held the big .45, muzzle down. In the silence, Bernhardt heard two metallic

140

clicks as the hammer came back. At the sound, he felt his throat suddenly go dry.

"Just do what I tell you," Bacardo said. "When you get the machine, say you're—" A pause, for thought. "Say your name's Artie."

"Artie?"

"Artie." With his ear close to the door, Bacardo gestured for silence. He listened for a long moment, then drew back the bolt and opened the door. Repeating firmly: "Artie."

10 P.M., PDT

Brian Chin nodded acknowledgment to the maître d', then turned to Fabrese. "We can have the booth." He gestured to a nearby alcove. The archway over the alcove was a miracle of Chinese ceremonial carving, a fantasy of intertwined dragons, all of it gold-leafed, accented in Mandarin red. A heavy red velvet curtain was drawn back to reveal a polished ebony table set for two: ivory chopsticks, museum-quality bowls and plates, white linen napkins, fancifully folded.

"Or we can have a table."

"How about a table?"

Chin nodded approvingly. "My family owns this place," he said, "so there's nothing for us to fear. Still . . ." He turned to the maître d', nodded to the open dining room. One table, specially set, had been moved apart from the others. "Please . . ." Chin bowed slightly, gestured for Fabrese to follow the maître d'. On a Saturday night, even though it was ten o'clock, the restaurant was almost full. Two waiters followed Fabrese and Chin, ceremoniously seating them, then withdrawing. A moment later a waitress appeared, bearing an Imari teapot. The waitress was small, a perfectly proportioned porcelain doll. She wore a traditional floor-length red gown trimmed in gold brocade. When the tea had been poured, Chin nodded dismissal. The waitress withdrew to stand against the far wall. At a nod from Chin, she would approach again. Fabrese swept the restaurant with an appreciative stare. "How long's your family had this place?"

"Three—no—four years."

"My God, it looks like it's been here forever."

Chin smiled: a gentle up-curving of his mouth, nothing more. In his thirties, Chin was a slim, fastidious man who seldom raised his voice and never laughed out loud. His face was an impassive oval; his eyes revealed nothing.

"The restaurant *has* been here forever. Eighty years, I think. Maybe more. But my family came to America only five years ago."

"You came from Hong Kong."

Chin nodded, but said no more. Because most immigrants from Hong Kong were poor and therefore undesirable, they bore a certain stigma that Chin found distasteful.

"When you say 'your family'—" Fabrese frowned, broke off. How should he say it? The Chinese, he knew, turned aside direct questions. Just as, in the Mafia, certain questions were asked with great care.

Once more, Chin's mouth described a small, knowing smile. "When I say 'my family,' I mean my actual family. Your meaning, I know—professionally—is different."

Fabrese nodded as both men eyed each other over their teacups before Chin returned his to its saucer as he said, "We hear of changes in New York these days. Many changes, in the New York families."

It was, Fabrese knew, an opening, a suggestion that now they might discuss business. Meaning that the time had come: either take the chance, take the gamble, or else call it a free Chinese dinner. One way he could win, the other way he could lose—everything. No, not everything, not if he kept ahead of the game. If he found the package, got that far, he could still cover himself, still come out on the right side. Prove Bacardo was skimming, give the package to Cella, and everybody won.

Everybody but Bacardo.

Or else he could take the package and run, fuck them all. Go down deep into Mexico, live happily ever after. If they ever found him, he'd die rich.

Now, though, sitting across the table from Brian Chin, he must begin. But slowly, carefully. Because everything could depend on this young Chinaman who dressed like an undertaker and whose eyes were as blank as two black stones—the gangster from Hong Kong who sat across the table sipping tea from a porcelain cup.

"The reason I wanted to see you," Fabrese began, "is that our people in New York sent me out here on what you might call a secret mission. You know—" He contrived a smile. "CIA stuff. Cloak and dagger, you might say."

Chin's smile, too, was contrived.

"It's the kind of a deal," Fabrese went on, "where the less I tell you—the less you know—the better for both of us. See?"

Chin allowed his eyes to briefly close as he nodded—once.

"You know that Benito Cella is taking Venezzio's place. Cella'll be the new *capo di tutti,* that's all set. There'll probably be a meeting of the council—the five New York families—in about a month, that's what they're thinking now. And then it'll be official. So what I'm telling you is off the record. You understand."

"I understand."

"So between now and a month from now, there're some loose ends to clean up."

"Yes, I would think so."

"Venezzio was in prison for almost ten years. He ran things from prison, no problem. Tony Bacardo—do you know him?"

"I know the name."

"Yeah, well, Bacardo was Don Carlo's number one. And I was number two." Once more Fabrese smiled. "Don Carlo gave the orders to Tony, and Tony gave the orders to me."

143

"Ah, yes." Now Chin's smile was subtly more appreciative. "Some things never change."

"Now, though, I'll be with Cella. That's all set."

"And Salvatore Perrone? Will he still be with Cella?"

"Ah." Caught by surprise, Fabrese blinked, felt the first sharp flick of anxiety. Then, as if the question interested him, nothing more, he spoke casually: "You know a lot about our organization."

For a moment Chin made no reply as, attentive to his task, he made a small ceremony of replenishing their tea. When he had sipped once more from his cup, he said, "Did you and Perrone come to San Francisco together?"

As it always did, the second flick from fear's whip cut deeper than the first. *Perrone in San Francisco.* Was it possible? Yes, certainly possible. Wherever Bacardo went, Cella would have people watching. He should have guessed.

But how did Brian Chin know? A Chinese numbers hustler, a hood from Hong Kong who'd got lucky in the heroin trade, how much did Chin know?

What else did Chin know?

As if to explain, Chin said, "There was a lunch today, at Fisherman's Wharf." Chin spoke very softly. Then, having expertly inserted the slim blade, he smiled again.

A lunch—yes, there would be a lunch for Perrone. Ricca, the San Francisco don, Benvenuti, from Los Angeles. And someone from Nevada, someone from San Diego, all of them, each with a couple of capos, the perfect chance to show clout, charter a jet, fly up to San Francisco, buy Perrone a drink, tell him that, yes, they were with Don Benito, have another drink. Then the tape would reverse: back into the limos, back to the waiting jet, back to L.A., or Las Vegas, or San Diego.

For Fabrese, now, there was just one chance, one single sliver of blue. He must lean closer, act out a grave warning. Saying urgently: "None of those guys at the lunch—especially Perrone—none of them are supposed to know I'm here. I hope you didn't . . ." He let it go meaningfully unfinished.

This time, Chin's smile seemed to reflect genuine amusement, however muted. "I know of the meeting only because San Francisco is really a very small town, and news travels fast." Indulgently, he shook his head. "I'm not in the loop."

"You didn't tell anybody about this, then—us meeting."

"No one."

Pretending to a relief he didn't feel, Fabrese smiled. "I didn't mean to—you know—give you a hard time. It's just that I've got to be careful. I already told you that."

"Cloak and dagger, as you say." Chin nodded appreciatively. Then, gently: "Spying is a dangerous game, there is no question." Gracefully, he gestured to the table. "Would you like to begin? I've already selected the menu. I hope you don't mind."

"No. Fine. Thanks."

Chin nodded to the waitress. Then, to Fabrese: "What is it, exactly, that you need from me?"

As if he appreciated the invitation to plain talk, Fabrese leaned forward again, lowered his voice, spoke as one confidant to another: "What I need are maybe four, five of your people to do some surveillance work."

"Just surveillance?" As he spoke, Chin nodded his thanks to the waitress, who was serving their soup.

"Just surveillance."

"For how long?"

"Probably just a day or two. I know you're up on electronics. That's why I thought of you."

Chin nodded, sampled the soup. "Ah. Excellent." He looked at Fabrese. "It's bird's nest soup, you know. Wonderful."

"Jesus." Fabrese stared down at his soup. "I thought it was a gag, bird's nest soup."

Chin's smile was subtly amused. "Many people think that."

"Well . . ." Tentatively, Fabrese sipped a spoonful, then looked surprised. "Well, it's great. Just great."

"This surveillance—would it be on some of your people?"

Fabrese had prepared himself for this question. "Tony Bacardo came to San Francisco yesterday. He could've come here because of some money that can't be accounted for. I'm not saying Tony's skimming, that's not it. But Don Benito, well, he sent me out here to keep track of Tony, make sure there're no loose ends when it comes time for Don Benito to take over the five families.''

"So Tony Bacardo doesn't know you're in San Francisco."

"God, no. That's what I'm *telling* you."

"Perrone—he doesn't know you're here, either."

"Perrone is what you might call a diplomat, coming to town to shake hands, do a lot of smiling, mend a few fences. I'm undercover. Like I said."

Chin waited for the waitress to serve the next course, then said, "You say you'll need four or five of my people."

"There's two women, a mother and a daughter. They live on Thirty-ninth Avenue. I need to have them watched."

"Ah—good. They live out in the avenues, as we call them. A lot of Chinese live out there. Do they live in a house?"

"Right. A row house."

"You've been there, then. To their house."

"I was there today."

"You talked to these two women. They know you."

Fabrese nodded. "They know me. Which is why I need you."

"And the other people?"

"There's just one more, besides Bacardo—a man. Tall, kind of stooped, early forties, I'd say. He wears gold aviator glasses. You know, stylish. But he's not much of a dresser. Corduroy pants and sweaters, like that. Tweedy, maybe. He's a friend of the women."

"You have no name for him."

"No."

"License plate?"

"I forgot that part."

"Does he live with the women?"

"I don't know. I don't think so."

Chin allowed a reflective silence to pass before he said, "That's all, those four."

"That's all."

"And when should these stakeouts start?"

"As soon as possible."

"Tonight?"

"That'd be great."

Once more, Chin sampled food from the several small plates placed on their table. Then: "My people—should they be armed? Is it that kind of a job?"

Promptly, Fabrese shook his head. This question, too, he'd expected. "It's not that kind of a job. I just want answers, that's all. No guns."

"If there are guns, then I would double the number of my people."

"No guns. Period."

"Then I can't see any problem, once we decide on how payment should be made." Now Chin's face was impassive, as if his entire attention was focused on the prawn he was conveying to his mouth.

"Well, there're two ways to go," Fabrese said. As he spoke, he touched the breast pocket of his jacket, where he carried an envelope fat with cash. "I could give you something up front, right now. Say ten thousand, to show good faith. Then you could tell me whatever you figure, after everything's finished. That's one way."

Chin turned his attention to the small task of blending seasoned snow peas with rice as he asked, "And the other way?"

"The other way, after everything's finished, and I'm back in New York with Cella, I tell him that I never could've done it without you. When he mentions money, how much you charged us, I tell him that you wanted to do him this favor, a little something from you to him, one top guy to another top guy. You know."

"Ah, yes," Chin said. "Yes—I know."

11 P.M., PDT

They lay as they always did in the afterglow, her body finding the full length of his, the fit that had never failed. It was the prelude to pillow talk, for Bernhardt the most meaningful moments.

And it was now, in these moments, sooner rather than later, that he must ask her to move in with him. "You're here all weekend," he would begin. "So why shouldn't we—"

No.

More than mere logic was required. This overture must come from the heart: "The more we're together, the more I want us to be together. So why don't we—"

He'd done it again, lapsed into logic, mere argumentation.

He'd written plays, one good enough to be produced off Broadway. But he couldn't find the words to begin.

Had it been this way with Jennie? They'd been walking from the town up to campus, he and Jennie. The distance had been less than a mile. It had been early in May, only a month before graduation. Before them, life had spread out with infinite promise, a magic tapestry woven just for them. Of course, they would go to New York. He'd already had a play produced at the Yellow Springs Area Theater. And an off-Broadway company was interested. So they would go to New York, the two of them. His mother, who'd lived in the Village and who'd taught modern dance in her loft, would help them find a place to live. Then, full of hope, they would begin making the rounds. Of course, they would expect rejection at first. But they would sustain each other until their turns came: bit parts for Jennie, an off-Broadway production of *Victims*, the play he'd begun writing while he was still a senior at Antioch.

And, incredibly, hope had burgeoned, become reality. Jennie began getting small parts. And, yes, *Victims* had run for three solid, successful weeks at the Bransten Theater.

But they hadn't known it would happen like that, not when

they were walking up to the campus on that soft, warm night in May. Then, that night, they could only hope—and plan.

And part of the plan, it turned out, had been marriage.

They'd seen *Two Women* at the movie theater in town. As they'd walked up the gentle hill from the town to the theater, talk about the film had turned to talk of the future—their future, in New York. Together they would pursue their dreams, hers to act, his to write and direct.

And so, by the time they got to the campus, they'd agreed that they would be married. There'd been no proposal, no acceptance. There'd only been a few quiet words spoken between them. They'd—

"Hey." With one finger, Paula was poking him in the ribs. "Hey, you're off somewhere."

It was a standing joke between them. If he was uncertain about a business decision or searching for a line of dialogue that would illuminate a scene, he often drifted off. In the light of day, Paula could clearly see the preoccupation in his eyes. In bed, in the darkness, she could feel the change in his body, their flesh in intimate contact.

He drew her closer, kissed the point of her chin, then lightly kissed her lips.

"Sorry."

"It's those ladies, isn't it—those ladies in distress."

He knew where the conversation would go. Paula was determined to work with him, doing investigations. He needed help, she reasoned, and she needed something to do. She was very quiet about it, very patient—but very determined. Meaning that now, in the afterglow, she would persist. "I have the feeling," she said, "that you'll take them on."

He considered. Then, somewhat to his own surprise, he heard himself say, "There'd be money in it. A lot of money."

"Like, five figures?"

He calculated. "At least."

Now she was calculating, too. "After five figures, you realize, comes six figures. As in a hundred thousand dollars."

"I know . . ."

"You sound a little—" She broke off, searched for the word. "You sound a little apprehensive. But maybe a little tempted, too."

"My car needs a new set of tires."

"Alan . . ." Now she traced a light line with a forefinger that began at the base of his throat and then ventured down. Meaning that, this time—this six-figure time—Paula would stop at nothing to get the story from him. Thank God.

11:45 P.M., PDT

When he'd finished the story, he realized that he was no longer turned toward her. Instead, even though her head was still cradled in the crook of his arm, he lay on his back, staring up at the ceiling. He'd been talking, uninterrupted, for more than a half hour.

"Are you telling me," Paula said, her voice rising incredulously, "that you've got five thousand dollars of this guy Bacardo's *money*? This—this hood?"

"He's not a hood." Reacting to her criticism, he spoke sharply. "He's a big shot."

"Okay. So he *hires* hoods."

Bernhardt made no response.

"Jesus, Alan." She raised herself on one elbow to look down into his face. "Jesus, if something should go wrong, you'd be in trouble with both the goddam Mafia and the goddam law."

"There's something I didn't tell you."

"Oh?"

"I told Bacardo that I might give the money back. I've got a number to call."

"Then for God's sake do it. Make the call."

He studied her face in silence. Two months ago, give or take,

Paula had begun pressuring him to let her work with him. "You're turning down business," she'd said. Adding fervently: "You don't have enough time to direct, worse yet. Or write. Or even act." In the end, Paula had prevailed. She'd started doing surveillance, fifteen dollars an hour. He'd charged the client forty—for surveillance jobs imaginatively, conscientiously well done. It was another reason, come to think of it, why she should move in with him.

"Alan?"

"Hmmm."

"Are you mad at me?"

"Of course not. I'm just trying to decide."

"I don't see what there is to decide."

"I've already looked at this from your point of view, which is the worst-case scenario. But there's another scenario."

She lowered her head back into the crook of his arm. With both of them staring up at the ceiling, she said, "And what's that?"

"Now you're mad."

"I'm *not* mad."

"That's the way you always talk when you're mad."

"And how's that?"

"It's—" He hesitated, then ventured, "It's haughty."

"Haughty?" Suddenly she laughed: a sharp, sudden peal. *"Haughty?"*

He lay in silence—waiting. Finally, as he knew she would, Paula said, "Okay. So what's the best-case scenario?"

"It's interesting, you know . . ." He spoke reflectively, subtly teasing her. "You've only been doing surveillance for a couple of months. But already you're talking different. You act different, too. Do you realize that?"

"Different in what sense?"

"For one thing, you swear more."

"Hmmm . . ." Paula was considering the point.

"Back to the best-case scenario," he said.

"Hmmm."

"Tomorrow I call C.B. I tell him there's a thousand dollars in it, win or lose, for a day's work. I'll tell him it's dangerous, that he should bring his guns. For C.B. that's a come-on. Next I'll buy a shovel. Then about, say, eight o'clock tomorrow night, we get under way—me and Louise in my car, C.B. in his car. We start out for the delta. Of course, C.B. and I'll have walkie-talkies, homers, the whole thing. Louise will give me directions as we go. We'll get to the appointed spot about ten, ten-thirty. We'll check it out very, very carefully. If there's a problem, we'll leave. Run, in other words. If there isn't a problem, we dig up the jewels. Maybe we take them to a hotel, a suite, so we can all keep track of each other. Then, Monday morning, we take the stuff to the bank, put it in a safe-deposit box. In due time, with me riding shotgun, Louise sells some of the jewels. That's when I get my ten percent.''

"If you and C.B. got greedy, what'd prevent you guys from taking the jewels away from Louise?"

"Nothing. But she's got to trust someone. And she knows it. She also knows that time is of the essence.''

"What about—"

"Let me finish this. I'm making it up as I go along, but so far it sounds pretty good.''

In spite of herself, Paula chuckled. "The creative mind at work.''

"Let's say," Bernhardt went on, "that something goes wrong. You talked about the law. Okay, let's say we get picked up by some deputy sheriff on suspicion. What's going to happen?"

"I hate to think.''

"What's going to happen is that I tell him the absolute truth. I say that Louise hired me to help her dig up an unspecified item at an unspecified location somewhere in the San Joaquin delta. Period.''

"That's the law. What about the Mafia? If Bacardo is scared enough to run, then—"

"I don't think Bacardo's scared. He's just being cautious. He wants to check out this Profaci guy.''

"Who's probably a hoodlum, after the jewels."

"I don't think that's what worried Bacardo. He's got politics on his mind. Job tenure."

"Mafia politics."

Bernhardt considered, then decided to say, "Don't knock Mafia politics. They play rough—but they play by the rules."

"Mafia rules."

"Naturally."

They lay silently for a moment. Finally Paula said, "If you're going to ride with Louise, then I should ride with C.B."

Bernhardt snorted. "I knew you were going to say that. I *knew* it."

She made no reply.

"If there's any danger, it'll come from the Mafia. We're agreed on that. And if that should happen, then guns are the only way out. And Louise, unarmed, becomes a liability. The same thing would apply to you. You'd be a liability, just like Louise. If C.B. and I were alone, and something went wrong, we'd fire a shot over their bow and run—probably for the police. But if we have to hang back to protect the womenfolk—" Aware of the risk, he let the image dangle.

A mistake.

"The womenfolk, eh?" Her voice was grim. "I assume that, as always, you chose your words with care."

"A little joke. Frontier humor."

"I know how to shoot. You taught me, if you'll recall."

Now they lay neither together nor apart. Finally Bernhardt ventured, "If you really want to help, there *is* something you could do."

"Oh? What's that? Load the flintlocks?"

"If it plays out according to the script, then we'll have to leave Angela behind. Louise's orders, no compromise."

"And you need a baby-sitter."

"This is no kid. She's twenty, at least. And beautiful. One of those blond California beauties."

"Long-legged, I suppose. Great boobs. A world-class ass. Right?"

Bernhardt decided to make no reply, a tactical withdrawal in the face of unpredictable hostile action.

SUNDAY, APRIL 22nd
8:30 A.M., PDT

As he ate the last of his croissant, Bernhardt said, "Why don't you take Crusher to the beach for an hour or two?"

"Crusher gets in fights at the beach," Paula said. "You know that." It was a cool response. Between them, the question of the treasure was still unresolved. It had been unresolved when they'd gone to sleep last night, a mistake that still hung heavily between them in the cold light of morning.

"Crusher gets in fights everywhere. That's what Airedales do."

She considered the answer, then decided to say, "If you had it to do all over again, would you still adopt him?"

"I never *did* adopt him. I was only supposed to keep him over a weekend, while his master arranged bail. So then the guy jumps bail. The last I heard he was in Majorca, having a ball."

"Let's say you knew how it would happen. Would you still take Crusher?"

"No comment."

In a voice that was carefully pitched to the neutral, Paula said, "Are you going to call C.B.?"

"Yes," he answered, meeting her gaze squarely. "And Louise, too." He let a beat pass. Then: "Dammit, Paula, I've—"

From the front of the flat Bernhardt's office telephone warbled. After the fourth ring the answering machine's message began, followed by a woman's voice. As the message went on, Bernhardt saw amused resignation register in Paula's face as she poured herself a second cup of coffee.

"There she is," Paula said. "One of your ladies in distress, I'll bet."

"Is that small, resigned smile meant to suggest that we can resolve this thing, resume our previous relationship?"

"The Mafia's man in San Francisco . . ." Now reluctant amusement touched the corners of her mouth as warmth began to glow in her eyes. In the office, the caller's message was ending, followed by a tone, then silence.

"You know you're going to call her back."

"But not until I've finished my coffee." As he spoke, he raised the cup, drank the last of his coffee.

"Make the call," Paula said. "I'll put the dishes in the sink."

"You're a good sport." Smiling, he rose, went around the table, kissed her meaningfully beneath her ear. She smiled in return, briefly stroked the inside of his thigh.

"Hmmm . . ." It was a sensual murmur, soft and interested. Should he lift her to her feet, kiss her in earnest, suggest a Sunday morning change of plans, a detour to the bedroom? Was that her meaning?

"Make the call," she repeated.

"Hmmm . . ."

"Then we'll see."

He smiled, kissed her again as, sensing the change of mood, Crusher had come to stand close beside them. Whenever they made love, it was always easier to close the bedroom door on Crusher.

He kissed her neck again, straightened, smiled, and walked down the flat's long hallway to his office, the room that was originally a front bedroom. As predicted, the voice on the tape was Angela Rabb's. Would he please call her? As soon as possible?

He copied down the number, made the call. "Angela?"

"Yes—Alan?"

"Yes."

"I hope it's not too early on Sunday morning. But Tony Bacardo called about a half hour ago. He said he had to go back to New York. But he said you—"

"Let's not talk about it on the phone, Angela. Can you come over?"

"Of course. Mom, too?"

He hesitated, then said, "Why don't you come by yourself? I think your mother should stay near her phone."

"I'll be right over."

9:20 A.M., PDT

Bernhardt's flat was on a hill so steep that only perpendicular parking was allowed on one side of the street. Driving slowly up the hill in low gear, vainly looking for a parking place, Angela passed Bernhardt's building and continued up to the next block, which was almost level, with parallel parking allowed on both sides of the street. Here she had a choice of parking places. As she braked to a stop in front of one of the spaces she saw a light blue sedan climbing the hill behind her. The driver was a young Chinese man. He, too, was slowing, obviously also looking for a place to park. As he passed her he looked straight ahead, ignoring her. Now he was stopping, maneuvering his car back and forth, into a parking place, just as she was.

At almost nine-thirty on a Sunday morning, in this quiet residential neighborhood on the northern slope of Potrero Hill, nothing stirred except for her and the Chinese man.

When she'd left her mother's house, she'd seen a blue car following at a distance. Watching the car in her mirror, she'd seen it turn off, disappear. The car had never come close enough for her to see the driver, and it had been impossible for her to identify the car's make.

Parked now, with the front wheels curbed, she switched off the engine, put the shift lever in park, set the brake. Three cars ahead, the blue sedan was still maneuvering into a tight parking place. Irresolutely, she looked back over her shoulder, down the steep slope of the next block. Alan Bernhardt's flat was midway down that block, across the street. There were two choices: get out of the car and walk directly down the hill to Bernhardt's building, or else wait for the Chinese man to make a move, commit himself. Through the windows of the two parked cars that separated them, she could make out the shape of the man's head. Now with the car finally parked, he sat motionless behind the steering wheel, looking straight ahead.

From behind her came the sound of an engine laboring up the hill. It was an old station wagon with a wind surfer and a mast strapped to its roof rack. As the station wagon slowly pulled even, Angela saw three teenagers inside, two boys and a girl. The station wagon was stopping less than twenty feet beyond the blue sedan. Quickly Angela got out of her Tercel, locked the door, and walked diagonally across the street, then down the hill a half block to Bernhardt's building. As she pressed the bell button she looked back the way she'd come, but the crest of the hill concealed both the blue sedan and the station wagon. In the Sunday morning quiet, she heard youthful laughter, doubtless the teenage wind surfers. From inside Bernhardt's flat she heard a dog barking: Crusher, Bernhardt's unruly Airedale.

As she touched the button a second time the door opened. With a firm grip on the dog's collar, Bernhardt smiled a greeting, stepped back to make room for her in the interior hallway. He wore jeans, running shoes, and a Monterey Jazz Festival sweatshirt.

"It's okay," Angela said. "I don't mind if he jumps up. I like Crusher. Really."

"All right . . ." Bernhardt released the dog, who immediately jumped up at her so high that his forepaws struck her shoulders. The Airedale was wriggling all over, a paroxysm of delight. As Bernhardt closed the front door he said, "Crusher loves people, as you already discovered yesterday. He hates dogs—male dogs, anyhow. But he loves people."

"He's great." As Bernhardt forced him down, Angela began scratching the dog behind both ears. Wagging his tail vigorously, Crusher raised his head to her, adoration in his eyes.

"He likes that," Bernhardt said. "You've got the touch. Have you had dogs?"

"Only one, when I was a little girl. I loved him."

Bernhardt took hold of the dog's collar as he gestured Angela into his office, the first door off the hallway. Then, sternly blocking the dog's entrance to the office, Bernhardt pointed down the hallway as, on cue, a woman's voice called out to the dog from the rear of the ground-floor flat. Hearing the voice, Angela nodded to herself. Yes, there was a woman in Bernhardt's life. Among the regulars at the Howell Theater, no one had been sure. They'd known only that, years ago, Bernhardt's young wife had died a violent death in New York.

As they sat down facing each other across Bernhardt's desk, he said, "I was going to call you this morning."

She nodded. "I knew you would. But Mom—" Disconsolately, Angela shook her head. "She's not sleeping. This thing—" Once more, she shook her head. "It's getting to her, Alan. I—God—I'd've called you two hours ago, if I'd listened to Mom. That's when Tony Bacardo called. About seven-thirty."

"Did he tell you he was going back to New York?"

She nodded. "He called from the airport."

"What else did he say?"

"He talked to Mom, not me. And she—she's so upset, it was hard to pin her down. But apparently Bacardo wants to know who Profaci really is—who he is, and who sent him. And for that, Tony's got to go back to New York."

"Is it still true that only your mother and Bacardo know where the jewels are?"

For a long moment she looked him full in the face. Plainly, she was deciding whether she must trust him fully. Finally she spoke in a low, cautious voice: "I know now. She told me yesterday. It was—" She searched for the words. "It was all she had to leave me, that's what she said. You know, like a will."

Bernhardt rose from behind the desk and went to the window. His slice of the cityscape was still covered with morning fog; today would be a late burn-off. On the street outside an old station wagon with a wind surfer on top was coming down the hill. Across the street, a barefoot neighbor wearing pajamas and a bathrobe was furtively retrieving his Sunday paper from the ivy that bordered his front stoop.

Like a will . . .

From the hallway he heard the clicking of Crusher's toenails; the dog was returning. From the kitchen he heard the clink of dishes being washed. Should he have invited Paula to sit in? On her first surveillance assignment, she'd chased off a murderer, saved a woman's life. Was she feeling like a scullery maid, not a member of the firm?

Bernhardt turned away from the window as Crusher came into the office, went to Angela, presented himself. "Excuse me a minute. I want you to meet my—ah—partner." Bernhardt walked down the long hallway to the kitchen where, yes, Paula was bent stubbornly over the sink, ignoring him. Her face was cloudy.

"I want you to meet Angela, see what you think."

She looked at him with mild suspicion.

"Come on." He tugged at her. "Quit sulking."

"What makes you think—?"

"Come *on*." Bernhardt found a towel, pulled her away from the sink, waited while she dried her hands. They went together to his office, where he made the introductions.

"Paula knows the whole thing," Bernhardt said. "She—" He hesitated, then decided to say, "She has some reservations." He turned to Paula for confirmation. She said nothing, revealed nothing.

"It's the Mafia involvement," Bernhardt explained. "It worries me, too. I don't really know much about them, but I sure don't want to tangle with them. And neither does Tony Bacardo."

"He told Mom that we should talk to you. He said you'd know what to do." When Bernhardt made no response, Angela turned to Paula, one woman to another. "If this doesn't work out for my mother, I don't know what'll happen to her. She's only forty, but—" As if her thoughts caused pain, Angela winced, shook her head. Then: "She's had a hard life. When she was about ten years old, her mother started to drink. My mother couldn't wait to leave home. She was only nineteen when she got married. And it—it didn't work. My father— well . . ." She shook her head sadly. "He—he died. Later, I mean, after they got divorced, he died. It was drugs. His father was one of those Hollywood hustlers—a producer, supposedly. And—" She broke off, sat for a moment with eyes downcast. Then, recovering: "And my stepfather—Jack Castle—died, too. But he was older. He was an actor, and he was good to my mother. But then he died. And he had a lot of debts when he died. So Mom struck out again, I guess you'd say. And then she came to San Francisco just a few years ago, with Walter Draper. I was sixteen when we moved up here. And it—it was terrible, living with him. When he drank, he—he—" In obvious anguish at the memory, she broke off.

"I know about that, Angela," Bernhardt offered gently.

"Yeah . . ." Eyes downcast, she nodded disconsolately. "Yeah, I remember how ashamed I was, telling you about it. Afterwards, I mean, I felt ashamed. I didn't even really know you when I told you about it."

"Sometimes that's best," Paula said. "Sometimes it's easier to tell a stranger."

As she spoke, Bernhardt searched Paula's face. Had he told her that Walter Draper had abused Angela? He couldn't remember.

For a moment Angela, too, was searching Paula's face. Then, speaking softly, as if all hope was gone, Angela said, "The reason I'm telling you all this, I want you to know how it is with my mother. It—it's hard, you know, when your father's a gangster. It's very hard.''

"And without those jewels . . ." This time, Bernhardt's quick scrutiny of Paula's face was covert.

They sat in silence for a long moment. Then, turning to Bernhardt, Angela said, "Mom says that it's all right with Tony if you get the jewels. She says that he trusts you. And we trust you, too. That—that's why I called you this morning. I mean, I thought that maybe the two of us—you and I—could get the jewels, talk Mom into letting me go. Ten minutes digging, that's all it would take."

"Angela . . ." Somberly, Bernhardt shook his head. It's not the digging. You *know* it's not the digging. It's the Mafia.''

"But my mom—what about her? This is her last shot, Alan.'' She spoke doggedly, with rigidly controlled passion. Angela Rabb, Bernhardt decided, had guts.

Bernhardt looked first at Angela, then at Paula. In Angela's eyes, he saw a low fire, steadily burning. In Paula's eyes, he saw—what?

What did they see in his eyes, one of them hardly out of her teens, one of them his lover, his friend—and, yes, his associate.

"Did Bacardo tell you that he'd given me money?'' Bernhardt asked, looking at Angela.

Her first reaction was a puzzled frown. Then she said, "Mom talked to him, not me. But she didn't say anything like that.''

"Well, he did. He gave me five thousand dollars.'' He realized that he was speaking defiantly, as if to challenge her—her, or Paula.

"Five thousand . . ." Angela stared at him incredulously. Then, seeking confirmation, Angela turned to Paula, who nodded. The two women exchanged a long, searching look before Bernhardt spoke again, another challenge: "And it's not enough, Angela. It's not nearly enough.''

"Yesterday,'' she said, "you and I talked about a contingency fee. I asked Mom about it last night. She wasn't sure. But now—this morning—she wants to do it. That's what she told me to tell you—that a contingency fee is okay."

"If we did it that way," Bernhardt said, "it'd be ten percent." As he said it, he looked at Paula. Her answering gaze revealed nothing.

"Ten percent is fine." Angela's prompt reply suggested that she had been prepared to go higher.

Bernhardt rose from behind his desk again, went to the window, looked out. Across the street a high-styled, long-legged blond woman was waiting patiently while her golden retriever was meticulously sniffing a sidewalk tree. Bernhardt had spoken to the woman several times, once, memorably, when Crusher had picked a fight with the golden. The woman, he'd later learned, was a producer on the Channel Six News.

"Alan . . ." It was Paula's voice. He turned, saw her also standing. Crusher, too, was on his feet, looking expectantly from him to Paula. Just as Angela was looking at them.

"Excuse us a minute," Paula said, speaking to Angela. Then Paula turned, walked down the hallway to the dining room, where they could shut the door. Crusher chose to remain in the hallway, awaiting developments.

"What're you going to do?" Paula asked, sotto voce.

"I think I'll do it."

"Good." She nodded decisively. "That poor woman. You've got her life in your hands. Literally."

Bernhardt shook his head incredulously as he stared at her. "Was I imagining it last night, or were you saying that I should stay away from this?"

"That was before I realized what the stakes were."

"The *stakes*? Jesus, the stakes are—"

"*Shhh*." She put her forefinger to her lips.

"You're becoming very unpredictable, you know that?"

"How about 'flexible'?" She smiled at him, then gestured with her head toward the door. "We should get back. The poor kid, she's obviously hanging by a thread."

"Yeah, well, *I'm* hanging by a thread, too."

Now her smile suggested the eternal female: inscrutable, subtly superior, and, yes, sometimes smug.

"My plan," Bernhardt said, "is to tell Angela that I'll take the job. Then I plan to tell her that, at the first hint of trouble, I'm out. Gone. Long gone."

"That's my plan, too."

12:05 P.M., PDT

Seated in his tiny office behind the restaurant, Brian Chin tapped the computer's keys, watched the symbols materialize on the screen: ALB for Alan Bernhardt, the third person on Fabrese's list. Another sequence, for the Delta data base: ALB, age 44, born NYC. Profession: theatrical director, actor—and private investigator. Time in secondary profession: three years with Dancer Associates. Currently an independent, less than six months' tenure. Followed by Bernhardt's address and phone numbers.

And, finally, Chin's own private project: JIF for Jimmy Fabrese, 321 West 87th Street, NYC. Profession: supervisor with Acme Dry Cleaners, a suspected front organization for organized crime. In a supplementary organized-crime data base Fabrese was rated a soldier in the Venezzio family, nothing more, no connection with Benito Cella. Sipping tea from a porcelain cup, Chin tapped F7, saved the document, left the computer switched on, ready.

But ready for what?

Were there enough pieces to work with, add the essential element of intelligence, make a preliminary pass at a pattern, therefore a plan? He decided to let his head fall back against the soft leather of his executive chair, decided to let his eyes close—decided to work with the pieces of the puzzle currently at hand, a preliminary alignment, a tentative juxtaposition.

Begin, then, at the beginning: begin with Fabrese, who'd somehow stumbled onto a valuable secret.

Begin with Fabrese, end with Fabrese, the small-time hood who was probably in over his head.

Switch, then, to the real players: Louise Rabb, the principal. Also Angela, probably Louise Rabb's daughter, probable last name also Rabb. Then focus on Alan Bernhardt, the wild card.

Chin was pleased at the precision with which his people had performed. And pleased, additionally, with the performance of his electronics. Fabrese had left the restaurant at ten-thirty last night. By eleven forty-five, two men and two cars had taken up positions at Thirty-ninth Avenue, where they'd reconnoitered thoroughly, communicating with Chin by cellular phone. "Mother" had been the code name for Louise Rabb, "Chick" for Angela.

Most of the houses on Thirty-ninth Avenue were row houses, each one attached to houses on either side. But the Rabb house was only attached on the south side, with a service way on the north. The living room was in front of the house, on the same side as the serviceway. Therefore, after getting Chin's approval, one member of the team had easily been able to drill a quarter-inch hole of sufficient length to accommodate a spike mike.

With almost every word being recorded, the two women had talked in the living room for almost two hours before they'd finally gone to bed. Charles Ng, the leader of the team, had brought the tapes to Chin, at his home on Russian Hill. The time had been three A.M., but Ng, on his own authority, had decided to awaken Chin. It had been the correct decision. By five-fifteen, Chin had pieced together the whole story, assuming he was correct in deciding that "Profaci" was really Fabrese. The only puzzle had been the identity of "Alan," but that question had been resolved when Angela, followed alternately by two cars, had driven to the Vermont Street address this morning, thus establishing Alan Bernhardt's identity.

Chin opened his eyes, leaned forward, began making random designs and word combinations on a legal pad, always a helpful exercise whenever psychic overload threatened.

Across the top of the sheet of paper, in Chinese characters, he doodled

一百萬一百萬元

a million dollars in jewels, somewhere in the delta south of Sacramento.

Buried treasure, the stuff of legend: pirates on the Spanish Main. Genghis Khan, his elephants laden with chests of plunder, the riches of the eastern world.

The legend—and the reality: a third-rate hood, two frightened women, and one part-time private eye, apparently an actor. Plums, ripe for the picking.

But first, planning was required, the life-or-death difference. So, while Ng presided at Thirty-ninth Avenue and Gregory Barrows, a Caucasian, was calling the shots at Vermont Street, Chin took stock:

As of now, noon on Sunday, a bright, clear April morning, the situation was static, in equilibrium. Bacardo was still in the air, flying to New York. After more than two hours spent with Bernhardt, Angela had just returned to her mother's house. During her absence, there had been no sound from inside the house at Thirty-ninth Avenue, despite the fact that Louise Rabb was still inside. Conclusion: except for her daughter, there was no one who could help Louise Rabb.

Back on stakeout after six hours' sleep, Ng had just reported that, once again, the two women were in the living room, in urgent conversation. In Ng's opinion, Louise Rabb was close to the breaking point. Angela, returning from Alan Bernhardt with good news, was trying to reassure her mother. She'd been home for less than ten minutes, during which time Chin had listened while the conversation from inside the house was being recorded. Clearly, Angela had come to an agreement with Alan Bernhardt. If everything went as they hoped, they would be "ready" tonight. Meaning that—

On the desk, the phone warbled. The console revealed that Barrows was calling from the Bernhardt stakeout.

"Go ahead," Chin said.

"Al is leaving. There's a woman and a dog with him. His wife, I'd say."

"Al" meaning Alan Bernhardt.

"Are you set up with Wayne?"

"I think so. Al has to go down the hill. Wayne's down there."

"Does Al park his car on the street?"

"Yes. There's no garage."

"Then be sure and install a homing device."

"I already have," Barrows answered.

"Good." Chin broke the connection. Locked on the homer, Barrows and Wayne Gee would follow Bernhardt, a rolling tail.

Chin waited for a dial tone, consulted an electronic memo screen, called Ng's number.

"Anything?"

"The other one," Ng said, groping. "The man."

"That's Al."

"Right. Looks like he's going to get someone for backup. That's what the women are talking about."

"He's moving now."

"This Al," Ng said, "he's the main man, it sounds like. What he says, they do."

"Hold on." Chin put Ng on hold, contacted Barrows. "I'd like to send someone with a spike mike to make an installation at Al's while he's gone. How does it look?"

"Iffy, I'd say," came the prompt response. "He lives in a lower flat, and the building's attached on both sides. The front's right on the sidewalk, maybe a five-foot garden with a few rosebushes. At night—late—maybe it'd work. Not now, though. It's a residential neighborhood. You know, kids playing, lots of action. Especially on Sunday. Everyone's out front, washing their cars."

"How about the back? An alley?"

"I don't think there's an alley. I'm almost sure, in fact."

In silence, Chin made his calculations. The conclusion: A fake cable system installation might work—but not on Sunday.

"Okay, we'll hold off on the mike. Where's Al going?"

"Hard to say. Upper Market, as of right now."

"Okay. I'll be here for at least an hour. Keep in touch." Chin switched back to Ng, gave instructions that he should be informed minute to minute if anything changed at Thirty-ninth Avenue. Then Chin poured himself a fresh cup of tea, sighed, gently massaged his eyes as, once again, he leaned back in the chair. The time for decisions had come.

First, as to Jimmy Fabrese: percentagewise, what was the probability that Fabrese had, in fact, come to San Francisco on a secret mission for Benito Cella? Chin considered, decided on ten percent.

Next, what exactly was Louise Rabb's connection with the Mafia—and therefore the treasure? Based on the taped conversations, it seemed that when Louise's father had died, he'd left his daughter a fortune buried somewhere in the delta. Therefore, to calculate risk, it was essential to know the identity of the father. But the data bases on Louise Rabb led nowhere. Born Louise Frazer, mother Janice Frazer, father unknown. Married Jeffrey Rabb, one child, Angela. Divorced after five years, husband now deceased. No credit rating, no police record, no civil action during those five years. Married Jack Castle, no children, husband deceased. C-minus credit rating during the marriage, middle-five-figure income, no police record. Residence, North Hollywood. Moved to San Francisco four years ago, shared residence with Walter Draper. Credit unrated. Changed name from Louise Castle to Louise Rabb. Renting current residence, one year. Estimated net worth, mid-four-figures, no more. Chin had requested a check on Janice

Frazer, but the computer's first pass had revealed nothing usable. Tomorrow, with more mainframes up, additional information would doubtless develop, hopefully including the name of Louise Frazer/Rabb/Castle/Rabb's father, the grand prize.

But tomorrow could be too late.

By tomorrow, according to the tapes, the jewels could be in a safe-deposit box, beyond reach.

Whatever was done, therefore, must be done tonight.

With Fabrese?

Or without Fabrese?

It was a question that depended on the efficacy of the data base that contradicted Fabrese's claim to represent Benito Cella. The service that provided the data base was reliable, especially for corporate intelligence. But how reliable could a data base be that outlined the structure of organized crime? By definition, the information was hearsay, gathered for law enforcement and the media. But now, with Venezzio just dead, how could—?

Chin's telephone rang softly. It was the third line he'd programmed for the Rabb operation—the number he'd given Jimmy Fabrese.

Yes, it was Fabrese's voice: abrupt and abrasive: "Brian? This is Jimmy."

"Yes . . ." He couldn't bring himself to say "Jimmy."

"How's it going?"

"I think," Chin said, "that we're making progress. It'll take a few hours before everything comes together. But I think I can see how this is going to develop."

"That man—the tall one with the aviator glasses, needs a haircut. What about him?"

"We're working on that now."

"Where are you? The restaurant?"

"Yes. But I don't think we should be seen together here."

"You mean . . .?" As Fabrese let the question die, apprehension clouded his voice.

"I'd just like to be careful. Are you still at your hotel?"

"Yeah. But I want to get some handle on this, Brian. I've got to call some people back east, put them in the picture."

"How soon do you have to call them?"

"It's already four o'clock back there."

"Ah . . ." Chin pretended to consider. Then, speaking carefully: "I think it's clear that your suspicions were correct. There *has* been some skimming."

"Th—there has?" It was a quick, spontaneous question, revealing sudden unease. Then, transparently trying to recover, Fabrese spoke brusquely, on the offensive: "That's what I was saying yesterday. There's skimming. No question."

"I know. I was confirming what you said."

"How'd you find out? Did you talk to Louise? If you did, then you fucked up, Brian. I didn't want her to know we're—"

"She has no idea that I know. None."

"Well, then, how'd you—?"

"The woman," Chin interrupted smoothly. "Louise. Who was her father?"

Instantly, a silence descended. Just as, instantly, Chin realized the mistake he'd made. *Was,* he'd said. Not *is.* But *was.* For such a mistake, a man could easily die.

But to correct himself would compound the danger.

Finally—ominously—Fabrese said, "Why're you asking about Louise's father?"

There was no time to consider, no time to invent a story. Now—here, now—only the truth would serve:

"You wanted the two women put under surveillance. Of course, we used electronic listening devices. We heard them talking for almost two hours last night. And today—Sunday—they've been talking."

"And they talked about Louise's father?" Fabrese spoke softly, cautiously, as if the mere mention of the father meant danger. "Is that what you're saying?"

Improvising now, taking his moment-to-moment cue from Fabrese's unease, strength in pursuit of weakness, the Chinese way, Chin said, "It would be wise for us to lay our cards on the table, Jimmy. Don't you think so?"

"Well, sure. But I told you yesterday that I've got to be careful. I can't—"

"You suggested that Benito Cella had sent you out here to find out whether Tony Bacardo might be skimming Mafia funds. You said your investigation was made necessary by the death of Carlo Venezzio. You also said that Bacardo was Venezzio's number one. Correct?"

"Yeah . . ." It was a hesitant response.

"So," Chin said, speaking now with the assurance of a teacher reciting well-remembered lessons, "if we begin drawing lines, and we connect the death of Venezzio to the arrival in San Francisco of Tony Bacardo, and then we connect those lines to Louise, and then, finally, if we add perhaps three hours of anxious conversation between the two women you asked me to watch, then it's possible to draw some conclusions."

"These conversations you keep talking about. What d'you mean, exactly? What'd you hear?"

"What I mean exactly," Chin said, "is that when I piece together what the two women are saying, it seems obvious to me that Louise's father has just died, leaving her a fortune in—"

"Hold it," Fabrese cut in. "Right there. Hold it. Either we meet and talk about this, or else we each get to pay phones. You don't know what you're messing with here."

"Oh, yes," Chin answered. "I know what I'm messing with. The question is, do *you* know what *you're* messing with?"

"I'm not going to talk on this line anymore. Fuck it."

Chin sighed, glanced at his watch. Mafiosi, someone had once said, were stupid and paranoid and greedy. Also vicious and religious and patriotic.

"It's exactly one o'clock," Chin said. "There's a park on Kearny and Sacramento. That's in Chinatown. It's called Prospect Park, mostly for children to play. I'll meet you there in fifteen minutes. From your hotel, it's ten minutes by cab."

"I'll be there."

1:25 P.M., PDT

Seated on opposite ends of the bench, surrounded by the shrieks of Chinese children at play, they stared at each other in silence. The pleasantries had been brief, unsmiling. Now, each man having made his final calculations, Fabrese was the first to speak: "What I want is for you to pick up where you left off on the phone. That's all you have to do. Just tell me what you heard, never mind trying to guess what it means. I'll take care of the guesswork."

"Ah." For the first time since they'd sat down together, Chin permitted himself a small, private smile. "But guesswork, you see, is the most enjoyable part of the process. Imagination, you see." He tapped his forehead. "Exercise for the mind."

"You said you used electronics—listening devices. Have you got what they said on tape?"

Projecting elaborate regret, Chin shook his head. "We tried, of course. But the quality just wasn't there."

"Okay." Fabrese's gesture was abrupt: a gathering anger, gracelessly suppressed. "Okay. Go ahead."

"My impression, as I said on the phone, was that Louise Rabb's father had just died. He was a mafioso—a very powerful mafioso. And he left a fortune in jewels for his daughter. The jewels are buried within a hundred miles of San Francisco." Chin broke off, looked blandly at the other man. "Does that agree with what you know—or suspect?"

"Never mind what I suspect. Just get to it."

Chin's smile was gentle, cat-and-mouse complacent. "My conclusion, you mean."

"That's what I mean." Fabrese spoke grimly.

"Well, the conclusion is obvious. Louise's father, I think, was Carlo Venezzio, who arranged to have a treasure buried for his daughter. When Venezzio died, it would be natural for Tony Bacardo to help Louise get the treasure. So he arrived in San Francisco Friday, two days ago. My guess is that Bacardo miscalculated what was necessary to get the jewels. Or perhaps he had second thoughts. Or perhaps—" The meaningful pause accentuated the final possibility. "Perhaps he realized that he would need backup—someone besides the daughter and the granddaughter of Carlo Venezzio. Someone, I imagine, who was familiar with guns."

Struggling to overcome the tremors of both excitement and fear that began in the pit of his stomach and would soon be exposed in his face, Fabrese made no reply, permitted himself no expression beyond a narrowing of his eyes, a tightening around the mouth.

"In any case," Chin said, "Bacardo is now in New York, or soon will be. And the two women are in their house on Thirty-ninth Avenue. And you—" Chin smiled gently. "You're here." The smile lingered as Chin added, "You're here, and you're worried. Or, at least, you are very concerned."

"Never mind me. What about the tall guy with the aviator glasses? I thought you were going to tail him, too."

"We haven't been able to track him down. But we've got two people at Louise's house. So if our friend goes there, we'll have someone available to—"

"I get the feeling," Fabrese interrupted, "that it could all come down tonight."

Chin nodded. "Yes, I have that feeling, too. If they get the jewels tonight, they can get them to a safe-deposit box in the morning."

"I also get the feeling," Fabrese said, "that the tall guy could be the muscle—the one with the gun."

Once more, Chin nodded.

2:40 P.M., PDT

When Bernhardt had finished, C. B. Tate sat perfectly still, quizzically staring. Then, in exaggerated wonderment, he shook his head. "For a mild-mannered actor," he said, "you do seem to have a knack for connecting with some pretty awesome characters."

A big, massively built black man, Tate spoke with a deep, rich feel for the rhythms of ghetto patois, his native tongue. Born in the projects south of San Francisco, a survivor of three years spent in the California correctional system, Tate had been saved ten years ago. His messiah had been a cigar-chomping bailbondsman named Bernard Feigenbaum, who knew a gladiator when he saw one. For six years, Tate had backed up Morey Edelstein, Feigenbaum's only living relative younger than fifty. Edelstein had been a skip tracer and freelance bounty hunter who enjoyed the game of running down bail jumpers but who feared the physical violence that often followed. Since one of Tate's talents was violence, he and Edelstein soon reached an accommodation. If Tate made him look good, Edelstein would pay Tate a bonus equal to a quarter of Edelstein's take, apart from Tate's own take. But, one rainy Friday night in Baltimore, having tracked down a stripper known as Charlie who also dealt in cocaine, Tate had missed a straight razor when he'd searched the lady—and Edelstein had paid with his life. After the funeral Tate told Feigenbaum that he intended to set up shop for himself, bounty hunting. Feigenbaum became his first client.

"So what d'you think?" Bernhardt asked. "Interested?"

"A thousand dollars . . ." Tate spoke with the richly textured resonance he always reserved for the discussion of substantial sums of money. In addition to the Sausalito houseboat in which they now sat, Tate also maintained a Corvette, two ex-wives, and three children, one of whom was determined to be a doctor.

"Anything beyond the thousand?" Tate asked. "Bonuses? Incentives?"

Bernhardt shifted his gaze to the houseboat's floor-to-ceiling window that offered a perfect view of San Francisco in the distance and the blue of the bay sparkling at eye level in the foreground. Finally Bernhardt said, "If I get lucky—very lucky—I could come up with a hundred thousand, plus what I got up front. That'll take a month, minimum. If it happens, I'll give you ten percent." He considered, then amended: "Anything over twenty-five thousand, let's say, I'll give you ten percent— when I get it. *If* I get it. Otherwise—" He pointed to the envelope that lay on Tate's coffee table. "Otherwise, that's it. A thousand dollars for you, four thousand for me. Up front."

"We got a deal. Coffee?"

"Thanks. Cream. No sugar."

"I remember." Tate rose, walked to the open kitchen counter, put on a burnished copper kettle. Next he went to a small cupboard and took out a loose-leaf notebook and ball-point pen. Whenever they did business together, Bernhardt always wrote the terms and conditions in the notebook, duly signed and dated. The practice, both men realized, was one reason for a friendship that had begun almost five years before, when Bernard Feigenbaum, a little-theater buff, had goaded Tate into trying out for the lead in *The Emperor Jones*, presented by the Howell Theater and directed by Alan Bernhardt. Of all the fledgling actors Bernhardt had ever directed, Tate had projected the most kinetic energy, the most raw, smoldering power—and the most instinctive control. When the *Sentinel*'s review came out, Tate read it twice, smiled his characteristically complex smile, and announced that his acting days were behind him. Unless, of course, Hollywood called.

Tate made their coffee, served it, scanned what Bernhardt had written, signed the agreement, then consulted his watch. "It's almost three o'clock. What time d'you figure to start?"

"I'm thinking that we leave San Francisco about eight. It's a three-hour drive, at least. Allow, say, a half hour to look around, another hour to get the stuff. That'd be about midnight. Meaning that we get back to San Francisco about three o'clock. All of us—you, me, the two women, and Paula—we all stay together at my place until the banks open tomorrow morning. Once the stuff is in a safe-deposit box, our job's done."

"You said 'Paula.' How's she fit in?"

"The mother—Louise—doesn't want the daughter—Angela—to go along. But she doesn't want to leave Angela alone, either. So I figure we'll leave Angela at my place. She and Paula will wait for us there."

"How about that dog of yours—Crusher? Maybe we should take him with us."

"I don't know . . ." Dubiously, Bernhardt shook his head. "He's not very disciplined. Besides, I'd like to leave him with Paula and Angela at my place."

Tate considered, then nodded approval. He wore a close-cropped beard, black flecked with gray. Whenever a problem engrossed Tate, he habitually stroked the beard. It was a mannerism that placed on display a massive custom-crafted gold signet ring. "By the way," he said, gesturing in the direction of the main yacht harbor, where Paula and Crusher had last been seen. "Where are they?"

"She's taking Crusher for a run up in the headlands. Then they'll come back here. I told her to give us an hour."

Approvingly, Tate nodded. "Good diplomacy, Alan. As always. Not to worry, though. I don't mind talking in front of her. Paula's first class. I'm a fan."

"I know. But this thing—" Bernhardt considered. "There's a lot that can happen."

"Is she willing to play bodyguard?"

"We've already talked about it. My flat is secure. It's attached on both sides, you know. And Crusher raises hell whenever a stranger comes to the door."

"Can Paula shoot?"

"She can. But she might not. She's got guts, though. She really has."

"Like I say, I'm a fan. Why don't you guys get married, file joint tax returns?"

Bernhardt looked at the other man thoughtfully before he said, "I think about it. A lot."

Tate nodded decisively. "Good. You can take my Corvette on the honeymoon."

For a moment Bernhardt looked intently into the other man's face. "Thanks, C.B. I'm touched."

Affecting diffidence, Tate nodded brusquely. Then, back to business: "So we've got the mother and the daughter covered. What about us?"

"You've still got your Ford, haven't you?"

Tate nodded again. "That's my bread-and-butter car, man. You know—low profile. The Corvette, that's for my image."

"Okay." Bernhardt paused, calculating distances and times and weekend traffic patterns. Then, still calculating, he said, "Louise lives on Thirty-ninth Avenue, near Taraval. Let's say you and I meet there about five-thirty. We'll take Louise and Angela over to my place, where Paula and Crusher'll be waiting."

Silently, Tate nodded agreement.

"We'll pick up a couple of flashlights and two walkie-talkies with spare batteries and a shovel at my place. We should have a couple of hours, to get our signals straight. We'll leave at eight. I'll take Louise in my car. She'll give me directions as we go. You'll follow me."

"This Louise lady, she must be a trusting sort. I mean, what's to prevent us from taking the jewels, once she tells us where they are?"

"She's got no choice. She's got to trust someone."

"Two women alone." Tate shook his head. "It's sad."

"Angela won't be alone for long. Believe me."

"What about Louise?"

Bernhardt shrugged, drank the last of his coffee, went to the window that offered a view of the city. "Louise's had a hard life. Her mother was a drunk and her father was a gangster."

"Yeah. A rich gangster, though."

Still looking out across the bay, Bernhardt shrugged, remained silent. With everything set, all the plans made, he was aware of a heaviness, a reluctance. Was it caution—or fear? Never before had he ventured into territory so uncharted, potentially so dangerous. The Mafia, that dark, baroque brotherhood that still took blood oaths—was it logical to assume they would allow a fortune in jewels to pass into the hands of the bastard daughter of a dead chieftain? The five thousand dollars from Bacardo—what was its true significance? Was it conscience money? Blood money? What better proof of Bacardo's fealty than to present a fortune in jewels to his new masters? What better—?

Behind him, Bernhardt heard Tate say something. As Bernhardt turned inquiringly to face the other man, Tate repeated: "Second thoughts?" He spoke quietly, gently probing.

"That's exactly what I'm having. Second thoughts."

"I don't know much about the Mafia. Is their arm as long as everyone says?"

"I think so. Anyhow, I sure don't want to cross them."

"Is that what we're doing—crossing them?" As he said it, probing, Tate kept his gaze sharp-focused on Bernhardt's face.

"I didn't think so, not originally. Now I'm not so sure."

"Bacardo could be stepping out of the line of fire—and paying you five thousand to take his place? Is that it?"

In spite of himself, Bernhardt guffawed. "C.B., you've got a gift. You really have."

Modestly, Tate lowered his eyes—and smiled. Then he said, "The sensible thing, it seems to me, is for us to keep the back door open. First sign of trouble, we blow retreat."

"Easier said than done, especially if Bacardo decided to switch sides and give the stuff back to the Mafia. He knows where the jewels are. There could be a half dozen hoods waiting for us."

"Why would they wait for us? If he tells them where the stuff is, why wouldn't they take the stuff and split? Why stick around?"

"To punish us. Anybody who goes after what's theirs, the Mafia punishes them. That much I know."

"Well, shit, Alan—" Dubiously, Tate shook his head. "Shit, I don't mind a good fight, maybe a little shooting. But this—" He continued to shake his head. "This, what you're saying, you're making me nervous."

"You want to forget about it? I trust your instincts, C.B. If you want to bow out, I will, too."

"You'd give back the money?"

"I'm sure as hell not going to keep it if we bow out."

"What I'm trying to figure out . . ." Tate let his eyes wander reflectively away. "What I'm trying to figure out is how much I'm risking for a thousand dollars. Or, best case, eleven thousand. I mean, it's pretty good money, no question, for a night's work. But . . ." He let it go meaningfully unfinished; his eyes strayed to their single-page contract, still lying on the coffee table.

Having seen this scene played out before, Bernhardt decided on an early capitulation. "The thousand, that's it, up front. But the other, why don't we say twenty-five percent, instead of ten? That way, best case, you get twenty-six thousand."

"Ah . . ." Obliquely gratified, Tate nodded. "Yes, I think that's more like it." Then, directly: "That's okay with you? For sure?"

Bernhardt nodded decisively. "For sure. The more I hear myself talk, the more sure I am." He reached for the notebook, made the change, initialed it, passed it to Tate for his initials.

"What about guns?" Tate said. "You've got that three-fifty-seven magnum, I know. What about that sawed-off of yours?"

Bernhardt grimaced. "That makes me nervous, that gun. If I'm ever caught with it—" He let the rest go eloquently unfinished.

"It's up to you," Tate said. "I've got two Browning nine-millimeters. I'll bring them both—and a rotary clip. And I can bring a shotgun, too, if you aren't bringing your sawed-off."

"Okay, I'll bring it. In the trunk of the car."

"You got buckshot?"

Grimly, Bernhardt nodded. "Yes, I've got buckshot. And I'll—" He felt the houseboat move, heard Crusher barking excitedly. Paula and Crusher had returned. As he rose to greet them, Bernhardt glanced at his watch. They'd been talking for more than an hour. Meaning that, in less than four hours, they would begin.

5 P.M., PDT

"It appears," Chin said, "that they plan to move tonight. Probably about eight o'clock."

"How many of them?" Fabrese asked. "How many cars?"

"Two cars, I should think. The tall man will go first, with Louise. They'll probably go in his car."

"What about the second car?"

"Apparently they've hired someone to drive a second car."

"What about the girl—the daughter?"

"Her mother won't let her go after the jewels. She'll stay behind."

"So it's two guys with guns, plus Louise."

"Right." Just as he'd decided not to reveal Bernhardt's identity, so Chin had decided not to mention Bernhardt's plans for guarding Angela. He'd also decided not to mention Bernhardt's Airedale, conceivably the night's wild card. Airedales, he'd once read, had been bred to fight bears.

They sat in one of Chin's cars, a low-profile Buick, five years old. The Buick was parked on Geary Street, three blocks from Fabrese's hotel. As they talked, both men stared straight ahead. On a warm spring afternoon, downtown San Francisco was quiet, given over to Sunday strollers and window shop-

180

pers paying tribute to the elegance of the closed shops that clustered around Union Square: Nieman Marcus, Coach, Shreves, Saks. Beyond the square to the east, the city's skyscrapers towered, their windows catching the glow of a sun that would soon set over the ocean to the west.

"Three hours . . ." As he spoke, Fabrese touched the butt of the .38 Smith and Wesson Chief's Special thrust in his belt. Chin had given him the revolver an hour ago, assuring him that it worked perfectly. And, yes, the gun was cold, untraceable. When Fabrese had offered to pay for it, Chin had only smiled: that small, unreadable smile that seemed to change significance as each hour passed.

Eight o'clock . . .

Three hours . . .

Meaning that now, right now, he must decide, up or down. Sitting in a strange car in a strange city, beside a Chinaman with a smile that meant nothing, he must decide: Make one grab, connect, and everything he wanted was there, handfuls of jewels, a million-dollar score. Take the chance, make the grab, drop off the face of the earth, rich.

Or else, like Bacardo, he could get on an airplane, go back to New York—alive. Go back to New York, keep his eyes open. He'd done it once, turned up something that was worth millions. He could do it again. He could—

"—seems," Chin was saying, "that you must make your plans."

"I need someone," Fabrese said. "I've got to have someone with me. A shooter."

"Ah . . ." Discreetly, Chin nodded. "Yes, I was about to say—you need someone with you."

Fabrese turned to look directly at the other man. Chin was still staring straight ahead, his face in profile. How old was Chin? Thirty? Forty? Where had he learned to talk like he did? In college? Benito Cella, it was said, had gone to college. Which was one reason, others said, that Cella was so dangerous. No one knew what Cella was thinking—until it was too late.

Still gazing impassively straight ahead, Chin said, "These

women—and the man, too—seem to think the jewels will bring a million dollars."

Still with his eyes fixed on the other man's face, Fabrese made no reply.

Three hours . . .

Less than three hours, now. Minutes, ticking away. Life-or-death minutes.

"But Tony Bacardo," Chin continued, "apparently decided it was too risky for him to go after the jewels. Which, I think, meant that he couldn't keep his job *and* help the two women get the jewels." As he spoke, Chin turned to face Fabrese. He was no longer smiling. "Is that how it appears to you?"

Fabrese swallowed. Then, nodding reluctantly: "Yeah, that's how it looks to me."

"You, though, have no such concern about your job."

Fabrese made no reply. Helplessly, he could only look at Chin—look, and wait. Suddenly the touch of the revolver thrust in his belt offered no comfort, no hope.

"Which to me means that you don't intend to return to New York."

"Listen, never mind about where I—"

"It's interesting," Chin broke in, "that neither you nor Bacardo can really operate here on the West Coast. Not unless you want to risk exposing yourself." He paused, then said softly, "If Charlie Ricca, for instance, knew what you planned, he would certainly contact Benito Cella for instructions. Ricca's real purpose, of course, would be to ingratiate himself with Benito Cella. Just as—" Another delicately timed pause. "Just as, according to you, I am ingratiating myself with Cella when I help you with your, ah, undercover operation."

Once more Chin paused, this time glancing at his watch. Then, almost as if he regretted the necessity to brush aside the web of lies between then, he gestured delicately as he said, "Two and a half hours, Mr. Fabrese. We can't afford to waste any more time on inventions, even though I've enjoyed watching you improvise. Americans, I find, are very good at improvisation. Unlike the Chinese." As if in regret, he sighed.

"Your plan is to get the jewels for yourself, and then run. Undoubtedly, you plan to leave the country. You needed me, or someone like me, to track Bacardo, in an effort to locate the treasure you somehow discovered was buried up in the delta. You needed someone totally unconnected to the Mafia. And you came to the right person. I have a first-class organization, and I have first-class electronics. For instance, after we talked last night, I called up on my computer screen practically the whole of Louise Rabb's life story. And then, as you know, I was able to install a listening device in Louise Rabb's living room. That device will continue to operate until approximately this time tomorrow, which should be plenty of time. Also, we placed a tiny transmitter—a homing device—on the car they'll use tonight when they leave for the delta. That way, we can remain a half mile back from both their cars, no problem."

We, Chin had said.

They both sat half turned, facing each other. Now, gravely, Chin nodded. Saying softly: "Yes, Mr. Fabrese. *We.* You heard correctly."

Fabrese drew a deep breath. First, a futile denial, he shrugged. Then, bitterly resigned, he nodded. "Okay. We."

"Fifty-fifty."

Fabrese stiffened. *"Fifty-fifty!* You're—you're fucking dreaming."

Chin shrugged. "If you think about it, you'll see that I'm being generous."

"Generous?" Outraged, an involuntary reaction, Fabrese once more touched the .38. Seeing the gesture, amused, Chin's small, smug smile returned as he said, "I've got the scanner, Mr. Fabrese. That's what's needed to track the homer attached to their car. And I've got the manpower. What do I need you for?"

"You son of a bitch. You do that—grab the whole thing—and you're a fucking dead man. I make one call to New York, and you're dead. I'm a hero. And you're dead."

"Just as now, perhaps, Bacardo is a hero. He is, perhaps, tell-

ing Mr. Cella how you plan to take this treasure for yourself."
Chin spoke slowly, with painstaking precision. How perfect
the pleasure, methodically deflating this pompous, bleating
Italian insect, a man in name only, no manners, no courage,
nothing but bluster. "Call me Jimmy," the insect had once
said. It was an affront that, now, he would address.

"I'm willing to take my chances with the Mafia," Chin said.
Then, maliciously: "Are you?"

"You bastard. I come to you with a straight deal, everything
on the table. And you do a—a goddam number on me. You
think I'll sit still for that? You think because it's your city, your
turf, you can—"

"Excuse me, but everything was *not* on the table. What you
told me—the nature of your mission—it was a lie."

Unaware that he'd done it, Fabrese had drawn the .38; the
pistol was between them, a few inches beneath the point of
Chin's right shoulder. Chin glanced down at the gun, saying,
"I loaned you that revolver, Mr. Fabrese. Do you think it's polite to point it at me?"

"I'll point it wherever I goddam fucking well want to point
it, you son of a bitch. And you'll like it." But, as Fabrese spoke,
the pistol began to drop lower—and lower. Calmly—contemptuously—Chin pointed to a cellular telephone mounted on the
console between them.

"I have only to make a call," Chin said, "and as many men
as I need will be here in a few minutes. I will choose two of the
best, and they will do exactly as I tell them, tonight." Letting
the words register, Chin stared at the other man—and waited.
With amusement, he watched the predictable succession of
emotions register on Fabrese's face: the fury, the bluster, the
greed. And, finally, the uncertainty, then the fear. Meaning
that, yes, Fabrese was about to capitulate.

5:50 P.M., PDT

"Of course," Chin was saying, "We'll have to play it by ear. But we should have a plan, a best-case scenario. I've often found that very helpful."

Fabrese scowled. "Meaning?"

"Let's decide what we *want* to have happen tonight."

Still seated in Chin's Buick, Fabrese shifted restlessly, looked at his watch. The time was almost six o'clock; dusk was about to fall. Downtown San Francisco was settling in for a quiet evening. The Sunday afternoon strollers were returning home, the theaters were still closed, and the restaurants had not yet begun to fill.

"Jesus Christ. What've we been *talking* about for an hour?"

Ignoring the other man's outburst, plainly a product of nerves, Chin began again: "I will go with you. Only me. We will use this car, which is in perfect condition. However, we must allow time to fill the tank. Then we will go to my home. You will stay in the car. I'll go upstairs and change clothes. I will wear running shoes, jeans, a dark jacket, and a black stocking cap—the costume, in fact, of the midnight prowler." As he spoke, Chin glanced at Fabrese's impeccably cut blue blazer, gray flannel trousers, gleaming white shirt, striped tie, and tasseled loafers. "If you like," Chin said, "there is probably still time to stop by an army surplus store, for you."

Impatiently, Fabrese brushed the suggestion aside. "Never mind about me."

"If digging is involved," Chin said, "which there clearly is, and if you should get dirty, and then you return to your hotel, you would be conspicuous." Once more, driving the Buick with one hand, Chin consulted his watch. "We have time. And a surplus store is on the way."

As spiteful as a spoiled child, Fabrese shrugged. "Whatever."

"So," Chin said, continuing, "I'll go upstairs, as I was saying, and I'll change—while you stay in the car. In a few minutes, I'll join you. I'll have a Colt .45 automatic in a shoulder holster under my jacket, and I'll have three extra clips of ammunition. I'll be carrying a nylon duffel bag, like athletes carry. I'll have an M-Sixteen rifle in the bag, along with flashlights. The rifle will be broken down, and I'll have three extra ammunition clips. Hopefully, the bag will be large enough to accommodate both the rifle and the container for the jewels. Of course, we'll also take a shovel, which is in my garage."

"Jesus," Fabrese said, "you've got an M-Sixteen? What're you expecting? A goddam war?"

"Every day," Chin answered, "it's proven that firepower is what our business is all about. At least at the street level."

"No question."

"By seven o'clock," Chin said, "we'll be ready." He pointed to the locked glove compartment. "There's a scanner in there, which will lock onto Bern—onto their car. By using that, and this"—he pointed to the cellular telephone—"we'll be in good shape."

"What about having two of your guys follow us, for backup?"

Chin shook his head. "No. The more people know about this operation, the more danger we face. I'm not talking about danger from the police. I'm talking about danger from your people. You'll be in Mexico, or wherever, with your share. But I'll be here. I don't plan to be killed by one of your famous hit men."

Fabrese made no reply. Only his hands, tightened into fists, hinted at the fear he felt.

"We will park, if possible, within sight of the Rabb house, on Thirty-ninth Avenue. I expect the tall man to arrive there about seven-thirty. He'll be driving a brown Honda station wagon. There was some conversation about a woman coming with him, to guard Angela while we're all gone. Another man—his name is C.B.—will also arrive about seven-thirty, in another car. A Ford. At about eight o'clock, Bern—" Vexed with himself, his second faux pas, Chin broke off, began again: "At about eight o'clock, I expect the tall man and Louise to leave. They'll be in the car with the homing device. The Honda. I expect the other car to follow, keeping the first car in sight. I would expect them to have walkie-talkies, and probably car phones. But they probably—''

"Why do you expect that?"

"Because they're pros," Chin answered. "Or at least so we must assume."

"This tall man—the man they've talked to—you know who he is, don't you?" It was a soft-spoken, hard-edged challenge.

Calculating carefully, Chin let a moment pass. Then: "I have suspicions, no more."

"Okay, then, who do you *suspect* he is?"

"I don't deal in speculation."

"Bullshit. That's *all* you deal in. With you, it's all smoke and mirrors."

"Our time is growing short. Do you want to bicker, or do you want to make plans?"

Muttering an obscenity, Fabrese shrugged again, gestured angrily. "Go ahead."

Ignoring Fabrese's anger, Chin said, "If the homing device is working properly, we can stay as far as a mile back, and still have a fix on them. I would expect them to cross the Golden Gate Bridge, then drive to Vallejo, and go on to the San Joaquin delta region. I would expect them to arrive at their destination between ten and eleven. From what Louise has been saying to her daughter, I don't think it'll take them very long to dig up the treasure. When they've got the jewels, they plan to return to San Francisco, either to Louise's house or maybe to the tall man's place. He lives in a flat on Potrero Hill. All of them, including Angela and possibly a female PI, will stay together all night. Tomorrow morning, they plan to go to the bank as soon as it opens. Once they put the jewels in Louise's safe-deposit box, of course, the game's over."

"So how're we going to hit them? Do you mind telling me?"

Now Chin's smile appeared to express genuine amusement. "We'll have two hours to make those plans while we drive.

However, I'm thinking that, if a good chance presents itself shortly after the treasure is dug up, that may be the time. It's probable, though, that they'll be on high alert then." As he spoke he pointed ahead. "There's the surplus store. I'll wait for you in the car. Be quick, please."

Ignoring the order, Fabrese said, "All right, so they'll be on high alert. So what then?"

"It depends. We may want to wait till they get back to the city. We'll hit them after they leave the cars and before they get inside their house. Ideally, at the precise instant when whoever is inside the house—Angela, and the female detective—opens the front door of whichever house they choose to spend tonight in. That way, the two men will be off balance, trying to protect both the women and the treasure. And themselves, of course."

Grudgingly Fabrese nodded agreement. Repeating: "Of course."

8 P.M., PDT

"Don't worry," Bernhardt said, smiling at Angela, making a joke of it. "With Crusher, how can you lose? Besides—" He slid open his center desk drawer, took out the .38 revolver he'd recently bought, put it on top of the desk. "Paula's gun," they called it. "Besides, there's this." But when he looked at Louise, he saw fear in her gaze, fixated on the revolver. Aware of the older woman's apprehension, Paula took the revolver, checked it, slipped it into her outsize handbag, out of sight. As if to offer reassurance, Angela moved closer to her mother, but said nothing.

The five of them were clustered together in Bernhardt's office, all of them standing. In the hallway, hearing his name, Crusher came to attention. Bernhardt glanced at his watch, then looked at C.B., who nodded. Yes, it was a few minutes after eight. Time to go. Bernhardt excused himself, went to the canvas satchel he'd packed and put in the hall closet, on the floor. Out of sight of those in the office, with only Crusher in attendance, Bernhardt zipped open the satchel, checked the contents: his Ruger .357 Magnum revolver, a half-filled box of .357 cartridges, the illegal sawed-off shotgun, a small plastic bag containing a handful of twelve-gauge buckshot loads, two walkie-talkies, and two four-cell flashlights. Another plastic bag contained extra batteries for the flashlights and walkie-talkies. A roll of two-inch duct tape, a survival knife, and a coil of half-inch white nylon rope completed the inventory.

He took the holstered .357, checked the load, then clipped the holster to his belt, on the left side. After years of faithful service dedicated to Dancer and Associates, Herbert Dancer had presented him with the top-of-the line Ruger, a "lifetime weapon," Dancer had pronounced, pompous as ever. With some satisfaction, less than three months later, he'd told Dancer that he was quitting to open his own agency. To his credit, Dancer hadn't mentioned the Ruger.

He settled the revolver at his belt, zipped up the satchel, zipped up his leather jacket, hefted the satchel, closed the closet door. Back in his office, he turned to Louise, who was dressed incongruously in a magenta nylon jacket and light blue stretch pants. She wore sneakers that she'd borrowed from Angela. Fixed on Bernhardt, Louise's eyes were unnaturally large. Her mouth, Bernhardt saw, was almost imperceptibly quivering. Louise was scared.

Bernhardt went to Paula, kissed her on the mouth, then smiled. He turned to Angela, said good-bye. Standing close beside her mother, Angela nodded, swallowed hard. Bernhardt went into the hallway and waited for Louise and C.B. to precede him out into the darkness.

As he walked beside Louise to his station wagon, Bernhardt

zipped down his leather jacket, exposing the walnut butt of the Ruger, close to his free hand. He scanned the sidewalk, the street, the nearby shrubbery. Walking ahead, C.B.'s close-cropped head was also in motion, side to side. Louise, walking rigidly, stared straight ahead, her eyes fixed. Bernhardt unlocked the right-hand door of the Honda while Tate dug in the canvas satchel to produce the walkie-talkies. Bernhardt zipped up the satchel, threw it in the rear seat, gestured for Louise to get into the car on the passenger side. Then, to test the radios, Tate walked down the sidewalk, crouched down behind a car to make transmission difficult. The radios checked out perfectly. When Tate returned, Bernhardt beckoned him down the sidewalk, out of Louise's hearing.

"So far," Bernhardt said, "all I know is that we're going across the Bay Bridge, and pick up Highway Eighty, going toward Sacramento. Louise has a map, and she's going to guide me. I think you should stay far enough back of me so that there's at least one car between us."

Tate nodded. "I agree." Like Bernhardt, Tate wore a leather jacket, open enough in the front to let him draw the nine-millimeter Browning automatic he carried in a shoulder holster. With his dark clothing and dark skin, standing with his legs slightly spread, heavily booted feet firmly planted, every line of Tate's body suggested a solitary guerilla, alert to the danger that he sensed the darkness concealed.

"If we should get separated and something goes wrong with the radios," Bernhardt said, "I'll wait for you at the Nut Tree, at Vacaville. I'll be in the parking lot."

"Right."

"Have you got the shovel?"

"Jesus, Alan, you already *asked* me that."

"Okay . . ." Bernhardt realized that, like Tate, his own body was taut; his own eyes had been constantly scanning the darkness.

"So," Tate said, "shall we do it?" In the question Bernhardt sensed Tate's elemental anticipation, facing danger.

Tate's anticipation, his own reluctance.

"Sure," Bernhardt answered. He touched the other man on the arm. "Let's do it. Keep your head down."

Tate smiled. "Yeah. You, too."

9:30 P.M., PDT

"I think," Chin said, "that they've turned off. You'd better slow down, get in the right lane." Chin switched on the flashlight, shone it on the map spread across his knees. For the last hour, the scanner's digital readout had held steady at 45 degrees. But now the scanner read 117 degrees. Conclusion: As expected, Bernhardt had turned off the freeway and was now traveling southeast on Route 12, the secondary road that led to Rio Vista and the San Joaquin delta region that lay south of Sacramento.

As, yes, the upcoming sign overhanging the freeway showed the Route 12 turnoff three-quarters of a mile ahead.

"There," Chin said, pointing. "Route Twelve."

As Fabrese slowed the car and switched on the turn indicators, Chin clicked off the flashlight. Bernhardt's Honda, he estimated, was about a mile ahead, traveling at reduced speed. So far, driving first in the city, then on the Bay Bridge, finally on the eight-lane freeway, it had been impossible to determine which of the drivers following Bernhardt was the one called C.B., probable last name Tate. But on Route 12, at night, the backup car would be revealed.

"Go east," Chin ordered as, into the freeway exit, one arrow pointed to 12 West, the other to 12 East. As they made the turn and swung onto the road to the east, Chin glanced at a wrist compass. Yes, they were traveling on a magnetic heading of

120 degrees, almost a dead match to the 122 degrees that now showed on the scanner's LCD display.

"Don't go too fast," Chin said. Ahead, the road narrowed to two lanes. As it began a gentle curve to the east, he could count taillights ahead: four cars, one of them Bernhardt's—

—and one of them C.B. Tate's, the backup man Bernhardt had called a samurai.

ISLETON, a sign read. 27 MILES.

"Is that where we're going?" Fabrese asked. "Isleton?"

"I have no idea."

Fabrese flung a hostile glance at the other man as he said, "Is that like you've got no idea who the tall man is? Is it like that? Bullshit, in other words?"

Chin made no response, concentrating instead on the scanner. Beneath the LCD display the scanner featured five small lights that showed the intensity of the homing device's signal. Three lights lit, the manual instructed, would translate to about a mile separation. Five lights suggested a half mile or less. One light meant that the signal was almost lost.

A million dollars in jewels and gold coin, the prize for interpreting these numerals and lights correctly. But make a mistake, one mistake, and the game changed, all bets canceled. Unless Fabrese believed that the treasure was within grasp, everything came tumbling down.

No, not everything. Because, back in the city, Charles Ng was about to actuate the second phase of a plan that, almost exactly twenty-four hours ago, had been nonexistent.

Simplicity . . .

Always, simplicity was the key.

And, yes, silence—the patience to listen, and the wisdom to analyze and make plans.

Followed, most essentially, by courage—the remorseless courage required to kill without hesitation, without mercy, without remorse.

All that the plan lacked was the exquisite taste of revenge. For all the indignities Fabrese had forced him to endure, there would be no payback, no final words, no parting smile.

9:40 P.M., PDT

In the mirror, Bernhardt saw two sets of headlights behind him, one car passing another car. Guiding the Honda with one hand, he held out his right hand for the walkie-talkie. Sitting beside him, Louise dutifully handed over the radio.

"C.B.?"

"Right here," came the prompt response.

"What are there, two cars between us now?"

"Right. That last one that passed us, I bet he was doing eighty, the dumb son of a bitch. I couldn't see inside the car."

"Anyone hanging back behind you?"

"Not that I can see. Maybe we should slow right down to forty, thirty-five, see who passes us, who don't pass."

"That'd indicate that we're suspicious."

"You mean we *aren't* suspicious?"

Bernhardt made no reply.

As, closing the distance, a car from the opposite direction came abreast of Bernhardt, whizzed past, leaving the black void of the night ahead. Immediately, the car behind Bernhardt pulled out, roared past. Inside the car Bernhardt had a quick glimpse of two men, both staring straight ahead.

"That's one between us now," Tate said. Then: "How much farther?"

"I'll get back to you." Bernhardt switched off the walkie-talkie, handed it back to Louise. He took a moment to decide what he must say. Then, glancing quickly at her face profiled in the dim glow of the car's instruments, he said, "We've been driving for an hour and a half. How much farther?"

"It's—I think it's about thirty, forty miles. Maybe a little more."

Bernhardt drove for a time in silence before he spoke again: "I think it's time that you tell me where we're going. I haven't pushed it, up to now. But C.B. and I have to know what we're getting into, what kind of terrain. We have to make plans."

Still staring straight ahead, Louise said nothing. Since they'd turned onto Route 12, she'd hardly spoken, except to answer questions or give cryptic directions.

"Louise?" The question was hard-edged, probing, demanding. The message: decision time had arrived, the point of no return. If she didn't extend her trust now, Bernhardt would abort the operation.

"I'm scared." Louise shook her head. "God, I'm scared."

"I'd think it was pretty strange if you weren't scared."

"You aren't scared."

In the darkened car, Bernhardt smiled. "When did I say I wasn't scared?"

She glanced at him, a quick look haunted by dark, dangerous demons. She began to speak, then broke off.

"If you want to turn around," Bernhardt said, "that's fine. But you've got to decide now. This country . . ." He gestured to the lowlands that surrounded them. There were no houses, no lights. Like the desert, the wetlands of the delta were unproductive, therefore unpopulated.

Therefore, tonight, potentially dangerous.

"This country," he repeated, "we shouldn't be out here like this if you're having second thoughts."

"I'm not having second thoughts. I'm just scared. Plain scared."

"I'm not asking whether you're scared. I'm asking you for a decision, go or no go. Now."

She turned, searched his face. Briefly he turned to meet her gaze, then returned his eyes to the road ahead and another pair of headlights approaching. In the mirror, checking, he saw the headlights of the car that C.B. had allowed to get between them, a strategic decision. Bernhardt glanced at the odometer. He would give it five more miles. Then he would—

"We go through Isleton," she was saying, speaking in a low, cowed voice. "Then we turn north, and follow the estuary. It—" She swallowed, searched his face one last time. "It's a little town. It's called Fowler's Landing. It's about ten miles from

Isleton, maybe less. It—it's where my grandmother was born."

"Ah . . ." Encouraged, Bernhardt nodded. "Yes, I see."

For a moment she lapsed into silence, as if his response had released her from the necessity of saying anything more. But then, still speaking brusquely, a command, not a request, he said, "Okay. So what then?"

"Then we—we go to the graveyard. That's where it's buried. In the graveyard."

"Jesus." In spite of himself, Bernhardt smiled out into the night. Repeating softly: "Jesus." Then, explaining: "It's all there, isn't it? The buried treasure, the little town out in the middle of nowhere—the graveyard, at midnight."

She made no response.

"This graveyard," Bernhardt said, "how's it situated?"

"I—I don't know what you mean."

"Is it in town? Out of town?"

"It's on the outskirts of town. There's a gravel road on the east side of town."

"How big is Fowler's Landing? How many people?"

"I think it's about three thousand people, something like that."

"Is it incorporated? Does it have its own police force?"

"I—I don't know. I haven't spent that much time there. Neither did my mother. When she was still a little girl, her family moved to Sacramento. She grew up there. Then, later, they moved to Cleveland. When she was eighteen, maybe nineteen, my mother left home. She'd saved her money, from working in the dime store. Ever since she was in high school, she worked. And she—"

"Wait." Bernhardt raised a hand. "Let's go back to the graveyard. You know how to get there, I assume."

She frowned. "Well, of course I do. I just told you how to get there, didn't I?" She spoke primly, with feeling. It was the first time since they'd left San Francisco that she'd spoken decisively.

"The graveyard—are there trees around it?"

She hesitated, then spoke tentatively: "A few, but not many."

"How long ago did your mother die?"

"It was six years ago."

Bernhardt nodded, then said, "You have directions—instructions—on how to locate the jewels."

"Yes . . ."

"Are the instructions clear?"

"I—I don't understand."

"There must be measurements. You know—a hundred feet due north of a certain tree, something like that."

"Well . . ." She nodded. "Yes, there're directions. They aren't very complicated. Once we get to the cemetery, it should take just a few minutes to dig it up."

"And you're satisfied that the instructions are perfectly clear, perfectly understandable."

"Yes, I am."

"Is there a fence around the cemetery?"

She nodded. "Yes. It's an iron fence. Very old, all rusted. The delta, you know—it's very damp."

"Is there a gate?"

"Yes, there's a gate."

"Locked?"

She shook her head. "No. At least, not that I remember."

"How long has it been since you were here, Louise?" He asked the question sternly, as if he were prosecuting her.

"It's been years. Two years, at least. But Tony Bacardo was here just yesterday."

He nodded, held out his hand for the walkie-talkie. He pressed the "transmit" key, heard Tate's acknowledgment, relayed Louise Rabb's information. As the two men spoke, a sign materialized beside the road: ISLETON, 10 MILES. POP. 6,040, ELEV. 12 FEET.

"Another twenty miles," Bernhardt said, speaking to Tate. "Any sign we're being followed?"

"Who's to say? There're three or four cars strung out back there. But they're just headlights in the mirror."

"In Isleton, in town, let's pull over and stop, talk about this."

"Right. You pull over. I'll drive past you, then walk back, get into your car. In back."

"Good."

10:20 P.M., PDT

"It sounds to me," Tate said, "like the two of you should park not too close to the gate of the cemetery. Hopefully, you should get your car out of sight. I should also park out of sight, but in a different direction, not close to your car. You should take the shovel, the two of you, and go into the cemetery, and dig up the loot—while I keep out of sight."

They sat in Bernhardt's station wagon. Staring straight ahead, acutely alert, Bernhardt sat behind the steering wheel. Half turned in the seat, Louise was looking back at Tate, who sat in the rear seat. Behind Tate, the shovel angled over the seat. Bernhardt's canvas equipment bag was in the baggage compartment behind the rear seat. Like Bernhardt, Tate was scanning the cars that passed and the few pedestrians abroad in Isleton on a humid Sunday night in April. The Honda was parked in the center of town, on the north side of the square. Bernhardt looked at Louise, whose attention was still sharp-focused on C. B. Tate. Was she reassured by the big, burly black man? Or was she frightened? Did she distrust Tate because he was black? Did she, therefore, fear that Tate would kill them and take the treasure? As if she sensed Bernhardt's unspoken questions, Louise now looked at him directly, fully. The message in her eyes was abject confusion compounded by fear and longing and, yes, suspicion.

To explore, probe the open sore, Bernhardt asked quietly, "What d'you think, Louise? How's that sound to you?"

"I wish Tony was here," she blurted. "Him and his people, with their guns. I wish they were here."

"I do, too," Bernhardt confessed. "But they aren't. And if we're going to do this, we do it tonight. Now. Right now."

Bitterly, unpredictably, she snorted, a harsh, rough exclamation. "We've got to do it. It's all over with me if I don't get those jewels. You know that." She spoke as if she were challenging him.

"Okay, then." He twisted behind the steering wheel to look squarely at Tate. "Okay, let's do it. You want to take the sawed-off in your car?"

"It's whatever you say, Alan. It's your show." Inscrutably half smiling, Tate spoke so softly that his voice could have been a caress. Bernhardt recognized the mannerism. When violence beckoned, Tate grew still, focused inward.

"Take the sawed-off," Bernhardt said. He watched Tate rummage in the canvas bag, come up with the shotgun, broken down into three pieces. Deftly, Tate assembled the gun, loaded it, slipped a handful of extra shells in the pocket of his jacket. Seeing Louise's eyes grow large as she watched, Tate smiled reassuringly, patted the sawed-off affectionately. "This," he said, "is big medicine. With one of these, nobody bothers you."

She said nothing, gave no sign that she'd heard. Unconcerned, Tate opened the rear door, got out, slipped the sawed-off up inside his jacket, concealed.

"See you at the cemetery." Tate waved once, then moved down the sidewalk to his Ford, parked a block away.

11:10 P.M., PDT

"They're moving," Chin said. "Let's go. Slowly."

Fabrese started the Buick's engine, put the car in gear.

"Not too fast," Chin said as he studied the scanner. They were passing a lopsided sign that advertised motel rooms with phones and TVs. The scanner's digital readout showed Bernhardt's car at 347 degrees, traveling almost due north. Ahead, Chin saw Isleton materializing: a random collection of buildings surrounding a nondescript town square. Except for the lights of the town, there was only darkness.

"You'd better slow down," Chin said. "We've got to find a road out of town that runs north."

"It can't be too much farther now. Christ, there's nothing *out* here."

"Which means," Chin said, "that we must be especially careful. If we're only three cars on a deserted road, we're vulnerable." They were approaching the Isleton town square now. The streets were almost deserted; in the whole downtown district, there were only two traffic lights. "There." Chin pointed to an intersection ahead. "That must be it."

"Fowler's Landing? That road?"

"Yes."

As they made the turn, Chin saw one of the scanner's five indicator lights blink off, leaving only two still lit. "Speed up a little." He glanced at the speedometer. "They're probably doing fifty-five or sixty."

As Fabrese increased their speed, the lights of Isleton quickly faded behind, leaving a darkness that surrounded them on all sides. Using a small flashlight to scan the map opened across his legs, Chin verified that they were traveling a road that followed a levee built along the western bank of the estuary that bordered Isleton, the largest town on the San Joaquin delta. Fowler's Landing, the next town, didn't show on the map.

The spike mike tapped into Louise Rabb's living room had recorded a reference to Fowler's Landing. But then the two women had gone into another room, probably the kitchen. At that distance their voices had been unintelligible. Later, though, there'd been talk of a grave.

"Christ, it's dark out here." Fabrese's expression was uneasy as he stared resentfully out into the darkness. Except for the two cars far ahead, pinpoints of red taillights, the road was deserted. "This is the goddam middle of nowhere."

"Perhaps you have lived too long in New York." As Chin said it he glanced at the scanner, then at his compass. Yes, the two headings corresponded: 330 degrees. And, yes, Bernhardt and Tate were holding a steady sixty, about a mile and a half ahead.

"I have a feeling," Chin said, "that they're going to Fowler's Landing."

"Well, then," Fabrese said, his voice heavily sarcastic, "Don't you think maybe we should make some plans, figure out how we're going to handle this? For instance, that M-Sixteen. Don't you think we should pull over and get it out of the trunk? The way I see it, that M-Sixteen might be all the edge we have. But it sure as shit won't help locked up."

"You're right, of course. But you should consider that, if we have it here, in the passenger's compartment, and we're stopped by the police, we would have to kill them."

Fabrese took his eyes off the road, looked at the other man. Chin allowed himself a small smile. The message: yes, Chin would do it—kill a policeman, no questions asked. Suddenly Fabrese felt himself go hollow at his center. How had it happened that he was driving down this dark, deserted two-lane road, heading for a tiny town he'd never heard of, taking orders from a Chinaman he hadn't even known a week ago? All he'd had was a name and a city: Brian Chin, available for hire, an independent operator with an organization that ticked like a watch.

Strange bedfellows, someone had once written.

Dead bedfellows?

Now Chin was nodding. Saying quietly: "All right. Pull over."

As Fabrese braked the car to a stop, Chin reached across, took the keys from the ignition, swung the passenger door open. There was a thump as the trunk lid came up, another thump as the lid slammed down. Carrying the compact rifle, Chin reappeared beside the car and got back in. He handed over the keys, glanced at the scanner as the Buick's engine came to life. Only one of the five distance calibration lights shone.

"Hurry," Chin urged. "We're losing them. Floorboard it."

As the car surged forward, screaming through the gears at full throttle, tires shrieking, rear end fishtailing, Chin braced himself as he turned the rifle upside down, checked the magazine. Yes, the tab showed twenty cartridges, a full load. He drew back the bolt, let it slam forward, set the safety, and tested it. The rifle was ready to fire. He propped it on the floor, with the barrel between his thigh and the door panel. The car was rocking precariously as it gathered speed: eighty-five, and still accelerating. The scanner still showed only one light; the heading was still constant. Ahead, the road was completely dark, with no winking taillights.

"That's fast enough for this road," Chin said. "Back off."

"What's the scanner say?"

"It says back off, dammit."

Fabrese glanced at the speedometer; the needle touched ninety. He eased off, gripped the wheel more firmly. Asking: "So what *is* the goddam plan? I say we should wait until they start digging, then hit them."

"Are you willing to kill them?" Chin asked the question quietly, frowning slightly as he spoke, as if he were puzzled. "All three of them? Is it worth that much to you?"

"For half a million, I'm ready to kill them." But as he said it, Fabrese felt conviction dissolve, fall away. Only the emptiness was left, most certainly revealed in his face, himself betraying himself, his own worst enemy. It had always been like this, the prisoner of his own fear, a nameless desperation that numbed the senses, left him helpless.

Never had he killed anyone. Never.

On the scanner, the second light came on. Then, quickly, a third.

"Slow down," Chin ordered sharply. "Fifty. Forty-five. *Now.*"

As Fabrese stepped on the brake, Chin spoke calmly, concisely: "If we can, we will do as you say. But we must be careful. The woman, surely, will be present, wherever it is that they dig. And one of the men, too. But the other man will probably be the lookout. So we must be very careful. Very deliberate." As he spoke, Chin saw the lights of a town materializing ahead. Just as, a half hour ago, Isleton had materialized on the eastern horizon.

Fowler's Landing.

Certainly, Fowler's Landing was just ahead.

There were four taillights ahead now. And a shift in heading. Bernhardt was slowing for the tiny town, and now turning thirty degrees to the north, away from the levee road.

"Slow down to about twenty," Chin said. "We're close now. Very close."

11:40 P.M., PDT

Except for one tavern that had attracted a small cluster of cars and pickups, the single main street of Fowler's Landing was deserted. Downshifting, Bernhardt spoke into the walkie-talkie: "We're in town. Where're you?"

"Maybe a mile behind you," Tate answered.

"Any lights in your mirror?"

"There was one pair until a few minutes ago. Then they either doused their lights or else turned off. Jesus, this place is empty. I never *been* in a place like this."

Bernhardt smiled, a surprise to himself. "What's the matter, C.B.? Afraid of the dark?"

"Man, maybe that's it. Seems like I want to feel the pavement, see a few streetlights, even if they're busted out."

"Well, just think about—"

"There," Louise interrupted, pointing to a narrow road that led off into the night. Repeating urgently: "There, that's the road to the cemetery."

"How far on that road?"

"Two miles," she answered. "Maybe three." Her voice was hushed. In the dim light, her eyes were awed. Bernhardt saw her swallow once—twice. Watching her, he felt the sudden emptiness of fear.

He turned onto the road, stopped, switched off his lights. Leaving the engine running, he keyed the walkie-talkie again. Saying: "We're on the last leg, C.B. When you get into town, you'll see a tavern on your right. It's the only place that's open, as far as I can see. Drive two streets past the tavern, then turn right. You'll see me, parked. When we see each other, I'll move out. Louise says the road is gravel once we get away from town. I'm going to use my parking lights."

"How far should I stay back?"

"Maybe two hundred yards, something like that."

"Right."

"How're your butterflies behaving?"

"No comment."

There was a short silence. Then, still staring straight ahead, Louise said, "You're friends, the two of you. Aren't you?" In her voice, Bernhardt could clearly hear a kind of puzzlement. In her forty years, had she known many blacks? Any blacks?

"That's right," he said, "we're friends."

"Is he a private investigator, too?"

"No. He's a bounty hunter. A very successful bounty hunter."

She frowned. "What's that mean—bounty hunter?"

"If someone is arrested, the judge sets bail. If the bad guy can put up ten percent, a bailbondsman posts the rest of it with the court. If the bad guy jumps bail, the court issues a warrant, and the bailbondsman pays C.B. to go find the bad guy and bring him back."

She nodded, then said, "The woman—Paula. She works for you."

Bernhardt considered, decided to say, "She works for me part-time. Otherwise—" He hesitated. "Otherwise, we're friends. Good friends."

"She seems very nice. Pretty, too. Very pretty."

"When she got out of college, she tried acting, down in Hollywood. She was off to a good start. But then she made the mistake of marrying a scriptwriter." Ruefully, he smiled. "Don't let Angela marry a scriptwriter. She—"

In the mirror, he saw headlights, quickly replaced by parking lights. Tate had found the turnoff. Bernhardt spoke into the walkie-talkie: "Okay, here I go. Let's see how the parking lights work on this road." He put the Honda in gear, moved out. The graveled road was narrow and uneven, but there was enough moonlight to avoid the worst of the potholes. Ahead, in the direction of the levee, Bernhardt saw a low-lying whiteness.

"Fog," Louise said.

"Do you think it'll come in over the cemetery?"

"I don't know. I've never been here at night."

Now they were passing a cluster of buildings on the right: apparently a house surrounded by several one-story warehouses.

"That's a catfish farm," Louise said. "As far as I know, except for stores that sell bait and tackle to weekend fishermen, that's the only business around here that amounts to anything."

"How much farther?"

"I think we're about halfway."

Bernhardt relayed the information to Tate, adding, "There's

fog ahead, it looks like. It's coming from the water—the estuary."

"I see it," Tate answered.

"Anything behind you?"

"Nothing." Then: "Maybe the fog's a plus."

"Maybe," Bernhardt answered.

"How much farther?"

"Less than a mile." Bernhardt looked at Louise for confirmation.

She nodded, licked her lips, nodded again. She raised her hand to point ahead. "There. It's right up there, across the road from that little grove of trees."

"This road—does it continue on, beyond the cemetery?"

"I'm not sure. I've only been here twice since the funeral." She considered, then spoke defensively: "See, I haven't had a car since my mother died."

"The checks from your father quit coming. Is that it?"

"They came, but not so often. And not so big. My father didn't like my choice of husbands. And he didn't like Walter, either. Walter Draper, the guy I was living with in San Francisco."

"So he cut back on your checks."

She made no reply.

"Do you have any idea how deep the stuff's buried?"

"No."

"Bacardo came up here yesterday to look things over. Could he guess how hard it'd be to dig it up?"

"He didn't think it'd take long. Fifteen minutes, maybe."

"I keep wondering," Bernhardt said, "whether he could've gotten the treasure when he came up here. I keep wondering whether he's made Cella a present of it, to show his loyalty." Without waiting for a response, Bernhardt went to the walkie-talkie again: "C.B."

"Right here."

"There's a little grove of trees up ahead, right across from the entrance to the cemetery. If possible, I'll park in there, out of sight. The road probably goes on. See if you can find a place beyond the cemetery to park so you're concealed. Then take the guns and walk back to me. I'll wait at my car for you. If everything looks all right, Louise and I'll go into the cemetery. You can stay near my car, out of sight."

"If there's going to a problem," Tate said, "it'll probably happen after we get the stuff."

"I know."

"If I were them," Tate said, "considering the terrain, and how this is pretty much a moonscape out here, I think I'd figure on bringing, say, four cars. I'd blockade this road ahead and behind. That's unless I got turned on by the idea of hiding my guys behind tombstones, something colorful like that."

Within two hundred feet of the iron fence that surrounded the cemetery, Bernhardt downshifted to first gear. Lights out, they were crawling ahead.

"Okay," he said into the walkie-talkie, his voice hushed. "Okay, here we go. It looks like I can get the car maybe half out of sight."

"Hmm."

Bernhardt gave the walkie-talkie to Louise, stopped the Honda at the small grove of trees. Yes, there was room enough between two large sycamores to conceal most of the car from casual observation. Bernhardt backed in between the two trees, switched off the engine, put the transmission in park, then turned to Louise. "If you want to do it, you can tell me now where the stuff is. You can stay in the car while I get it. You'll have C.B. here with you." As he spoke, he twisted, opened the duffel bag, withdrew two flashlights.

"I can't tell you where it is. I mean—" She drew a deep, tremulous breath. "I mean, I *can* tell you, but then you'd still have to look for it. And that'd take time."

As he waited for her to go on, he saw Tate's Ford come into view, slowly passing from right to left. As Tate drew even, Bernhardt saw the big black man raise a forefinger—then two fingers, the victory sign. Bernhardt watched the Ford pass beyond the cemetery and then disappear, blocked out by the trees that concealed Bernhardt. Finally the walkie-talkie crackled to life.

"There's no place where I can get the car out of sight," Tate said. "No cover, except for those trees you're in. I'm coming back to where you are."

"Okay," Bernhardt said. "Let's just get it done, the sooner the better."

"I agree. Definitely, I agree." And, moments later, the Ford appeared, running with only the parking lights.

Acutely aware of his own anxiety, the growing fear that somewhere in the darkness there was danger, Bernhardt swung open his car door. Ordering brusquely: "Okay, let's do it." He took a flashlight and the shovel from the station wagon, closed the doors, gave the second flashlight to Louise. He walked to the front of the Honda. Also out of the car, Louise came to stand timidly beside him. Bernhardt looked at her one last time, handed her the walkie-talkie, her assigned task. He forced a smile. Then they were walking across the gravel road to the graveyard.

11:45 P.M., PDT

"Nothing," Fabrese said, peering out into the darkness. They sat in the Buick. They were parked on the shoulder of the gravel road, lights out. "Are you sure they're stopped?

"They've been stopped for two or three minutes." As Chin spoke, he glanced again at the scanner: all five lights were lit. Bernhardt's car, then, was less than a half mile ahead, invisible in the dark, featureless landscape. Conclusion: the quarry had gone to ground. Without doubt, Bernhardt's car was parked in the small grove of trees just ahead, the only identifiable feature of a dark, desolate landscape. Chin was aware of a sudden breathless constriction across his chest. He recognized the feeling. It was the excitement of the hunter, closing in for the kill. He switched off the scanner, touched the breech of the M-16, close beside him. Was the rifle set for single shot, not automatic fire? He glanced down, verified that, yes, the rifle would fire single shots. And, yes, the rifle was still on safety, with a round in the chamber.

"So what do we do?" Fabrese demanded. "Walk? Do we walk from here? Is that what you're thinking?"

"No," Chin answered, "I think we should drive ahead. But slowly. Very quietly, very slowly, without lights. I think another hundred yards, and we'll see their cars."

"Okay." Fabrese put the Buick in gear, began their slow, blind progress. In the last several minutes fog had begun to drift around them. Was it an advantage? For whom—which side? "Okay," he repeated. "But as far as I can see, you've fucked this whole thing up. If we had two cars, one of us could stay here and the other one could go ahead, beyond them. Then we'd have them bottled up. Another M-Sixteen, an Uzi, one of those, and we'd blast the shit out of them."

"That's one way," Chin answered calmly. "A war—three bodies, two cars shot up, all before we knew they really had the jewels. Is that your plan?" For the first time he allowed the contempt he felt for this repulsive little man to surface.

11:59 P.M., PDT

"There." Louise's voice was a low, ragged whisper. "There—that one. It's my—my mother's grave. The jewels are buried—" She fell silent, one last hesitation, facing the abyss. "They're buried behind the headstone."

"Ah . . ."

A million dollars' worth of jewels. Mafia treasure, his for the taking.

Holding an unlit flashlight in his left hand, Bernhardt propped the shovel against his thigh, took the radio from Louise.

"C.B.?" Spoken softly, cautiously.

"Yeah?"

"I'm starting to dig. It shouldn't take long. Anything?"

"I'm not sure . . ." In Tate's voice Bernhardt heard uncertainty. Or was it fear? Had he ever known Tate to be afraid? Of anything?

"What's that mean?"

"I thought I heard a car, coming from the direction of town. But now I don't hear anything."

"You should get away from our cars. Why don't you come here, inside the cemetery? We're on the north side, left from the gate. You go to your right, keep some distance between us. You can get down beside a tombstone. That way you can—"

"A *tombstone?*" Suddenly Tate's voice erupted in a spontaneous guffaw. "You know what? I just realized that I'm superstitious. Like, graveyards at midnight—hiding behind tombstones—all this goddam fog, suddenly. I mean, let's dig this stuff up, then get back to the bright lights."

"Jesus, C.B. Come *on.*"

"Okay. Here I go."

Bernhardt returned the radio to Louise, then stood motionless, staring through the gathering mist in the direction of the gate. The dim figure of Tate materialized, an outsize wraith disappearing now behind a large headstone. Tate, packing his two nine-millimeter Browning automatics, one with a twenty-shot rotary clip. Tate, with Bernhardt's sawed-off, a walking arsenal.

Bernhardt calculated that perhaps a hundred feet separated them.

"Here." Bernhardt gave his flashlight to Louise. Then he hefted the shovel and stepped behind her mother's tombstone. "Shine it down there. Just for a second."

She obeyed. The grass behind the tombstone was undisturbed.

"Ah . . . good." Hearing himself say it, the words sounded like a benediction—a soulful prayer for final fulfillment. As the light winked off, he drove the spade into the hard, unyielding earth, stepped on the shovel with his full weight, turned a meager shovelful. He drove the shovel again into the earth—and again. Finally, with a foot-high mound of raw dirt beside a circular hole, he felt the shovel strike something solid, heard the dull thunk.

"Jesus," he breathed, "there's something there."

Just as, from the walkie-talkie in Louise's hand, he heard Tate's metallic voice:

"Alan."

Even in the single whispered word, Bernhardt could hear it: the life-or-death urgency of survival, kill or be killed.

"*Gimme,*" Bernhardt hissed, putting out his hand for the radio. "*Quick.*" Then, with the radio pressed to his ear: "C.B.?"

"There's a car, coming the way we came. It's stopped now, engine turned off. But I can see it. And—" He broke off. There was a moment of agonizing silence. Then: "They're getting out of the car, coming down the road. Two of them."

"Can they see our cars?"

"Hard to tell. They will, though, before they get much closer. One of them, it looks like he's carrying a rifle. Maybe an M-Sixteen, one of those. You know, heavy duty. This goddam fog, all I can see is shadows, like. Ghosts. They're walking on either side of the road. You know, like skirmishers. How close are you to getting the stuff?"

"I think I've just found it. Anyhow, the shovel hit something solid."

"Their timing is right on, then. Makes you wonder whether—"

The sharp crack of a single shot split the night like the crash of lightning.

"God—*damn*." It was Tate, on the radio. "The guy with the rifle, he fell back a little. Then he let the other guy have it."

"Jesus . . ." As he spoke, Bernhardt realized that he was staring down at the hole behind the tombstone. Repeating solemnly: "Jesus."

"Now the guy with the rifle, looks like he's going to make sure. He's—"

Another shot.

"Yeah," Tate breathed. "He made sure."

Bernhardt had fallen into a crouch. But he wasn't crouching behind the tombstone to protect himself. Revolver in hand, he was crouching in front of the hole he'd dug, as if to protect the treasure. Louise was close beside him.

"Don't let him see you, C.B.," Bernhardt breathed. "If he's got an M-Sixteen, you've had it. That goddam sawed-off, it's no good beyond—"

"*Wait*," Tate interrupted, his voice hardly audible now. Repeating urgently: "*Wait*. Hold on. This guy, the guy with the rifle, he's—yeah—Christ, he's going back to their car."

Bernhardt realized that he was gulping incredulously. "Are you sure?"

"He's just strolling along, carrying the rifle like he's real comfortable with it, like that. And—yeah—he's getting in the car now. You want my advice, get that goddam loot, whatever it is, and let's go home."

"What's he doing now?"

"He's starting the car, I think. And—yeah, there go the

headlights. Looks like he don't care, now. Looks like he's finished up here, and he's going home." Tate's voice was louder now, more confident.

Still pressed close to Bernhardt, Louise began to mutter, "It's a trick. They're all around us, in the dark. They waited for us to find the jewels. And now they'll kill us." She began to cry: dry, desperate sobs. Then, fervently thankful: "Thank God I didn't let her come."

For a moment Bernhardt stared at her incredulously. Angela, she meant. She thought they were going to die. She was grateful that it would be her, not her child.

Suddenly Bernhardt put the radio on the ground, took up the shovel, began furiously digging. Whispering, "Shut up. They aren't going to kill us. So shut up."

As, to the west, he saw the flash of headlights. The intruder—the murderer—was backing and filling on the narrow gravel road until, finally, he could go back down the road toward Fowler's Landing, taillights winking.

Again and again now, the spade was striking something solid. The treasure, surely the treasure. Mafia gold. The walkie-talking was crackling; Tate was transmitting. Breathing hard, Bernhardt snatched up the radio.

"Well?" Tate demanded. "How much longer?"

"A couple of minutes, no more. Shut up and let me dig, why don't you?" And to Louise: "You shut up, too. And get your head down. If you're worried, get your goddam head down." He laid the radio on the grass behind the grave and began desperately digging. Three more shovelsful, then four, and he took up the flashlight, shone the light down in the hole. A white cylinder was visible, half uncovered.

A million dollars encased in a white sewer pipe. Gleaming in the flashlight's beam like a bleached skull.

"My God," Louise breathed. "My God, there it is."

Bernhardt laid the shovel aside, fell to his knees, began scraping at the dirt with his hands.

"Hurry," Louise breathed. She, too, was on her knees, working with her hands, clawing the dirt.

"Wait." He kicked at the half-exposed canister. Feeling it shift, he grasped it with both hands, felt it shift again. Flat on the ground now, he twisted the canister—and felt it come free. On his knees, he was holding it in both hands: the million-dollar prize. Somberly, he presented the trophy to Louise. Then he keyed the walkie-talkie.

"Got it," he breathed. "We *got* it, C.B."

"All *right*." It was a jubilant response. Then, urgently: "So let's *go*, man. This place, it's giving me the creeps."

"I'm going to fill in the hole first." And to Louise: "Take it to C.B. Wait there for me."

Obediently, she rose, took the canister with both hands, as if she were serving at an altar. In the dim light, her eyes were rapt.

Bernhardt began filling the hole, urgently bent to the task. From the surrounding darkness, in the mist rising from the graveyard, how many eyes were watching?

How many bodies would the authorities find tomorrow?

Hastily, he finished the job, replaced the sod, tramped it down. In two hours, they would be back in San Francisco: the five of them safe at his flat, guarding the treasure.

Bernhardt slipped the flashlight into the pocket of his jacket, loosened the .357 in its holster, picked up the shovel and the radio. Now he was walking between the tombstones in the direction of the gate. To the left of the gate, inside the cemetery, he could make out two figures: Tate and Louise, waiting for him. Together, they would go to their cars. When they were under way, he would call Paula on the cellular phone, tell her they'd found the treasure.

Or, more precisely, tell her they'd found a length of white plastic sewer pipe, capped at either end, that rattled when it was shaken.

A small cylinder that, already tonight, had cost one man his life.

They gathered at the gate: Louise with the canister, the men carrying the guns, the radios, the shovel, and the flashlights.

"What about that dead one?" Tate asked, his voice pitched low. "What'll we do about him?"

"Where is he?" Bernhardt asked.

Tate led them from the gate to the graveled road, where he pointed in the direction of Fowler's Landing. "He's just off the road, on the left shoulder. Two hundred feet, maybe."

"Here." Bernhardt gave Tate the shovel, then began walking down the road. Yes, he could make it out: a lifeless, shapeless, blood-drenched bundle with head and hands attached, the eternal caprice of death by violence. The victim lay on his back, one arm flung wide, one leg tucked beneath the other leg, as if he'd pivoted as he fell. The head and the torso were covered with blood, soaked with blood, clotted with blood. A revolver lay about a foot from the right hand.

As he stood motionless, frozen, Bernhardt felt his stomach convulse, felt the bile begin to rise. He bit his tongue, doggedly shook his head, moved the flashlight beam from the face down to the torso, the legs, the feet, then back again. The victim was dressed as Bernhardt was dressed: dark jacket, dark jeans. The shoes, though, were tasseled black loafers, Gucci style. And beneath the roughly cut outdoor jacket, call it army surplus, Bernhardt saw a gleaming white collar and silk tie. Conclusion: this well-dressed man had gotten costumed for the part—the hunter, tracking them in the darkness.

Bernhardt straightened, took an uncertain step to his right, toward Tate and Louise. The sooner they were in their cars, under way, the safer they would be.

But in seconds, if he could bring himself to do it, he might discover a wallet, an ID. If this man had come to kill them, then he must know the assassin's identity—a deep, primitive necessity.

Urgently, he beckoned to Tate, who immediately put the shovel aside, said something to Louise. Then, carrying the double-barreled sawed-off, Tate quickly covered the distance between them, shone his flashlight down on the body.

"Jesus."

"Here . . ." Bernhardt bent over the body. "Let's roll him over. I want to get his ID."

Both men found a grip on the dead man's jacket, nodded to each other, heaved in unison—then stepped quickly back as the grotesque shape seemed to momentarily prop itself on its side before, suddenly capitulating to gravity, it flopped face-down on the gravel, one arm almost touching Bernhardt as it came over, crashed to the ground. Once more, gritting his teeth, Bernhardt touched the body, feeling below the belt, above the buttocks—

—finding, yes, the rectangular bulge of a wallet. Fumbling, he withdrew the wallet. Should he thrust it in his own pocket, to be examined later, back in San Francisco?

No. Not later. If the police questioned him, found him with the wallet . . . even the random possibility numbed him with fear. Causing him, therefore, to leave the body as it lay and beckon to Tate, who was pocketing the dead man's revolver. They strode quickly to the Honda. Still cradling the white plastic canister in both arms, a maternal embrace, Louise stood motionless beside the car. Bernhardt put the wallet on the car's hood, waited for Tate to shine a light on it. Then, compartment by compartment, he emptied the wallet, spread out the contents: folding money, lots of it, a driver's license, a few business cards. All the documents agreed: name, James Fabrese, residence, New York City. As Louise, still cradling the canister, drew close, Bernhardt took the driver's license from its plastic sheath, held it close to the flashlight.

"Come on, Alan," Tate urged, "let's move it. Let's take the money, toss the goddam wallet and the gun. Let's—"

"Profaci," Louise said. She spoke in a small, cowed voice. "The picture on the license. It's Profaci."

"Jesus." Bernhardt looked at her. "You're sure?"

She nodded silently, conclusively. Yes, she was sure. Dead sure.

Bernhardt looked at her for one last long moment. Then he

nodded to Tate, who began stuffing the documents back into the wallet. "Here." Tate handed over the money.

Bernhardt momentarily recoiled from the blood money. Then he saw all the fifties, all the twenties, a few tens.

"Go on. *Take* it, Alan."

"What the hell," Bernhardt muttered. He took the money, folded it, thrust it into his jacket pocket. Saying to Tate: "We can't toss the wallet and the gun, not here. Our prints are all over both of them."

"Okay." Impatiently, Tate thrust the wallet in his own pocket. "We get to the causeway back beyond Isleton, I'll pull over, toss it all in the water. Okay?"

Bernhardt hesitated.

"Alan—*shit*—come *on*. Let's *split*, for God's sake. Snap out of it, will you?" It was an order. An angry order.

As he looked at Tate he felt himself coming back to himself, once more sharp-focused, ready. It had been the blood—all that blood—and the odor of death, sights and smells that had stunned him, left him helpless.

"Okay." He gestured Louise into the Honda, slid the shovel into the station wagon, got in behind the wheel. "Here." He handed the walkie-talkie to the woman. "Put the jewels on the floor." He started the car, watched Tate get into the Ford. Bernhardt held out his hand for the radio, spoke to Tate: "Let's run on parking lights for a mile or so, then switch on the headlights."

"Right."

"Okay, here we go." Bernhardt put the car in gear, moved out. As they passed the body on their left, Louise was staring straight ahead. Her face was pale and drawn.

"Are you sure about him?" Bernhardt asked. "Profaci—you're sure it's him?"

"I'm positive."

"He worked for your father, is that what he told you?"

She nodded. "And Cella, too. Benito Cella."

Bernhardt glanced into the mirror. Yes, Tate was just pulling out, leaving the grove of trees behind.

The grove and the graveyard, disappearing in the mirror, leaving only Tate's parking lights, pinpoints in the darkness.

"I have the feeling that this can't be true," Louise said. As she spoke she looked at him intently, as if for reassurance.

"The treasure—is that what you mean?"

"Yes. The treasure."

"Well," Bernhardt said, "there's something rattling around in there." As he spoke, he glanced down at the canister lying on the floor at the woman's feet.

A fortune in jewels . . .

Yet, with the prize actually in hand, something to touch, something to hold, the probability that the treasure actually existed seemed more remote, not less. It was, after all, only three pieces of white plastic pipe that someone had once filled with something, then sealed up with plastic glue, the same glue children used, making plastic models.

"How do we get it open?" she asked.

"We have to use a saw. I've got one at home." He glanced at his watch. The time was almost twelve-thirty. Should he call Paula, tell her the news? The call would wake her, perhaps startle her, frighten Angela. And when Paula asked him for details, and he couldn't tell her about the dead man, not on the air, she would worry.

Therefore, he must not make the call.

Half past midnight . . .

They'd gotten to the graveyard a little before midnight. In a half hour, they'd dug up the treasure—and seen a man die.

Meaning that, somewhere in the night, a killer was waiting.

2 A.M., PDT

Bernhardt flipped the turn indicator, checked the mirrors, made the turn onto Vermont Street—the last turn. Four more blocks and he'd be home. At two o'clock, Potrero Hill was deep in sleep. As he downshifted to first gear for the last steep climb, he took the radio from Louise, a ritual that had become a reflex.

"Get close to me," Bernhardt said, speaking to Tate. "It could be that they're waiting at the house." As he said it he looked apologetically at Louise. All during the night he'd tried to avoid alarming her as he spoke to Tate on the radio. But if Louise was frightened, she gave no sign.

"When we park," Bernhardt said to her, "I'll put everything in the canvas bag, including the canister. We'll leave the shovel in the car. You'll carry the bag. I'll go first. Then you. Then C.B., in the rear. Have you got that?" As he spoke, they entered the final block, going uphill. His building was on the left, midway in the block. Because of the steep slope, parking was perpendicular to the curb, on one side of the street. There was one parking space left, only three doors from Bernhardt's building. He maneuvered the Honda into the slot, took the radio from Louise.

"You'll have to park in the next block, C.B., on top. It's level, so there's parking on both sides of the street. We'll wait for you in the car."

"Right." Behind them, Tate's Ford passed, climbing the hill.

Bernhardt checked the Honda's doors; yes, all four were locked. He switched off the walkie-talkie, unfastened the short antenna, put them into the canvas bag along with the flashlights. "Okay." He held out his hands for the white plastic canister. Louise lifted it from the floor. There was a momentary hesitation, an instinctive, elemental reluctance to surrender the canister, with whatever wealth it contained. Then she handed it over. He leaned over the seat, put it in the bag. He zipped up the bag, hefted it. Yes, Louise could handle it, no problem.

"Is this when—" She broke off. Then, almost timidly: "Is this the dangerous time?"

"I don't know, Louise. I just don't know. All I want to do is get the three of us inside the house with the jewels. We get inside, we lock the doors and draw the drapes, we make sure Crusher's on the job, and we wait until the banks open. Then we celebrate." He hesitated, then added, "That's assuming, of course, that we haven't done all this to bring home a tube filled with pebbles." As he spoke, he saw movement in the street above them: a figure coming toward them in the darkness. Tate? Bernhardt realized that his hand was on the butt of the .357. The figure was coming down the middle of the street, Wild West style. It was—

Yes, it was Tate. Bernhardt exhaled softly, gestured toward the passenger door. He spoke quietly. "Okay . . . get out. I'll hand the bag to you." He lifted the bag into the Honda's front seat, gave it to the woman, then got out of the car, went around to Louise's side as Tate joined them. Tate carried the sawed-off close to his right leg, muzzle down. His head was in constant motion, scanning the area. All of the homes in the block were either single-family dwellings or two-flat buildings, almost all of them attached to their neighbors, almost all of them built with their front facades less than ten feet from the sidewalk— just enough space for a small front garden. Most of the front gardens were protected by ornamental fences or chest-high hedges. Between the Honda and Bernhardt's front door, therefore, they would be constantly within range of a concealed gunman. One full automatic burst from the M-16 and it would all be over, winner take all.

Bernhardt spoke softly to Tate: "I'll go first. Then Louise. Then you."

Impassively, Tate nodded. Back in the city, his own turf, Tate was once more the black samurai, the calm, cold, deadly street warrior, ready for a fight.

"Okay," Bernhardt breathed, "here we go." He began walking on the sidewalk, up the hill to his building. As he walked, he drew the .357.

They passed the first building. It was a two-flat building, like Bernhardt's. There were two more houses to pass on this side of the street, both single-family dwellings. The two homes had low hedges in front, perfect for a gunman to hide behind. But if it happened that way, at this range, one blast from the sawed-off could cut a man in two.

They were passing the second home, the last one. Then, feeling his knees go weak with relief, Bernhardt was turning onto his own short flagstone walkway. He held the .357 in his right hand; in his left he held his keys ready. Had Paula bolted the door? If she had, a probability, he would have to ring the bell to wake her. He would have to—

He was on the small front stoop when he smelled it: a strong, acrid chemical odor.

And, at that same moment, he became aware of an unfamiliar silence from inside the flat.

There was no barking—no anxious whining as Crusher recognized his step, welcomed him home.

There was only silence.

A silence, and the odor.

Carrying the canvas satchel, Louise was standing close to him, sensing that something had suddenly gone wrong. But Tate shouldered her abruptly aside, demanding in a low, urgent whisper: "What?"

"It's—there's something—"

And then he saw it: one of the three bay windows in his office, broken out. The drapes were drawn, the room was dark—and the window almost entirely shattered.

"Here." Tate pushed Louise against the house beside the door, out of harm's way. Then, to Bernhardt: "You going to try the door?"

Bernhardt nodded, his eyes fixed on the doorknob. Saying, "You guard my back."

"Right." With the shotgun ready, Tate turned to face the street. Bernhardt cocked the .357, two fateful clicks, incredibly loud in the silence. With his left hand he returned the keys to the pocket of his jacket. Then, very slowly, as if the prospect of touching the knob were repugnant, Bernhardt extended his left hand until he was touching the knob—slowly rotating it— hearing the click of the latch—

—and feeling the door move.

Unlocked.

The door swung inward at Bernhardt's touch.

"It's open," he whispered. As he said it, he saw the wood splintered above the latch.

Still standing with her back against the wall, just as Tate had left her, clutching the canvas bag close, Louise began to cry. Bernhardt waited for Tate to acknowledge what he'd said, one short nod of his black bullet head. Then Bernhardt stepped to the other side of the door—

—and slowly pushed it open, exposing only his hand and forearm.

The interior of the flat was dark and still: a lung-searing cave, a terrible blackness, a void without sound or life or hope.

Tate muttered a heartfelt obscenity, then said, "That's gas, man. Tear gas, something like that. *Shit!*"

"You stay here," Bernhardt said. "I'm going in."

"You won't get very—" Tate broke off, coughed. "*Shit.* You'd better—" A car was coming: headlights, from up the hill. It was a panel truck, a newspaper van on its early rounds, dropping off bundles of *The Sentinel* at two o'clock in the morning.

The Sentinel . . .

Tomorrow at this time, how would the front page read? *Potrero Hill Massacre?*

Bernhardt's gaze shifted from the disappearing truck to the open door of his flat—and finally to the wide-eyed woman who stood motionless, clutching the canvas bag close to her body.

A fortune in jewels . . .

If they called the police, questions would be asked, evidence would be impounded.

Should he call Hastings or Friedman, the homicide lieutenants who were his only real friends on the force?

Call them and tell them what? Tell them the truth? How far did friendship stretch? A million dollars' worth? Would—

"Jesus, Alan, let's not just *stand* here."

Suddenly angry, eyes stinging, voice choking, Bernhardt confronted the other man. "Shut up, why don't you? Why don't you just shut up?"

And instantly, hearing himself say it, he heard the echoes from so long ago: himself a child on the playground, aggrieved, fists bunched, about to lash out.

Tate's response was a grunt, meant to soothe. "You want me to go in, see how far I get?"

"No. Wait." Bernhardt holstered his revolver, took off his jacket, stripped off his shirt, stepped over a low hedge to a water tap. He soaked the shirt, stepped back over the hedge, held the shirt to his face. Would it help? In the movies, yes, it helped. But here? Now?

He nodded to Louise, then to Tate, a mute apology for his angry words. Then, with the .357 in his hand, he stepped across the threshold.

The first room on his left was his office. The door was standing open. In the pale light from a streetlamp he saw what he hoped to see: nothing disturbed—

—no bodies lying on the floor.

The next two rooms on the left were bedrooms. The first was the guest room, where Angela would have slept. The bed had been slept in, but the room was empty.

The next bedroom was his—his, and Paula's.

He realized that fear was dragging at his steps as he came close to the door. Yes, the door was open, wide open. His eyes were streaming; his throat was on fire. But he could breathe without choking. The draft created by the open front door was helping.

Another step and, yes, he could make out shapes in his bedroom: tangled blankets on the bed—

—and the shape of something on the floor between the bed and the closet. It was a shape smaller than a body, a human body.

Gritting his teeth, he switched on the light.

It was Crusher.

The Airedale lay on his side, as if he were sleeping—peacefully sleeping, eyes closed.

Sleeping?

Or unconscious, but still alive?

Bernhardt knelt beside the dog. Yes, he could feel faint respiration, a rising and falling of the brown and black fur beneath his hand. Bernhardt stepped to the window that opened on an airshaft, threw up the sash. For now, these next minutes, it was all he could do for the dog. Quickly he stepped to the nightstand, where Paula would have kept the .38 revolver he'd given her. But as his fingers touched the knob of the drawer, he saw it: the gun, lying on the floor between the nightstand and the bed. He thrust his own gun into its holster, picked up the .38, checked the cylinder: five cartridges, all unfired. Plus one empty cylinder, for safety.

He thrust the .38 in his belt, knelt again to put his hand on Crusher. Yes, the dog was still breathing. Bernhardt straightened, decided to switch off the bedroom light before he ventured into the hallway. The dining room and kitchen were at the rear of the flat. As he stepped into the dining room his foot struck something on the floor. He stooped, picked up a small metal canister. It was, certainly, a tear gas canister. As, yes, he saw it: one of the dining room windows, broken out. He put the canister down, went into the hallway. The door that led to the rear garden was partially opened. Even in the uncertain light he saw the wood splintered around the lock. It had been a coordinated attack, then: two canisters of gas, one in front, one in back. Then, front and back, they'd broken in the doors. Men in gas masks, carrying guns. A raid, executed with swat-team precision. They'd taken Paula and Angela—and left the dog for dead.

He pulled the broken back door open wide. He could feel the fresh breeze in his face. Crusher would be grateful. If Crusher lived, he would be grateful.

Moving quickly now, he was striding down the hallway to the front door.

Just as, in his office, the phone warbled. Once. Twice. Should he answer? No; instinct warned against answering. He was at the door of his office. Three rings. He waited for the fourth ring, followed by his brief spiel on the answering machine.

Then came the voice, talking to the machine. It was an educated voice, an affected, studied voice, carefully modulated: "I know you're in there, Mr. Bernhardt. If you'll just answer, we can get on with things."

They were out there, then. Somewhere in the night, close by. Watching. Whoever had Paula, they were watching. The answering machine was silent now, but the tape was still running. He had only moments to make his decision: pick up the phone, or else—

—or else what?

Or else snap this slender thread that connected him with whoever had Paula?

The thought translated into instant action. Without fully realizing that he'd done it, he was at his desk, holding the phone to his ear, pressing the button that cut out the machine.

"Mr. Bernhardt?" It was a soft-spoken, polite inquiry.

He took the wet shirt away from his face, coughed, managed to say, "Who's this?" Then he discovered that if he took the phone to the broken-out window, he could breathe well enough to speak normally. Allowing him to demand: "Who's calling?"

"We have the women," the voice was saying. "We are all together, in one room. I am looking at both of the women. When you and I are finished with our business, you can talk to Paula Brett. Would you like that?"

He realized that, irrationally, his instinct was to deny his tormentor the satisfaction of admitting that, yes, more than anything in the world, he wanted to talk to Paula, to know she was unharmed.

"What we want, of course, are the jewels. Were you successful at Fowler's Landing? Did Louise direct you to the jewels?"

"Do you expect me to answer that, you son of a bitch?"

"Mr. Bernhardt . . ." It was a pained response. "We have much to talk about, you and me. Name-calling only wastes time."

Bernhardt urgently beckoned Tate and Louise into the office as he spoke into the phone: "If you bring those women back now—right now—we won't press charges. That's all I've got to say."

There was a silence. Standing close beside him, Louise lowered the canvas bag to the floor, as if to divest herself. Her eyes were wide as she began to slowly shake her head. Balefully, Tate began to swear, his voice a low, purposeful monotone. In the darkened room, Bernhardt gestured for Tate to pull back the drapes that covered the broken-out window, for more air circulation.

"I'm assuming," the caller said, "that, in fact, you now have a million dollars in jewels. I, on the other hand, have the two women. Fabrese is no longer a problem. Therefore, this whole affair can be managed with no loose ends. We can—"

"You killed Fabrese."

With the words, Tate broke off swearing as his black eyes searched Bernhardt's face. Louise, crying, sank numbly into Bernhardt's desk chair, the jewels forgotten.

"Of course," the caller said, "I would never answer a question like that. However, I will say that things are simpler with Fabrese dead. Much simpler. Don't you agree?"

"Are you part of the Mafia?"

"No." It was an amused response. "No, Mr. Bernhardt. I'm not with the Mafia. That much I'll tell you."

"You killed Fabrese at Fowler's Landing. Then you left. You didn't go for the jewels. You left."

"I prefer to operate in my own territory."

"San Francisco . . ."

"Yes, San Francisco." The speaker allowed a silence to pass. Then, in an aloof, supercilious voice he said, "You're beginning to think, I can see that—put things together, make connections. Good. I prefer to deal with intelligent people. And you, obviously, are intelligent."

"And you're an Oriental—an educated Oriental. Chinese, I think. And you've obviously got an organization. That makes you a local Chinese gangster."

"Ah . . ." The voice projected pleasure. "Ah, yes, that's good. Very good. You have an educated ear, I can see."

"I'm an actor. My business is voices."

"An actor . . ." A moment's silence. Then, plainly pleased, titillated: "San Francisco—there's such a variety here. Don't you agree?" It was a benevolent question.

Suddenly overwhelmed by the incredible irony of a fortune in jewels lying at his feet while he made small talk with Paula's kidnapper, Bernhardt began to slowly, helplessly shake his head. Was it denial? Desperation? Was it fatigue compounded by fear and shock and the terrible helplessness of abject indecision?

Once more, the voice began: "You have a trained ear, Mr. Bernhardt. And I also have a trained ear. I can hear indecision in your voice, and weariness, too. You've had a very long night, and you've had a nasty shock, too. Therefore, I am going to hang up now. I'll give you a few hours, so that you and Louise can make your decision. Then I'll call you back, and we will make the arrangements. Perhaps you should try to get a few hours' sleep. It'll clear the mind."

"My mind's clear. And I—"

"There are two things to remember. First, don't call the police, try to involve them. This goes without saying, especially since you would be in a very awkward position, trying to explain how you came into possession of a fortune that belongs to the Mafia. Don't you agree?"

Bernhardt made no response. Remarkably, standing close to the broken-out window, with a breeze blowing through the flat from the back door, he was unaffected by the gas. He put his hand over the phone, spoke to Tate: "Crusher's in the back bedroom, out cold. Carry him in here, where there's more air. See if you can help him get on his feet."

Tate blinked. "Crusher?"

Suddenly furious, another irrational cheap shot directed at Tate, he came back angrily: "Crusher, goddammit."

Tate shrugged, laid the shotgun on the desk. After making sure that Bernhardt was aware of the sawed-off lying there, Tate left the room. He moved smoothly, alertly, as if he were integral to the whole: a jungle predator, gliding through the forest. Yes, this was Tate's natural element: danger everywhere. Danger, and death.

On the phone, the voice was saying, "The other point is, don't try putting the jewels in a safe-deposit box, as you plan. That, I would consider a hostile act. Paula and Angela would suffer accordingly."

"You goddam—"

"I should make it clear before I hang up," the voice was saying, "that, whatever happens, I don't plan to kill the women. That would be counterproductive. However—"

"You son of a bitch, you'd—"

"However," the caller interrupted smoothly, "I'll certainly disfigure them. As you've guessed, I have an organization. Which is, in this case, fortunate. Because I myself would be incapable of, let us say, chopping off a finger or two, and perhaps cutting off a nose. But I can assure you that I have people who—"

Breathing hard, aware that he was trembling now, beginning to lose it, Bernhardt banged down the phone. Then, instantly, he realized that now he could not talk to Paula; he'd ruined his chances of talking to her. At the thought, he felt himself racked by a sudden sob.

They were still in darkness; the entire flat was dark. The front door was closed now, and bolted. But the back door was open for ventilation. Now, carrying Crusher, Tate appeared in the doorway of the office. The dog's head lolled, his legs flopped uselessly below Tate's arms. Tate held the dog tenderly, gently.

"There." Bernhardt pointed to the floor close to the windows. "Put him there. And open the other two windows. Leave the drapes drawn, though." As Tate obeyed, Bernhardt knelt beside Crusher. Was the dog still breathing? Yes: short, shallow breathing. Would there be brain damage, after being unconscious so long? Irrationally, Bernhardt wished he'd asked the caller how long ago they'd attacked. The vet would want to know.

"Put the desk lamp on," he ordered. When Tate obeyed, Bernhardt rolled back the dog's eyelid. It was a useless gesture; he had no idea how the pupil should look. He lifted the limp head an inch from the floor and let it fall as he watched for a reaction. Had there been a blink? He lifted the head again, let it thump down again.

Yes. Certainly it was a blink, an involuntary response to pain. Frantically, Bernhardt began slapping the dog on the head, the body, the rump. With every blow, there was a blink. And now, a miracle, there was a small whine, a protest. The Airedale's eyes fluttered, finally came open.

"*Hey,*" Bernhardt chortled. "Hey, it's okay. He'll be okay."

"Jesus." In mock despair, Tate shook his head. Repeating: "Jesus. Dog lovers. You—"

Struggling for self-control, choking on her sobs, Louise demanded, "What're we going to *do*? Who was it on the phone? What'd they say? What'd they want?"

Massaging the dog now, Bernhardt spoke over his shoulder: "They want the jewels. They've got Paula and Angela. And they want the jewels. Ransom, in other words."

"Chinese?" Tate asked. "Did you say Chinese?"

Looking down at Crusher, who sighed once, contentedly, and then closed his eyes again, Bernhardt nodded. "Chinese gangsters. I'm almost sure."

"So what'll we do?" Tate asked mildly. "What's the plan?"

"The plan," Bernhardt said, shifting his gaze to the satchel. "The plan is to find out what's in that canister."

3:15 A.M., PDT

"My God," Tate breathed, "there they are." An awed moment of somber silence passed. Then he murmured, "It's like getting religion, something like that. Only better."

They stood staring down at Bernhardt's desktop. The cut-open white plastic canister and the hacksaw Bernhardt had finally found in the basement lay together on one corner of the desk. Bernhardt's papers and memos and mail had been stacked on another corner. Countless multicolored facets of hundreds of gems reflected light from the desk lamp, a foot-long swath scattered across the center of the desk. A dozen-odd gold coins were mixed with the jewels.

"My God," Tate whispered again, his voice still hushed. "Look at that, would you?"

As if he were reacting to the tension that suddenly filled the room, Crusher lifted his head, blinked, tried to get to his feet. The forepaws were manageable, but the back legs were failing. With a sigh, the dog shook his head, let his front legs splay as he went back to sleep.

"My God," Louise echoed. "My God, look at them." Hesitantly, she stepped forward until, with timid fingertips, she touched the jewels, finally using a forefinger to describe a small furrow from one end of the swath to the other. Then, as if to give the others their turn, she politely stepped back.

"You'd better put them away," Tate said, "get them out of sight."

The words jolted Bernhardt back to reality, back to the terrible tyranny of the truth: the vision of Paula, a kidnap victim, held hostage by a smooth-talking Chinese who, most certainly, was capable of ordering her disfigured and then dumped out on the street, dazed and bleeding, marked for life—ruined for life.

Carrying the .357, with the .38 still thrust in his belt, Bernhardt strode quickly down the long, narrow hallway to the kitchen. He tested the strength of the chair that propped the back door closed. Then he opened an overhead cupboard and took out a brown paper sack and, an afterthought, a clear plastic grocer's bag. He would order Louise to put the jewels in the plastic bag, which they would slip into the brown paper bag. Then, together, they would decide on a place of concealment, a place Louise could keep constantly in sight.

4:20 A.M., PDT

"Louise . . ." Vehemently, Bernhardt shook his head. "*Forget it. I'm not going to call the police, just pick up the phone and call. Not until I've had a chance to talk to a friend of mine—a lieutenant, in Homicide."

"But—" She, too, was shaking her head, a blind denial of an impossible choice: a fortune that would keep her for life, in exchange for her only child, held hostage. "But we can't just do nothing. We can't—"

"We've got to assume," Bernhardt said, measuring every word for maximum impact, "that Mafia money bought that treasure. God knows, that's what the police'll assume. And the first thing that'll happen, believe me, is that the police'll confiscate the jewels. Then, sure as hell, while they're conducting their investigation, they'll pull my license. Then they'll—"

"If you won't go to the police, then I will. I've got nothing to hide. *Nothing.*"

"You might not have anything to hide," Tate said, "but you've sure as hell got lots to lose."

Louise turned to stare at the big black man who still stood guard at the windows of the office, shotgun ready. "I've got a lot to lose either way," she said bitterly. "Either I lose my daughter or I lose a million dollars."

Stoically, Tate refused to answer. Instead he looked away toward the street, slightly shrugging. For this kind of dilemma, these negotiations, Tate had no gift, no patience.

"If you want Angela back," Bernhardt said, "if that's all that matters, then you've got to give up the jewels. There's no other way."

Fixed on him, her eyes went blank, gave no indication that she'd heard.

"If that's what you want," he said, "then that's what we'll do." He let a beat pass, for emphasis. "We'll *do* it. They're going to call back, I don't know exactly when. But when they do call, I'll tell them we're ready to do business. It's up to you."

There was utter silence as both men watched the woman's face, searching for a sign. When her face remained expressionless, a frozen mask of despair, Tate spoke softly: "How about you fudge a little, Louise?" As he spoke he looked pointedly at the paper bag filled with treasure. Louise was sitting on one of Bernhardt's visitor's chairs. The paper bag was on the floor beside her chair.

Frowning, puzzled, Louise focused on the black man. Looking down at her, Tate smiled. It was a cheerful coconspirator's smile, Tate's particular gift. "You skim off a handful, give these bad guys what's left. You take a handful, give Alan a few diamonds, who's to know?"

For a moment, their eyes fixed on Tate, Bernhardt and Louise speculated in silence. Then Bernhardt said, "There might be another way." As he said it, he looked at his watch. The time was almost five o'clock.

"Another way?" Louise's voice was timid as she searched Bernhardt's face for some faint sign of hope.

Bernhardt spoke to Tate: "I'm sure this guy is Chinese. He practically admitted he was Chinese. And he spoke like an educated man. He's obviously got an organization, and it's odds-on he's based in San Francisco."

"Yeah . . ." Plainly, Tate was intrigued, his thoughts racing ahead. But then he frowned, shook his head. "Those Chinese guys, though, they play for keeps. They're smart, too. And they're tight. Very, very tight. Your skin is the wrong color, you don't get within miles of those guys. Which is why I never take a warrant on them. They just go to Chinatown, and they disappear. And nobody—*nobody*—can find them, not unless you're Chinese. Believe me." Tate shook his head. "Believe me, I know what I'm talking about."

"My point, though, is that there can't be many guys in the Chinese underworld who answer this guy's description. Maybe there's only one."

"Yeah, well—" Tate shrugged. "Well, okay, you know somebody on the Chinatown detail, I suppose you could come up with a short list of names. But then what? You might get a name, and maybe you even get an address. But then what'd we do? Blast our way in, rescue Paula and Angela?" Grimly smiling, Tate shook his head. "I don't think so."

"Still," Bernhardt mused, "if we had a name, that'd be a start."

"When's this guy going to call back?"

"I've no idea. He said he'd give us time. He even said I should get some sleep. I don't think he's going to rush it. I get the impression he thinks time is on his side."

Tate glanced at his watch. "Four more hours and the banks'll be open."

Grimly, Bernhardt shook his head. "No. If we do that—put the stuff in a safe-deposit box—then that's the end. They'd start cutting on Paula and Angela. He said if we—"

"They're watching us, aren't they? They're out there somewhere right now, aren't they?" Louise's voice was cowed, trembling on the ragged edge of hysteria. Wide-eyed, blinking spasmodically, she was staring at the drawn drapes. A breeze was blowing through the broken window: a ghostly hand behind the drapes.

When Bernhardt answered her, he spoke with grave deliberation, an attempt to steady her, force her to face facts. "They probably *are* out there, Louise. I'd be surprised if they weren't. I'd also be surprised if your place isn't bugged."

"But—" She frowned, a denial. "But one of us—either Angela or me—we've been home almost all the time, since Tony Bacardo came. No one could've gotten in to plant a bug."

"They don't have to get inside. All it takes is a little luck."

"But—but I thought it was Profaci. I thought—" Suddenly she sharply shook her head. "Fabrese. Whatever his name is, I thought he told them what we were doing. I thought they were in it together, Fabrese and this other one. The Chinese."

"They probably *were* in it together," Tate said. "Then, when the Chinese guy saw he didn't need Fabrese anymore, he killed him." He shrugged. "It's called trimming the overhead."

Louise fixed her stricken stare on Tate. Accusing him: "You act like this is a joke, the way you talk."

Tate made no reply, gave no sign that he'd heard. Instead, cradling the shotgun, he turned again toward the street, listening. From outside came the sound of an engine: a car, going down the hill. In the silence that followed, Bernhardt leaned back in his desk chair, let his eyes close. Instantly the images began: Paula, bound to a chair, with one arm free. They would be in a damp, musty brick basement in Chinatown. She would be seated beside a small wooden table. Overhead, a single bare light bulb hung from a cord cast a cone of light on Paula and the table, leaving the rest of the room in shadow. Now her tormentor—the man on the phone—stepped out of the shadows to stand close to the table, looking down on Paula. Then two other figures materialized out of the gloom: two men, both Chinese. One of the men held a hatchet. Impassively, he advanced on the helpless woman, grasped her free arm. He began—

"—got to give it to them," Louise was saying. "Angela—I can't risk it, having Angela hurt. I've got to give it to them."

Bernhardt looked at Tate, a long, searching moment. Then, in unison, both men turned to face Louise. Under their scrutiny, she drew herself up, squared her shoulders, brought her knees together, clasped her hands in her lap, lifted her chin a defiant half-inch. Saying again, firmly: "I've got to give it to them. Angela—I've got to do it for Angela. If they hurt her, ruin her looks, I could never live with myself. Angela's only twenty. She—she's got her whole life to live. She—" As if she were confused, Louise broke off, dropped her eyes, let herself go slack in the chair. Then, in a dull, defeated monotone, as if she were confessing to something shameful, she said, "All my life, I heard Carlo Venezzio. That's all I heard. But only in whispers. My father—" She said it as if it were an obscenity. "God, what is it, being a father? A couple of times a year, without even telling us he's coming, he drives up to the house in a Cadillac. He tells the driver and another guy riding in front to stay put. Then he gets out of the car, all smiles, carrying a goddam stuffed animal. Is that being a father? A million dollars' worth of jewels and gold stuffed into a sewer pipe—is that all there is?"

"Well," Tate said, "it all depends on where you're sitting, Louise. My neighborhood, where I grew up, they'd think they were in heaven, living your life."

Once more she stared at Tate, her face unreadable. Then, exhausted, she dropped her eyes. Muttering: "I've got to get some sleep. Whatever happens, I've got to get some sleep." She looked down at the paper sack, on the floor beside her chair. She seemed to study it for a moment. Then, as if she were deeply reluctant, she picked up the sack, folded it over, and rose to her feet. "I want to go to the bathroom," she said. "Then I've got to go to sleep."

"Sure." Bernhardt stepped out into the hallway, pointed out the bathroom and the guest room. "That's where Angela was sleeping when—" Angry with himself, he broke off, waited for her to use the bathroom. When she reentered the hallway he smiled, took her into the bedroom. The pattern of the blankets clearly showed where Angela had lain. Even though the bedroom window was closed, there was almost no odor of tear gas.

"Shall I open the window?" he asked. "For ventilation?" Then, reading her hesitation, he said, "There're stops, so it's impossible to open the window more than six inches at the top and bottom. Also, it's on an airshaft." When she nodded hesitantly, he opened the window, wished her well, and closed the door. He went into the office, stood for a moment looking down at Crusher, who still slept. Bernhardt bent down, lifted the dog in his arms as he spoke softly to Tate: "Let's go back to the dining room."

"Right." Tate switched off the light in the office, checked the chair jammed against the front door, and followed Bernhardt down the hallway. Once in the dining room, Bernhardt bent down again, put Crusher on his feet, tried to hold the dog steady, standing on all four paws. The dog sagged; his legs began to splay. His eyes were glazed, half open.

"Here." Tate put the sawed-off on the floor. "You hold him." He slapped the dog sharply—left side of the head, right side, left, right. Now he shook the dog's head sharply from side to side. The dog protested weakly, tried feebly to pull away.

"Do it again," Bernhardt said.

Two more slaps, and the dog's protest was stronger. His eyes were open, for the first time focused, no longer glazed.

"Okay." Tentatively, Bernhardt released his supporting embrace, first the dog's front legs, then the hind legs.

"*Hey.*" Tate said. "Lookee there—he's doing it, making it. Way to go, Crusher." Whereupon the dog sighed, let his eyes close as he settled to the floor, once more to sleep.

"He's going to be okay," Bernhardt said. "Don't you think so?" As he spoke, he went to the dining room door, closed it.

"Yeah," Tate answered, laconically nodding. "Yeah, I'd say he'll be all right."

The two men went to the dining room table. They sat side by side with the sawed-off on the table between them.

"So?" Tate spoke so softly that only Bernhardt could hear. "So now what? We lay back while Louise hands over a fortune? Is that it?"

"This guy's talking about disfigurement. And the way he says it—the feeling I get—that's what he'll do." He paused, his eyes locked with Tate's. Then: "If Louise wants to hand over the jewels, I'm not going to stop her."

"Yeah, well—" Tate drew a long, lugubrious breath. "Well, it's her call. Except that I still like the idea of us skimming off a little cream. Christ, it's not like there's any accountant looking over our shoulders."

"I'll see what she says."

"That lady . . ." Tate shook his head, a gesture that expressed both irony and futility—and, yes, a certain sadness, reflecting on the human condition. "When you think about it, she's in a pretty shitty corner. But she's got guts, seems like to me. She's—what?—stubborn, I guess I'd say." As he said it, Tate smiled, looked slyly at Bernhardt. "Like you. You're stubborn, too."

Bernhardt returned the smile. At five o'clock in the morning, he was too exhausted even to frame a properly modest response. Then, back to business: "Listen, C.B., you don't have to stay for the whole show. I mean, you're welcome—I'd *like* to have you stay. But I've got my thousand dollars' worth."

"When d'you figure this Chinese guy's going to call?"

"I've no idea. Sometime in the next few hours, certainly."

"You have to arrange a swap. That can get tricky."

"Maybe," Bernhardt answered. Then, tentatively, feeling his way: "Or maybe not. If I take this guy at his word, all I've got to do is deliver the brown paper sack, and then back off until he releases Paula and Angela."

"And that's it? The end? Seventy-five thousand for you and twenty-five for me—you're going to walk away from that?"

"We have to get the women back. Then let's see what happens."

Tate studied Bernhardt carefully before he said, "You've got an idea. I can see it in your face. I know that expression."

"Call it the germ of an idea."

"The cops?"

"No," Bernhardt said, impatiently shaking his head. "We've been *through* this, what'll happen if we call the cops."

"I wasn't saying *call* the cops. I was saying *talk* to the cops. Your buddy in Homicide, that's what I meant."

Yawning, Bernhardt looked at his watch. "Listen, C.B., I've

got to sleep." He gathered himself, rose to his feet. "If you want to stay, fine. Take my bed. I'll sleep on the couch in the living room."

"So it's not the cops. It's something else."

Bernhardt knelt, took Crusher in his arms again. Straightening, he shook his head. "No," he answered, "it's not the cops."

"Something else, then."

"No comment."

MONDAY, APRIL 23rd
8:25 A.M., PDT

When she was a little girl, her bed had been a place of refuge, her safe haven, her secret place. Pull the blankets over her head, remain very quiet, and the goblins would pass, slouching off toward another part of the forest. Whenever her parents had punished her, that rare occasion, her bed was her sanctuary of sobs. Even when she was in her early twenties, married to the wrong man for the wrong reasons, an emotional disaster, she'd found refuge in bed, burrowed down among the covers, sobbing as she tried to make herself even smaller than she felt as she listened to her husband, drunk, prowling the house beyond her bedroom door as he mouthed bits of obscene dialogue that, sometimes, she recognized in the screenplays he wrote, the low-budget thrillers that had made him rich.

The Scylla of childhood traumas and the Charybdis of a disastrous marriage . . .

And now, once more burrowed in a nest of blankets, terrified, her eyes closed, Paula listened.

Just as, last night, once she and Angela had gone to bed, she'd listened. She'd listened, and Crusher, lying on the floor at the foot of the bed, had also listened. Once, soon after she'd gone to bed, she'd heard Crusher growl. Frightened, she'd taken the revolver from the drawer of the nightstand. But then Crusher had subsided. Reassured, she put the revolver away, settled down, closed her eyes—finally drifted off to sleep. The time, she calculated later, must have been about eleven-thirty.

Then there'd been the sound of a crash, a confusion of breaking glass, of wood splintering, of hostile voices raised—Crusher barking, Angela screaming. Eyes streaming, blinded, nose and throat seared, choking, gagging, she'd groped desperately for the nightstand, the drawer, the revolver. But just as she found the revolver something struck her forearm, a numbing blow. Then she'd felt their hands: two men wearing gas masks, fugitives from a horror movie. They'd pinned her against the wall, one of them with his forearm jammed against her throat. The men had spoken in Chinese: short, indecipherable words. From the next room had come the other sounds: Angela, furiously swearing, other Chinese voices shouting her down, finally silencing her.

And, worst of all, she heard Crusher. The dog was whimpering, not barking. Her first coherent thought, irrationally, had been sorrow for Alan, when he found Crusher dead on the bedroom floor.

While, in the eddying clouds of yellowish gas, in darkness, the four men, all Chinese, went about their business.

Military precision was the catch-all cliché.

They'd even brought two raincoats and two pairs of oversize sneakers. She'd only been wearing panties, no bra, no nightgown. Roughly, they'd bundled her into the raincoat, told her to hurry as she buttoned the coat, then slipped her feet unwillingly into the shoes. During the time it had taken her to dress, that part of her mind still capable of lucid thought told her that, of its kind, this kidnapping was a model of precision.

Just as, now, the same still-rational segment of her mind was calculating the odds on her own mortality. The handicapper's conclusion: fifty-fifty that she would be dead by this time tomorrow.

Slowly, Paula let her eyes come open.

It was a tiny bedroom, barely large enough to accommodate a double bed, a dresser, two nightstands, and one small armchair.

A Chinese man sat in the armchair. He was a slightly built man, unhealthy looking. His hands were small, his neck was skinny. He wore a heavy wool sweater, corduroy trousers, and slightly soiled white running shoes. Cradled in his lap he held a large automatic pistol.

"You're awake. Are you all right? I was told to ask." His voice was bland, his eyes were expressionless.

I was told to ask . . .

Implying, perhaps, a criminal organization. Suggesting, therefore, that the odds on her living another day might have improved, however minutely. An organization might act more rationally.

"I have to use the bathroom."

"Ah." He nodded, rose, went to the closet. Yes, it was the same raincoat they'd given her last night. He took the coat from its hook, tossed it on the bed, returned to his chair, resumed his previous position. As she maneuvered into the coat without exposing her body to him, the inward image of an old soft-core porno film perversely materialized: *How to Undress in Front of Your Husband.*

8:40 A.M., PDT

When she opened the bathroom door and stepped out into the short hallway that led back to the bedroom, two men were waiting in the hallway. The newcomer, about forty, was also Chinese. He was dressed in designer jeans, beautifully burnished loafers, and a hundred-dollar Madras shirt. His black hair was expensively styled. He was smiling politely. He was unarmed.

"You're Paula."

Gathering the raincoat closer, she silently nodded. She was barefooted, and the uncarpeted hallway floor was uncomfortably cold. Slowly, she advanced on the two men, who stood opposite the door to the bedroom.

"I'd like to put my shoes on. And I'd like a comb."

As if he were puzzled, the newcomer frowned. "Did you look in the medicine cabinet?"

"Yes. There's no comb."

Chin hesitated. Then, tentatively: "You're welcome to use my comb." As if to confirm the offer, he touched the back pocket of his perfectly fitting jeans.

"No, thanks." With body language, she tried to express disdain.

"Well, then." With the air of someone reluctantly turning to business before the preliminaries had been properly concluded, Chin gestured for her to enter the small, sparsely furnished living room that opened off the hallway to the right. "Well, then, if you'll just go into the living room . . ." He gestured politely, then said something in Chinese to the other man, who went into the bedroom. Carrying the tennis shoes, he quickly reappeared. He gave the shoes to Chin, who was following Paula into the living room. Chin gestured her to a couch and gave her the shoes.

"This house is unoccupied," Chin said, "and the gas is turned off. That's why it's cold." Then, slightly raising his voice, he spoke again in Chinese. Moments later, followed by another Chinese man carrying a pistol, Angela appeared. Like Paula, she wore a raincoat and tennis shoes. Beneath the raincoat, Paula saw the hem of a nightgown. Did Angela feel more secure, wearing a nightgown beneath the coat?

As Angela sat beside her on the couch, Paula quickly surveyed the room, which was furnished with the nondescript couch, one mismatched armchair, and a glass-topped coffee table placed in front of the couch. Except for a wooden chopping board, a meat cleaver, and several neatly folded bath towels, the coffee table was bare. There was only one large picture window, completely covered by closely drawn venetian blinds. The oak floor was uncarpeted. There was a musty odor of emptiness: stale air and dust and disuse.

When Chin spoke again in Chinese, the two guards took up

positions standing against the wall. Each man stood impassively, arms crossed. Each man held an automatic pistol.

For a moment Chin stared thoughtfully at the two women. Then, as if he had ordered his thoughts and was about to make a boardroom presentation, he began to speak:

"About six hours ago—call it two-thirty—I talked to Mr. Bernhardt. You'll be glad to know that, yes, they found the jewels. Or, at least, I assume they found the jewels, since they didn't deny it. So—" Chin permitted himself a small, self-satisfied smile. "So that's the first problem solved. As things worked out, it was necessary to kill Jimmy Fabrese. There were many reasons, which I won't get into. However—" He turned his attention to Paula. "However, as matters now stand, taking it from the police point of view, it appears that Mr. Bernhardt killed a member of the Mafia in cold blood, so that he could get to the jewels—which, of course, belong to the Mafia. Mr. Tate and Mrs. Rabb, of course, would also have very serious problems. But the authorities would probably go after Bernhardt first, as the mastermind. They—"

"Alan wouldn't do that," Paula flared. "He's no killer."

Chin nodded. "I agree. And, in fact, it's true—he didn't kill Fabrese. But he'll have a difficult time proving it, I'm afraid. Fabrese was killed by a two-twenty-three bullet, two of them. The two-twenty-three-caliber cartridge is incredibly powerful. Bullets from that cartridge, at close range, go right through the body. So there would be no ballistics evidence to exonerate Mr. Bernhardt, because the chances of recovering the bullet are almost nonexistent. However—" He paused to refocus his thoughts. Then: "However, back to the treasure, which is now at Bernhardt's flat. As you know, the plan was to put the jewels in a safe-deposit box. The banks open in about a half hour. Of course, I have people watching Bernhardt's flat. They have orders to prevent either Bernhardt or Tate from reaching their cars, even if it means killing them in broad daylight on Vermont Street. Do you understand?" Chin directed the question at Paula.

"Have they been hurt?" Paula demanded. "Are they all right?"

"As long as they agree to turn over the jewels, they won't be harmed. But if they don't give me the treasure—well . . ." Pantomiming deep regret, Chin sighed, shrugged, spread his hands. "Well, you may as well know that if they refuse, then—" He gestured to the cleaver and the cutting board. "Then I've told them we'll use that to chop off some of your fingers. Three fingers on each hand, I think. And probably part of your nose, too. For the nose, we'll use a straight razor."

Slowly, desperately, Paula began to shake her head, the ultimate denial. "You're bluffing. You're trying to scare us." As, beside her, Angela began to softly sob.

"You would be making a serious mistake," Chin said, "if you believe that I'm bluffing. On the contrary, this is business. Strictly business. In exchange for the slight risk of being arrested, I stand to gain a million dollars or more. Those are once-in-a-lifetime odds. I'd never forgive myself if I didn't take the gamble."

"You've kidnapped us. That's the death penalty."

Chin chose not to reply.

12:05 P.M., EDT

When Bacardo had finished talking, Cella continued to walk with his customary deliberate stride. Cella wore a pearl-gray fedora, a dark blue cashmere topcoat, a white shirt, and a striped silk tie. Because his hands were clasped at the small of his back, his head was pitched forward as he walked. Two well-dressed bodyguards followed Bacardo and Cella at a distance of not more than twenty feet. At noon on a sparkling

April day, with trees greening and plants blooming, Central Park South was a festival of diversity: young, old, rich, poor, reflective, boisterous—and, yes, drugged-out or insane. Or both.

Just ahead, three black teenagers, two boys and a girl, were sprawled on a park bench.

"Have you got three fives?" Cella asked.

"I think so." Bacardo took out a sheaf of bills, riffled through them. "Yeah. Three fives."

Cella gestured to the teenagers. Bacardo nodded, made the deal, sat beside Cella on the bench as the three blacks pranced gleefully away. Cella folded his arms, leaned back, crossed his legs, adjusted his creases. Looking straight ahead, he spoke quietly, judiciously:

"It's good you told me about it, Tony. We never did much business together, the two of us. But I always liked the way you handled yourself. I always figured that without you, Don Carlo would never've gotten as far as he did."

Also staring straight ahead, Bacardo made no response. With his eyes he briefly followed two young women as they passed. Both women wore tight-fitting jeans that clung to buttocks and pelvis. At age sixty, Bacardo reflected, the spectacle was more provocative than he could remember from earlier years.

"What it comes down to," Cella said, "is whether she's entitled to that much money. Don Carlo's family—Maria and the kids, even though Maria's a pain in the ass—they're entitled, no question. But if we paid off every bastard kid our guys had—well—it just wouldn't work."

Watching the two women disappear behind a screen of pedestrians, Bacardo decided to make no reply. Cella, he'd decided, liked to work out problems as he talked.

"I remember Janice Frazer," Cella said. "God, she was something. That body—incredible. You remember?"

"Sure," Bacardo answered. "I remember."

"But she turned into a rummy, you say."

"Afraid so."

"And her child is forty years old." Incredulously, Cella shook his head.

Bacardo sighed. "Yeah, I know. Time gets away from you."

Cella sat silently for a moment, thoughtfully eyeing a horse-drawn carriage slowly making its way south on Fifth Avenue. The horse looked old and tired, plodding along with its head hung low. How old was the horse? Twenty? Older? Would the owner of the carriage work the horse until he dropped? Were there work rules for horses?

Finally Cella spoke: "So these jewels—are they dug up by now, or what?"

"I don't know. I was going to call the PI—Bernhardt. But then I thought I should talk to you first."

"You think, though, that they're dug up."

"I'm guessing, but I'd say yes. I mean, as far as I could see, everything checked out according to what Don Carlo said. So why should they wait?" Bacardo shrugged. "Get a shovel, dig up the stuff, put it someplace safe."

"Hmmm." Judiciously, Cella nodded. Then, quietly, he said, "What I don't understand, Tony, is why you didn't do the digging."

Expecting the question, Bacardo was prepared. "That's what I went out there to do. I mean, it was Don Carlo's dying wish, about those jewels. But then Louise said there was some-one on my tail." As he spoke, Bacardo turned to look directly at the other man, hopeful of making eye contact. But Cella still sat impassively, eyes straight ahead. Waiting.

Meaning that everything, then, had been said. Everything but the words that would decide it all—

—loser say his prayers.

"He told Louise his name was Profaci," Bacardo said. "And he said you sent him out to San Francisco."

Cella frowned. "Profaci? He said Profaci?"

Decisively Bacardo nodded. Repeating firmly, "Profaci."

"Huh . . ." It was a calculating monosyllable. Beneath a frown, Cella's pale eyes were narrowing.

"I figured the name was a fake," Bacardo said. "But just the fact that someone was out there dogging me, I figured I wanted to come back, talk to you."

"This guy—how'd Louise meet him?"

"He rang her doorbell. She said he weighed maybe a hundred sixty, maybe forty years old, lots of dark hair, narrow face, kind of pale. Good dresser. Rough talking, no manners."

Ruefully Cella smiled. "Like about twenty of our guys, give or take."

Bacardo considered, decided to say nothing. Once more, a make-or-break silence fell between them before Cella turned on the bench to finally face the other man squarely. Cella began speaking slowly, deliberately: "When you said you wanted to go out to the Coast, I have to tell you that I got a little jumpy. I mean, Carlo wasn't cold, and there you were, going off to the West Coast on personal business. You know what I'm saying?"

"Sure." Conscious of the relief he felt, finally with everything coming down on the table, Bacardo nodded deeply. "Sure. I'd feel the same way. Exactly."

"Which is why I asked Sal to go out there, to see some of our guys, see what they were thinking, with Don Carlo out of it. I figured that if you really were taking care of personal business, there wasn't any harm. You see what I'm saying."

"Sure." Once more, emphatically, Bacardo nodded. "Sure I see. Absolutely."

"So when you first said it, about this guy on your tail, I thought maybe it was Sal, free-lancing."

"No." Once more, decisively, Bacardo shook his head. "No, it didn't sound like Sal. I mean, forget about the description, this guy sounds like he's a weasel. And Sal's no weasel."

Cella smiled: his first smile since they'd gotten out of their cars and begun walking, almost an hour ago. "No, Sal's no weasel."

Bacardo nodded—and waited while Cella made his decision. Finally Cella said, "What I want you to do is find out who this Profaci really is. I mean, he's out there in California telling people I sent him." Grimly, Cella shook his head. "This is exactly the kind of thing I won't have. Do you understand what I'm saying, Tony?"

Bacardo nodded gravely. It was the first direct order he'd gotten from Cella, an important moment. "I understand. I'll get right on it. Immediately."

"Good." Benignly now, a change of pace, Cella smiled. Repeating: "Good. Keep me posted. You've got my personal number."

"Right."

"About this other thing, the stuff Don Carlo meant for Janice's girl, well, now that I've got the whole picture, no more guessing games, let's just see what happens out there. I mean, if the woman—Louise—if she and this Bernhardt can work things out, get the jewels with no help from us, then I don't see any problem, especially if all this stays between us, doesn't get around. You understand what I'm saying."

Bacardo's answer was solemn. "I understand."

"I mean, okay, Don Carlo was out of line, giving her that much. But on the other hand, Don Carlo was the most important *capo di tutti* ever. At least in terms of organization, the bottom line, he was a goddam genius. And the more I think about it, the more I think it wouldn't be smart for me to start off filling Don Carlo's shoes by going after his daughter."

Once more, Bacardo nodded. Adding: "His granddaughter, too."

"Yeah. Right."

Bacardo drew a long, grateful breath. "So it's okay, then. We're all square."

Cella nodded, smiled—offered his hand, the seal of agreement, all that was required. As he shook the other man's hand, Bacardo bowed his head slightly, the requisite obeisance. From this moment, he was Cella's man, a loyalist.

"I appreciate it, Don Benito. And from Don Carlo, too—thanks."

"Ah, ah." Still smiling, Cella lifted a playful forefinger. "Just 'Benito,' remember? Like this, just the two of us, it's 'Benito.' "

"Benito . . ." Tentatively.

"Benito." Decisively.

10 A.M., PDT

Bernhardt picked up the telephone on the second ring. "Alan Bernhardt."

"Mr. Bernhardt."

Yes, it was *his* voice: quiet-spoken, urbane, faintly accented, studied.

"Do you recognize my voice?"

"Yes," Bernhardt answered grimly. "I recognize you."

"Have you slept?"

"For an hour or two." As he said it, he glanced at his watch: exactly ten o'clock. They'd been in his office for more than an hour, their eyes fix-focused on his desk, on his telephone.

"Will you please tell me your situation?"

"My situation?"

"You and Mrs. Rabb and your black friend, are you all together there?"

"Yes. We're in my office, in the front of the house."

"And the jewels? Are they also there?"

"Yes."

"Are they what you expected?"

"It's not what I expect. It's what Mrs. Rabb expects. They're her property, not mine."

"You've discussed our conversation with Mrs. Rabb."

"Of course."

"And what have you decided?"

"We've decided to do what you want."

"Are you recording this?"

"No," Bernhardt lied. "I don't have a recorder that tapes off the telephone."

"I suspect that you do."

"Suspect what you like."

"In my business one assumes the worst, and plans accordingly. Therefore I must assume that you're recording this. I must also assume that you have plans to win this contest."

"My plan is to get Paula Brett back. Mrs. Rabb's plan is to get her daughter back."

"In exchange for the jewels."

"In exchange for the jewels."

"All the jewels?" The question was subtly tainted with ironic good humor.

Bernhardt decided to make no reply.

"I think of myself as a realist," Chin said. "I expect others to also act realistically. Therefore, I'm assuming that, before you turn the jewels over to me, you will have deducted, say, ten percent of the total. That is acceptable. In fact, to act otherwise would be stupid. And dealing with stupid people, I've found, is a losing proposition. I'm sure you agree."

Bernhardt made no reply. Across the desk, an earphone in one ear, Tate was monitoring the tape machine. As he listened, Tate's mouth up-curved in a small, knowing smile.

"So much for the, ah, commission arrangements," Chin said. "Let's go back to you and your black assistant and the plans you're most certainly making. You're obviously an astute man. Just as obviously, you're familiar with San Francisco, which is actually a very small town. Here, everyone knows everyone else. Therefore, after we transact our business, it might be possible for you to guess at my identity. You might decide to go to the police with your suspicions. With a recording of this conversation as evidence, plus Miss Brett and Miss Rabb, who could identify me, the DA might decide to indict. It's certainly a possibility. But before I went to trial, Mr. Bernhardt, assuming that you chose to stay in San Francisco—or for that matter, in this country—I can absolutely guarantee that you

would be dead long before the judge dropped the gavel."
There was a short silence as the tape continued to spin. Across
the desk, Tate's broad, muscle-ridged face was a study in concentration. The small, intrigued smile was still in place.

"Do you believe me?" Chin asked quietly.

This time, Bernhardt realized, a reply was required; the time
for silence had passed.

"Yes," he answered, "I believe you."

As, across the desk, Tate was nodding reluctant agreement.
Seated in a chair with the brown paper bag containing the jewels on the floor beside her, Louise stared wide-eyed at Bernhardt's face. Her posture was so rigid that her muscles might
have been in spasm. Her expression was numbed.

"Well, then." There was a new note of crispness in Chin's
voice. The actual negotiations were about to begin. "Shall we
make our plans?"

"Yes."

"Your car, I assume, is the brown Civic station wagon that
you used last night."

"Yes."

"It's now parked at the curb near your building."

"Yes."

"What I want," Chin said, "is for you to take the jewels to
your car. There's a homing device on your car. It has a magnet,
of course, and it's stuck to the front part of your gas tank, on
the driver's side. Do you understand?"

As Bernhardt answered in the affirmative, he saw Tate's face
come alive with aggrieved vexation. A homing device—accounting, of course, for the night's sequence of events, including the murder of Fabrese.

"I want you to put that homing device, with the jewels, in
whatever container you choose. Do you have a car phone?"

"Yes." Bernhardt gave him the number.

"Good. The time is now ten-fifteen. I'll give you a half hour
to take your ten percent. Are the stones unmounted?"

"Yes."

"But they're cut."

"Yes."

"Good. What I would suggest is that you dump them out on a flat surface and count them. Then, simply deduct ten percent of the total, numerically. I know a little about gems, and I can tell you that a random division is best. Size alone is not always the most important criterion. It's quality that really counts."

"I'll keep that in mind," Bernhardt said acidly. Tate smiled appreciatively.

"At ten forty-five," Chin went on, "I expect the three of you to be in your car. You can begin driving toward Golden Gate Park. Use any route you like. Of course, we'll be tracking you with our scanner. We'll give you directions as we go. Be very careful, obviously, not to break any traffic laws."

Bernhardt gritted his teeth. "Thank you."

"I'm told you have a sawed-off shotgun. I don't think you should bring that, since it's an illegal weapon. If you should be involved in an accident, and the police saw that gun, we'd all be in trouble."

"I'll think about it."

"Once you're inside Golden Gate Park," Chin said, "you'll be given instructions by phone. At some point, we'll tell you to put the jewels in a trash container. Then you'll be told to drive to a point about a mile from the trash container. You'll wait there until we have the jewels. If everything is satisfactory, you'll be told where you can find the two women. They're now in a small row house in the Outer Sunset district, not too far from the Rabbs', in fact. There'll be three keys under a small planter box to the right of the front door. One key opens the door. The other keys unlock two pairs of handcuffs. The women, you see, are in the basement. They're handcuffed to a large water pipe."

"They'd better not be hurt."

"They won't be. Incidentally, how's your dog?"

Bernhardt looked down at Crusher, lying in front of the room's small gas fireplace. "He'll be all right."

"Good. Well, there's lots to be done. Incidentally, if there's any communications problems, you're to go back to your office and wait for me to call you there. Understood?"

"Yes."

"Excellent." The line clicked, went dead.

10:32 A.M., PDT

With the curtains drawn in the office and the jewels strewn across the desktop in a multicolored swath, Bernhardt looked at Louise. "I make it two hundred sixty-three altogether," he said. "And twenty gold coins."

"So that's twenty-six jewels for us," she said, "and two gold coins."

Bernhardt nodded agreement, saying, "You make the division." He handed her the ruler they'd just used to separate the jewels for counting. "Then we'll—"

"Jesus," Tate blurted, "you want my opinion, you're both crazy. My God, take a goddam *handful*, why don't you? Who the fuck's to *know*?" As he spoke, his eyes were fixed on the treasure. In that moment Bernhardt saw an indefinable nakedness in Tate's face, something elemental, therefore arresting. Just as, in his own face, he could feel the tug of a companion expression. Here—now—life had suddenly come down to its elemental parts, no longer a civilized whole.

"No," Louise answered, for the first time speaking calmly, firmly, finally in control of herself. "No, we're not going to do that." As, methodically, she began to count. Her lips, Bernhardt noticed, were moving.

12:12 P.M., PDT

"I have to tell you," Tate said, "I find this amazing. I mean, shit, we've just dropped a fortune in jewels in a goddam trash can. And here we are—" Sitting in the front passenger seat of the Honda, Tate swept the surrounding greenery of Golden Gate Park with a muscular arm. The gesture exposed the big nine-millimeter automatic in its shoulder holster slung beneath his right arm. An identical gun, Bernhardt knew, was slung under his left arm. "Here we are, hoping that this goddam Chinaman is going to give us a—"

The telephone mounted between the seats beeped.

"Yes?"

"We have the goods," Chin said. "No problem. Are you ready to copy the information I have for you?"

Bernhardt took his ballpoint pen and notebook from his pocket. "Go ahead."

"The address is twenty-four-twenty Noriega. Do you remember my instructions concerning the keys?"

"Of course."

"Well, then, our business is concluded. Perhaps, Mr. Bernhardt, we can do business again. In my line of work, it's not practical to advertise. But I think you'd be impressed. Meanwhile, though, I'll sign off."

Bernhardt slammed down the telephone, twisted the key in the ignition, started the engine. In minutes he would see Paula, touch her, hold her close.

12:35 P.M., PDT

With Tate beside him, Bernhardt turned onto the 2300 block of Noriega and saw a cluster of girls on the sidewalk. The girls wore matching red sweaters, white blouses, and plaid skirts, uniforms of a Catholic girls' school. Across the street, a Chinese woman wheeled two babies in a double stroller. Farther down the block, in a driveway, two men wearing grease-stained T-shirts were working on a vintage car. Beneath the raised hood, both men leaned far into the engine compartment. It was a typical April afternoon in the Sunset District, where endless blocks of small segmented row houses rose and fell with the terrain that had once been a vast expanse of sand dunes.

In the next block, in a house like all these others, Paula and Angela were shackled to a water pipe.

"Pretty benign," Tate said. "So far."

In the 2400 block now, Bernhardt slowed the Honda, began checking house numbers. Yes, there across the street: 2420. It was a small stucco house painted pink with white trim. The architecture was fake Spanish, suggested by a few terra-cotta roof tiles and hand-hewn beams tacked to the stucco facade. The single large picture window was covered by white venetian blinds. A few neglected plants were dying in the barren ground of a small front garden. Like most San Francisco houses, it was built on a narrow twenty-five-foot lot over a ground-floor garage. The overhead garage door had three small windows, all frosted. A few circulars littered the narrow concrete steps that led up to the front door. The tightly drawn blinds, scruffy garden, and yellowing circulars all suggested disuse.

Bernhardt parked the Honda so that it blocked the driveway. He switched off the engine, set the brake, turned to look at the house. Tate, too, was silently staring, both of them alert for signs of life from inside.

Bernhardt spoke in a low voice: "I feel like I don't want to go in." It was an admission of the ennui that had overtaken him, left him incapable of rousing himself to act. He could only struggle helplessly with the monstrous horror bursting in his imagination: Paula, shackled to the water pipe, eyes wide and empty, lying in her own blood. Dead.

"Yeah . . ." Tate nodded reflectively, an unexpected expression of rough-cut sympathy. "Yeah, I guess I know what you mean. Still . . ." He tripped the door handle, then waited for Bernhardt, moving woodenly now, to do the same. "Still, we came here to wind it up. So let's get about it."

Obediently, Bernhardt got out of the car, went around to join Tate, who stood on the sidewalk looking at the house. Then, in unison, both men scanned their surroundings: middle-class San Francisco on an amiable, secure Monday afternoon. Except for three small children playing on the sidewalk nearby, there were no Chinese to be seen. Carefully, both men verified that, of the dozen-odd cars parked at the curb of the 2400 block of Noriega, none were occupied. Only one car was in motion: an orange pickup driven by an overweight Caucasian male.

"Okay." Bernhardt drew a last long, tremulous breath. "Okay, here we go." He stepped forward, mounted the front stairs. Yes, there was the small rectangular planter on the porch railing that the voice on the phone had described. Like the shrubs and flowers in the front garden, the plant in the green pot was dying. With Tate beside him, a two-man crowd on the small porch, Bernhardt lifted the ceramic container, set it aside—

—and, yes, saw the keys: one door key, two small handcuff keys.

Was he offering up a small prayer of thanksgiving? Addressed to which deity?

Was there, after all, a beneficent God?

Soon—in minutes—he would know.

He handed the two handcuff keys to Tate, who carefully pocketed them, then stepped back. It was a deferential withdrawal, as if he'd just viewed a body lying in state, and was now stepping respectfully back.

Aware that his hand was trembling, Bernhardt managed to fit the key to the lock. He turned the key until the latch clicked. Then, slowly, he pushed the door open. He pocketed the key, opened the door wide, drew the .357. With Tate close behind, he stepped into a small, pastel-painted entryway. Had there been a sound from the garage below? Could there still be guards in the house, a failure of communication after the jewels had been handed over?

Bernhardt moved into a small living room as Tate swung the door closed behind them. The house had a shut-up, musty odor. Except for two chromium-plated kitchen chairs, a small coffee table with towels spread across it, and a threadbare couch, probably left behind by the previous tenant, the living room was unfurnished. The small Spanish-style fireplace was littered with refuse. The floor was bare, badly scratched and spotted. Bernhardt stood motionless in the middle of the room, listening. Standing beside him, Tate also stood motionless, staring into the hallway that led back to the rear of the house.

Bernhardt spoke in a whisper: "Let's—"

"*Shhh.*" Holding a Browning automatic in his right hand, Tate raised his left, a warning. Then, silently, he inclined his head, his gaze fixed on the floor just ahead. The message: he'd heard something. But when Bernhardt listened, he heard nothing. Now Tate frowned, shrugged. Whatever sound he'd heard, the house was silent now.

"Did you bolt the front door?" Bernhardt whispered.

Frowning, Tate nodded abruptly. The message: of course he'd bolted the door.

Nodding in return, holding the .357 ready, Bernhardt advanced slowly, soundlessly into the hallway. There were four doors. One of the doors, Bernhardt knew, led down to the basement and garage, at street level. The first door on the left, opening out, was a closet. Bernhardt grimaced to himself. Of course, the basement door would open inward, not outward.

Holding his breath, he pushed open the second door—

—and saw the flight of rough wooden stairs leading down.

He looked back at Tate, who nodded. Yes, Tate was ready. As always, Tate was ready.

Slowly, step by step, Bernhardt was descending the stairs. Whoever was down there would see his feet and legs before he saw them.

One step—two—three. If they were there, handcuffed, they would—

A thump. Another thump. An incoherent voice, muffled.

Paula.

Four more steps down and he was in the basement. The garage was in the front of the house, the utility area in the rear. Paula and Angela sat close together on the concrete floor. They were handcuffed separately around a drain pipe that served two laundry sinks. Incongruously, both women wore identical raincoats and cheap white tennis shoes that looked new. Both were gagged with wide strips of adhesive tape. Above the tape, Paula's eyes were enormous.

Without words, choking incoherently on his own rage, Bernhardt holstered the .357, dropped to his knees beside Paula, cradled her head close, an awkward embrace. Her eyes were streaming. "Goddammit," Bernhardt muttered. "Goddam them." He felt Tate's hand on his shoulder.

"Here." In his big outstretched palm, Tate offered the two handcuff keys. Bernhardt took one, grasped Paula's handcuffs, turned them to expose the keyhole. Yes, the key fitted. A moment later she was free. On their knees, they were hugging each other fiercely, she mute, choking and sobbing, Bernhardt suddenly laughing half-hysterically. Beside them, also on his knees, Tate was freeing Angela. Now, still laughing incoherently, Bernhardt touched the adhesive tape covering Paula's mouth. "You want me to do it? Or do you?"

Her response was a nod to him, signifying that he should tear the tape off. He pulled her to her feet, steadied her for a moment, drew a deep breath.

"Okay—here goes." With his fingernails, he lifted the edge of the topmost strip, waited a moment, then ripped it free.

Suddenly a childhood scene came back: his mother, ripping adhesive tape off for him, so many years ago. *Ouch time*, she'd called it.

Now he was working at the second strip, ripping it away. Awkwardly, with fingers still stiff from the handcuffs, Paula took a handkerchief from her mouth, threw it from her. Then, crying and laughing, she was kissing him. Never had he held her so close.

2 P.M., PDT

Sitting beside Bernhardt in the bank's small customer lounge, Tate chuckled. "I get the feeling we're under surveillance." As he spoke, he winked at the video monitor.

Bernhardt smiled faintly, looked Tate over critically. "Not surprising. We both need shaves. Not to mention showers and clean clothes."

"And sleep, too. Don't forget sleep."

"How could I forget sleep? Christ, I'm out on my feet."

"How's Paula doing?"

"She'll be all right. She's at her place, sleeping."

"Has she still got that gun?"

Bernhardt nodded. "Yes."

"That's a very gutsy lady. A lot gutsier than she looks."

"I know . . ."

"What'd about Crusher?" Tate asked. "What'd the vet say?"

"They'll keep him for a couple of days. His lungs're congested, but they say he'll be all right."

"Ah . . . good."

Bernhardt yawned, settled himself in his chair, considered closing his eyes. It had been fifteen minutes since Louise and Angela had been buzzed back into the bank's vault. They'd carried their jewels in Louise's purse.

"When they make a TV movie of my life," Tate said, "this goddam caper will take top billing. I mean, just think—a fortune buried up in the goddam swamps by a Mafia kingpin. A guy's killed, for reasons that still aren't clear since the murderer obliges us by disappearing in the goddam mist with his killer rifle. So, surprise, we dig it up, a fortune in jewels. But then, slips, a Chinese hoodlum who's apparently an electronics freak—and who probably offed Profaci or Fabrese or whatever the name was—kidnaps Paula and Angela after he takes out Crusher. And when all the smoke settles, pardon the expression, and nobody gets disfigured, what'd you end up with?" Despairingly, Tate shook his head. "You end up with two diamonds and one ruby and one gold coin. We latch on to—what?—two hundred and sixty-three jewels and twenty gold coins, whatever the count was, all spread out on your desk like we were little kids showing off the loot we got on Halloween, trick or treating. So now, sitting here, your end of the action wouldn't even cover your thumbnail."

"You're forgetting five thousand dollars. One thousand of which went to you."

"Plus twenty-five percent of what those three jewels and that gold piece bring, let's not forget that."

"You want to divvy up now?" Bernhardt asked, an amiable challenge. "I'll give you whichever stone you want. You'll be getting a third, not a quarter. So I'll keep whatever the gold coin brings. What d'you say?"

"You mean now? Settle up right now?" Taken by surprise, Tate reflexively surveyed the interior of the bank, a bastion of privilege. "Here?"

"Why not here?"

"Jesus, Alan, you're a real player, aren't you?"

"What d'you say?"

"I don't know shit about jewels."

Bernhardt smiled at Tate's discomfort. "I don't know shit either. So what d'you say? One way, you have to wait for me to sell them to get your cut. This way, it's all settled."

Responding to the challenge, Tate matched Bernhardt's smile. "What the hell? Let's do it."

Bernhardt took the double-folded envelope from his shirt pocket. Carefully, he emptied out the three gems, two diamonds and one ruby. "Here." Cupped in his palm, he held out the gems. Gingerly, Tate took them in his own hand.

"Jesus . . ." Now bemusement twisted Tate's smile. "Jesus, we're playing blindfolded here." Then, frowning: "I read somewhere that, carat for carat, a good ruby's worth more than a good diamond."

"Then take the ruby." As he said it, Bernhardt saw Louise and Angela emerging from the vault. "Hurry up. Here they come."

"Ah, shit." Recovering his habitual nonchalance, Tate casually plucked a diamond and a ruby from his palm, passed them to Bernhardt. "Diamonds are forever, right?"

"So we're square, then." Bernhardt returned the two remaining gems to the envelope, then to his pocket.

Tate nodded. "Square." Carefully, he began folding his own diamond inside a parking citation he discovered in an inside pocket. Then, as he watched Louise and Angela coming slowly toward them, he asked, "So is this the end? Case closed?"

Also looking at the two women, Bernhardt answered with coldly measured precision, "No, it isn't the end. This case is still open."

"Ah . . ." Quizzically, Tate studied the other man's face. Yes, he'd seen Bernhardt look like this before. Bernhardt wasn't especially street savvy, and he'd never pretended to be very tough. But Bernhardt was determined. When Bernhardt looked like he looked now, someone was going to pay.

"So," Tate said, probing. "So you going to need me, or what?"

"I don't know," Bernhardt answered, his eyes going reflectively into far focus.

"You—ah—you want to be careful with these Chinese guys.

They got their own style, you know. They blow somebody away, they never even change expression."

Rising to his feet as Louise and Angela came closer, Bernhardt made no reply.

5 P.M., PDT

Bernhardt eased the door of her apartment open, stepped inside, softly closed the door, and bolted it. He went to the small living room, then stood motionless, listening. It was a small apartment, only one bedroom, a bath, a large living room with a dining table at one end, and a small kitchen that opened on a counter. The building had originally been a Victorian mansion, in later years divided into four apartments. The coved ceilings were high, the woodwork was intricately carved, the fireplace was framed and mantled in marble. Two of the windows in the living room were curved glass, with stained glass at the top. Paula came from a life of privilege. An only child, both her parents were college professors; her father was a nationally recognized economist. The furnishings she'd chosen for the apartment reflected her background: impeccably restrained taste, a good eye for proportion—and money in the bank.

"Alan . . . ?" From behind the half-open bedroom door, her voice was blurred by sleep. Or was it exhaustion?

"Yes." He went to the bedroom door, pushed it open. She lay on the far side of the double bed, her knees drawn up. She was facing him. Her hands on the counterpane were tightly clenched. Her brown hair was tousled. In her pale, drawn face the dark eyes were abnormally large: waif's eyes. Without speaking, he sat on the bed, stroked her hair back from her forehead. The time was five o'clock. After he'd taken Louise and Angela to their home, the end of his responsibility, he'd brought Paula here, to her own place. He'd waited while she'd taken a long, hot shower and got into bed. She'd taken an over-the-counter sleeping pill. When they'd gotten into bed together and he'd held her close, he'd whispered the same endearments a parent would whisper to a child, trying to make the memory of something terrible go away. Before she finally went to sleep in his arms, he'd whispered that he would have to leave her for a few minutes, once she'd fallen to sleep. In reply, she'd murmured something unintelligible.

"How'd you sleep?"

She tried to smile: a small, wan, wistful attempt that quickly faded. "I'm not sure I *did* sleep."

"Did you hear me go out?"

"No."

"Then you slept."

"What time is it?"

"A little after five."

"Can you stay here tonight?"

"Sure. Of course." Once more stroking her hair, smiling into her eyes, he swung his legs up on the bed to lie beside her, on top of the bed clothing.

"How's Crusher?" she asked.

"He'll be all right. He's at the vet's for at least tonight."

"Poor Crusher. He's the only one who was really hurt."

"I'm glad to hear you say it."

She tried another smile as her eyes began to close.

"Listen," he said, "I've got to go out again in a few minutes. There's a call I have to take."

Her eyes came heavily open. "Can't you take it here?"

"No. But I've just got to go around the corner. Then I'll be right back." As he spoke, he glanced at his watch. In sixteen minutes, exactly, he must be ready to take the call.

Watching him, her eyes came into sharper focus. She began to frown, an expression of suspicion. "Alan . . ." She let the rest go meaningfully unsaid. Signifying that she suspected why he must leave her.

"Before I go—" It was a tentative, elusive beginning. "I want to ask you about the Chinese guy who did the talking. Can you describe him?"

"Alan, for God's sake, don't go after them. You—my God— you and C.B., you wouldn't stand a chance against this man. It—it's creepy, how much power he projects, how much evil. He never raises his voice, but everything he says is menacing. And he's got an organization. Last night, it was like a military operation."

"How old is he?"

"Thirty-five to forty-five, I'd say." Then, as he'd taught her, she recited the rest of it: "A handsome man, very urbane. Medium build, probably a hundred sixty, no more. Good dresser. Very intelligent. And very vain, I think."

"He's got to be the one I talked to on the phone. If I had to pick one word, 'urbane' would be it. Smooth talking, never raises his voice, even when—" About to repeat what the voice on the phone had threatened, he broke off.

But in a low, hushed voice, she finished it: "Even when he was threatening to cut off my fingers, he never raised his voice. Is that what you were going to say, Alan?" As she spoke, the terror remembered returned in a rush, once more haunting the shadows deep in her eyes. But then, just as quickly, her eyes cleared. She set her small jaw, drew a deep breath, then spoke fervently, furiously: "The bastard. The goddam smooth-talking bastard."

He smiled. On the road back, Paula had made the first turn. *The lady's got guts,* Tate had said.

Yes, the lady did indeed have guts.

Bernhardt moved close, kissed her once, hard. Then, exclaiming as he looked at his watch, he rolled off the bed. "I'll lock the door. Back soon—a half hour, no more."

"Alan . . ."

"Gotta go." He waved, strode quickly to the door.

5:50 P.M., PDT

"So what you're telling me," Bacardo was saying, "is that Fabrese was putting the arm on Louise, to try and get to the jewels. So when you got the jewels, dug them up, Fabrese was following you, going to hijack the jewels. He called himself Profaci. Is that what you're telling me?"

"He was definitely following us," Bernhardt answered. "And Louise is sure about the alias." As he said it, he saw two teenage boys walking purposefully toward the phone booth. Bernhardt turned his back on them, spoke into the phone: "What he intended to do, that's supposition."

"And this Chinaman took Fabrese off your back. Then the Chinaman just walked away."

"I assume it was the Chinaman that killed Fabrese. But we didn't actually *see* him at the graveyard."

"The treasure," Bacardo said. "How was it packaged?"

"It was in a white plastic sewer pipe. About a foot long, sealed on the ends. Maybe five inches in diameter."

"How'd you get it open?"

"We used a hacksaw." As he said it, Bernhardt realized that he was being tested. The conclusion: Bacardo had handled the treasure, and probably assembled the jewels, and sealed them in the canister. Meaning that, probably, Bacardo had taken a count of the jewels.

And, yes, Bacardo's next question was the proof: "What was in the container? What kind of jewels? How many?"

"There were two hundred sixty-three jewels. They were all cut, but they weren't mounted. And twenty gold coins."

"So Louise took twenty-six jewels and two coins, you say. And she gave the rest to this goddam Chinaman. All because of threats he made on the phone." It was a flat statement of fact heavily laden with contempt.

Bernhardt made no response.

"You *let* her hand everything over."

"They were going to chop off her daughter's fingers, for God's sake. And Paula—the woman I happen to be in love with—they were going to do the same to her. Chop off their fingers, and cut off their noses, too."

"So you just rolled over, you and this nigger you hired. You let this Chinaman get away with a goddam fortune. You put three jewels in your pocket, like it was some kind of a tip, and you—"

"Listen, Tony." Bernhardt drew a deep, tight breath. "The way this Chinese guy operates, I wasn't going to take chances. And neither was Louise. Okay, so she lost a fortune in ill-gotten gains. She can still—"

"What's this 'ill-gotten gains' shit? What's that supposed to mean?"

"You know what it means. It means hot money. It means we can't call the police. It means that—"

"What you don't seem to get," Bacardo cut in, "is that this fucking Chinaman has made fools of us. I don't know what game Fabrese was playing. I've got my suspicions, knowing Fabrese. But whatever game it was, we'd've taken care of it. Us. Not some goddam Chinaman. So this Chinaman is way over the line. He's whacked one of our people. And then, for Christ's sake, he hijacked a fortune that belongs to the daughter of a don. He's—"

Furiously, Bacardo broke off. Then, ominously quiet: "He's making us look terrible out there on the Coast. And that's not going to happen, Bernhardt. You got that?"

Bernhardt made no reply. Suddenly he realized that the Mafia, like every successful enterprise, was acutely conscious of its image. He smiled to himself at the wayward thought. While, outside the phone booth, two women had joined the teenage boys. All four were frowning. Bernhardt shrugged, pointed to the phone, pretended to frown with helpless vexation because of something he was hearing on the phone.

"—positive about all this?" Bacardo was asking.

"I'm not sure what you mean."

"What I mean is, after we hang up, I'm going to make some

calls. I'm sure—absolutely sure—that we aren't going to roll over on this. I mean, something like this—nobody does this to us. The first thing I did today—I got back in town last night—I laid all this out with my boss. Everything. That's what I came back here for, to get square with the boss. You *know* that. And we're square, him and me. He said it was okay about Louise and the stuff. Which means—" For emphasis, solemnly, Bacardo paused. Then: "Which means that what's happened is that this Chinaman has rubbed my boss's nose in this. You understand what I'm saying?"

As Bernhardt heard the words he felt it begin: a sense of danger, an awareness that the chain of events was inexorably tightening around him. Around him, and Paula, too.

"What I'm telling you," Bacardo was saying softly, "is that you'd better be ready to back all this up."

"Everything I said is true." Bernhardt was satisfied with his voice: calm, measured, firm.

"And your girlfriend. She knows what this Chinaman looks like. Is that right?"

"That's right. But I don't want her—"

"When did you give the stuff to this Chinaman? What time?"

"It was about one o'clock this afternoon. Our time."

"And—" A pause, to calculate. "And it's a little before six out there."

"Right."

"Okay." Another pause. "I've got to make those calls. Something like this, we can't waste any time. Tomorrow at this time, the stuff could already be fenced. You understand?"

"Yes. But—"

"Have you ever heard of Charlie Ricca?"

Charlie Ricca, the Mafia's man in San Francisco. Handsome, ostensibly affable, a stereotypical glad-hander. Natty dresser, full head of iron-gray hair, sparkling blue eyes, big grin. Charlie Ricca, mobster, always seen at the head of his entourage.

"Yes." It was a cautious monosyllable. "I've heard of Ricca."

"Okay. Tonight, you be where we can call you. And your girlfriend, too. Both of you."

"Listen, Tony, she's in no shape to—"

"Give me a phone number for tonight."

"Well, Jesus, it's—" Helplessly, he gave him Paula's number.

"Is that your office?"

"No—Christ—I already told you, I'm staying with—"

"Okay. I've got to get off. Remember, it's Charlie Ricca. Got it?"

"Yes, I've got it."

"All right." The line clicked, went dead.

8:30 P.M., PDT

"Is it the money, Alan? Is that it?" In the question, there was an unmistakable undertone of accusation. Paula had spent last night in the anteroom of hell. She couldn't bear the thought of returning, risking the same terrible trauma.

"It's—" He shook his head doggedly. Then, earnestly: "It's everything. Sure, some of it's the money. Seventy-five, a hundred thousand dollars—I'd be a hypocrite if I denied it. But, Jesus, this guy should be punished for what he did to you and Angela."

"The police punish criminals, Alan. Law enforcement. Not private detectives."

"This whole thing, right from the beginning, has been outside the law," he answered. "I've always known that. *You've* always known that."

"But it's Louise's decision, if she wants them punished. Not yours."

"Yeah, well . . ." He sighed heavily, regretfully shook his

head. "Well, the truth is, it seems to be the Mafia's decision now. Apparently the head man—Benito Cella, I guess—has decreed that Louise can have the jewels, no problem. So when these Chinese gangsters copped the jewels, that's now seen as a challenge to the Mafia. Plus, a Mafia soldier was murdered, never mind that he was probably playing a double game. It's—" Bernhardt gestured, threw the ethics question up for grabs. "It's like these goddam spy novels. Nothing's what it seems."

They sat at either end of Paula's living room couch, each twisted to face the other. Paula's legs were tucked up beneath her robe. There were dark smudges of fatigue under her eyes and tension lines around her mouth. Her voice was roughened with fatigue. Both of them, Bernhardt knew, were exhausted. And, worse, they were in disagreement. Perhaps serious disagreement. Would this be their first fight?

Finally Paula spoke: "It's the money you took from Bacardo. That's when it all started, for you."

"That's not really true. It started when Angela called. And I distinctly remember that you—"

Paula's door buzzer sounded. Bernhardt's eyes flew to the door; yes, the dead bolt was in place.

"Don't answer it," Paula whispered. Also fixed on the door, her eyes were wide.

"Paula, I've got to answer it. I don't have a choice."

"It's them. The Mafia." They were standing now, both of them facing the door.

He stepped close, touched her arm. "Go into the bedroom. Let me talk to them."

"I'll go into the bedroom—to get dressed." She turned away, strode purposefully into the bedroom. Beneath the white terrycloth robe, the movement of her body, taut with indignation, was incredibly provocative.

Once more the buzzer sounded. Longer. More insistently. *Was* it the Mafia? He'd given Bacardo Paula's phone number, not her address.

"Just a minute." He went to the coatrack, slipped on the

light poplin jacket that would conceal the .357 still holstered at his belt. As he went to the door he checked the time: 8:40. A little more than two hours had elapsed since he'd talked to Bacardo.

"Who is it?"

"It's Charlie Ricca." The voice sounded casually matter-of-fact: a neighbor, come to visit.

"Just a minute." Bernhardt retracted the dead bolt, released the lock. He drew a long, deep breath. Then, with the .357 loose in the spring holster, he turned the knob, opened the door.

Yes, it was Charlie Ricca. The tabloid image was definitive: the pink-jowled face glowing with health, the jovial blue eyes snapping, the thick gray hair meticulously styled with a Hollywood flair—and the affable, photogenic smile. Only the clothing was unfamiliar. Instead of a thousand-dollar suit and a hundred-dollar tie, Ricca wore a designer leather jacket, cavalry twill trousers, and beautifully burnished ankle-high desert boots. The two men standing behind him also wore leather jackets.

"Mr. Bernhardt? Alan Bernhardt?" As he spoke, Ricca extended a thick, muscular hand. "Charlie Ricca." As they shook hands he said, "You're expecting us. Right?"

"Yes . . . right." Bernhardt stepped back, gestured the three men inside. In the small, delicately furnished living room, the three men in their bulky leather jackets projected an aura of impassive power. Ricca was a short man, thickly built. The other two men were bigger and taller. The three men together evoked an aura from a bygone era: two impassive, stone-eyed Nazi storm troopers and their quick-witted, personable officer.

"This is Jimmy." Ricca gestured to one of the men, who nodded and smiled. Incongruously, Jimmy's smile and his lowered eyes suggested a certain shyness.

"And this is Al." Unsmiling, the other man nodded once, then looked away.

"Would you—" Bernhardt cleared his throat, began again: "Would you like to sit down?"

Ricca looked at his watch, then nodded. He took the room's most comfortable armchair, gesturing the other two men to the sofa. Bernhardt sat facing Ricca, who crossed his legs, adjusted his trouser creases, and smiled at him. Beneath his leather jacket Ricca wore a western shirt with pearl buttons.

"So you're a private eye." The remark was an expression of both amusement and easygoing condescension. It was the same mix of reactions that Bernhardt often got from the police.

When Bernhardt chose not to reply, Ricca shrugged, saying, "Well, Tony Bacardo seems to think you're all right. That's good enough for me."

Using as much acting skill as he could muster to lace the single word with irony, Bernhardt said, "Thanks." As, suddenly, a flash of insight illuminated the incongruity of the scene: a photogenic mobster, two dead-eyed thugs, and himself seated in Paula's bandbox Victorian living room, making small talk. How had it happened?

There was, of course, a one-word answer: money. And the companion word: greed.

"Tony said a woman saw the guy," Ricca said. "So is this her place?" As he spoke he looked at the closed bedroom door.

Bernhardt nodded. "This is her place. She's getting dressed. Last night she was teargassed and kidnapped. Then she was handcuffed to a goddam water pipe, she and Angela. So I don't want her to—"

"Who's Angela?" Ricca interrupted abruptly.

"Angela Rabb." He paused. Then, low-keyed, for maximum impact: "Carlo Venezzio's granddaughter."

"Ah . . ." Ricca nodded thoughtfully. "Yeah, I see."

Watching the other man's reaction, Bernhardt realized that, yes, Carlo Venezzio's reach extended beyond the grave. Every discipline had its pantheon of deities.

"So can both of them, the women, identify this Chinaman?"

"Yes. But—"

The door to the bedroom opened. Paula was dressed in a sweater, jeans, and slippers. She hadn't bothered with makeup. Ignoring the other two men, Bernhardt introduced her to Ricca, who rose to his feet, politely offered his chair. Coldly, she declined. Bernhardt began again: "But I don't want Paula to get involved in whatever you're going to—"

"Hey, no problem." Smiling, Ricca reached in a side pocket, produced a photograph, handed it to Paula. "Is that the guy?"

She hardly glanced at the photo before she nodded. "Yes— that's him." Her voice was wan, but her eyes were dark with hatred. On his feet, Bernhardt took the photo from her. It was a grainy telephoto shot of a Chinese man standing with his arms folded. He was leaning against a sports car, staring off into the distance. He was slightly frowning, as if he were impatiently waiting for someone. Yes, the man in the photo fitted Paula's earlier description: regular features, medium build, well dressed, seemingly suave and self-confident.

"Who is he?" Bernhardt asked.

"His name is Brian Chin," Ricca answered. "He came over here from Hong Kong maybe eight years ago, something like that. He's kind of a free-lancer, does a little drugs, a little loan-sharking. The old Chinese guys, the regular families, they don't have anything to do with Chin. He doesn't give a shit. When Tony called me about all this, I right away thought it was Chin. He's very smooth, very smart. And he's got an organization. He takes these guys from Hong Kong, doesn't pay them shit. And girls, too. It's the same with girls. He gets them from Hong Kong. Beautiful girls, never more than twenty years old." Smiling meaningfully, he looked at Paula. "These girls, they—"

Bernhardt cut in angrily. "Okay, so he's the one. Brian Chin. Now what?"

Amused, locker-room-lascivious now, Ricca lazily shifted his gaze to Bernhardt, then back to Paula. "Ah . . . so that's how it is, eh?"

Grimly, Bernhardt made no reply.

Ricca allowed himself another moment of supercilious amusement aimed at Bernhardt. Then, suddenly, he rose to his feet. "Okay, let's see what happens. I've got some more guys downstairs, and three cars." He looked again at Paula, smiled, bowed mockingly before, all business now, he turned to Bernhardt. "You carrying a gun?"

"Yes."

"A permit?"

"Of course."

"What kind of a gun?"

"It's a Ruger revolver. Three fifty-seven."

"Okay." Ricca nodded approval, then strode to the door. "Okay. We'll go downstairs, see where we stand."

10:20 P.M., PDT

"I'd just as soon we weren't doing this, you want the truth," Ricca said. "The way I see it, Tony Bacardo fucked up. Maybe Carlo Venezzio fucked up, too; that's not for me to say. But anyhow, when the don died, Tony should've gone right to Don Benito, got the word, up or down. Tony should've had more sense than to come out here all by himself, chasing his tail. He goes to Don Benito, lays it all out. Then he brings a crew with him, does the job right."

Bernhardt made no reply. They'd been talking alone for almost an hour in the rear seat of one of Ricca's cars. The car was parked on Grant Street, in Chinatown. Point by point, Ricca had insisted on knowing everything, even the smallest detail—including the two gems and the one gold coin, safely zipped in an inside pocket of Bernhardt's poplin jacket. Twice during the last hour one of Ricca's men had come to tap on the car. Ricca had gotten out, conversed briefly with his underling, then returned to sit beside Bernhardt.

"What I'm saying," Ricca continued, "is that Bacardo comes out here, makes a mess. Then he went back to New York and did what he should've already done, which is touch base with

Cella. So now . . ." Ricca spread his hands. "Now we've got to clean up the mess. The problem with that being, tomorrow at this time there could be a goddam war here. And all because Bacardo didn't—"

"A war?"

Once more, Ricca's hands expressed aggravated impatience, protesting the vicissitudes of the executive life. "If the word gets out that Chin whacked one of our people and stole from us—stole big—then we don't have any choice. One of our guys goes down, somebody pays. A guy steals a dollar from us, we get ten dollars back. There's no other way." Faintly smiling, he turned in the leather seat to face Bernhardt. "That's why we're having this little chat. Chin took the first shot. Now it's our turn."

"You mean—?" He cleared his throat. "You mean me, too?"

"Sure I mean you. Christ, this guy took a fortune off you and kidnapped your lady friend. Am I wrong?"

"No. But—"

"You called Tony, asked for help."

"I told him what happened," Bernhardt said. "But I—"

"Yeah, well, however it happened, the guys in New York want it fixed. And that's what we're going to do. We're going to—"

Two taps on the roof of the car. Ricca swung his door open, got out of the car, let the door swing closed as he listened to the man called Al. Speaking in low voices, the two men gradually moved away from the car as they continued to talk, their backs to Bernhardt, heads bowed, concentrating. The pattern of their conversation was plain in pantomime: first Al gave Ricca important information, then Ricca gave Al long, detailed orders. Next Ricca required that Al repeat the orders he'd just received. Finally, in agreement, they nodded, then turned away from each other. Back in the car, Ricca spoke to Bernhardt with the same intensity he'd just focused on Al.

"Everything's all set. What's happened, four of our guys're over at this Chin's house. He lives on Russian Hill, just an ordinary house, nothing special. He's got a wife and two kids—

young kids, eight, ten, something like that. And his mother lives there, too, in an in-law apartment. Chin's got a restaurant here in Chinatown. Great place, first-class food, not too expensive, considering what you get. He's got an office in the back of the restaurant, behind the kitchen. The only way to get to the office is through the restaurant. The back door is steel, and the windows look like jail windows. They've even got bulletproof glass. Chin always has at least two guys with him. They're like Al and Jimmy—assistants, you might say. Anyone wants to see Chin, he's got to go through the kitchen, get past those guys—those guys, and a couple of TV cameras. See?"

Bernhardt nodded. "I see."

"Sometimes those guys help out in the kitchen, if Chin's there and the restaurant is busy. Otherwise, they just hang around. It's a pretty good layout," Ricca conceded. "Very secure. Like I say, Chin's smart. But, anyhow, what we're going to do—" Ricca broke off, gestured to Al and Jimmy, who had come to stand in front of the car. At the gesture, the two men got into the front seat, Jimmy behind the wheel. As the car's engine turned over, Jimmy spoke over his shoulder: "Everything's set."

"Okay," Ricca answered. "Good." As they pulled away from the curb, Ricca spoke to Bernhardt: "We'll be at Chin's restaurant in a minute or two. We'll pull up right in front. You'll go in alone. You'll—"

"Alone?"

Impatiently, Ricca nodded. "Sure, alone. That's the only way it'll work, the only way they'll let you in. By the way, you'd better give Al your gun. Otherwise, they'll just take it off you. See?"

Aware of his growing apprehension, the fearful certainty that giving up his gun symbolized a lack of control, a surrender that could cost him his life, Bernhardt unclipped the holster and handed over the gun. The man called Al accepted the gun with chilling indifference.

"You walk into the restaurant," Ricca said, "and you give your name to the maître d', whatever, and you say you want to see Brian Chin. Tell them it's business. That's all: just say it's business. Be very polite, but—you know—very definite. Pretty soon they'll take you back to the kitchen, where the two guys will pat you down, maybe ask for some identification. When you see Chin, you tell him to call home. That's all you have to do."

"Your men will be there, at Chin's house. Is that it?"

Ricca smiled. "That's it. They're there now, no problem. Apparently the wife forgot to set the alarms." The smile widened. "I love that. Chin's an electronics freak, everything wired. So then his wife forgets to push the button."

"What'll Chin hear on the phone?"

"That's the beauty of it." The smug smile was still in place. "He'll hear what you heard from him: turn over the jewels, and everything's cool. Otherwise, we chop off some fingers. You like it?"

Unable to reply, his answer choked by the conflicting surge of emotions, Bernhardt could only stare straight ahead. He was aware that, suddenly, he was holding himself so rigidly that the muscles of his back and shoulders had locked up.

Exactly what he'd heard . . .

He and Brian Chin, together in Chin's office. Chin, calling his home. Chin, opening a desk drawer, withdrawing a pistol. Those were the images of fear, of terror.

But there was another image: the swath of jewels, a sparkling crescent that spread across his desk like multicolored bits of cold fire.

And—yes—the final image: the screams of two Chinese children as their mother's fingers fell to the floor. Their mother's fingers, or their fingers.

As Bernhardt began to shake his head, he realized that Ricca was speaking again. Almost lost in the confusion of blood pounding in his ears, the other man's words were hardly audible: "He calls home and gets the word, then you tell him to get the jewels, which are probably in his safe at the office. Or maybe they're in his house, better yet. Then you bring him out to the car. He goes in the back, between me and you. You and

Al pat him down, then put him in beside me. Then you get in the car, in back. Got it?"

Was he nodding? How could he know, since his mind and his muscles had disconnected, left him helpless to—

"If his two people come out with him," Ricca was saying, "then everything's off, it all hits the fan. Be sure and tell him that. Tell him if there's any shooting, then his wife and kids pay."

Without realizing that he meant to reply, unaware of his own words, Bernhardt protested: "You're sending me into a goddam trap, a one-way ticket. You—Christ—why don't *you* phone Chin?"

Ricca shook his head. "This way there's more clout. It's like if one general wants another general to surrender. He doesn't call the other general on the phone. He sends a go-between. A high-level officer, like that. It's—you know—it's protocol."

11:05 P.M., PDT

Watching Chin with a director's eye, Bernhardt could only admire the other man's expertise. Even the smallest nuance enhanced the image of the inscrutable Oriental villain. The eyes, the hands, the body language, the voice—everything worked. The phone call had taken ninety seconds, no more. During the entire time, sitting behind the elaborately carved ebony table that served as his desk, Chin's black eyes, utterly without expression, had never left Bernhardt's face. Now, with elaborate delicacy, Chin replaced his phone in its cradle. As, still, his eyes were inexorably locked with Bernhardt's.

When he finally spoke, Chin's voice was very soft and precise, projecting the icy self-control that had never deserted him: "Before I decide what to do, I must know whether Charlie Ricca is free-lancing, as opposed to acting on orders from the Mafia."

"I can't—" Bernhardt felt his throat close, forcing him to begin again: "I can't tell you that. All I can tell you is that there's a car outside with three men in it. They'll take you to your home. That's where you give them the jewels."

As if he accepted the statement, Chin nodded thoughtfully, almost dreamily. Then his gaze sharpened, focused on Bernhardt.

"I could, of course, kill you. Or I could hold you hostage, as I did the two young women. The only difference being—" Benignly, Chin smiled. "The only difference being that, secretly, I would have agonized if I'd had to order the women maimed."

Bernhardt made no response.

"You're a brave man, Mr. Bernhardt, to come here like this." Gravely, Chin nodded approval. "Yes—very brave. Or else very foolhardy."

"I've always thought that bravery and foolhardiness are two sides of the same coin."

"That's bravery in the heat of battle. Doing this—coming here like this—that was done after careful calculation." A meaningful pause. Then: "In cold blood, one might say."

"To be honest, I didn't have much choice." Hearing himself say it, Bernhardt was bemused by his own words. Why was he confiding in this suave, smooth-talking sadist who was dressed in a double-breasted suit and spoke like an imitation Harvard graduate?

"How is it that you don't have a choice?"

"I took Mafia money to help Louise get those jewels." And, having said it, he could only continue: "The Mafia doesn't forget. I've learned that."

"I do not forget, either. You understand?"

Once more, Bernhardt remained silent.

"I feel a little sorry for you, Mr. Bernhardt. From now on,

wherever you go, there could be someone following, with orders to kill you."

"Orders from you?"

Chin only smiled. Then he rose to his feet behind the desk. He went to a framed Chinese landscape hinged to the wall. From a small wall safe he took a black silk pouch secured by a golden cord—surely the jewels. He closed the safe, twirled the dial, swung the landscape back in place. Holding the pouch in the palm of his right hand, Chin gestured to a steel door set in the wall behind his desk. "That door leads to the alley. I would have no difficulty leaving by that route. Four of my men in two cars would enter the alley. They would be heavily armed. When they were ready, I would take these"—he bounced the jewels in his hand—"and leave. No one would be able to stop me, least of all Charlie Ricca."

Also standing, Bernhardt nodded. "I believe you could."

"I'd kill you, of course, before I left."

Bernhardt felt the center of himself fall away. But, as if the sensation were stage fright, those last desolate moments before the actor steps onto the stage, he felt himself retreating into a let's-pretend persona: the cold, controlled investigator, in command. Saying quietly: "If you kill me, you've still got to deal with Ricca. And the law, too." He looked meaningfully at his watch. The time was eleven-twenty. Ricca's deadline was eleven-thirty.

"You'd better decide," he said. "You've got ten minutes."

Chin smiled, then spoke reflectively: "When I turned thirty, I decided it was time to marry and have a family. As you doubtless know, my business interests include bringing people from Hong Kong." The small smile widened slightly. "Call it the import business, if you like. One aspect of the business is women—very young, very beautiful young women. Therefore, when I decided to marry, it was natural that I would choose one of these women. Her name is Gah Bou, which means Little Fawn. She bore me two children, a boy and a girl. I'm very fond of these children. If Ricca should harm Gah Bou, I could bear it. But if those children were harmed, all because of a bag of jewels—" Still smiling slightly, perhaps wistfully, he looked down at the silk pouch. Then, to Bernhardt: "I'm ready. Are you ready?"

"I'm ready."

1:10 A.M., PDT

With his eyes on the jewels, Ricca spoke to Bernhardt: "Do you know how many there're supposed to be?"

"Two hundred thirty-seven jewels," Bernhardt answered. "And eighteen gold coins."

"Okay . . ." Ricca gestured to the jewels, which were piled on a newspaper spread on a chrome-and-formica kitchen table. "You count them. Count them good, because you're responsible."

Bernhardt turned to Brian Chin, who stood beside the table. In his impeccably cut double-breasted suit, Chin looked incongruous in the brightly lit kitchen. "Have you got a ruler?"

Chin moved his head to his wife, a silent command. She went to a drawer and produced a plastic ruler. Bernhardt thanked her, then turned his attention to the jewels. The four of them—Bernhardt, Ricca, Chin and Gah Bou—all stood around the table. Ricca's eyes were fixated on the jewels, avidly watching them reflect the light as Bernhardt counted. Also watching, Chin stood impassively, arms calmly folded. Jimmy, one of Ricca's men, stood in the doorway of the kitchen. The .45 caliber Colt automatic Jimmy held was lowered, trained on Chin's legs. Al and another of Ricca's men were in the living room, guarding Chin's two children and his mother. In the two cars parked at the curb three more Mafia gunmen stood watch.

During the time it took Bernhardt to complete his count, no one in the kitchen changed position. From the living room,

Bernhardt heard a child's voice. It was the boy, asking an unintelligible question about his guard's gun. The guard's answer was also unintelligible.

Finally Bernhardt nodded, spoke to Ricca: "They're all there."

"You sure?"

"Shall I count them again?"

Impatiently, Ricca shook his head. Then he spoke to Chin's wife: "You go into the living room, sit with your kids."

She looked at Chin, who nodded. She turned, left the room. She wore blue jeans and a gray cashmere sweater. The movement of her perfectly proportioned body was superb.

"Okay." Ricca pointed to the jewels, spoke to Bernhardt. "Put 'em in the bag." Ricca eyed Bernhardt's waist-length poplin field jacket with its elastic waistband. "Will they fit in a pocket?"

"I don't think so." But, a surprise, the black silk pouch could be carried in one of the jacket's two bellows pockets.

"Ah, good." Satisfied, Ricca nodded. Then, as if the disappearance of the pouch had liberated him, brought him back to the business at hand, Ricca turned to Chin, spoke briskly:

"What we're going to do now," he said, "is we're going to go outside, me and Jimmy and you and Bernhardt. I've got three men outside, in two cars. There's a Lincoln and an Oldsmobile. Two of my men are in the front seat of the Lincoln. The third man is behind the wheel of the Olds. Bernhardt'll get in the back seat of the Lincoln. You'll get in beside him. I'll get in beside you. Jimmy—" As Ricca spoke, Jimmy came to attention. "Jimmy'll get in the front seat of the Olds, beside the driver. Al—" Ricca gestured to the living room. In response, Chin nodded. Yes, he knew Al's name. "Al'll stay here. Another guy stays, too."

"Is this a one-way ride?" Chin asked. His voice, Bernhardt realized, was dead level. His face was impassive. Once again, Brian Chin was giving a magnificent performance: ice water in his veins, no fear showing, even facing death. While, certainly, his thoughts were running wild.

Ignoring the question, Ricca said, "When we were coming here, I saw a couple of cars following us. They were your guys, weren't they?" It was a low-keyed question, matter-of-factly asked.

Gravely, Chin nodded.

"And when we patted you down in front of your restaurant, before you got in my car, you were carrying a mini walkie-talkie. Which you've still got in your pocket."

Once more, Chin nodded.

"Okay." Satisfied, Ricca also nodded. He drew a large auto-matic pistol from beneath the sports jacket he wore. He pulled back the slide, checked the load, released the slide, eased off the hammer. "Okay," he repeated. "Now, I want you to call your guys, tell them we're coming out. Tell them Jimmy'll come first. Then Bernhardt. Then you. Then me. You probably have some kind of a signal that'll tell your guys how you want them to handle this. Maybe your guys have Uzis, something like that. But if you tell them to start a war, rescue you, some shit like that—well, naturally, you'll be the first to go. First you, then your family."

"I expect to be the first to go no matter what happens." Still Chin's voice was dead level; his eyes revealed nothing.

Ricca's smile was directed at Chin. The smile was genuine, Bernhardt realized. Signifying a simple professional respect. How many gangsters could face death so calmly? Still smiling, Ricca shook his head. "Maybe not. We've got a way to go, you and me. You want my advice, you'll take it one step at a time. Don't do anything dumb." When Chin made no reply, Ricca gestured impatiently. "You going to call your guys, or what?"

Chin let a long, thoughtful moment of silence pass before, with measured deliberation, he took a tiny portable radio from an inside pocket. He extended the antenna, punched out a number. Then he began speaking in Chinese. Startled, Bern-hardt looked at Ricca. But Ricca only nodded. The message: he'd expected Chin to speak in Chinese. In less than a minute, Chin returned the radio to his pocket, nodded to Ricca.

"Okay." Ricca looked first at Bernhardt, then at Jimmy.

"Ready?" When each man nodded, Ricca spoke to Bernhardt directly: "You better get that three fifty-seven in your hand, unless you're some kind of a fast-draw artist."

Bernhardt drew the gun with his right hand; with his left hand, once again, he verified that, yes, the jewels were safe in his jacket pocket.

"Okay," Ricca repeated, "let's go, like I just said, in that order. You first, Jimmy. Then Bernhardt."

Nodding, Jimmy began moving out of the kitchen and into a short central hallway, leading the way to the front door. When Ricca reached the archway to the living room he spoke to Al: "You and Freddy stay put. I'll call you on the phone, tell you when." Momentarily Ricca swept the grandmother and mother with a look of practiced intimidation. "Anybody gives you a problem, Al, you shoot. Got it?"

Al nodded. "Got it."

"Good." Ricca motioned for Jimmy to open the front door and begin descending the outside stairs, followed by Bernhardt, Chin, and Ricca. At the curb, the man riding passenger in the front seat of the Lincoln was getting out of the car. In his left hand he carried a sawed-off shotgun. With his right he pulled open the car's rear door, then stood with his back to the car. His head was in constant motion; he held the sawed-off with both hands, ready. As Bernhardt followed Jimmy down the single flight of concrete steps to the sidewalk, he saw a car turning onto the quiet residential street. On both sides of the street, cars were parked in almost every available parking place. The car in motion could carry Chin's gunmen, a flying wedge: cavalry, in the vanguard of the main attack. On these stairs, how close behind him was Chin? When the shooting started, Chin would certainly throw himself on Bernhardt's back.

UNDERWORLD SHOOTOUT IN QUIET RUSSIAN HILL DISTRICT, the headline would read. Followed by the subhead: MAFIA BATTLES CHINESE GANG, PRIVATE INVESTIGATOR DIES CARRYING A FORTUNE IN GEMS.

Traveling slowly, the oncoming car drew abreast of the Chin

house. Two figures were inside: two men, Caucasians, both facing forward, incurious. Ahead, Jimmy was on the sidewalk. As, yes, the car was peacefully passing, proceeding up the block. Three more steps down, and Bernhardt, too, stood on the sidewalk. Now the passenger door of the Oldsmobile swung open. At the Lincoln, Jimmy turned back to face Bernhardt. Jimmy held his big automatic with the muzzle raised, the approved pre-combat stance.

"Okay," Jimmy said, jerking his head to Bernhardt. "Get in the car. *Move.*"

As Bernhardt stooped, Jimmy hissed, "Be careful of that goddam gun. Don't let him grab it off you." Bernhardt nodded, shifted the .357 to his left hand as he slid into the car, holding the revolver between his thigh and the door. The bulk of the jewels in his left pocket pressed against the Lincoln's door, a palpable presence. Incredibly, since he'd left the shelter of the house and begun descending the front stairs, he hadn't been aware of the jewels: a million dollars, in the pocket of his jacket.

A million dollars, and already one dead.

Now Chin was sitting close beside Bernhardt. Also guarding his pistol, Ricca entered the car. Jimmy slammed the door, exchanged a look with Ricca. Both men nodded. Jimmy straightened, went to the Oldsmobile, got in beside the driver. In the front seat of the Lincoln, the gunman on the passenger side turned to face the three men in the rear seat. He held a large-caliber stainless-steel revolver similar to Bernhardt's. Trained on Chin's chest, the revolver rested on the back of the front seat. Still holding his .357 along his left thigh, Bernhardt twisted to face Chin. Ricca, too, was facing Chin. Impassively, Chin stared straight ahead. Once more, Bernhardt could only marvel at the role Chin was portraying with such incredible composure.

Suddenly Ricca spoke: the boss, briskly taking charge. "Okay. So far so good. Now, Brian, I want you to get in touch with your guys again." Ricca gestured to the pocket that held Chin's miniature walkie-talkie.

"Oh?" Chin's eyebrows rose a fraction of an inch. "Why is that?"

"They're around here somewhere, right?"

Chin considered the question, then gravely nodded.

"How many cars?"

"Two."

"How many men?"

"Four. Two in each car."

"So they're—what—within a block or two, something like that?"

"Yes." Chin's inflection suggested a delicate irony, a supercilious superiority to Ricca's streetwise patois. Repeating mockingly: "Something like that."

"Okay." Pleased, Ricca nodded. "So here's what I'm going to do, Brian." A pause, for added weight. "What I'm going to do, I'm going to give you a choice. It's you or one of your guys, take your pick."

"You mean—" Chin frowned, began again: "You mean either I die or one of them dies?"

Ricca smiled. "You got it. And, at that, you're getting off lucky. If I was calling it, you wouldn't get a choice."

"Orders from New York," Chin said.

Grimly, Ricca nodded. "That's right, asshole. Just so I'm sure you know what this is all about, what you did was hijack jewels that belonged to Carlo Venezzio. So you robbed from our people. And that's like a death sentence, you rob from us. And then, Christ, you kill one of our soldiers. Plus, you kidnap Carlo Venezzio's granddaughter. And for all that, Cella's willing to let you live." Marveling, Ricca shook his head. "To be honest, I don't get it. I mean, something like this happened and I was running things, I'd kill two of your guys, not just one. And I'd take two million dollars, plus the jewels. But Cella, he's—you know—a statesman, whatever you want to call it. He doesn't want to start a war out here, not when he isn't even the official head man yet. So you're lucky, Brian. Believe me, you're the luckiest Chinaman around."

"When I killed Fabrese," Chin said, "he was in the process of hijacking those jewels. I stopped him."

"The answer to that one," Ricca said, "is that I couldn't care less. This whole thing is a mess, and all I want is to get it over with. So I'm obeying orders. No more, no less. So you decide, Brian. It's your move."

"And if I should refuse to make the call—then what?"

"Then we all drive out by the ocean, and we put a bullet in your head."

"And if I make the call?"

"You tell the guy to get in the Olds, in back. Then you tell the rest of your guys to go home."

"And then?"

"Then we all go out to Ocean Beach, like I said. Same plan, different faces. By the way, tell your man to bring a gun with him."

"A gun?"

Ricca nodded. "We take it off him. See?"

"Ah . . ." In turn, Chin nodded appreciatively. "Yes, I see. That's the gun you use."

Ricca smiled: a small, smug smile.

"Very clever," Chin conceded.

"Thanks." Ricca looked again at his watch. "I'll give you exactly two minutes to decide."

Chin nodded, drew a long breath, took out the miniature radio.

1:50 A.M., PDT

For more than a mile they'd been driving south on the Great Highway, with the ocean on their right. Out to sea, Bernhardt saw a fog bank: a low line of white lying between the dark of the sky and the dark of the ocean. Since Chin's gunman had gotten into the Oldsmobile, no one had spoken. It was the most oppressive silence Bernhardt had ever experienced: a burden of impossible weight that smothered the soul. Yet the silence served somehow to soften the enormity of their mission: cold-blooded murder. Only the barrel of the stainless-steel revolver trained on Chin gave proof of the truth to come: the execution of one human being by another.

No, not another. Not by just one of them. They would all be executioners, all conspirators. It was, Bernhardt knew, an enormity that would always haunt him, never set him free. When he'd been a child, at odd times in odd places, he had sometimes been overtaken by a sudden shift of reality, a strange, isolated, frightening objectivity: who was he, really? How had he come here, now? Of all the possible combinations of time and place, how had it happened? It was as if he'd separated from himself, a spectator to his own fate.

A spectator? A helpless spectator?

No. Not helpless. Here, now, he must—

"Okay," Ricca said, "this looks good. Signal that we're pulling over." As the Lincoln slowed, then began to rumble on the gravel shoulder of the Great Highway, Bernhardt saw the Oldsmobile's turn signal come on. Slowly, the two cars came to a stop, separated by only a few yards. With his eyes straight ahead, his shoulder and thigh in contact with Chin's, Bernhardt could feel Chin's whole body tighten. Chin's gunman was riding in the back seat of the Oldsmobile, with Jimmy's gun on him. Did the gunman know what awaited him? Chin's orders to the unknown man had been given in Chinese; their content would never be known. Had Chin told the man to resist? Submit? In their native language, had they said good-bye?

The Lincoln drew to a stop. Still holding the .357 along his left thigh, secured, Bernhardt realized that he was using his right hand to cover the jewels in his jacket pocket, as if to protect them.

A treasure in jewels . . .

Three days ago he hadn't known the treasure existed.